MW01267943

chapter one

chapter one

Costa Rica

Yousef Alqamoussi

CROWN
PRESS

Published by Crown Press LLC.
PO Box 43435
Detroit, MI 48243.

Cover design © by W Design and Development.
Author photograph © by Agnes C. Fischer.

ISBN 978-0-9790706-4-8

Library of Congress Control Number: 2018900483

10 9 8 7 6 5 4 3 2 1

Printed in the United States of America.

contents

April 21, 2016

Dear Editor,

    It pains my fucking heart that I have to sit here and beg you to notice me. That your opinion about these words will ultimately dictate the value of my work. Fuck you. Who the fuck are you to determine the value of genuine human expression?

    I mean, I know what you want. You want commas and periods, sentences and paragraphs, big multisyllabic words of "experimental", "ethnic", "experiential", "no erotica" writing. But I really don't feel like impressing you, sir or ma'am, and I'd rather just give it to you straight. So here it is:

    I wrote a book. It's a collection of thoughts that sound exactly like this letter. Some may call it a cross between Joyce's <u>Ulysses</u> and Holden Caulfield's grieving despondent spirit. Others may say it's the voice of a generation, a 21st-century "Howl" or <u>Naked Lunch</u>. Frankly, I don't quite care what they think. It is what it is. Take it or leave it.

    I hope you'll read this and be impressed and call me and tell me it's the work of a genius and that you can't wait to get it off the press. That'd be great. If you don't, I'll probably just send it to like thirty other people and after that, I'll probably give up and print it myself. But it would make my life a hell of a lot easier if you would just print the fucking thing already. I hate kissing ass.

    Thank you for your time and dedication to all that you do.

Sincerely Yours,

J. Musi

preface

4/17/16 The problem is this: I am too much of a free spirit. All beliefs and values have vanished or collapsed. All goals have been accomplished or abandoned. And this has placed me in a position of infinite choice: the choice to do everything and to do nothing. The choice to go anywhere and to go nowhere. The choice to spend my time or to waste it. The choice to race past the clouds or to watch them go by. And here begins the next chapter of my life, one of a potentially infinite and utterly absent future.

4/18/16 Here you are, Mr. Reader. Wondering when exactly I'm going to get on with it. When does the *story* start? Have we reached the rising action? And at our holy climax, will the fearless protagonist experience his much-awaited epiphany and cross the barrier of no return? And will his holy choice dissemble into a series of stumbling falling actions which finally descend into a seemingly settled but vaguely uncertain resolution? And will his sacrifice be an emblem and a guide for future generations? Because that is what you want, isn't it? That is what you do. You search for a plot, a meaning. You scan these lines for structure, rummaging for linearity between the paragraphs and grammatical sensibility. Organization and style. Plot and character. Setting and mood. Don't waste your time. These are thoughts. You know thoughts? Listen to *your* thoughts and tell me when one paragraph ends and another begins. Discern *your* comma splices from your sentence fragments from your run-ons. Tell me how *your* protagonist fares in the end, if not crumbling in the wet white sheets of a hospital bed or choked and gagged by strangling arteries of cheese and bacon or sliced by grate metals and crooked glass in the driver's seat of your precious Toyota Honda Lexus Prius. My my my, aren't *you* quite the craft.

chapter one

4/19/16 Sometimes I ask myself, why would anybody ever want to read this shit? But then I remember <u>Sorrows of a Young Werther</u> and <u>Anne of Green Gables</u> and <u>Beloved</u> and anything by William fucking Wordsworth and <u>To Kill a Fucking Mockingbird</u>. And I think, well it's better than *that* shit, for *sure!* And then I think of all the brilliant nonsense like Ginsberg's "Howl" and Burroughs' <u>Naked Lunch</u> and all the abstract art like three squares and a circle and crosses dipped in piss and I figure, well, might as well write it. It can't be worse than *that* shit, right? If you're going to appreciate *that*, then you might as well enjoy *this*. Might as well, right?

4/24/16 There is in me an insatiable thirst for a quest. For discovering things greater than ourselves. Beyond that is a murky darkness which beckons me to its call. I seek movement for movement's sake. There is no destination except the verb of motion. I seek to chart the uncharted. I seek to capture the unspoken and unrealized. There is a swelling urge to go. To go for the sake of going. To return only once going has fulfilled itself and accomplished itself. I seek to dive into the unknown and allow its wisdom to take me away. And when it is finished with me, it will bring me back and things will never be the same again.

5/4/16 I am drowning in the black guck of mucky hatred. And I am poisoned by this paralyzing stagnation. My life has become a tiny puddle in the road. Water seeks motion, yet it is confined to this crack in the ground. As time passes, it accumulates dirt and dust. It grows murkier, muddier, stinkier, dirtier. Flies lay their putrid eggs in its basin. And there is nothing left to do but to wait to evaporate, atom by infinite atom.

5/21/16 Today I went to a skate park to practice riding my skateboard on something a little less rough than these Michigan roads. When I beheld those glorious angles my bowels shifted in mortal terror. I was afraid to fall. But as I watched these fabulous "dudes" work their wheels I witnessed that the old saying "we all fall down" is nowhere truer than at this skate park where every young man woman and child— some no older than five and others whitehaired— all fall down. They

all fall down and they get right back up onto their
wheels. They all fall down, and you know who falls down
the most? Only the best. The great ones fall more often
than they succeed, yet you would never remember that
they fell. And so I began to fall. And the less I was
afraid to fall, the more I was able to do. Within twenty
minutes I was half-piping. Within forty minutes I was
riding five-foot-tall ramps. And falling. And right before I left as I was attempting one last ride I took a
holy fall and slammed my hip and scraped my elbow. But
what joy! What pride to be among the fallen! I rewarded
myself with pizza and left the park proud to have fallen
and prouder to have gotten back up. So I blasted back
down I-75 against the cool winds of the sunset evening
electrified by Michael Jackson's "Bad" and "Beat It" and
"Scream" and "Dirty Diana" and "Smooth Criminal" and
"You Rock My World" and it's all ripping vocals ripping
chords ripping guitar ripping hearts and I'm tearing
down the fast lane celebrating my splendid victory. Sure
my elbow was sore and at one point I even considered
hospitalization. But then my better half said to me "go
put a Band-Aid on it you little bitch" and I remembered
what it was like to be alive again.

5/23/16 I'm starting to wonder if all this chatter
really matters. I mean, what's the point here? Do you
honestly even care? Why would you? Is there anything
here of any true substance? I mean, YOU could write one
of these as easily as I could, couldn't you? In the end,
who cares about my overpriced "Angela" bagels and fallen
skateboards and un-ironic hot dogs and sick meditations?
I swear to you. I have NO I DEA where I'm going with all
of this. But I'm going. It feels right somehow to keep
going. And I'll keep going until going fulfills itself,
whatever that means. So you can drop all this nonsense
and go on with your day if you wish or you're welcome to
come along. But I must forewarn you: I'm not making any
promises.

6/25/16 This question may upset you, Dear Patient
Trusting Reader, but I wonder: how do I know when this
thing is finally over? I mean, at what point will I know
that I've written exactly enough of what this whole
thing is actually supposed to be and stop? Because I
honestly don't know. I believe that when it is finished

my Muses will tell me, at which point I'll simply write
the date and time of that precise instance and say
"That's it. I think I'm done." And that will be it. So
be on the lookout for that, I suppose.

    7/26/16 5:05 PM.
That's it. I think I'm done.

chapter one

8/14/16

And so I suppose now, my Fellow Reader, comes the
moment I assume you've all been waiting for— the Magnum
Opus of this merry tale of absurd and inflammatory nonsense in which our Holy Protagonist sets out for adventure to find himself and seek a moment of astounding
enlightenment amid daring trials and tribulations and
perils and dangers and gallant quests and encounters
with fascinating people and enlightening conversations
and unforgettable sights and upon return from this great
and wild journey a new discovery of himself and the
world around him and an opportunity for you Oh Holy Noble Reader to live vicariously through these incredible
experiences and to dream of YOUR one day when YOU will
have the courage to undertake such a journey yourself.
So sit back and enjoy the ride because Costa Rica has
been one zany insaney psychobrainy fuck of a holy trip.

On that fateful Saturday afternoon I sat in the
guest room of my house (which in an Arab home is the one
strictly reserved for guests that nobody EVER sits in
and is reserved only for visits from the Ambassador and
the one day when a local family will come to ask for
your daughter's hand in marriage) staring at my brand
new Hoodoo Red Osprey Porter 46 Pack, crammed to capacity with things I had anticipated to need for my trip to
Costa Rica. Sitting there apprehensively, I couldn't
quite stomach the fact that the next week of my entire
life was packed right here into this red-orange backpack
that by some miracle would have to suffice for so long.
I had been packing since Wednesday, actually, by col-
lecting things I wanted and neatly laying them out on my
brother Kal's bed in the other room which since his move
away from home has served as a new shared family desk
and is only cleared off when he comes back to visit. Sad
but true. So I had collected what I considered "bare
essentials" and when Saturday morning had come around I
had stuffed what I could into this large-but-not-quite-

large-enough new bag of mine and had experienced a very
powerful realization in the process: that when you are
packing the rest of your life's near-future into a single backpack, you have to make some real-life decisions
and you learn a lot about yourself in those moments. So
of the very few things I had set aside for packing, I
could only fit about 70% of them into the bag and spent
two hours shaving away the 30% I couldn't take, which
included extra underwear and socks, my Rubik's cube, and
swimming shorts (which HOOOLY FUCK what a mistake that
was! Going to Central America in August without swimming
shorts turned out to be like going scuba diving without
an oxygen tank, as you my Humble Reader will readily
discover).

What added to my thrilling apprehension on that Saturday afternoon just hours before my connecting flight
to Atlanta was that besides the fact that I was arriving
in Costa Rica— a place I still could not confidently
place on a world map— on Sunday, August 7th at 11:40 AM
at Juan Santamaria Airport (SJO) in San José, I had AB-
SOLUTELY NO IDEA what was going to happen next. Adam and
I had simply booked the flights and decided that we
would figure it out from there once we arrived. The only
information I had that could help me had come from a
phone call that I'd made the night before to a young
woman named Eliana whom I'd met at Rosie O' Grady's in
Ferndale during Salsa Sunday a few weeks prior. "Eli"
was a vibrant, kind, well-spoken, and titanically-
bosomed yet unquestionably unattractive American woman
who taught foreign language in the city and had lived in
Costa Rica for a year. After dancing together I had
chatted with her and somehow the topic of my upcoming
travels to Costa Rica had come up and she told me that
she'd lived there and we exchanged numbers and now here
I was calling her on the night before my travels trying
to construct some semblance of reality about this place
I was going to. So in her own impressive strikingly eloquent way she spoke with great regard about this amazing
place called Costa Rica and she suggested that I avoid
the northeastern Caribbean coast and instead that I head
down to the southern Pacific coast and visit Manuel Antonio and Uvita / Punta Uvita and that I head inland as
well and visit Volcan Arenal and nearby La Fortuna and
Monteverde which was just south of there and that I enjoy all the great things there were to see. And as she

spoke I took my printed black-and-white map of Costa
Rica and highlighted in orange all of these little names
on the map knowing absolutely nothing about what I was
highlighting. Then I asked about the rain, for all
weather forecasts I saw GUARANTEED 100% chances of se-
vere thunderstorms all day and night all over Costa Rica. But Eli assured me that we were actually going some
time before the wet season and chances were that the
mornings would be sunny and sometime near the mid-
afternoon the clouds would start to move in and by
nighttime the rain would come but we would have most of
the day to enjoy our time. Then I asked with great concern about the water and food there, for I had read
online (yes, on the "internet", the number-one source of
universal truth) that EVERYTHING would make you sick and
that you should stick to bottled water because local
water wasn't safe to drink. She was very surprised I had
read that because she had lived there and had NEVER had
a problem. So that was reassuring. So I thanked Eli for
giving me all of this awesome firsthand information and
I told her that I'd love to get together following my
trip to catch up and she said that would be great.

And so, with only these bits of information the hour
of reckoning descended upon me and I hugged my sister
and father and hugged my mother and she did the Quran
ritual as I stood by the door and made me pay $1.00
which I call the Travel Tax because my mom makes me pay
it as charity so it can protect me and I reluctantly
produced four sweet quarters and deposited them into the
charity sack and Mikey my youngest brother took my bag—
my life— and threw it into the back seat of his gold
Jeep and we were ready to go. But right before we left I
remembered that I had forgotten my new athletic sunglasses upstairs so I ran up to get them and my mom
scolded me because I'm such a forgetful damn fool (which
you will discover very quickly and horrifically as this
tale unfolds) and I kissed my mom again and waved to her
as she stood apprehensively at the window and we were
off.

Mikey is an angry driver and in some ways a sort-of
unhappy young man so he spent most of the ride fuming at
the stupidity of other drivers and irate at how the universe didn't tick and tock to his preconceived whistle.
And when we arrived I hugged him or shook his hand I
don't remember and I entered the McNamara Terminal at

DTW and in less than ten minutes I had navigated the
steaming aggravated colon of airport security and had
squeezed firmly out of the other end onto a long escalator into the terminal.

Lugging this big red bag which would soon become the
best friend I ever had I approached the big screens to
locate the gate to my flight. As I searched for Flight
DL 2659 to Atlanta I heard someone behind me call out my
name and I wondered, who in the hell would know ME at
the airport? Then suddenly to my incredible delight I
saw two large bearded security men approach me and they
were Michael Darini and Harry Burrows, my childhood
school friends, and I was really so happy to see them.
We talked and it turned out that both of them worked as
airport staff and they told me that I was looking good
and when I told them they were looking good too they
laughed at how ridiculous that sounded and said I was
just saying that to return the compliment, but in truth
I wasn't, for I had always liked these guys. I had known
Mike since the first grade and he is the son of a Lebanese father and a Korean mother and I've always really
liked him and we had also gone to middle and high school
together and I had attended his wedding and now here he
stood before me large and smiling and with this fucking
awesome long Confucian-looking East Asian beard (Listen,
Confucius somehow comes up a lot in this little spiel of
mine so be prepared to hear that name a lot) and looking
cute as ever. And I had met Burrows in middle school and
he was a die-hard Dallas Cowboys fan and we were friends
throughout middle and high school and during my last
four years as a teacher I have taught two of his sisters
and the youngest of them is absolutely the cutest little
button of sweetness you ever did see. So the guys had to
go and I wished them well and as they went on to their
jobs I watched them go and then headed for my gate.

Once I had located my gate and knew where it was, I
had well over an hour to kill so I went to the bathroom
and then headed back toward the center of McNamara Terminal and there as if seeing it for the first time I
beheld the absolute spectacular beauty of this architec-
tural marvel. In the center was this amazing fountain
with a streaming water-show so I admired that for a moment. Then I noticed that right next to it was this phe-
nomenally-designed little booth and café which was all
white and metallic and it was labeled with a lovely red

square and in the center the word "illy" in white and
this was an espresso bar. I thought, how absolutely delightful a nice cup of mocha espresso would be right
now. So I approached the line and this lovely black girl
with the most genial spirit helped me pick out a cup of
coffee from the menu. I had trouble deciding which of
two options I wanted so she helped me choose one and
once I had paid for it and taken a seat facing the amazing water-show fountain she approached me with BOTH cups
of espresso, one free of charge. I was in awe and en-
gulfed with the love of humanity and her generosity and
was so thrilled that my trip was already off to an amazing start. So I sat watching this water admiring the
flow of the universe and reflecting upon Alan Watts and
Bruce Lee and nature and sipping these two orgasmically
delicious cups of espresso and knowing that if there was
a heaven it most likely looked like this.

And now it was time to board Flight DL 2659 to
Hartsfield-Jackson Atlanta Intl Airport and I had spent
the last hour seated playing with my baoding balls— also
known as Chinese stress balls— because I liked how they
moved and they relaxed me. And I think subconsciously I
also needed them a bit because like every other fucking
square area of human gathering in this country there
blared a TV and it was blasting into our faces the
"news" and we had no choice but to watch this "news"
because we in America have corrupted any semblance of
truth in the world and coiled all of our facts and information down to teen gossip and mortifying slander and
wouldn't you know it! To my illustrious surprise! There
he was! Donald Trump! On the "news"! On the big screen!
Who would have thought! So I sat there unable to tear
myself from the glaring hatred of this mutant orange
ape-troll and thank GOD CHRIST AND BUDDHA I didn't miss
what he had to say toDAY because you sure can't cock-
fucking miss anything THIS enlightened sage has to say!
But then it was boarding time so as I approached seat
22D I was elated to see that I had been assigned an
aisle seat and even MORE elated that seated in 22E next
to me was this adorable blonde cutie whom I greeted
chivalrously and sat beside. I had never sat beside an

attractive woman on a plane before, let alone a sweet
southern belle, so this was quite a stroke of luck. During the flight she and I talked but she was tired and
didn't really feel like talking much because she had
gotten off work just before this flight and was having a
long day but from the little conversation we DID have I
discovered that she was from Atlanta and was pretty familiar with the area! So since I had an overnight 12-
hour layover there I asked her where she recommended I
go for dinner and to hang out and she suggested midtown
because it was safe and clean and not sketchy like down-
town. So I thanked this sweet cutie and wished her luck
and finally I arrived in Atlanta!

For some reason I had assumed priorly that the airport would offer some kind of check-in or valet service
or something where I could leave my bag for a couple of
hours as I went out to the city to eat. But ATL Information politely informed me in a West-Indian accent that
no such services actually exist. Now this changed things
because it meant I would have to carry this huge bag all
across Atlanta and that was risky and burdensome and as
if reading my mind my mother messaged me (wow what a
fucking stream of alliteration that was back there. Not
intentional) and told me it was a really bad idea to
venture across town with a blazing orange-red travel
case because that made me an obvious target for trouble.
I assured her that it was all under control and I decided to wear my bag as a backpack rather than a handbag
(which the Osprey Porter 46 Pack allows you to do) and
that would help me seem less conspicuously a tourist. So
I got my round-trip train ticket for the MARTA and
hopped on headed for midtown Atlanta.

As the train departed on the Red Line about fifteen
stops from the airport I was surprised to discover how
"hood" this city was. I mean it was "hood" enough to
recoil a fella from Detroit, you know what I mean? That
was one thing that I should've known coming in. Another
thing I TOTALLY should've known was how steaming humid
this fucking place was, and that dressing up in a long-
sleeve button-up and jeans was a ridiculously bad idea.
So I sat there sweating and feeling stank as group by
group of these fellow train riders appeared more hood
and ghetto and ratchet with every ascending stop. One
chick in particular really grossed me out in her way-
too-small-girl-cover-your-wiggly-waist-lovehandles polo

and her damn-dat-booty-big-but-not-da-good-kinda-big
jeans and this stupid little plastic see-through backpack made just for everyone behind her to turn their
horrified attention to all the dumb shit she carried
around all day like her Cheetos and her M&M's and her
Almond Joys—

That's enough. I arrived at the midtown stop which
was on 10th street I believe and I got off and it was
steaming hot and I was sweating and alone in the hot
Atlanta night and I was lugging around this really heavy
big bag and wondering how the hell I was supposed to
carry this around all night and all week and go uphill
and downhill (yes, not only is midtown Atlanta very
sparsely designed and concretey, but it's also HILLY)
marching to the drippings of my sweat. And at that moment for the first of many times on this trip the all-
too-familiar feeling of Traveler's Dread descended upon
me and I wanted to go home and I missed my mom and it
was hot and I was scared and I wondered why I was doing
all of this and what the hell I was doing here and holy
shit fuck this. But then with some deep breaths and the
expert advice of Google Maps I regained my bearings and
headed uphill toward midtown. And let me tell you something, folks: midtown Atlanta kinda sucks and is certainly not designed for the common pedestrian. And ho-
mie, coming from a fella from DETROIT, that's GOTTA say
a LOT! So I marched on toward a meal and as I passed by
a park a homeless black man with the God of Hope (or
crack) beaming in his eyes sang to me "you ain't nothin'
but a hound dog..." and I gave him a little jitter of
recognition and shook to his singing and he was elated
and kept going and I sang the rest of that great song to
myself until I reached the next intersection and saw
some people on different corners eating and mingling so
I assumed I had reached the midtown city center.

I walked around this vast hilly concrete-caved town
and found nothing open except for a Burger-Fi and a sushi restaurant on the corner. And right before I was
about to go in I figured, why not take one quick walk
around the block and see if anything else is open? But
as I walked just a bit longer around this mammoth block
I gained nothing of options and only increased in heat,
exhaustion, thirst, sweat, and frustration. Now it
wasn't all as miserable as I make it sound, come to
think of it, but I did find myself quite disappointed by

this nationally-renowned city of Atlanta. I was hoping for some kind of jazz or blues bar or even a semi-authentic southern restaurant where I could try something unique. But my two options were fucking burgers and mother fucking sushi of all things. Yet just as I neared the sushi corner I saw right next to it a place still open and the menu looked Italian. A man standing outside smoking a cigarette noted my interest and said "You should really try this place, voted best pizza in all of Atlanta" (I would later discover that he was the restaurant's owner, but that doesn't mean he wasn't right). I honestly didn't want to travel on such a heavy stomach of pizza or pasta but my options were indeed limited so I told him I might just try the sushi next door and with a twinge of disgust he shook his head and opened the Italian restaurant door, ushering me in and declaring "It's not even real sushi. It's cooked".

So I found myself inside this modern Italian restaurant where everyone was quite friendly and polite and a few parties of people were just getting their orders. I was seated against the wall at a table for one and immediately my order was taken. I ordered a personal pizza margherita with mushrooms and a drink and then I saw a "seafood salad" on the menu which looked kind of interesting and I was happy to finally be seated in a cool place with good food to eat and cold water to drink. So I rested amiably with my big-ass Hoodoo Red Osprey Porter 46 Pack joining me in the seat next to me and at the table to my left sat three men, two Americans and a Frenchman or Spaniard or something, and they talked about sports and countries and Hillary and Trump and other such trivialities. I eared into and out of their conversation and watched American Ninja Warrior as it blared unabashedly from the TV at the bar across the restaurant. Then my "seafood salad" arrived and it turned out to be a small jumble of boiled seafood such as shrimp and scallops and octopus and calamari and it had been sprinkled with salt and too much lemon and I found it slightly grotesque. So I picked at the shrimp and a few scallops and gagged on a piece of octopus and then set the fucker aside and downed some water and was greatly disappointed at this sorry excuse for a salad. Fortunately the pizza was to die for and I ate with such delectable gusto until I couldn't eat anymore. But the explosive satisfaction of this phenomenal pizza soon

went sour when I received the check and realized that,
tip included, this meal had cost me nearly $40.00! I was
quite pissed and sad because that was such a waste of
money which I really needed out in Costa Rica. I mean,
that was a whole day's spending out there! But it was
more than that that upset me; it was that we have so
much money to throw away that we can afford to purchase
a $40 meal and throw half of it into the garbage (for I
hadn't been able to finish the pizza and had all but
disposed entirely of the "salad"). I had ordered what
could gracefully feed a family of four in four-fifths of
the world and spent what could be an entire family's
fortune for days. It was more than what I had spent and
ordered that bothered me; it was that I threw it all
away so mindlessly.

I paid grudgingly and left the whole of this shit
town behind me and got back on the MARTA and rode back
quietly to the airport and truly, cousin, that's all the
fuck there is to say about Georgia's fucking Atlanta.

And now I was back at Hartsfield-Jackson Atlanta
Intl Airport with a hefty bag and sweaty clothes and a
heavy stomach and a pocket already emptier than I ever
wanted it to be and a whole night ahead of me before my
9:39 AM Flight DL 900 to SJO. But the better— FAR better— part of my stay in Atlanta was yet to come. As I
rode the airport floor escalator or moving walkway or
moving sidewalk or travelator or whatever its technical
name is, I realized just how colossal this airport really was. And now that it was well past midnight the traffic had died down greatly and I could really enjoy the
place with a softer pace and keener eye. Riding the moving sidewalk with a moment to think, I came to discover
that this airport was absolutely FULL of gorgeous art!
Giant photographs along the walls, ceiling-high statues
in the middle, and all African-themed works of indescribable creativity and beauty. Enormous murals of African color and pasture and trees and elephants and lions and cultural costume. Statues of deities and mothers
and families and heroes and glory. So I glided through
these endless terminals absorbed in the African beauty
of these humbling monoliths, amazed that such grandeur

could be strewn about in this airport of all places. And with every passing inch of moving sidewalk I was further pleasantly startled by the sheer magnificence of these ancient cultures and I wanted to view and admire them forever.

I arrived back at my terminal for the next day's flight and realized that it was well past midnight by now and the place was all but completely empty. Shops, restaurants, and even bathrooms had been closed down for the night. As I passed by each gate I slowly came to notice that besides the three or four night-shift workers cleaning about, I was the only person there! I found this discovery awfully exciting and went about finding a gate waiting area with a clean corner where I could sleep for the night. Before that, I had to get myself ready for bed. So I found an open restroom and went inside and arranged myself for the night. First I changed out of my sweaty clothes into some fresh underwear and a shirt and shorts and put these awfully stupid long-sleeve shirt and jeans the fuck at the bottom of my bag where I didn't ever see them again until well after this whole trip was over and I was back home and unpacking my bag. Then I took a few paper towels and ran then under water and pumped a bit of hand soap onto them and proceeded to a bathroom stall where I scrubbed my crotch and upper thighs from all the sweat and breeding bacteria which could turn this whole trip into an itchy rashy quest from hell before dawn had cracked. I applied some deodorant, peppered my package with baby powder, brushed my teeth and flossed, and washed my face. Then I looked into the mirror and smiled like a dumbass for I was ready for bed! Lugging my big bag I returned to the terminal and as I was heading back I overheard a commercial from the airport television announce that Hartsfield-Jackson Atlanta Intl Airport was "the busiest airport in the world". I wasn't sure I had heard that correctly until the little girl from the commercial repeated it. And I looked around and beheld this vast silent eerie place— "the busiest airport in the world"— entirely empty, and it made this night's rest all the more special and sweet and surreally delightful. I found a nice corner on the floor against the wall where I could charge my phone and I took out my travel pillow and my water bottle and I laid down for my night's rest.

In no time at all it became obnoxiously apparent to
me that achieving sleep was going to be harder than I
thought, for you see the airport's televisions were
still blaring on at a dizzyingly loud volume. Now it
seems that during the day-to-day commotion of the airport such a volume would seem appropriate, but in this
overnight calm it was downright offensive. And of all
the things that you could blare from an airport television wouldn't you know it had to be the "news" and the
"news" kept playing reruns of the previous day's
"events" like what this senator said about that con-
gressman and how this superstar was caught driving drunk
and how trumping the trump of trumpeten would trumpa
tumpa trump-trump. I covered my eyes with a bandanna
(which little did I know then that bandannas would become very thematic during my upcoming sally) and put on
my headphones and played a 12-hour white noise video on
Youtube and since "fan white noise" wasn't loud enough I
switched to "rainforest thunderstorm" and wouldn't you
know it, even THAT wasn't enough to fade out the blaring
orange voice of this Republican apefuck and I swore to
all that was holy that of all the things to come from
this entire beautiful trip what I was going to enjoy
most of all were not the forests and animals and people
and mountains and volcanoes and oceans and beaches and
fruits and foods and moist bronze Latin asses and boobs
no no no. What I was going to enjoy most of all was that
for approximately seven precious dulce days or so I
wouldn't have to hear the bone-scraping voice or see the
flesh-melting corkscrewed orange face of this indescribably hideous fucker fucktard, of this metacosmic mistake
of semen-and-egg fusion, of this volcanic heat-heap of
steaming creamed wet-orange demon dung. In all of God's
Heaven-on-Earth Costa Rica, that would be the very best
part of it all.

I slept for a bit, probably two hours, and then woke
up and relocated to a chair where I think I got in another hour of sleep. But soon it was 5:00 AM and the
commotion of early travelers was rising so it was time
to get up and get a move-on. I packed my things up once
again and admired how the airport slowly came back to
life with the bustling of hurried travelers. I walked
out to the bathroom and washed my face and brushed my
teeth and peed and exited into the terminal with revived

excitement prepared to arrive in a few hours in Costa
Rica!

I bought some breakfast and ate in a small airport
cafeteria while reading the book I had brought along
with me for the trip: The Dharma Bums, by Jack Kerouac.
I love reading Kerouac when I travel because he so magi-
cally captures the spirit of travel and adventure so I
read that and ate amid families feeding their children
and rugged college travelers giggling for no sensible
reason and fleeting business folk striving to transcend
time and space in pursuit of whatever it is they think
they're accomplishing. Then I had a few hours to wander
the airport and I realized that there was yet MUCH more
art to be seen, such as an ENTIRE gallery of local children's art, paintings created by fourth- and fifth- and
sixth-graders, and some exhibits too of art made from
animal parts like carved elephant tusks of ivory and
leather purses from deerskin and rugs from leopards and
other such beauties that are only beautiful until you
realize what suffering and malicious murder had been
inflicted upon a formerly living creature just for the
sake of the human ego. We are some sick fucks, my
friends, and you need to go to the Hartsfield-Jackson
Atlanta Intl Airport and see why.

Then to kill more hours I paced up and down the terminal and drank lots of water from my CamelBak Chute
1.5L Sky Blue water bottle which was too big for the
water bottle fountain so I had to squeeze it in and risk
cracking the bottle or damaging the fountain (which the
bottle was supposed to "fit into") but luckily nothing
happened and I'd drink and pee it out again and then it
was time for Flight DL 900 to SJO so I headed to my gate
and to relax I played with my baoding balls and then I
was on the plane!

Once again I discovered to my elation that seat 36C
was an aisle seat so I took out my book and phone and
headphones and put the rest in the overhead compartment
and next to me at the window seat in 36A was a real nice
chubby young man with a beard and it was nice to sit
beside such a jovial fellow. Then another cool young
rustic long-haired dude took 36B and we were three dudes
on our way to Costa Rica. I would later learn through
conversation that the nice chub in 36A was off to meet
his wife there and was hoping to explore some potential
property before Trump becomes president. As for the

gruff dude in 36B, he had just broken up with his girlfriend in South America not too long ago and had roamed
the continent for a while and was now slowly making his
way around the world and for some reason was heading to
Costa Rica. As the plane prepared for takeoff everyone
got onto their personal screens and of all the films and
shows and songs that they could've chosen from, they
almost all ended up choosing John Oliver's episode on
"Donald Trump" or "Trump's Wall" and there I was on this
plane with rows and rows of screen after screen watching
this squirrely-looking British man spew our nation's
much-deserving hatred and I found it hilarious that when
we can choose anything at all we still choose to absorb
ourselves in the marvelous disgust of this fucking orange Neanderthal.

Personally I had had enough of it all so I just read
more of The Dharma Bums and closed my eyes for a rest
and meditated a bit. Then I got on the screen myself and
began watching Hail, Caesar, but well over an hour into
the film I realized that it wasn't sitting so well with
me and I just wasn't into it so I turned it off. Snacks
and drinks came around so I ate and drank and then after
returning to my book I started watching another movie, a
Spanish film called Magallanes, which was about this
former assassin-turned-taxi driver who picks up a passenger who turns out to be a girl from his past and he
stalks the ever-loving shit out of her and I was very
intrigued and wanted to finish it but we were landing so
I saved it for another day. And ladies and gentlemen,
now comes the meat and bones of this merry tale, the
moment of truth, the landing in San José, Costa Rica!

chapter one

When I arrived at customs I was a bit shocked by the
length of the line ahead of me. It looked to be at least
an hour-long wait. So I texted my mother first and told
her we had landed and she praised Allah. Then I texted
Adam my travel buddy from Utah and informed him that I
had arrived and said: "Deplaned but customs line is insane" and he replied "Yes it was for me too but they're
prtty quick. I'm outside the airport. Theres a band
playing, I'm right next to em" and I was ecstatic. Then
I texted my buddies the "3 Blind Mice" and I said: "I
see what looks like a misty volcano from the airport
window and a band is playing as u leave the gate" and my
buddies W and Doc were geeked. So now it was time to
wait and the line was moving relatively quickly and
since my bag was so heavy I just laid it down in front
of me and as the line moved I'd nudge it forward with my
foot and in retrospect I'm sure some people must've
thought that was weird and partly gross but I didn't
notice or care because here's something you're going to
learn about me very quickly: I'm a naïve guy when it
comes to such social etiquette. But the catch is this:
I'm not naïve because I don't know any better. I'm naïve
because I don't care what people think of me anymore.
And though I totally possess the capability to zoom out
and observe and critique myself through the eyes of others, I've grown extremely desensitized to this sort of
extrospection and frankly have NEVER benefitted from
such self-consciousness. So now I just do whatever the
fuck I want and leave it to others to exercise the self-
consciousness part for themselves.

So as I neared the front of the line and the customs
officers' booths I grew a tad bit restless and annoyed
with how many Americans and English speakers were in
line because I didn't fly all this fucking way across
the world to be spoken-to in fucking American English! I
came here to acquire the Spanish language and Latin culture so this was starting to seem like a disappointment.

So to pass the time I played for a bit with my baoding balls and then read a couple more chapters from The Dharma Bums while continuing to nudge my bag forward inch by inch and it shoveled up airport floor dust and when it started to annoy me I picked it up and started to carry it forward instead. Then I finally reached the front of the line and that was so easy to get by and before I knew it the whole security process was over and there I was past the sliding doors into the blaring heat of the Central-American bustle and boil and exiting the airport into the next chapter of my life.

As I passed the sliding doors out into civil Costa Rica a few things immediately struck me: the sheer number of people waiting outside for the arriving travelers; the long lines of little brown men flashing big white cards with long Latin names; the enthused families and friends with beaming white smiles and gleaming eyes; and then, beyond that, a seemingly infinite sea of white shirts and brown feet bulging from the tan sandals of taxi drivers, all out flailing their hands and charming the arrivals with smiles and offers of "best deals". Yes, this was the Mexican bullfight of the taxi drivers, the swarming school of avid anchovies. So with every jutting hand and face of taxi mayhem I raised my palm and announced "grácias, grácias", signifying politely that I wasn't interested. But in all, the whole matter was profoundly hilarious. Then I called Adam on Whatsapp to notify him of my arrival and after a little bit of confusion there he was swimming toward me from my left through a yelping sea of taxi anchovies and we hugged brotherlyly and it was great to see him.

So let me tell you a bit about Adam because if you don't know this amazing human being then a) your loss, and b) this strange Costa-Rican yarn won't make a whole lotta sense. I met Adam in the tenth grade on the Lowrey basketball court where so many of the guys would meet to play after school pretty much until sunset. If I'm not mistaken, he asked if he could drink from my water bottle (or I from his) and immediately we clicked and have been dearest friends ever since. It turns out I had completely forgotten (and Adam had fondly reminded me) that we had been friends in the second grade as well, in Ms. Garrison's class at Maples Elementary. God, that Garrison was a screamer, but according to my mother she was an excellent teacher but I wouldn't know. What I DO re-

call is that on the last day of second grade as we were
coming single file down the stairs Ms. Garrison was crying as we passed by her and I thought that very odd because until that moment the only emotion that woman had
ever expressed was sheer werewolf rage. But back to Adam. So we had a great deal of awesome experiences together back in high school like in Mrs. Nichols' speech
class where we performed a great number of different
extraordinary speeches such as transforming the class-
room into a boxing ring and demonstrating how to box. It
was also in Mrs. Nichols' speech class that we met and
befriended Sam Picot, a Colombian-born Lebanese fellow
who to date remains the wisest man I ever met. I remember we met Sam, shamefully, when he had stood up to give
a speech for the first time and his heavy Colombian accent was so foreign to us that Adam and I cracked up
laughing. But later the gorgeous Amanda Naim scolded us
for being such dicks and we felt so remorseful that we
chatted him up the next day and realized just how low
and foolish we were, for this was THE smartest and wisest guy we'd ever know. Sam once said "I'd rather be
alone and one with myself, than nothing but a shadow
around others". I mean what fucking tenth-grader talks
like that! Adam and I partied through high school gradu-
ation, remained college friends, worked together at All-
Star Valet which I later quit and he almost owned,
stayed in touch after I completed college and he realized with clarity of mind that the American college educational system was a corrupt ordeal and quit and moved
on to things that mattered, and since his move to Zion
National Park in Utah he and I have remained very close
friends and I even visited him there last year. Up until
that time Adam had done more traveling than the average
person would ever do in a lifetime, visiting Australia,
Morocco, Spain, Yemen, Jamaica, Norway, Canada, the rel-
ative whole of the United States, and now here I was
embracing my dear childhood chum halfway across the
world in Costa Rica! Who would've thought!

So while he had been waiting for me to arrive (Adam
had landed about three hours earlier) he had done some
research and asked the airport front desk and the car
rental reception and the taxi anchovies and a cop and
gathered that in terms of transportation we had three
possible options: 1) we could rent a car for a daily
fee, which would cost a lot and burden us with the re-

sponsibility of a vehicle, BUT would grant us tremendous
transportational freedom; 2) we could take a taxi to
Jacó (which I still knew nothing about, except that less
than twenty-four hours ago Adam had texted me the following: "Riva Jaco in Jaco, Costa Rica is where we're
staying on the 7th and 8th") which would cost roughly
$80.00 between the two of us, or 3) we could rough it
out by local bus for a few hours longer and it would
cost like $8.00. Yes, EIGHT DOLLARS! But before making a
decision he was hungry so we decided to eat and walked
over to an airport café just outside and there was a
lovely young Latina there who took our order. We each
ordered some kind of spicy sandwich and a bottle of water and sat down to eat amid other Latinos and travelers. Then Adam asked me if I wanted to use American cash
for spending or convert to the country's local currency
which I came to discover was called a "colon", or
"colones" in plural. And I was absolutely flabbergasted
by this name of all names for a national currency because why would you call your money fuckin "COLONes"
dammit? "Yes hi I'd like to buy some toilet paper" "certainly sir that will be 7,000 assholes please" "sí
grácias cabron" like seriously?? We laughed about that
and ate and I didn't finish my food so Adam ate his and
took a crack at mine and it was all pretty good. Then we
had to ask a police officer to escort us back into the
airport so we could exchange some cash and at the currency exchange was this adorable bespectacled Latina and
her smile was just so sweet. God I love Latin women as
you will sure as your ass soon discover.

So after a bit more research and thought we decided
that the best course of action would be the local bus,
so we took our bags— Adam's bag was less full and I was
quite jealous because I wished I could know how to pack
so lightly for a whole week— and walked over to the bus
stop. Of course every taxi anchovy on the block swarmed
us meep-meep-meeping to give us a ride for the unbeata-
ble low price of $80.00 and we politely declined until
we got on that bus. So the plan was to take a bus from
the airport town of Alajuela to the capital city, San
José (approx. twenty minutes), and then to board a long-
distance bus from San José to Jacó (approx. three hours)
and there we would be! So in no time we had boarded our
first bus and were seated somewhere toward the back and
a few things became glaringly apparent to me. First,

chapter one

Costa Rica is fucking HOT! Humid! There wasn't any air
conditioning (hah...air conditioning. You fool...) and
I'm a sweater, dude, a sweaty sweaty fellow. So I took
out my bandanna to mop my brow every few seconds and
sweat is very much going to be a fact of my life from
this point on and a tremendous figure in this plot's
unfolding. So that was the first thing. Second, this bus
was busy and crammed. And uncomfortable. And I realized
that in many ways I was out of my comfort zone and wondered for how long I'd feel that way (to which the answer is, boy you ain't even scratched the SURFACE of
discomfort. Come to think of it, every limit you've ever
thought you had is about to be tested and every fear
brought forward and you sir are in for one rowdy fucking
ride).
    Our bus arrived in San José and we quickly got off
and went around the block to find the main bus terminal
where we could take our next bus to Jacó. We were jovial, excited, and energized. And hot. So I did another
thing that would become an iconic crux of this zany adventure: I tied my sweaty bandanna around my head to
uphold the stream of sweat from my brow which otherwise
LITERALLY cascades down my nose, cheeks, and face. And
when Adam beheld this short muscular gruff-looking companion of his with a black bandanna tied haphazardly
around his head, he started to develop some cautionary
reservations. Let me explain why. So you remember a
while back that whole spiel I gave about careless naive-
ty and how while I SHOULD know better I often dismissively choose NOT to know better because I lack
fucks? Well, Ice is correct in noting that hiking
through the barrios of a third-world Central-American
country with a bandanna around your head and a fat-ass
brand-new Hoodoo Red Osprey Porter 46 Pack isn't exactly
a call for peace. In fact, it is by all accounts a dec-
laration of war. And maybe marching through the crime-
ridden poverty-stricken barrios of this city capped like
a chapo may not be the best course of action for two
weary travelers. Yes, I knew that. Of COURSE I knew
that. But I shrugged it off because I don't like sweating.
    Sure enough, a great staple of my personal life
reared its ugly head just forty steps away from our bus:
the great personal curse of misplacing and forgetting my
shit. Yes, this is something I literally. Always. Do at

home. Remember earlier how I forgot my sunglasses up in
my room as I was leaving for the airport? Yes. I honestly can't recall a time that I've left my house WITHOUT
running back in to get something. Wallet, phone, keys,
water bottle, book, socks...you name it. And so here I
was around the block from our bus and what do I notice
missing from my pockets? You guessed it: my phone! Yes!
Left back on the bus on my seat where I had placed it
between my legs rather than putting it in my pocket. My
heart sank down to my ass and I went pale and as soon as
I shuffled around to run back and find that bus Adam
grabbed me and held out my phone laughing and said "Dude
you left this right on your seat". I felt like the dumb
fucking idiot that I am because here we were out in Costa Rica and just twenty minutes from the airport I'm
already losing my shit. Disgusting. I thanked Ice and we
proceeded through the town of San José toward our next
bus station.

San José is a shit hole, my friends. Of all the people whom Adam and I had spoken to about this trip, exactly NOBODY had suggested we "stay" in San José. And
within moments, we could totally see why. Aside from the
oppressive humidity, this city was gross: piles and
piles of trash heaped along the curb; hookers and bums
up and down the streets; busted curbs and stores, homeless overload. One sight in particular, a big box lying
sideways on the curb with two torn tattered man-legs
jutting out of them, stands out to me above all of the
other homeless dishevelry. The "ta3teer" (تعتير), as it
is so precisely worded in Arabic, was beyond measure (I
used "ta3teer" because no English word I can think of so
perfectly captures the decrepit dilapidated atmosphere
that I'm trying to convey. Actually come to think of it,
"decrepit" and "dilapidated" are close enough).
As we crossed this wasteland of hopeless vehemence
we pondered naturally how much of a risk we were in. And
upon reflection, I told Adam something I had learned
over the years: "Ice, you know, I've come to realize
that to an unknowing stranger, I don't exactly look ap-
proachable". Adam laughed, for all things considered
this was quite true. If you'd never met me and didn't

know what a ditsy bookwormed silly little child I really
am on the inside, I wouldn't seem to you like someone
you'd want to pick a fight with. Though I'm short, I'm
muscular and stiff and I walk with a calculated gait and
a stern gaze and to a stranger I look like a guy who
isn't going down without a fight to the death. But Adam
also informed me, correctly, that while that may deter
MOST attacks, you must realize that in the unlikely
event that someone DOES decide to attack, then you can
count on that assault being disproportionately violent,
almost for THEM as an act of self-defense. Crazy but
true.

We arrived at the bus station amid shitty graffiti
and battered concrete walls and a police presence akin
to a military war zone. One graffito in particular was
downright hysterical, for it was a spray-painted image
of a huge hand with the middle finger up and the middle
finger was a penis. God, can you fathom that? What offensive genius! The middle finger jutting from the fist
as a furious circumcised cock! Brilliant! We laughed so
hard. Then we entered the station and I was hoping for
some air-conditioned relief from the heat but alas, this
was an open station with cool shade but no AC (and by
the way this hope for AC is going to drag on for DAYS
and become a true Odyssean quest for elusive reprieve).
We took the escalator up to the second floor and we ordered two tickets to Jacó and the cost per ticket was
3,300 colones (or assholes, because that's what fucking
colones are and I couldn't shake away that image no matter how hard I tried) and we paid the man and he gave us
back a receipt and since I hate receipts I threw the
receipt away because fuck it. So now that we had time to
kill we figured we could spend it buying me a pair of
swimming shorts, for on our way to the station Adam had
mentioned his eagerness to swim and I had said, "Well
have fun because I didn't bring my swimming shorts", and
he had uttered with outraged disbelief "ARE YOU CRAZY?"
And yes of all the things I DIDN'T pack into this fucking bag my shorts were one of them. We thought we'd go
around to some of these stores and check out the shorts
because this bus station was something like a mall. But
when we saw that these Billabong swimming shorts cost
74,000 and 80,000 and 68,000 colones, equal to tens and
tens of American dollars, we figured we could wait until
we got to town.

Then I needed the bathroom so we headed up to the third floor where the bathroom was and as I proceeded to walk in and pee, a man standing at the bathroom door said "doscientos" and I said "bien cómo estás" and he halted me and said "doscientos colones, señor" and I then realized that "doscientos" meant "two hundred" which meant that this son of a bitch was charging me to use the fucking bathroom. I told Adam that it costs money to use the bathroom, as if to demand his salvation from this absurd injustice, but he just thought that was an interesting thing to find in such a country. So I turned around and wanted to tell this guy "I got your dos cien colones right fucking here in the back of my pants, mother-pendejo!!!" but decided instead to just give the man the two coins and go piss. And after I had peed I washed my face with cold water and really felt the heat taking its toll on me because my clothes were growing damp and my bandanna was soaked and I just kept streaming nasty sticky hot sweat dammit and no amount of ice-cold water or shade was really serving any relief. And for a moment I really felt a surge of panic like this heat was going to consume me like a tsunami wave and suffocate me to death but I calmed myself and went back out there and Adam and I decided to take a short walk through the town to kill time. But talk about short, because no sooner had we gone down the block that we sauntered right back to the station to stay put.

And now it was time to check on our bus and make sure we were in the right place. We approached the shabby gate to the bus entrance and figured our bus ride was coming up soon and the man at the gate in a purple polo or something reminded us to have our tickets ready—

Tickets? We weren't given any tickets.

Then it all came to me. Yes, then it all made sense. Remember, my Noble Reader, that whole thing from earlier with the 3,300 colones and a receipt? And how "since I hate receipts I threw the receipt away because fuck it"? Yes, do you vaguely recall THAT shit? Well it turns the fuck out that that receipt wasn't just a receipt— fucking IDIOT— it was proof of purchase! And, in the vague context of this individual instance, MY FUCKING BUS TICKET!!!

AAAAAAHHHHHHHHHHHHHHHHHHHHHHHHHHHHHHHHHHHHHHHHHHHHHH
HHHHHHHHH!!!

Shit.

"Adam, I lost my bus ticket," I told him a little while later. He laughed a lot, but it is only while reading this right now that he will discover that "lost" is something of a falsity here. The TRUTH is that I'm stupid beyond rational conception and clumsy and futile and without his direct and constant assistance I would have died out in San José all by myself. We went back to the ticketing booth hoping to explain that I had "lost" my copy of the receipt and that the man at the booth just needed to print a new one for me. But since I didn't have the Spanish skills to articulate this complex conundrum, an English-speaking tico in the line behind me (a "tico" is a Costa-Rican native) kindly volunteered to explain for me. But there was nothing the ticket booth hombre could do so I had to buy another ticket.

Folks, all comedy aside, this was serious. I had almost lost my phone AND transportation within an hour of arriving in the city. This sort of carelessness couldn't last for eight more days. I had to start prioritizing and getting focused. So I concocted this ingenious plan where I would designate where my things "belonged" and then after I used those things I'd PUT THEM BACK WHERE I GOT THEM! Profound! So from this point on in my trip, passport and itinerary would go into my lower right pocket, money and wallet into my upper right pocket, and phone into my left pocket. And what I took out to use went back where I got it. Done.

Time for the bus to Jacó.

As we got on the bus to take our seats, the bus driver took our tickets and handed us a business card. Now I thought, what a strange-ass thing to do in a situation like this, what the hell would I want this guy's business card for? But with the last few episodes of idiocy fresh in my mind I decided NOT to throw away this business card and instead placed it in my upper right pocket along with the wallet and receipts, though I couldn't fathom what the hell I'd need it for. Adam was assigned to sit a few rows ahead of me on the right and so I moved to my row farther back on the left and sat before an open window. And for the first time since I'd

arrived in this glorious and sultry country I experienced a short whiff of relief when the bus sped off and
blew the hot Central-American wind into my damp face. In
no time at all, we had exited San José and were on our
way south to Jacó.

First it's the green. The lush verdant fertile leafy
grassy endless green. It douses you. It consumes you.
Green uphill, green downhill, endless gleaming green.
Green no lens but the eye-lens can behold. We drove
through the green, into the green, beyond the green.
Green resets you.

Then it was the color. Hilltops sprinkled with red
and blue and yellow and orange and purple boxes. Each
crest and valley tucked in its bosom those tiny colored
boxes. And these boxes were houses, and they were suffi-
cient. Color is the truth of Costa Rica. My eyes swirled
with wonder, captivated, spellbound.

We rode the waves of the earth, the hills of God.
White cotton clouds sailed the blues and greys of heaven
above us and beside us. Celestial mists of fog descended
upon us with cool caresses of peppered slumber. We sped
by neat rows and rows of coconut tree farms and beheld
the grace of shaded symmetry: endless shaded caverns of
lush canopy into the distant tranquil wilds of the
hills. I closed my eyes to capture it all inside of me.
And smiled.

After some time we arrived at the next town. There
was a brief exchange of passengers, on and off, and then
the driver came down the aisle to collect something from
each of us. When I beheld what he was taking, I laid
witness to my idiocy yet again: those business cards
from before weren't advertisements. They were proofs of
purchase in San José. In other words, they indicated
that you had paid in full for the trip to Jacó. I took
out my business card and handed it to him nervously; had
I thrown THAT away, I'd likely have been thrown off the
bus.

On the road again, we entered vast farmlands and
wide open fields. Adam kept his eyes to Google Maps to
make sure we got off at the correct stop. A cute little
black American girl seated before me turned around to
say hello and to ask for directions to her hostel in
Jacó and she was with a foreign boyfriend (my, how ironic. What a bunch of fat burger-packed powder-spoiled
ignorant nut-jobs we are, my Fellow Patriots. I mean,

the nerve I have to call him a "foreign" in his own
country [he was Latino, if not tico]. How is he any more
"foreign" there than I am?? We really need to get back
in touch with reality, my Fellow Patriots) and I
couldn't help them very much at all. Then after a stop
or two, Adam signaled to exit the bus and I got off with
him. And looking out into this vast endless road amid
farmland and a sky amassing for certain rain, I couldn't
understand how we were anywhere near the "coastal" town
of Jacó. But then Adam explained that the bus had been
on the correct route south but had suddenly taken a turn
to the west and this was the closest we could exit before being shipped off to another city. And I solemnly
recalled this poor black American girl and her "foreign"
boyfriend on a bus headed far away from Jacó and hoped
for all the world that they would get off soon. I'll
never know if they did.

We continued our route to Jacó on foot through farmland and through coastal forest where herds of cows and
great lizards in trees and strange birdcalls occupied
our humors for a while. And with the doom of rain upon
us we hoped to find our shelter soon. After twenty
minutes or so of anxious ambling we saw our surroundings
transforming from bovine farms and aged trees into narrow streets and congested cars and sauntering ticos and
we were suddenly in the town of Jacó!

I was instantly struck by the pulsing colors, the
moist warm bronze Latin bodies, the energy of these extraordinary people, the bustle of this little surf town,
the shacks and shops of towels, surfboards, souvenirs,
and restaurants buzzing with vivacious vibrato. Music,
drums, congas, maracas, and xylophones ignited each
passing block, rousing the dormant spirit. The road narrowed into a small yellow bridge and as we crossed it we
beheld to the south amid amiably sailing grey clouds the
tranquil rage of the Pacific coast and I was euphoric!
The waves lined up slowly but surely in tidy certain
rows of unstoppable force, and then spilled tamely onto
the dark beach sand. And my spirit spilled with them,
submitting to the will of a wise and motherly universe.

After walking one block we turned into a street between a two-story KFC and an open white bar-stage structure where a band was setting up and we crossed into a
small residential area. There at the next corner we ap-

proached a locked gate and I realized that this was our
hostel.

We were greeted by two large dogs— a white one and
an even larger black one— who barked demonically. Then
emerged from this small seemingly run-down box-shack a
white guy with a blond beard and a distinctly American
accent and he opened the gate for us and I thought, shit
I think you better not because I've never been EATEN BY
DOGS BEFORE! But the very second those two dogs caught
our whiffs they immediately calmed down and went away.
They would turn out to be the sweetest couple of dogs I
had ever met. And as for the blond-bearded Yankee? This
was Gary, and he ran the place. Gary shook our hands and
asked our names.

"Adam," said Adam.

"Joe," I said, and I felt Adam cringe when I said
that because he must've wondered disappointedly why I
introduced myself as "Joe" and not by my actual name.
The reason— and of course I had a reason— was simple,
but I'll explain that more a little later.

Gary welcomed us into Riva Jacó, the hostel, and we
entered this building that I could only describe as
"open"— three doors, numerous windows, bare bodies, all
exposed— and led us across what served as a living room
(it was a tile-floored large corner with a TV, a stack
of books, a computer, and some lawn chairs) to the
kitchen (a counter, sink, two fridges, two shelves of
strange ingredients and "Sucaritas"— which are Latin
Frosted Flakes— and a dish tray full of wet cups) where
he took out this old notebook and started explaining the
hostel's rules.

Adam listened while I gazed about in mortal terror.
This, I thought. This is where we are staying? The place
isn't air-conditioned! These rooms have no drawers or
counters! Where are the bathrooms? This place isn't air-
conditioned! I don't see the bathrooms or showers. Do
these dogs just roam around here all night? Where's the
fucking AC?? So Gary took us OUTSIDE of this lovely
shack into the "back yard" which included five or six
tents (these served as outdoor hostels and were actually
a step up from our accommodation), two wooden sheds each
with a showerhead and a knob (yes ONE KNOB. You KNOW
where THAT is going!), two more adjacent wooden sheds
with a toilet and some toilet paper, and a large metal
basin with a rusty mirror where you could view in full

sight your morbid misery. And inside, two rooms each
contained: two bunk beds, two oscillating fans, four
metal lockers which open vertically like ovens, and one
high window. And besides a few fluorescent lights and a
master bedroom for the owner/manager, that my friends is
JUST ABOUT IT FOR RIVA JACÓ!

Adam signed off and paid for our night's stay (well,
he didn't have the cash to pay right then so we were
allowed to pay the next day once we could find a currency exchange and get some fucking COLONES) and we proceeded into our room. Again, this was a grey square with
two fans (one of which was disheveled from dust and
rust), two bunk beds (of which the bottom bunks, and
arguably the cooler bunks in this non-air-conditioned
fuck-hole, had been taken already by two decent-looking
American girls whom we'd meet the acquaintance of rather
soon), and four rusted dented dark metal coffins (which
were positioned BEHIND the wooden door of this room. Let
me explain why that's a poor position. In order to open
any of these lockers you had to shut the wooden door to
the room completely. And if you didn't, then when you
opened these steel sarcophagi they would scrape right
into the door and groove out these nice evenly-carved
semi-circles, the proof of which had already carved four
quarter-inch-deep semi-circles as examples). We took the
uppermost locker and placed our stuff in it, secured it
shut with the white lock that I'd brought along, and
then headed off back to town to get something to eat.

On our ways out, we met Cecile and Rachel who were
extremely friendly and seemed like they'd make a pair of
decent lays for the night if we could score them. And
crossing the "lobby-kitchen" was this surf-body dude in
yellow-ish shorts and beard and long hair who greeted us
so lovingly and his name was Santiago, and he was a professional Uruguayan surfer here to compete at Jacó's
International Surf Competition (which I'll get to later). Gary was there again to say hello and he was very
friendly. And then. From the owner's master bedroom.
Emerged. This woman.

You think I'm about to fall in love, don't you. You
think this is going to become a classic tale of romance
in the Caribbean. It isn't. But when she emerged and
Gary introduced us to the hostel's owner, Laura, I found
myself a bit stunned by this woman. I wouldn't say Laura
was beautiful or even attractive. She was tall and slim

and lacked any defining womanly features. Her face was
plain and in fact forever pressed into a sulking "resting bitch face" as Adam called it, a term I learned for
the first time. But what struck me about her and really
stayed with me until this day were her eyes. And again,
it wasn't that they were BEAUTIFUL necessarily, because
in so many ways they weren't. But they were STRONG. They
were FIRM. They were grey and shallow but so deep at the
same time and they had the tranquil furious certainty of
a royal lioness. Yes, she impressed upon me the presence
of a queen lioness. She stirred something within me on
sight, and I don't think I ever conjured up the courage
to even speak to her beyond a few mumbling words. I
highly doubt if Adam would agree. But then HIS femme
fatale is to come later.

We left Riva through the steel front gates and Adam
used our assigned key to open it. Then I followed and a
few steps down the block Adam noticed I didn't shut the
gate behind me, so I raced back and closed it and assured myself I wouldn't forget to close it again. See, I
make mistakes but I learn from them very quickly. For
instance, as I returned to close the gate in question I
was carrying, and correctly so, my passport and itinerary in my lower right pocket; cash, coin (ticos use
LOTSA coin!) and wallet in my upper right pocket; and
phone in my left pocket. See? I learn. We proceeded down
the block and across the little bridge to all of those
bustling shops and realized with quite a start that it
was dark out! Yes, the sun had all but set and it was
night-time! I hadn't known before then that sunset in
Costa Rica was right around 6:00 PM, so this came as a
surprise. But as we continued about, the night did little to alleviate the strangling mugginess of this
coastal paradise. My clothes and bandanna, soaked in
sweat, bled out what they could no longer bridle and
spilled their hopeless carry down my limbs and face.
We were hungry so we searched for a place to eat.
Our options seemed unhealthy and boring: burgers, pizza,
and the occasional bar. Where were all the cool Latino
joints? The local meals, the fresh ocean seafood, the
Costa-Rican authentic cuisine? It seemed this place was

designed for and by Americans! We were quite disappointed and finally we settled upon a Middle-Eastern shop
that served falafel and hummus and chicken and other
"Israeli foods" (and if you don't know why I put "Israeli foods" in quotation marks then you, sir or madam, are
a very ignorant soul indeed). We ordered and ate this
pretty tasty food and drank this ice-cold refreshing
lemonade that seriously spurted up my spirits because
I'd never before experienced such euphoric refreshment.
Then we walked around a bit more exploring and returned
to the hostel to change and freshen up before going out
on the town to see what Jacó had to offer.

We started off then toward the Pacific coast and arrived in the pit of black night. Looking out, we could
vaguely make out the heaving white caps of rising waves
and hear their steady crashes against the shore. The
occasional vicious lightning crack-whipped in the distance, and murky thunder followed. We stood. The low
tide of the night created this vast moist flat wasteland
before us, descending into the black death of a godless
sea.

"Do you worry about walking out here," I asked.

"Why?" Adam replied.

"Isn't there a risk of getting bitten by a crab or
something?"

Ice looked down around his feet. "Absolutely," he
said, and looked back out into the ocean.

He talked, but I couldn't listen. The strangling py-
thon of Traveler's Dread was rising within me. The
night, the heat, the darkness, the solitude in a strange
land, the fear of injury, all surrounded me and
squeezed. I was tired and sweaty and itchy and stinking
and all I wanted was a quiet room with air conditioning.
I was terrified of the crabs and poisonous microbes and
sharp infectious shells and gangrene and AIDS that
trickled the grounds beneath me waiting to rise up and
tear down my soul before any medical assistance could
rescue me from their certain spate. And Adam talked and
I gazed out in mortal terror at this Lovecraftean horror
before me— this black icking damp tar wasteland of
coffined doom too surreal and dark for imaginary conception. This growling heaving ocean with raging white-
capped jaws surging toward me in black hate stretching,
aching to rise up above me with a roar of black evil and
swallow me up, gripping me with its forceful certitude

to drag me by my flailing limbs into its murky black depths where I'd swell with suffocation swelling floundering blimping with suffocation but she wouldn't let me die she would just hold me down there for hours and days and weeks and years and chuckle horrifically as I begged to die. Why was I here? I could have been home. In my soft non-bedbuggy bed. With my own room air conditioner. And my mother downstairs in peaceful slumber. And within three dialed digits of immediate medical attention. And just as it had all risen up to a ghastly scream in my trembling throat, it suddenly subsided and recoiled. And it was gone. I was back on a beach in Jacó with my main man Adam and a night to be had for the ages.

chapter one

Now just up the beach behind us right on the sand
was this absolutely fantastic-looking beaming-bright
club of sorts and it glowed colorfully in the midst of
the aquatic murks. It was loud and bright and bombastic
and kaleidoscopic and totally fitting for our night's
mood, so we ascended the beach and went there. It was an
open bar and nightclub with a Caribbean feel and palm-
tree-branch roofs and solid wooden tables and chairs and
even some pool tables and a DJ. So we looked around and
the place was fairly empty, and Adam and I ordered some
drinks. I admired the beautiful bartender with her sweet
young tender breast lustrous in the moonlight and Adam
tried to muddle through the strangely jambled service of
the bar. As we ordered, three girls at the bar kept eyeing us with what seemed to me, yet I doubted strongly at
the time, a far-too-eagerly lustful eye. One in particular with a black top was dancing in place and practically begging me to join, but I was too sweaty and hot and
thirsty to care at that moment. We went over and sat
down amid the blaring but jovial music and we chatted
about funny things. But these girls at the bar just kept
looking over at us and smiling and inviting us with a
zeal I'd never before quite witnessed.

Now listen to what I'm telling you here, folks: I'm
in this empty nightclub on a Sunday night and these
beautiful Latin girls are eyeing me down straight up
asking for it. And you're wondering what the FUCK I'm
doing not going over there and making my dreams come
true, right? Well, so was Adam. But to me, something
didn't seem right. Not at all, actually. Something about
these girls repelled me— something instinctual, something primal. Now looks were NOTT the problem, god
fucking dammit, because they were so deliciously
moisteningly sexy! I mean, the one in the middle who got
up to dance with her black-topped friend? She wore a
low-cut white top and a bright-colored skirt and my god
this woman charged my blood. She looked to me a bit like

Jennifer Lopez in a skirt but goodness with a FAR more fantastic body like this round melony rack and a more contained yet equally massive ass like a fucking spot-on ass. But my gut never lies, folks, and something told me not to approach these girls just yet. So Ice and I carried on our very cheerful and pleasant conversations discussing, in fact, girls and approaches and all of that and we kept these chicks in the corners of our eyes. But something still wasn't right, for even some time later a guy DID approach them and hug one of them and even dance with them a bit, but then he walked away. No, something wasn't right about this at all.

The power went out for a few minutes and then came back on. And so did these supercharged whores (by this point, their persistent glares and downright lascivious jabs were growing kind of gross with how slutty it all was. I mean, a chase is kind of nice, you know. But these girls were handing it over and it started to turn us off) who looked like our indifference was driving them crazy. After roughly an hour of this, some parties had gone and come and suddenly, in walks this woman with Megatits. MEGAtits, folks. And an ass for smashing coconuts open. She walks right in and greets the club staff and then hugs and kisses the three whores and Ice and I threw up our hands for this just wasn't making any fucking sense at all! And throwing this whole mindfuck all together Adam concluded that these were a pack of prostitutes getting off their shifts and grabbing some drinks off-hours and though at the time I found this to be a bit far-fetched I now believe with reasonable certainty that that is exactly what that was all about. It turns out in fact that Jacó was fucking SWARMING with hookers and streetwalkers but who knew? But after Miss WonderGuns had walked in we checked out completely and left, for all in all we had had a wonderful time laughing and drinking and talking very deeply. For you will come to discover just how deep and introspective and intellectual Adam and I can be.

We walked a bit more around town and though it neared 9:00 or 10:00 PM nothing much seemed to be going on at all. Here and there were a few little places blasting dance music but beyond that there was very little action to be seen. So after a bit more ambling we headed back across our trusty bridge there and down our street where on the corner a silhouette of a staggering

prostitute eyed us down (no, we couldn't see the eyes
but we sure could feel them) and at the next block we
entered our hostel and for the most part everyone had
just about turned in. By this point I was literally
soaked in sweat and fuming with rage and discomfort from
a humidity which I could've sworn was personally trying
to spite me. I mean it was downright offensive. I really
needed a rough shower before I even thought about going
to bed so I grabbed some underwear and a shirt and soap
and a towel and went right the fuck back OUTside where
the showers and toilets stood in wooden shacks beneath a
green canopy of leaves and as the skies sprinkled light
rain I entered the shower shack and disrobed and when I
saw the single knob that twisted only one way I put it
all together and understood that there was no hot water
here. I was going to have to shower in ice-cold water.
Now folks, that may sound to you in paradise first-world
la-la-land over there like some sort of miserable Chinese prison torture, but to me it was quite elating to
have discovered even a slight reprieve from this unspeakable coastal heat. Though without an alternative, a
freezing-cold shower was just what I needed.

So in order to survive this glacial ordeal I had to
strategize, of course, because I couldn't very well just
jump right into a stream of sleet-iced water. It would
almost certainly stop my heart! So I proceeded instead
to mentally isolate my body into parts and to wash each
part separately. I started with my head and face, wetting and scrubbing, wetting and scrubbing, and then proceeded down to my arms, torso, crotch and ass TWICE,
legs, and feet. I scrubbed each individual part with
body wash and then with the terror of a weeping boy before a sinister doctor's booster shot, I splashed the
smiting ice-water onto myself and literally yelped with
pain and delight. Yet freezing as that water was, no
sooner did it splash onto my steaming body that it was
immediately replaced by sticky hot streaming gucky
sweat. And before I had even turned the knob off from my
shower I had already become entirely streamed in sweat
once again. Infuriated, I brushed my teeth and hair before this rusted sink-basin and returned to my room in
my underwear and climbed up to the top bunk and lay in
bed dreadful and hopeless and feeling very much that I
wasn't going to be able to do this. After a brief and
painful surge of Traveler's Dread and wondering indig-

nantly how I could possibly fall asleep in such strangling heat I drifted off into silent blissful slumber
and I actually slept more deeply and pleasantly than I
had in the farthest reaches of recent memory.

I awoke the next morning after a long, restful, and
uninterrupted sleep to find Adam also awake and he gestured a greeting to me and descended the bed. I too got
off and Rachel beneath me, a young blonde American girl,
was still sleeping soundly so I tried not to disturb
her. I came out to the lobby area and there was Gary in
his lawn chair facing the TV and at the kitchen counter
stood resting-bitch-faced lion-eyed awe-inspiring Laura
statuesque and without a fuck in the world. I went out
the back door to the leaf-canopied patio area where the
showers and toilets were and there was Santiago, shirtless and jolly, seated with his all-too-stereotypically-
stunning blonde European girlfriend and Santiago greeted
me as if I were family and I felt the love of humanity
in this guy's soul. I washed my face and brushed and
peed and as I went back to my room for a minute Rachel
had woken up in nothing but an oversized white T-shirt
(and panties underneath, I hoped! Or hoped not!) and we
chatted quite a bit for ten or fifteen minutes. Rachel
was a young American girl who'd been traveling for
months and was just on-the-go and she was sweet and fun
to talk to. She was setting up to watch movies on her
laptop so I wished her well and left and then I crossed
back through the hostel to the front entrance where the
big black dog rested lazily before the door and Adam sat
in the shade reposed and sipping his morning coffee. I
took my coffee and sat beside him.

We talked. We discussed the trip so far as well as
books and family and travel and plans for this day's
trip. And as we talked, I noticed something: so far this
morning, I had not experienced ANY of the frustrations
and fears and difficulties of the previous night. How
could this be? The heat was still there, but I had accepted it. The hostel was the same, but I did not mind
it; in fact, I sort of liked it! Gary and Laura and Santiago were great. The dogs were beautiful. This coffee
was delicious. It was hot and sweaty and liberating to
be shirtless and careless, and I had slept like a baby
despite it all. I was in Costa RICA! And before Adam had
time to realize my change in spirit, he eased into a
conversation he must've been dreading all morning:

"So, do we want to stay HERE or do we want to go to another town?"

"Let's stay here," I said. "It's great."

"So if we stay here, we'll book another night at this hostel."

"Cool."

He hesitated. "...which means we will have one more night without air conditioning."

I smiled. "I know. It's alright."

It is hard to explain. Hard to believe. But there is something so rewarding, so tantalizing, about facing what you "can't" do— and then doing it!— and then looking back and wondering what exactly you were afraid of in the first place. Before that morning, I "couldn't" sweat. I "couldn't" shower in cold water. I "couldn't" fall asleep in a hot room. What else "can't" I do?

I was about to find out.

"So will our next hostel have AC?" I asked.

Adam checked HostelWorld to find out. "Yeah," he said. "There are plenty to choose from."

"Cool," I said. "Should we book there now?"

"Nah," he said. "We can do it in the morning."

So we booked another night at Riva Jacó and this may sound insane and impossible to you but I was kind of excited! And it wasn't the sort of excitement that you have when looking forward to pleasure, but a new and arguably more intense excitement of looking forward to difficulty and the chance to surmount it! And it was thrilling!

Adam spoke to Gary a bit about places to eat and to exchange cash and places to book some activities like ziplining and surfing and scuba diving. And since for the most part Jacó lacked street names, all directions were given as points of reference, the most obvious one being the bridge. "Go left past the bridge and it should be on your right", Gary would say. So I put on some military green shorts (because it was hot) and a grey tank top (because it was hot) and tucked my bandanna into my pocket and my other items— passport, wallet, and phone— into their designated pockets, and Adam threw on the red shorts and navy-blue cutoff that he would wear for most of this trip and topped his head with his tattered orange hat which only came off throughout this entire trip when it was time to sleep and maybe when he showered. We locked our bags up in the uppermost locker and we were off!

We first went out to exchange our American cash for colones (by now, I've come to terms with the fact that Costa-Rican currency is called "colones" so no more "asshole" jokes from this point forward, I hope). We found the grocery store where the exchange booth was located and after Adam exchanged HIS cash I went and exchanged all of the American I had and I handed it to the teller and said "dos cien...two hundred" and he counted it and said "doscientos cincuenta...two hundred fifty" and of course I the DUMB MOTHER FUCK had done it again. So he gave my $250.00 value back to me in colones— or DIDN'T, how would I know with MY genius counting skills— and we went off to find a place to eat. God, Kal my brother the CPA would kick me right in the balls if he knew, I thought.

A few blocks down we found this pretty cool tico joint and we went in to order breakfast. Adam ordered a coffee and an omelet and I got the huevos revueltos (scrambled eggs) and pintos con arroz (beans and rice) y un café negro (black coffee). I practiced my Spanish with the young lady who took my order and she seemed quite amused with my effort. Then I went over and found Adam seated in this densely shaded area of the restaurant and it was beautiful so I sat and our food came and we ate delightedly. The waitress suggested we add hot sauce (or salsa) to our food so we did and shit that stuff tastes so much better with salsa! So Adam finished his food and I didn't because it was too much for me so Adam ate what was left (which by my recollection this symbiotic scenario occurred during virtually every meal of this trip) and we finished our coffees and the waitress offered to take a picture of us together so we took it and it was great and then I noticed the itching ankles and shins and knew the mosfuckingquitoes had gotten me, those fucking parasitical scumbags. I want to grab one by its puny wings and light it on fire and fucking cum with delight as it roasts alive between my thumb and index finger (Sorry. As I wrote that I felt horrible and I apologize for that highly unnecessary and compoundly disturbing image. Moving on).

We headed back across the bridge and just around the corner from our hostel was this cool booth for booking adventures and tours. So Adam and I went in and there

was this plump cute young tica and we tried to engage
her in Spanish and she did what all of these other na-
tives do which is the second they sniff our touristness
they switch to English and it kinda sucks. Because to be
honest, I came all this way not to lounge around on the
beach and stalk booty but to experience the Latin culture and Spanish language so this was really starting to
nip that effort in the bud. So I decided that no matter
how these ticos responded, I was just going to keep
speaking in Spanish. So anyways, her name was Maria and
she was so cheerful and sweet and she helped us choose
our activities from this tremendous board of options and
we narrowed it down to ziplining and surfing. Adam inquired further into the details of the activities because one thing I've noticed about Adam is whether he's
meeting people or learning something new he always asks
a LOT of questions and he genuinely listens. I admire
this greatly about him. So finally after many questions
he settled upon booking ziplining and surfing and just
as we reached into our pockets to pay I turned to Adam
and with what I played off as disinterest but was actually mild fear I said "You know, Ice, count me out of
the surfing. I'm not interested. I'll watch". And Adam's
face twisted from surprise to shock to disgust to disbelief to anger so fast you wouldn't know what hit him.
And his answer to that was a simply-put "No, man" and a
"you're doin' it" and I laughed and knew better than to
argue with him.

So we waited as Maria made the necessary arrangements and we sat in this small booth and waited and in
the distance we saw a fucking IGUANA! Yes, just trudging
along an open green field was an IGUANA, people! A lizard the size of a CAT! It was remarkable. And as we
rested in the booth I saw that we were surrounded by
traditional Costa-Rican statues and masks and I looked
at them with fascinated wonder, for if you looked just a
bit more carefully at their art you'd realize how advanced and cultured and intelligent these Peoples of the
Americas really were. These were thinkers and masters
and civilized storytellers, kings and queens of vast and
glorious worlds, people in touch with the earth, with
nature, with themselves. They would have solved 90% of
our modern problems, our deepest griefs, if we hadn't
slain them by the millions a few hundred years ago all

for the specs of gold on their earrings. Unspeakable shame...

Maria had us all set and we were thrilled to discover that we were booked to do BOTH activities in ONE DAY, which completely freed up the next day because we hadn't any idea that there would be so much availability on-demand. So we were scheduled to zipline at 10:45 AM and then for surfing lessons at 2:00 PM, which couldn't have been more perfect. We had roughly forty-five minutes to get back to the hostel, change and get ready, come back for the zipline, stop into town for lunch, and be on the beach for surfing lessons all before dinner! THRILLING!

We went back to the hostel and geared up and I was sweating and reeking but to my amazement I didn't quite care anymore because fuck it, what can you do? And as we came trudging back around the corner to the booth I yelled out "Hola, Maria!" because I've always wanted to call out to a woman named Maria— I dunno. One of those things you just always wondered about doing, you know?— and Adam laughed a bit but Maria thought I was weird and a bit crazy but that's all because I AM weird and a bit crazy and in no time a shuttle was outside waiting for us! SO DAMMIT WE WERE OFF TO ZIPLINE DUDE!!!

chapter one

The best part of ziplining. THE. BEST. PART. Was
that the shuttle to get to and from there was air-
conditioned.

The NEXT BEST PART of ziplining was gliding on a
harness across a green rainforest above trees and slopes
and grass and certain death, several hundred feet in the
air, soaring like a bird at remarkable speed, flying
through the heavens between boundless green and blue,
embracing the spurs of wind and sun, exhilarating with
the dreams of our holiest gods, and of course pondering
the thousands of miniscule things that could go wrong
that could strip your soul away in an instant. It all
comes together as one; it is you and you are it.

On the shuttle sat behind us two young pumped dudes
ready for life and thrilled to be a part of it. Jason,
the more social of the two, lived somewhere in Florida
and was out here just having a good time. He taught
sports to little kids and apparently had settled upon
teaching after being out of a job for a very long time.
Gabriel, his buddy, was Dominican and didn't talk as
much. We chatted throughout the ride and arrived on a
large ranch bustling with activity. We checked in and
signed our names and the waivers that sealed our dooms
and then we got a wristband and went out to get harnessed. After a good large group of us was ready (including Jason, Gabriel, and a few American families), we
all loaded up into this big cart and a tractor dragged
us out across the fields and up a long muddy trail. Rain
sprinkled down on us and we wondered if we were going to
zipline through a sheet of rainshowers. More importantly, we wondered how much more risky this was to do in
the rain. We chatted on the way up and there was this
American couple and their two cute little daughters,
both around the ages of nine or ten, were such adorable
mannered girls.

When we reached the top, we got off and the group
from our cart merged with a much larger group of folks

that had previously arrived and they seemed to be a
sports team of sorts (also from the USA). And indeed
they were, as Gabriel and Jason verified, a women's college basketball team or something and apparently they
were VERY good and had just dominated in a game from
last night. So I suppose they were celebrating. So once
a good fifty or so of us were on the first platform we
stood beneath the gentle drizzle of rain as the staff
assembled and the head staffer began in his funny Spanish accent to go over the rules. First he introduced us
to all the other staffers and one of them was named Diego. And since the whole of us on this platform were ignorant stereotypical Americans, when we heard there was
a Mexican named Diego here (you realize he isn't "Mexican", right?) we all delved into the caverns of our
knowledge banks and uncovered all that we knew about
this ancient common Hispanic name. And what we came up
with to yell out at him with jeering laughter was "Go
Diego go!" and "Where's Dora, Diego?" and
"DIEEEGOOOOOOOOOOOOO!" and honestly by the look on Diego's face I knew 1) he did NOT like what we were doing,
2) this was NOT the fucking first time a group of asshole Americans had done that, and 3) If he had a chance
to accidentally let every single one of us fall to our
wet green deaths he would probably "do everything he
can" to stop the catastrophe but would sleep just fine
that night if he couldn't. So the staffers set out to
get to their posts where they would clip us from one
line to another as we descended rope by rope, platform
by platform, back hundreds of feet down to the ground.

There was some confusion in the order of the groups,
so the staffers decided to take the biggest group first
(this being the mostly black women's basketball team and
their two old white male coaches). BUT. For some reason
the whole team got to go except ONE of the two old white
basketball coaches and he had to stay behind because his
number didn't match or something. The staffer apologized
profusely but that didn't stop this old fart from complaining the absolute entire fifteen minutes or so of
our wait. "I'm going to miss the bus. Are you going to
pay for my taxi?" he'd ask. The staffer would apologize
pleadingly and the old white coach would respond, "Don't
tell ME, tell the folks down THERE." Lord knows how he
reviewed this whole operation on Yelp that afternoon
when he got his fat saggy ass some Wi-Fi. And I couldn't

help but listen to this old indignant turd and think
"Guy, you're in COSTA RICA on VACATION celebrating VIC-
TORY with about THIRTY YOUNG COLLEGE GIRLS atop a lus-
cious green RAINFOREST about to ZIPLINE in your fat yellow POLO...and THIS? THIS is the last straw for you?
THIS? THIS is the Great Affront? Having to "wait a second"? THIS is what's going to ruin your day?"

I wish we Americans could see what we look like out
there. I really. Really. Do.

Adam and I were among the last of the group to descend. Before us we watched about thirty or so hair-
flairing death-screaming college girls plummet to their
wits' ends. So when our turn came up Adam insisted I go
before him, so I did. I stood on the box ("soporte de la
caja", as I'd learn on my way down) and looked out.

Now folks, do this with me: stand on the box. You
are canopied by endless brush, and beyond that a grey
and trickling sky. You look down and behold the high
tops of towering trees, hundreds of feet beneath you.
Rain taps your helmet and your arms. "Lean back", the
staffer commands. And you must trust your life to this
single rope and the three metal clips that ring it. Beyond that, you are loose as the wind. Then..."Go!"

And so you go. You glide through the trees, the
wind, the rain at the speed of the hawks. You hear the
zipping of the rope against your clips, the wind at your
heels, the forest fleeting beneath you. You blaze
through the sky and directly toward a tree where a
staffer in blue catches you. "How was it?" he always
asks. "Excellent! WHOO!" you yell. Adam, quickly on my
tail, yells out in a cry: "This is WAY more fun than I
thought it would be!" and it is. You walk around the
platform, get clipped, "soporte de la caja", and then
"Go!" And with the ocean to your right and the thickets
of lush rainforest to your left, you do it all again.
Flying streaming gliding soaring in the spirit of the
eagle. And at the sixth or seventh platform, they tell
you that you should hang upside down on this one for the
picture, if you wish. I didn't do that. But Adam, of
course, who bears the testicles of the Great Plains Buffalo harnessed in his pants, glides TOTALLY upside down
and I catch the whole thing on video!

And after ten or twelve or so of these platforms,
you descend to the bottom where a jolly team of ticos
welcomes you back and asks about your ride. You are ush-

ered to a sink to wash up, and there they also have some
water and slices of watermelon and pineapple for refreshment. The fruits are swarming with gleeful bees,
but with good reason, for these delectable fruits are
seeping with cool sweet nectary deliciousness and who
could blame those poor bees for wantin' a piece of THAT
action?

We rested, reflected, laughed, and soon were back in
the crisp sweet air conditioning of the shuttle bus. As
we rode back Jason talked and talked and in truth I
don't remember a single thing he said and don't care to
dig my memory for it, but it was nice to hear somebody
talk I guess. And when we arrived back at the adventure
tours booth we wished them well and said "we should hang
out!" like we always say to people we fucking KNOW we're
never gonna see again and went on our way.

We had a couple of hours to rest up and get a bite
to eat before our surf lesson at 2:00 PM. But before all
of that, I really couldn't put off a pair of swimming
shorts any longer. So after a quick bite Adam and I ventured through the local shops looking for a place to buy
a pair. Now, there were shorts all over the place ranging from 27,000 to 50,000 CRC (about $50.00 to $80.00
USD) and frankly, with TWO pairs of swimming shorts sitting up in my bedroom at home, I couldn't justify the
cost. When after multiple ventures I found one for
$20.00, it didn't fit. But the lady at the store was
very helpful and did everything she could to help me
find an alternative. Finally, after great lengths of
effort, I settled upon yellow-and-green soccer shorts
(costing about $15.00) which weren't swimming shorts but
would effectively do the job. Well, sort of. And as if a
bandanna tank-topped vato wasn't enough, now I was
marching through Costa Rica in a bandanna, tank top, and
shorts representing Brazil during Olympics season.

"You're really askin' for it," Adam said.

Once I had the shorts we headed back to the adventure tours booth and once again with great glee I cried
out "Hola Maria!" and if it had been funny or even TOL-
ERABLE the first time around, this second time it was
foully annoying. In a few moments our shuttle arrived

and Juan our driver was one cool young tico. So since he
spoke almost no English at all, we took the opportunity
to practice our Spanish with him and we spoke at great
lengths about all kinds of things and WHO KNOWS what
either of us understood from each other.

Ten minutes later we arrived at Playa Jacó closer to
Playa Hermosa and we looked out at this vast ocean
steadily banking with waves of immaculate beauty. We
went under this white portable canopy and took off our
slippers and shirts and our instructor, Juan explained,
was on his way. So we took a moment to walk up to the
beach and dip our feet into the water and the temperature was absolutely PERFECT! Adam correctly identified
that since the sand was finer and bore a tinge of black
then it must've been volcanic, which indeed it was. So
we admired this vast ocean and this heavenly sky and at
one point with ecstatic excitement I cried out in discovery "Can you believe it! Between HERE and JAPAN
there's nothing but OCEAN! It's HUGE!" So we went back
to the canopy and there were a couple of pretty attractive girls up there surfing who came up for a drink of
water and a break and then returned to the ocean and
they were followed by a milfy Asian surfer with quite a
fine voluptuous bod and then a silver-haired man and
Adam put it all together and concluded that they were a
surfer family. Then from behind us emerged this super-
tanned dude with long dark hair and blond ends to his
shoulders and a goatee and this was Julián, our instructor. He was jolly and cool and cried out "Pura vida!"
and gave us a whole bunch of complicated handshakes with
fists and fingers and shit, and then before us were two
huge surfboards and he started to show us how to surf.
Step by step he explained the pretty technical process
of riding a board, catching a wave, achieving balance,
and riding out the wave to the end. Adam and I are both
quick learners so in no time Julián brought out our
boards and applied some surf wax and we put on our rash
guards (long-sleeved shirts to protect from the scrapes
of the board and sand) and it was time to surf!

As we waded into the ocean the smooth steady waves
embraced us candidly and the water rushed our senses and
our spirits. We waded farther and farther as Julián instructed us on how to proceed. We got on the boards,
centered and belly-down. We waited. He held down our
boards until the right wave came along. Julián turned us

around. "Foot up", "Paddle paddle", "Stand up!" and suddenly from behind me a strong sturdy force propelled me
forward. With my right foot in back I stood up and
leaned forward and centered my left foot and folks on my
very first try I rode a complete wave!

The rush was incredible. I screamed and hooted. It
was such an addiction and I paddled back craving more!
Adam was cheering and hooting and jumping around and
couldn't BELIEVE he'd never done this before! And it
turned out that both of us were very decent beginner
surfers due to our backgrounds in skateboarding and
snowboarding— for those same mechanics come into play
here— and we were ecstatic. After five or six runs I was
riding three or four waves IN A ROW! Then Julián asked
us if we were ready to go deeper and of course we were!
So it was time to get on our boards and hit the REAL
waves.

I watched with what grace, what calm, what submission Julián interacted with the water. For to resist or
to fight water in any way was a CERTAIN defeat. But
Julián knew the water. He was its child. He did whatever
it wanted, or he got out of the way. So if a giant wave
came his way, either he allowed the wave to take him
wherever it was going, or he dipped below it and let it
pass over him. No struggle. No conflict. Complete tranquil liquid submission. I saw this and watched admiringly this man's gentle surrender to the universe. For he
understood that the ocean, the universe, the flow always
wins. And those who try to order, to command, to con-
quer, to resist the flow, soon succumb to the flow. Yet
those who succumb to the flow by their own wisdom find
that the flow knows best, and they are at peace.

I wanted to learn what Julián knew. I wanted to see
into this mind of the flow, of the submission. He knew
water. He understood water. So as we swam out into the
ocean's great white-capped mountains I called out to
him, "So I want to learn more. Like, I don't understand
the water."

And Julián looked at me and he said with a look of
sheer bewilderment: "What do you mean?"

And I thought, "I sound crazy".

So I didn't bother to explain further and Julián
didn't bother to ask. And I assumed that this highly
intricate abstract philosophical concept which I've just
expressed to you must be something he knows intuitively

but isn't able to articulate. So I moved on and Julián ordered that we begin to "paddle out paddle out paddle out". I wasn't sure what he meant exactly but I knew what "paddle" meant so I did that after him. And as we swam farther out into high tide the waves grew monumentous and solid and reached five or even six feet high and you really had no chance against them. So they started tossing me sideways and I called out to Julián "how do I turn?" meaning, how do I paddle myself in the direction I want to go. And with great frustration Julián commanded "paddle out paddle out paddle out". I didn't know what that meant at all so I kept paddling but whatever it meant, I knew it didn't mean to just keep aimlessly paddling.

See, Julián had a very specific plan in his head. Direction, purpose, technique, objective...it was all in his head. But he wasn't articulating it. And Adam and I were aware enough to ask, but either he wasn't under-standing our questions or wasn't interested in answer-ing. So amidst this enormous chaos of tidal fury, he just kept saying "paddle out paddle out paddle out" and that meant NOTHING to me if I didn't understand 1) what "paddle out" means in surfer lingo, 2) what or why we are "paddle out"ing, and 3) what the objective is, like how do I know I'm doing the correct "paddle out". And then suddenly out of nowhere Julián cried "paddle in!" and I thought, "paddle IN? Fucker I'm still trying to figure out 'paddle out paddle out paddle out' and now you want me to 'paddle IN?'" But whatever I was doing was wrong because very soon I found myself drifted over fifty feet away and facing sideways and bombarded with waves and Julián looked concerned and the other surfers were giving me that look people give you when you're drifting into oncoming traffic at five miles per hour. So Julián swam to me and fished me out and I could tell he had really lost his patience. But in truth, I couldn't understand why HE had lost his patience. All he kept saying was "Look, you need to do how I taught you" and I wondered, when did he explain how to do ANYTHING like this, because I would have remembered that! If he could find the words— Spanish, English, or otherwise— to explain what we were doing perhaps I'd actually impress him. But he must've said "paddle out paddle out paddle out" over a thousand times and I still knew then and know now just as much what "paddle out" means as you do,

my Most Illustrious Reader. The bottom line was, Julián
was teaching a teacher and he couldn't teach. So I realized that unless I was gonna just bob out here like a
shipwreck survivor I might as well move on with my life.
I told Adam I was heading back and I semi-rode the waves
back to shore and that was more fun than "paddle out"
could ever fucking be.

I sat on the shore and let the tide caress my feet
and knees and I played with the dark ash-tinged sand and
watched the ocean, the mother of our planet, do her
earthly work. And it doesn't take very long of watching
the sea or the sky or the earth before time slows down
and you gently swirl into a new primal consciousness and
suddenly you and the rest of the universe all make perfect sense. So I sat there in the euphoric trance of the
sea and sand for what seemed like a beautiful cyclical
eternity and when Adam came back he was so damn geeked
and I was so happy to see him this excited.

We showered off and changed as the skies darkened
and it began to thunder and rain and after saying goodbye to Julián a Russian-ish girl named Nadine approached
us with a laptop and she was the photographer for the
Surfer Company which had authorized our lessons. She
showed us whole SERIES of high-quality amazing photos
she had taken of us surfing and said we could buy the
whole file for $25.00 and I said HELL YEAH because those
right there were high-quality shots of the first time we
ever surfed at one of the surfing capitals of the world!
We thanked everyone and Juan drove us back to Riva Jacó
where we had time to unwind and relax a bit, for we had
accomplished some of the most memorable activities of
our lives within the last eight hours and it was time
for us to sit back and revel in our grand and glorious
triumphs. Plus it was getting dark and starting to rain.

You are going to see throughout this merry little
yarn I'm spinning here that CLOTHES. CLOTHING. Was the
worst part of this trip for me. Clothes were my biggest
burden and my biggest regret, and thanks to Adam's
countless valuable talks with me on this trip about an
actual knowledge base in the world called "textiles", I
won't make that mistake ever again. See, everything I

had brought on this trip, all of my articles of clothing, were made of a DARLING little fabric called COTTON.
Yes, you may have heard of, even seen, even TOUCHED the
fucker at some point in your dig. Folks, this son of a
bitch likes moisture, likes bacteria, and likes humidity. So if he can get within a DAB of those things, he
will cling the fuck on until his dying day. So in the
sweaty humid moist mucking heat of Central America??
Yeah, this fucker was CHILL.

We got back to the hostel amid darkness and pouring
rain and I needed to wash up and change. Since it was
too early for a shower, I decided to just change into
dry clothes. So I took off my yellow-green Brazilian-
flag-colored shorts, and wouldn't you know it? They were
SOAKED. I mean they must've been made of SUPER COTTON,
because no matter how much water I squeezed out of them
they were still heavy as buckets. And THEN, to my phan-
tasmagorical horror, I found that they had FILLED with
sand. YES! INside. Like, the seams had little holes in
them and I guess during my mesmer on the beach the waves
had washed up sand INSIDE the shorts. I rinsed them as
best as I could but couldn't get nearly enough of the
sand out. So I hung them up to dry near the door and
cursed my life.

But one relief— hell, MIRACLE— of fabric I DID encounter was that my beloved pal Adam had correctly pre-
dicted my textile curse and had thoughtfully brought a
neon-green quick-dry microfiber towel. JUST FOR ME! I
was so excited and thankful, for it was the only item of
fabric I had that could dry by morning. I was so
thrilled. So after that, I just went about my usual
business: rinsing my body in ice-cold water, drying off
with the microfiber towel, walking out in my underwear
and brushing my hair and teeth, throwing on more sweaty
cotton, and chatting with all of the folks at the hostel. It wasn't until many days later that I would discover something: I had done ALL OF THIS. The WHOLE process. Without a second thought. Ice shower, roaming in
underwear, sweat and cotton, all as if it had been that
way my whole life! I felt not the slightest discomfort;
in fact, I was really enjoying it! In exactly 24 hours
at Riva, I had adapted to a life I could never have imagined.

I went back inside where Gary was signing in two really cute newcomer girls who did not wanna talk to ANY-

body. I welcomed them! YEAH! In my grey Hanes and white
tank top dripping in sweat, I just said "Hey ladies,
welcome!" Yeah, like I owned the place! And then I saw
ferocious Laura sitting by the television and she was
watching <u>Scent of a Woman</u> starring Al Pacino and it was
one of the most famous scenes of the film, the whole
"I'M IN THE DARK HERE!" scene (GOD what a powerful scene) and I stood and watched it. And there were Spanish
subtitles too so I got to practice my Spanish a bit as
well: "ESTOY EN LA OSCURIDAD AQUI!"
    Doesn't quite work, does it?
    I went into my room to find some pants and Rachel
was there on her laptop so as I put on some pants we
talked a LOT about her life and past and her travels
across the world and within Costa Rica. And nothing
about us both half-naked in a shared bedroom chatting
away struck me as unusual or sexual or even weird. We
just carried on as if we were in line at Kroger. Then I
left and saw Santiago the Uruguayan surfer dude and I
was so excited to tell him that Adam and I had gone
surfing! His response was ecstatic glee and he gave me a
whole bunch of weird fist-pump hand-slap high-five fin-
ger-wiggles and he almost hugged me with joy. So we
talked a bit about that and then he left all shirtless
and dude-y. Once he had gone I noticed that to my left
was a face of a young man I hadn't yet seen before, and
he was staring INTENTLY at me and I felt a bit weirded
out by it. But to break the ice and awkwardness (for all
he was really doing was nonverbally trying to initiate
conversation) I just said hello and introduced myself as
"Joe" and this fellow was named Elías. Elías had just
arrived at Riva and he was from Mexico City and Elías
was very interested in my conversation with Santiago
about surfing because, well, he had come to Jacó to
surf! So Elías and I talked and I was so impressed by
this sweet polite mannered young man and really felt so
blessed to have come to a place in the world full of
such incredibly heartwarming people like Rachel and Gary
and Santiago and Adam and Elías.
    When Adam came back from talking to some girl I
didn't even meet yet he asked if I was hungry and I said
"yeah let's eat". I introduced him to Elías and they
talked and then I went back to my room to get my wallet
and figured, hey Rachel's just sitting here maybe she'd
wanna come grab a bite with us! So I offered her to come

and she said yes! So now it was me and Adam and Rachel,
but then Adam also invited Eliás and now it was the four
of us and Adam asked Gary for a good tip on a place to
eat and he recommended a café "just across the bridge
(of course) and on the right", and then wouldn't you
know the four of us were off to eat!

We walked off together chatting into the sprinkling
night of Jacó. Adam and Rachel carried most of the conversation while Eliás and I contributed thoughtfully
whenever possible (or necessary). After a short walk we
arrived at the café of Gary's recommendation and we were
quite impressed! The place was astoundingly American
with purely American clientele and beer lists and menus
and a guitar duo of two SO AMERICANEY AMERICANS who were
creepy-looking but AMAZING guitarists and the whole café
was EXPLODING with color and lights and we took a seat
closer to the back corner. We got some waters and menus
and as we ordered and waited and ate and drank and paid,
Rachel and Adam continued talking and though I didn't
and don't recall anything of the conversation itself,
I'll never forget their voices— spilling over with zest
and zeal and laughter and the pleasure of conversation.
I'll never forget the profound guitar skills, the creaking jamming life-mapping passions of those two zany
American creeps at the stage. I'll never forget the
sheer soak, the psychedelic gorge of colors vibrant reds
and zesty oranges and drowning blues and bubbling purples and lush greens color pulsing color the whole of
Costa Rica was color. I sat back and admired this beautiful moment, this pause in the swing and swirl of our
pale blue dot, this rich reason why the whole of it all
is worth it in the end, why lying in our deathbeds many
years from now certain of the end and writhing in pain,
we might for the last second of the game smile and say
with our last chuckle, "but that was somethin', wasn't
it..."

We went back, laughing and chatting along the way.
We arrived to a slumbering hostel. I showered, scrubbed,
brushed and flossed, hung my microfiber towel out to
dry, checked my soaked shorts (still fucking SOAKED),
got into some fresh dry (for a second) clothes, climbed
up to my bunk, and drifted off to sleep. And at that
moment, if I were offered to do that every day for the
rest of my life, I wouldn't have hesitated to accept.

The next morning, seated outside in front of the hostel under the shade, sipping coffee with the black dog at the door in repose, and with my shorts hanging in the sun STILL without the SLIGHTEST indication of dryness, Adam had some bad news.

"So, how important is air conditioning for you?" he asked.

Here is what had happened. You may recall that the morning before, we searched up a few hostels at our next destination of Manuel Antonio and a few of them had air conditioning. Well, Adam had suggested we delay booking until the next day, and now the next day was here and we had only three hostel options: $12.00, $14.00, or $72.00.

And guess which one had the darling air conditioning.

But during my stay here at Riva Jacó I felt that I had learned something quite profound. I had learned that I could adapt. That as bad as it was, with time it wasn't bad anymore. That in such a short time, I had actually grown quite comfortable with this rustic rugged lifestyle! Yes, I was good now! I was a good old-fashioned vato, sí! A true tico, yes! Air conditioning and water and bugs and jungle HAH! Hola señor, pura vida mi amigo! Yes, I'd be FINE without air conditioning, I said. WHO CARES, I said. Ain't worth the extra CASH, I bellowed, SIIIIIIII...

Adam felt remorseful, for he had really wanted to grant me this single request. But alas, it was going to have to wait. So he booked our next spot in Manuel Antonio, and with our last sips of coffee it was time to go! We checked out of the hostel and said goodbye to sweetheart Rachel and brotherly Gary and Cleopatran Laura and the dogs and Elías wasn't there so we didn't get to wish him well and in truth I felt very sad to leave Riva Jacó behind and I mused fondly and humorously about the tortures of my first night there and how in just a matter of days I had faced oppressive humidity, freezing-cold showers, tremorous Traveler's Dread, bugbites, sunburn, heights, and exhaustion and surmounted all! I felt liberated and emboldened and excited to face the world! And you will see how THAT fared by later that afternoon.

chapter one

So with all my sweaty reeking cotton cloth shoved
into plastic bags I hoped we could get some laundry done
before we moved on to Manuel Antonio. Gary directed me
to the town's laundromat ("If you cross the bridge on
the left and go up a block it's like on the left behind
the pizza shop") so Adam and I figured that if we could
drop off the laundry, grab breakfast, and pick it up,
then we would make the 10:30 bus just in time. As we
headed out with our bags and just as we crossed the
bridge and a couple of stray dogs on this beautiful
sweltering sunny day I remembered— of course and without
fail the dreaded personal curse— that I had forgotten my
wet yellow-green "swimming shorts" hanging on the gate
back at Riva. Adam the good old sport who really put up
with a lot from me (or laughed his ass off about it in
amusement) offered to run back and grab the shorts so I
could catch the cleaners. I found the cleaners and
walked in with two bags of shit, a beaming smile, and an
"Hola" and I was greeted by an older gentleman who took
them off my hands kindly. And as I took the receipt
(Yup, can't lose THAT shit) and bid him well, I asked
how long it would take and he replied "en 5:00, mas o
menos". I jumped with a start, for by 5:00 PM we would
be on the beach in Manuel Antonio! I checked the time
and it was already almost 9:30 AM (wow, I hadn't realized the time at all) so I asked if there was any way it
could all be done in an hour, for we had a bus to catch.
The kind older gentleman with a white goatee and glasses
seemed so truly compassionately sorry but he didn't see
any way that this could be possible. Yet from behind him
one of the older tica washwomen intervened and they exchanged some words and he turned back to me and said "en
una hora" which meant this sweet woman had offered to do
it all for me in one hour! I couldn't believe it! I mean
this sweet darling woman was willing to go out of her
way just for me. And the best part of it all was that
this whole ordeal would only cost me 3,000 colones!— or
$6.00!— and I was elated! I thanked them all exuberantly
and then headed back out toward the bridge and as I saw
Adam crossing it toward me shorts in hand I explained
the situation and he was fine with it. But realizing
that my "swimming shorts" were far from dry I knew that
these had to be carried on to Manuel Antonio still sandy
and wet and that was fine. I wrapped them in a plastic
bag and we went to the previous day's restaurant and

50

pretty much ordered the same food again. As Adam took
his seat in the same chair as yesterday, I asked if we
could move to another table just to change it up a bit.
For even though we were back at the same great café to
eat the same great food, a little change in seating
could give the repeating event some distinctiveness.

So we sat and ate and my food took longer than expected to come out because it turned out they had mis-
placed my order ticket and they were so apologetic but
it was cool and when the huevos revueltos y pintos con
arroz y frutas y café negro came out I ate with my army-
green shorts and grey tank top and black bandanna and
unshaved face and apparently a resting-bitch-face of my
own (which Adam had taken the time to inform me about).
In fact, Ice duly noted that I was physically starting
to fit in a lot more than one could've imagined and when
I asked what he meant he took a picture and showed me.
And in truth, I looked rough and sweaty and stern and
violent and though I felt far from any of these things
no mugger or murderer would dare mess with me.

We arrived back at the cleaners right around 10:20
AM which gave us about ten minutes before our bus was
due. I waited as these two darling older ticas handled
my clothes with the love and care and dignity of humanity's mothers and I truly sincerely loved them. I stood
just outside of the cleaners with Adam trying to explain
to him the difference between "por" and "para" and a few
other complex Spanish grammarities and when the ladies
had finished my laundry they handed it all to me FOLDED
AND BAGGED! Crisp and NEAT! I WAS BLOWN AWAY! I tipped
these beautiful mothers of God and bid them well, and we
were off again to our bus stop.

We asked a pair of police officers where the bus
stop was and they directed us just down the street. But
where they told us to go there was no indication of any
bus stop. No booth or sign or bench or anything. We
stood around a bit waiting and then I asked someone in a
nearby store and he said that the bus stop was that empty parking space in the middle of the road. Now, I
couldn't understand how this grey scraped parking space
was a BUS STOP but Adam and I waited there under a tree
for a few minutes. But after a few busses passed by and
we called out to them "Manuel Antonio?" and they said
"no", we realized that what had most likely happened was

that our bus had already come and gone. And by that account, we had literally missed it by seconds.

The next bus was at noon. To most people who travel,
this is a catastrophe. This is the end of the trip. This
"ruined everything!" To us? It was a chance to catch the
Jacó International Surf Competition! So we headed south
a few blocks until we reached the beach, and before us
was this tremendous expanse of sand and ocean. In the
distance were the gleeful crowds of cheering national-
ists as their heroes mounted in conquest the wet bellies
of the curling sea. We walked and the sun bathed us and
the wind caressed us and we ventured step after step
through this gorgeous godly landscape. And after a while
we reached what had evolved into a lengthy creek that
descends and ascends to and from the ocean and it ran
like a shallow yet wide river. And since Adam was both a
BOSS and in slippers, he walked right through it and
delighted in the cool tickle of the running current. But
I, in black K-Swiss and cotton socks, attempted to trav-
erse this Mosesean stream cómo un águila (like an eagle)
and like Pharaoh instead, I flopped right into the center and SOAKED my shoes and socks. Seriously, are YOU,
my Most Gallant Reader, as fucking stupid and clumsy as
I am?? Well Adam is NOT, for he winced with pain and
empathy and knew full well how fucking screwed I was
because if a pair of athletic shorts took DAYS to dry in
this climate, how long would these SHOES take? Furious
and indignant, humiliated and abashed, I marched on
flopping through the sand hating myself and wishing the
sand would swallow me into the ground where I belonged.
Certainly it wasn't THAT bad, come to think of it. But
for a moment I really did feel that way.

After continuing our beautiful sandy stride, sans
the wet flopping squeaking shoes, we reached the vast
and galvanizing crowds of international pride and
watched with delight as surfers took to the waves like
daring knights. And with the gallantness and swiftness
and suavity of razor-edged swords they sliced the bellies of the raging tides, zipping them teasingly, har-
nessing them coyly, cupping their force, cradling their
might, and then falling to their frazzled destruction
with genial surrender. And as their warring gladiators
took to their gliding steeds the mountainous white-
capped caverns of marine combat, the sons and sultry
(sexy! If I may interject) daughters of their distant

homelands cheered them on with the vigor and esteem of times far-gone. From the sombrero-capped sillies of Mexico to the passionate fervors of Italy, from the confident poises of Sweden to the waving vitalities of South Africa, each nation cheered on the glorious warriors, the violent sea, and the wonders of human audacity.

And as we beheld these electrifying marvels, we saw coming up the beach across the whole worldly procession an adorable golden dog. Cute as innocence herself he marched along with aplomb and jollity distinctive only of a freeloving dog. He witnessed our delight, our pride and passion, our national flags, large and awave with the ocean, surfing the winds of the sky. And suddenly, stopping merrily before it all, with eyes agape and tongue and balls a-dangle, this little golden dog flung his tight perk asshole straight out into the air and with orgasmic focus squeezed out the richest creamiest moistest copious feces a sight ever before did see. Yes, with the pride of a Brazilian graffiti street artist he pressed right on and as his pulsating asshole churned out this behemoth train, a local tica from afar raced up behind him and scoldingly kicked some sand over his outstanding heap of brown dung. And so this merrily dog shat his holy shit right out onto the proud and cheering stands of this International Surf Competition and when his heart contented and his rectum recoiled he marched right on his merry little way into the distant expanses of Costa-Rican paradise.

Back at the bus stop, I started to feel my cheerful vitality fading. The beaming sun had compounded the heat, drenching me in gucky sweat that streamed ticklishly down my limbs and head. My soaked shoes aggravated my ankles and really pinched my discomforts in a keen sort of way, for there is no way to think straight in sopping wet shoes, my friends. My neck was aching quite sharply, and though at first I dreaded that I'd been bitten or stung by something, Adam identified correctly that since my neck and the rest of my back and shoulders were searing steaming red, what I was sensing was probably sunburn. Now you may vaguely wonder, Oh Most Patient Reader, who in the hell (other than Adam who doesn't

care about such things) would venture to the coasts of
Central America without sunscreen. But for weeks I'd
been monitoring the weather reports in Costa Rica and
ALL of them forecasted 100% chances of storms 100% of
the time! So I was falsely informed that I wouldn't need
protection from the sun because for all intents and purposes the sun wouldn't be there.

NOT what happened.

And you will discover too, sometime soon, why this
sunburn was EXTRA hilarious. Why sunburn plus super-sun
of the Central-American coast plus grey tank top equals
a shitstorm of embarrassing tan-line scar tissue. But
for now join me as I buy some water and hide in the
shade and strip off my sopping shoes and socks with in-
consolable rage! I put on a fresh pair of socks and when
I replaced my shoes I discovered that they were for the
most part quite dry! It turned out that these stupid
black K-Swiss were quite a fantastic choice for watery
terrain, for they were made of an imitation leather or
plastic or something and were water-repellent! So with
fresh socks I was pretty much good to go! What an indescribable consolation.

Our bus arrived and we sat toward the back beside
each other. Since my large and heavy bag wouldn't fit in
the upper compartment I rested it on my lap. It was
heavy and cumbersome but it would have to do. But Adam
wouldn't allow it so he tried to stuff it up there and
when it didn't fit he placed it in a small gaping space
near the bus door. Now I worried that in that position
it was an easy target for snatching, but Adam was on it
and remained quite diligent throughout the whole trip
guarding this prized treasure. And from this seat on the
bus I looked on at my Hoodoo Red Osprey Porter 46 Pack
yielding at the seams and I felt everything pause for a
minute. I looked on in wonder, for this single item bore
my entire life in its grasp. My clothes and shoes and
book and documents and toiletries and tools, all tucked
within its firm embrace. And I beheld this beautiful
pack admiringly and sensed its loyal compassion and knew
that on this trip, it was my dear and trusted friend.

And to the soothing rumble of the speeding bus I sat
soaking in the summer breeze and cooling my face with it
and Adam lowered the brim of his orange hat and tucked
his chin and that was the universal signal that he was
napping. And that guy, folks, can sleep through any-

thing. So I admired the breeze and gazed out as our bus
ascended the lush landscapes of the Pacific coast and I
read a few chapters more of <u>The Dharma Bums</u> and Kerouac
was on a natural adventure too and I closed my eyes for
a bit and in fleeting no-time we found ourselves on a
single winding road surrounded by towering trees and
forest and dense greenery. And every few minutes the bus
would stop and folks would get off and I noticed that
stops were becoming more and more sparse and distances
greater and greater and buildings farther and farther.
The skies assembled for rain and the trees grew thicker
and the green darker and the road narrower. Adam awoke
and checked his phone and shuffled about, for we were
almost at our next stop in Manuel Antonio. So I put my
book away and grabbed my bag and somewhere in the seemingly middle of nowhere the bus stopped and Adam and I
jumped off onto the side of the road.

I stood confused, alarmed. We had exited far from
any buildings or structures. There wasn't even a curb on
the road to stand on. Aside from the single asphalt
road, winding downhill, we were eclipsed by thick
charged towering green. We stood in the thickets of the
Central-American rainforest. The skies darkened. It began to rain.

Now folks, I don't know what to tell you about jolly
old candyland Michigan rain from where I come from, but
THIS rain HERE? This was rainforest rain. Got that??
Chances are unless you've either lived in such a region
or taken the boat tour beneath Niagara Falls, you've
never seen anything like this. Adam searched his phone
for our destination as I swiftly unfolded my tiny black
umbrella to shelter myself (I might as well have un-
wrapped a tampon and held it over my head). The rain
descended. Adam declared "This way" and started uphill,
back the way we had come. I followed. The rain increased. My umbrella held off what it could. The humidity descended like fog and stifled my lungs, then plucked
up the sweat from my baking flesh. My legs ached as I
struggled to keep up with Adam's chugging gait. The ascent uphill tugged the fibers of my legs with every
strenuous step. Speeding busses and cars flung by honking from around the winding corner as we pressed ourselves away from the coursing road and into the brush.
And then a grievous terror descended upon me. I cried
out to Adam, "Hey, is my bag waterproof?"

"No," he shouted back. And then, realizing it himself, he added "Neither is mine".

We climbed. Up and up against the showering sky.
Against spattering roads and clenching humidity and aching legs and a hopeless umbrella. I covered my head, but
then I thought of all my belongings in my bag which
would NEVER dry if they got wet out here so I covered
the bag and exposed my face. Adam just kept climbing and
climbing the son of a bitch will you just fucking find a
roof already? And somewhere up there, far ahead of me,
he stopped and stared at his phone. And when I reached
him panting and relieved for the pause he scratched his
hat as rain splattered off of its brim and he looked
back the way we had come and said "It says we missed it"
and I thought FUCK YOU AND FUCK GOOGLE AND FUCK COSTA
FUCKING RICA!!!

We started back downhill. It was muddy and by now
dangerously slick. It was hard to see through the dimness and the sheets of surging rain which fell with
mocking confidence. My umbrella now wretchedly staved
off what little water it could from my bag and I edged
my way down so as not to slip into the road and kiss the
four bottom rubbers of a flailing bus. And just when I
finally decided, fuck it I'll just die out here as
roadkill, Adam turned right and walked onto a pebbly
path and some few feet away was a tin roof which served
as the "lobby" of our hostel in Manuel Antonio.

This place was in shambles. Shambles amidst thickets
of forest amidst thickets of surging sky amidst thickets
of gelatine heat. White rickety rusted paint-peeled
crooked-poled shambles. Adam approached a shabby table
where a few guys sat chatting and laughing and from
among them rose a gentle effeminate pretty white boy
with a genial smile and a glowing heart. His name was
Devin and he ran the hostel. But I was far too embit-
tered and bothered to even greet Devin, let alone anyone
else at that table. As Adam made arrangements I took the
room key and headed off to our room which sat atop a
feeble-looking pile of slabwoods amidst a tall and dense
shrub. I proceeded to the left for the stairs and painted on a wall in big letters was the word "SHOWERS" with
a huge derisive arrow that pointed AWAY from the building deep into a green thicket of underbrush where as
hard as I looked I didn't see any showers. Is that where
the showers are? Or perhaps they're beyond my scope of

vision they're so far away! I ascended the rickety stairs, growing more infuriated with every step. I reached the platform of the second story to find wet clothing lined up haphazardly along the ledge. We approached our room— Number Two, I believe— and Adam struggled to get the door open. He jambled and jambled with this fangled key in this rusted-ass keyhole and I thought, well if you'd move over I can just PISS the door down. How the fucking hinges haven't powdered into dust already is an Abrahamic miracle. Finally, he decided to go ask Devin and I gave it a go and it opened because you just had to shift the door a bit to get it open. We entered this empty room— empty of life, of character, full only of space and emptiness. There were four beds: two closest to the door— which were already covered in and surrounded by heaps of feminine shit— and two to the rear, where we would sleep. There was a single oscillating fan and a wooden hodgepodge with a mirror slapped onto it and beyond that ABSOLUTELY. FUCKING. NOTHING.

I switched on the light and it didn't turn on. Adam tried it and it still didn't work. We unscrewed the rusted stained carbon-spattered lightbulb and Adam left the room to get a new one. There I stood to digest my present location. Wet and hot and drained and indignant, sad and alone and hopeless and feeble, the mounting Traveler's Dread this time consumed me. The "ta3teer"(تعتير) consumed me. The damp bleeding-moist heat consumed me. The lack of air conditioning and the jabbing insult of that pathetic fan consumed me. The physical and mental darkness of a burnt lightbulb consumed me. The lack of Wi-Fi and the solitude consumed me. The absence of lockers or a way to safeguard our stuff consumed me. The large crawling bug on the wall and my wet Hoodoo Red Osprey Porter 46 Pack and the sopping wet socks and shirt and peeling walls and busted platform outside with literal gaps in the floor and the rage of a world that doesn't give a fuck about you all consumed me. I unzipped my bag to check my belongings, but nothing had gotten wet. Not even my copy of The Dharma Bums, which had been tucked into the outside pocket. I undid my shoes and took off my socks and stood for a moment pacing the room. Adam returned and before he could screw the lightbulb into the ceiling I spilled it all out right before his feet:

"Ice, man. I mean. This is. I mean, I HAVE STAND-ARDS, you know. Like, this is. Like there's no AC and no Wi-Fi and no lockers and. I mean there is a STANDARD..."

Adam stopped. The look on his face caught me by surprise. "Whoa, man," he said. He set his bag down and examined me carefully. I sat down on my bed. He sat on the bed across from me.

We talked. It was the first time I had spoken like this, expressing such enraged dissatisfaction, but Ice wondered how long I'd been FEELING this way. He was aghast not just by my words, but by my DEMEANOR. By the sheer finality of my rage. The truth was, besides the natural moments of Traveler's Dread, this was the very first time I had felt this way. Sure, Riva Jacó had shocked me, but more so due to its entirely foreign atmosphere than its "standard". This was the first time I felt that a place or situation was "beneath" me. Why?

We talked. "But what do you mean by 'standard'?" he asked. "Is it a 'standard' set by society? A 'standard' set by—"

"No, it's a standard I set for myself," I explained. "See, my hotel or hostel or whatever is more than just a place to put my head down, Ice. It's a place I retire to after a long day. A place to relax. It's where I reset. It's where I shower and rest and sleep and unwind. And so, when the place I'm retiring back to is THIS...", indicating our surroundings, "and it's just as bad being in here as it is out there, then I wind up in perpetual unrest and can't relax. I need a pit stop and to know I'll be having one."

He listened with his usual sincere attentiveness. It is always refreshing and relieving to speak to Adam.

"To me, an accommodation should have a few basic things," I continued. "At least, it should be safe and clean. This place isn't, Ice. It's dirty and shabby and there are gaps in the planks outside, man. And there's no AIR CONDITIONING! And we can't lock our bags up, so are they just supposed to stay out HERE?"

"Okay...okay..." Adam said. "I mean, I told you it wouldn't have air conditioning and—"

"I know," I said.

"So for me, if there's a bed to sleep in, I'm good." He thought for a moment. Then he asked what seemed like a random question. "Have you ever backpacked before?"

"No," I answered. But then I thought "Well, what do you mean by 'backpacking'?"

"Have you ever lived and slept outdoors?"

"No," I said.

And that was when the lightbulb went on in his head and it all made sense. "So, when it comes to finding a place to stay, you gotta understand where I'm coming from" he said. "On the Appalachian Trail, for example, if I got thirsty, I had to go to the river, gather some water, start a fire, boil it, cool it, and THEN drink. A drink of water took forty minutes."

I had never thought about that. Perhaps you hadn't either.

"If I needed to take a shit, I had to hike into the woods, dig a hole, shit INTO it, gather dry safe leaves to wipe my ass with (for if the leaves weren't SAFE and NON-POISONOUS, well...), and then fill the hole back up. And if I needed to SLEEP..." and he really didn't have to say any more. "For me," Adam concluded, "a place to stay is a roof and a bed to sleep in. That's it." And I realized that compared to the circumstances he was describing, those other things truly were luxuries.

So we talked in the numb dimness of a rainy evening, to the tranquilizing sounds of steady showers. We talked about lodgings, accommodations, experience, life challenges, philosophy, tradition, society, religion. We talked and talked and I sat on the edge of the bed leaning forward attentively and Adam leaned back in his characteristic long recline and his hat's brim firm and low and his hands across his midsection, fingers entwined. We talked, and these were the moments that travel is all about. It's about leaving behind what you "know" to explore the unknown. About immersing yourself into the unknown so that upon return, you re-evaluate what you thought you "knew". Yes, I had a "standard". But upon what basis did I build it? Who said a place HAD to be safe and clean and neat and air-conditioned? Who said it HAD to score three stars or more on Yelp in customer service? Perhaps that's a luxury. Perhaps most people don't have any of those things. Perhaps most people don't have a roof and a soft surface to lie on, let alone fucking air conditioning. Perhaps my "standard" came from a world where air conditioning and television and Wi-Fi and electricity and Verizon and warm showers and concierge service were the baseline. Perhaps THAT

world wasn't in touch with the rest of the world around
it.

Perhaps I'm an ungrateful spoiled asshole.

We got up and stepped out of our room. The rain had
stopped and the clouds were breaking up, and from behind
them emerged inspiring seas of crisp sunlight. I texted
my friends the "3 Blind Mice": "Currently in Manuel Antonio. It's a rain forest. There is a lizard and a cock-
roach on the wall and green as life can be". I got into
my sandals and left my bag on my bed and felt so much
better after talking to Adam and reflecting upon my
state of mind. As we were leaving Adam expressed that
what he had most felt during our talk was guilt.

GUILT?? I wondered. Why?

He explained that had he booked one of those air-
conditioned hostels from the PREVIOUS morning then this
whole fit of frustration wouldn't have happened and he
regretted waiting for the next morning to book. And I
was touched because here was my dear buddy feeling
guilty for something that was nobody's fault, because in
life shit happens and it's okay. We left and then I had
the peace of mind to say hi to Devin and some of the
other folks there. And something funny happened to me
because when I met Devin I kept saying "How's it goin'
MAN" and "Thanks, BRO" and "Sure, BROTHER" and felt very
self-conscious about it, for you see Devin was quite
clearly a raging homosexual and I hoped he didn't think
I was trying to insult him by calling him by these mas-
culine terms all the time but that I was just speaking
as I usually do. I wish things like this— the social
norms of society and ways of addressing one another—
were more clear. But because we as a human race are
afraid of our differences we can't seem to have these
healthy conversations amongst ourselves about how to
address each other and it's pretty sad. So I hope one
day I'll learn how to address homosexuals.

Adam and I started our descent downhill toward the
bustling little town of Manuel Antonio which sat right
on the shores of this gorgeous holy Pacific Ocean, this
mother of earth which gently caressed and petted its
baby sands with the fortitude of a courageous queen

mother. We walked around looking for a place to eat and as we passed through the street we spotted numerous people on the curbs trying to sell us weed and a gang of tourists gawking stupidly and obnoxiously and borderline-hysterically at a few monkeys playing on a tree and many restaurants with charming ticos trying to serenade us inside. We spotted a beautiful-looking restaurant on a second-story terrace overlooking the ocean with a huge and delightful seafood menu, so up we went!

We took a seat near the beautiful ocean view with the clouds parting and spilling sunshine between them and a waitress came over to take our orders. As soon as she saw us struggling a bit with our Spanish she immediately switched to English and I felt I had had just about enough of that. So as she spoke I just kept struggling through in Spanish and insisting to continue with the practice, because in truth this is the only way to learn a language after all (I mean there are many ways, as I know, to learn a language but for purposes of the story I will say that this was the best way to learn). I saw on the menu whole fresh fish and the red snapper caught my eye and with delectable doting delight I ordered the red snapper filet with vegetables and a drink. Adam ordered as well and we sat talking and chatting and laughing with no mind paid to the sweat or the heat or the AC or any of the other things that seem to govern the course of our daily happiness but are silly mindless details for the spoiled. And after we had finished this absolutely fantastic meal and the jovial conversation that accompanied it we got up to go and while paying I spotted one of those childish gumball machines and suddenly I TOTALLY wanted a gumball! So for 100 colones (a small petty coin) we could have one and I felt thrilled! I gawked into this globe of fresh inspiring round color and delighted at the thought of a sweet mouthwatering gumball pulverized between the gnashing teeth of my drooling warm mouth and the delight was insatiable! And as Adam deposited his coin I thought, I REALLY want a red or a pink gumball. And sure enough, Adam got a red or pink gumball! INCREDIBLE! PROFOUND! DESTINY! With avid joy I took this glorious sign of the gods as an omen of heavenly Manna so with pompous gusto I placed my 100-colones coin into the slot and turned the knob and out came a gumball and wouldn't you know it? It was BLUE. And I thought, DAMmit I didn't want BLUE. With great dejection and the droop of a stray dog I took my gumball and ate it. But halfway down the stairs I was overcome with its delicious taste and forgot all about the color failure of my gumballic odyssey.

Behind us, the hostess laughed at us. We smiled and laughed too.

When we got downstairs we ran into another one of those charming tico serenaders whose job it was to lure us into this or that establishment. And this lovely señor of charming gaiety asked us "Where you from" and when we said we were Americans he vehemently protested. "No! You no have blon hair! No blue eyes!" and we thought, well you kinda missed the point of America there pal. We laughed and bantered a bit and then as the conversation slightly dipped into a silent pause he looked to his right and then to his left and then he said "Hey wee ga' son guud weeeeeeeeed" and we laughed our asses off and walked away. Passing by a few stores which bloomed with bright Caribbean color and later spotting a sloth hanging from an electric pole, we walked around town watching the purple-greying sunset of this clouding Pacific Ocean and tried to speak only in Spanish which was fun and hilarious as we delighted in the sweet coastal pleasurable charm that is the lovely Manuel Antonio.

chapter one

On the whole, the night was off to an excellent
start. The guests had gathered as a lively mass on the
white paint-peeled veranda of the hostel amid rickety
blue-tinged lighting and wood to enjoy the night. Americans sat heartily at the table talking and laughing. A
French trio cooked spaghetti and meatballs in the common
kitchen. A Mexican pair tried to teach a Spanish (from
Spain) group of girls how to salsa. And of course where
there is salsa there is ME and so there I was taking a
young girl by the arm and twirling her around a few
times before suavely retiring to my room to mop my
streaming sweat-stanked face.

I opened the door and upon entering my room beheld
the two other roommates with whom we would share the
night: both girls, both seemingly European. One was a
tall hunky blonde (by no means fat, but it was like her
bones were made of timber or something). The other was a
dark-haired faceless— in fact outright featureless
ghosty— girl of puny forgettable stature who had more of
the presence of a thin lazy cloud of grey gas than of a
human being. I said "Oh hello, ladies! How are you!" The
blonde responded politely but with a clench, as if bracing her purse to her chest. The greygas one emitted some
faint urch of compulsory reciprocation.

Weird.

I crossed their sleeping quarters into my own where
I proceeded to change out of one set of soaking-sweat-
wet cotton rags and into fresh new dry-for-a-second-but-
now-suddenly-soaking-sweat-wet cotton rags and proceeded
back to the chipping-white veranda to continue my steaming sulk, but not before I bade my lady company farewell, to which the timber blonde responded with an inar-
ticulate breathless "yaaaa" and the greygas ghost responded not at all.

Very weird.

When I returned, the salsa lessons were coming to a
close, the French trio had finished cooking and had be-

gun eating their spaghetti, a bustling group of young
Spanish girls were goofing off quite uproariously— playing all sorts of giggly goofy spontaneous cheerful games
of one childish form or another— and Adam was off in
conversation as he always is so masterfully. I, on the
other hand, don't quite dive into human interaction so
effortlessly. I then texted my friends the "3 Blind
Mice": "Spanish American Dutch and even a French girl
right now offered me beer. Camille. Teaching girls how
to dance. Miss u guys. No idea who I'll be by Sunday"
and then I sauntered around a stack of books and skimmed
their spines, and there I found a small chess set! After
finishing a short game of darts, Adam was down for chess
so we set up in the pitch-black steaming-hot mosquito-
ridden corner of the veranda amid tattered floorboards,
peeling white paint, and steady rain to the flashlight
of my cell phone. It was an interesting game we played.
We would drift around from focus to spontaneous conversation to interaction with others to silent inner
thoughts to physical distractions of light, sweat, mosquitoes, and rain, and back to momentary focus. We never
did quite finish that game, actually. But chess isn't in
fact about finishing at all. It isn't about who wins or
who plays best or even whose move it is. Chess is about
the silent intellectual banter, the casual friendly
stroll between two human equals in tangled puzzling exchange. And if chess to you is about check- or stale-
mate, about "e4...e5, Nf3..." and beyond, then my friend
you're missing the whole entire game indeed.

Eventually Adam and I drifted off from our game completely (which is the beauty of chess and of all great
conversations: it's most important to START them, whether you finish them or not) as I retreated to a sink to
wash the sweat-gack off my damn gucking face. Returning,
I found him deeply engaged in conversation with an el-
derly but highly convicted old dude who introduced himself as Ezekiel. Ezekiel then introduced us to his
granddaughter, an angelic little sweetheart named Samantha, who with the candor and vigor of the Utah mountains
from which they hailed thrust her deck of cards into my
face and said "Want to see a magic trick?" and then before I could answer declared "Pick a card!" So I picked
a card and watched this heartwarming little darling fum-
ble the damned fuck out of her deck of cards and completely jack up the whole trick, only to tell me "Let's

start again. Want to see a magic trick?..." to which I
smiled gaily and watched her with charming delight insult the very sanctity of magic card tricks. Then she
put that poor dishonored deck away and said she wanted
to play chess! Adam moved aside to another table to carry on his discussion with Ezekiel while Samantha situat-
ed her sweet self between me and this tiny wooden cell-
phone-lit chess board.

I set the board back up and moved my pawn, and when
Samantha moved her pawn clear across the board and over
my whole row of pawns and knocked over my bishop on c1,
I said "Ok, so let's put the pieces back..." (That move
is illegal, in case you aren't familiar with chess. That
move is very fucking illegal indeed). Then I proceeded
to teach Samantha, piece by piece and move by move, how
to play chess. "Okay," I said. "Take THIS piece. This is
called a ROOK. Some call it a CASTLE. It moves like
THIS..." and so on. And if you don't know, chess takes
anyone just twenty minutes to learn but over twenty
lifetimes to master. So after a while we went back and
tried to play a game and wouldn't you know, little Samantha played FANTASTICALLY! She really impressed me
with how quickly she had learned! So we played chess and
talked about school and about her little brother and had
quite a hoot. But then I got bored and sweaty and told
her I would be right back, so I retreated to the bathroom and doused myself shamelessly beneath the faucet as
if to wash out the sweat and my demon soul along with
it. When I returned, the veranda's dynamics had shifted
a bit, for Samantha had left the chess board and gone
about with her helpless deck of cards, and the five
Spanish girls were playing some kind of balancing game
and toppling all over each other with deranged laughter,
and Adam and Ezekiel were still at it, but this time
Ezekiel had leaned right into Adam and was doing all of
the talking and by the look on Adam's face, this was one
of those conversations that wasn't going to end before
bedtime.

So I stood around a moment and suddenly I saw one of
the Spanish gals wandering near the chess board, scanning it with interest, and then glancing around to see
who it was for. Adam beckoned to me and said "Hey, she
wants to play!" and I thought, what fun to play chess
and chat with a lovely little chica amid the showering
forests of the Pacific coast. So I approached her and

said "Hola! Quieres jugar?" and she said "Sí!" and I
thought, great! So we sat down and as we set up the
board suddenly Samantha popped her head up from behind
me like a deranged chainsaw slasher and screamed "I WAN-
NA PLAY!" And although my first natural impulse was
"fuck off you scampy little shit you're ruining this!" I
immediately gained my composure and responded somewhat
more diplomatically and un-insanely, "Well, Samantha,
you can! You will play the winner!" Samantha agreed and
as the young señorita and I began our game Samantha told
us all the fuck about her baby brother and other random
spontaneous facts about random shit like rocks and toads
and fingers. Meanwhile, I asked my young Spanish opponent "Cómo te llamas?" and she said "Soy Marta" and I
said "Hola Marta, mucho gusto!" and then Marta asked for
MY name and I said "Joe. José," and I felt Adam's potential rage searing down my neck for finding me once again
calling myself "Joe" and not my real name. But poor Adam
was too busy for that, for Ezekiel had gone off to fetch
the Book of Mormon and Adam was fucking done for the
night. Poor benevolent fellow. Serves him right for being so fucking friendly all the time.

Marta was quite an excellent chess player and put up
an intense challenge! We talked in Spanish as lovely
darling Samantha carried on driveling with pointless
facts and pulling Marta's hair and trying to scare the
shit out of us by going under the table and fucking with
our feet. And Marta kept clutching her stomach as if she
was in pain so I asked her, "Tiene dolor, Marta?" and
she said "Sí, poquito," and I thought, that sucks to
have tummy pain. Then Samantha popped out from behind
Marta and screamed into her face and I thought "Child,
it's yo ass's time fo bed!" But as Marta moved in for
the kill and REALLY had me in trouble I suddenly noticed
her king was exposed to a single-move checkmate. And
although she had me finished in two moves and heavily
outnumbered I carefully studied this seeming vulnerabil-
ity in her left flank and saw that indeed she was check-
mated in one move! So after she had moved right up to my
king I simply made my move and to both of our astonish-
ments I had won the game! We laughed and joked and she
went off to retire to her room and I wished her a good
night and better health. Then Samantha started setting
up the board thinking we were gonna play, but I gently
talked her away with hopes of a game for tomorrow. And

as she went off to go to HER room, I noticed that besides me and a couple of stragglers heading off, the
only people left on that white veranda were Ezekiel
romping off about Christ and the Book of Mormon and good
old Adam, hand over mouth, letting it all shovel
through. After I had cleaned up the chess set and was
off to go, those two finally DID wrap it up and Ezekiel
apologized for taking up the WHOLE of Adam's night talking about Christ Almighty and the Holy Book of Mormon
and Adam of course insisted that it was his pleasure and
it was no problem. Then Adam and I headed back to our
room with the Book of Mormon given to him by Ezekiel
tucked neatly under his arm.

The truth is, Adam really DIDN'T mind having spent
his night listening to a geezer preacher, as far as I
could tell. People genuinely fascinate him, for their
merits or their flaws. But also, Adam is full of insight
and he had much to say about the nature of his night's
dialogue. "Ezekiel is so full of conviction," he said,
explaining the irony of being so quick to doubt others
yet so certain of one's own beliefs.

"Have you read the Book of Mormon?" Adam asked me,
to which I responded that I had. It was alright. And
when we got up to our rooms we bid our lady-guests good-
night and they hardly answered, and I was wondering what
the hell exactly was up with Timber-Blonde and greygas-
ghost-bitch. But no time to wonder about all that; we
had a big day ahead of us! To the chirps of monkeys,
insects, and far-off howling drunks we drifted off into
silent slumber.

We awoke around 6:00 AM to the cascades of crisp
sunlight, moist green leaves, and the chirps of birds
and monkeys. It turned out that my crusade for AC was
all in vain, for the night had actually been downright
chilly! It's funny how our worries so often disappoint
and fall short of expectation. I got up, dressed (at
which point I noticed to my horror in the mirror that
yesterday's walk on the beach of Jacó had carved into me
a hideous casting tan-line. The shape of my TANK TOP! So
surrounding my white chest, back, and abdomen was this
brown-red calloused leather casting chiseled along my

arms, shoulders, and neck neck NECK!!!), and packed a
few things into my sling bag (especially water) and then
lugged my Hoodoo Red Osprey Porter 46 Pack out with me
to the quiet sun-crisped white veranda where breakfast
would be served and proceeded quietly and diligently so
as not to awaken the two rude cold-blooded toad-faced
EuroBitches in our sleeping quarters whom I had to cross
during my exit.

Walking down the blue-painted steps into the infinite green ocean of God's darling little craft, I beheld
with humbling wonder the mountainous towers of leaf and
wood gently rocking to the songs of the wind— the joyous
and hearty sounds of unfamiliar birds and primates,
sounds inspiring awe that I never before did hear. I
walked over to the white veranda where in the common
kitchen a tiny older tica and her younger assistant prepared pancakes and papaya slices for the guests. Coffee
brewed in the corner and glasses for water were in the
sink. Seeing me, the old tica greeted me affectionately
and with authority, ushering me to an outside table and
asking me to wait for a while, as the pancakes still
weren't ready. She did this, by the way, ENTIRELY in
Spanish without the SLIGHTEST regard for my comprehen-
sion. Luckily, I understood what she was saying. But it
was also nice to finally meet a local who wasn't going
to accommodate my tourist-ass bullshit.

When the food was ready I grabbed my plate of two
pancakes and papaya and skipped the coffee and went out
to sit at a table in the morning sunshine amid the green
moisture of the rainforest. And my Hoodoo Red Osprey
Porter 46 Pack contrasted so boldly and beautifully with
its surroundings that I had to take a picture. Adam soon
joined me with his food and coffee and as we ate we discussed numerous topics which I greatly enjoyed but now
sadly struggle to recall. Once we had finished we went
back to the common kitchen and at the sink we saw some
people had left their dishes unwashed and we wondered
who in the hell would do that in a place like this.
Like, were they thinking this kind tiny tica was going
to do it FOR them? Or perhaps the Manuel Antonio Rainforest Park Rangers would be summoned for the task! So
we washed our dishes and I think Adam washed the other
dishes too and we thanked the old tica and her helper
friend and proceeded to get to the Manuel Antonio National Park!

chapter one

We returned to our room to drop off our bags, and
without lockers or a place to keep them safe I really
wondered why I should entrust my whole life zipped up
into my Hoodoo Red Osprey Porter 46 Pack to the owners
of this hostel or around these two snobby EuroTramps in
the adjacent beds. But Adam felt confident and unworried
and I followed his lead and as we closed the door to
leave I watched as my dear Hoodoo Red Osprey Porter 46
Pack faded from sight and sincerely wondered if that bag
and its contents would be there when I returned.

It was 7:15 AM when we descended the winding road
into town and around the left bend into the park. Some
way down, a troupe of tour guides stood around at a bend
in the road trying to seem like they were just casually
out and about observing animals. One of them, a charming
hefty tico, greeted us cheerfully and asked us if we
wanted to see a sloth. We said, sure. So he directed us
to this nifty little telescope and we looked into it and
there in the glorious distance of the forest was a sloth
easing its way down a tree! Amazing! The tico suavely
and casually insisted that it was indeed amazing! And we
could see THIS amazing and countless OTHER amazings if
we hired a tour guide into the park for the fabulously
low price of 10,000 colones! AWESOME!

Go fuck yourself, we said in terms far more genial
and polite, and continued down the winding road into
town. We chatted merrily as we crossed the deserted
shops on our left and the gleaming Pacific beach on our
right until we reached the end of the road and turned
left.

There we found another troupe of park guides, cheerful as the merry day and deeply concerned for us. Approaching with the disquieted gravity of a pardoning
priest, their leader solemnly suggested that we hire a
guide for this park. Without a guide, we would miss everything. To that we politely declined and continued.
Uphill, closer to some grand hotels peeking out of dense
foliated greenery, another guide caught merrily up to us
in a skipping jog and a beaming smile and asked if we
were meeting our designated park guide INside or OUTside
of the park. When we informed him politely that we were
without a guide at all, the woe of the Holy Virgin Mary
befell him and he bemoaned our grave misfortune. Lucky
for us, however, the Good Lord had imparted unto him
great and glorious news, the Word which is He, where we

69

could find these saintly park guides to direct us through the unknown desolates of the Luciferous jungle. I had a mind to tell this browning fucker at which "desolates" I was about to direct my foot, but decided instead to laugh and keep going. But I must admit that such repeated cries for a park guide were slightly starting to concern me. I turned to Adam and said, "Do you think we should hire a guide?"

His response was profound: "We could," he said. "But I would rather we explore the park ourselves." Then he went on to explain with his usual experiential wisdom his reasoning for this. With a guide, he explained, we would certainly see more animals, plants, and wonders within the park. Informationally, it would be well worth our money. On the other hand, going without a guide offers us the chance to discover these things for ourselves. We could see 100% of the park, handed to us on a rigid, scheduled platter. Or we could see 10% of the park and mesmer in the awe-inspiring wonder of our own discoveries. "In the end," Adam said, "you don't know what you've missed."

His logic intrigued me and indeed made sense to me. "Sense", actually, is a strong word. In terms of "sense"— or even "logic" for that matter— I could totally see my brother Kal or my father or some other rational being listening to this "logic" and "sense" and then kicking us in the balls for it. (You know? I just realized that this is not the first time I imagine my brother Kal kicking me in the balls for my thought-infirmities. I'm not sure why. To me, he comes off as the type of guy who would kick people in the balls for being stupid. Time will tell). But pardon me for saying this: sometimes life isn't about "logic". It isn't about "sense". Sometimes life is about NON sense, about discovery in the midst of welcome chaos. Sometimes life is about doing what DOESN'T make "sense" so that you can discover new things and make "sense" of them later. And if I sound crazy to you now, perhaps this upcoming anecdote of our venture into Manuel Antonio National Park will shed some light on the matter.

In no time, we found ourselves quite close to the park. Vendors sold knick-knacks, coconut water, fresh fruit juice, and snacks. Adam needed cash so we stopped by a small bank-teller booth and bought our tickets.

Adam, who is a park guide himself at Zion National
Park in Utah, found himself completely astonished by the
organization, cleanliness, and operation of Manuel Antonio. For many minutes he expressed indignantly his frustrations with tourists leaving their trash, shit, piss,
and carvings all over Zion: how they strew their plastic
bags and Burger King plastic cups and plastic hotdog
wrappers and clots of diabetic feces all over the place
and how teenagers carved their stupid little names inside stupid little hearts against the walls of these
million-year-old monoliths of God. Yet here in this
"third-world country" (what a crock of a name for people
and countries who are in many ways so much more advanced
than we are), our bags were being searched for food and
drink, properly disposed of with exquisite professionalism in an air of dignity and jovial respect that permeated this profound paradise. And through his deep passion I too felt the shame of insatiable consumerism
strain my soul, for indeed the greatest crime of man and
his gods has been the notion that we are somehow separate from nature.

As we entered the park, tens of visitors were herded
about, organizing themselves into tour groups as brown
guides in brown shorts with telescopes tucked under
their arms sallied about orchestrating this experience
for them. With humble politeness, we ambled past the
bustling groups into the park, where we would orches-
trate our experiences for ourselves.

Manuel Antonio National Park begins on a road-wide
dirt trail with enormous mounting walls of dense tropical rainforest on each side. Near and far the vibrant
sounds of tropical life rile the ears and the heart. We
ambled slowly past brown men in brown suits directing
visitors who directed their screens and lenses and gadgets frenziedly into the distance to capture fleeting
moments of perpetual life. We caught snippets of de-
scriptions of birds, primates, and plants as we walked
amid children jumping with joy, amid tourists thrashing
their touristy tourism into God's silent heart trying to
tear what they could out of it and splack it back onto
their Facebook and Twitter and Snapchat and Instagram

pages for all to admire. Vying desperately to capture
life's moments as they pass, they prefer to artificially
harness them in pocket-sized window-boxes rather than to
hold out their arms and let the moments splash their
skins.

Let me be fair, though. I'm not saying everyone
there was doing that. I'm sure many people were just
appreciating what they saw. And certainly I'm guilty of
such instances myself. But what I described I did very
much see, and it was just as annoying and desecratory as
it sounds. Anyways, after a lengthy while of this nox-
iousness we reached a quiet smaller trail to our left
which led to a view of a small waterfall. So, to see the
waterfall and to escape the incessant touristiness of
these intrusive hoarders of moments, we turned left and
got away from it all.

If I am sounding snobby to you at the moment, I sincerely apologize. But this is something I really just
don't understand: what is our modern obsession with
"capturing moments"? What do you need to "capture" a
"moment" for? What makes a moment a moment is that it is
fleeting and never coming back. That is what makes it
special. That is what impresses it into memory and makes
it the valuable thing that it is. That's the whole
point. The SECOND point is, who in the fucking hell do
we think we are trying to "capture" a moment? Are we
really under the absurd impression that space and time
are things that can be possessed? Possession is an illu-
sion, my friends, and this desperate need to hold onto
fleeting moments is both futile and delusional. Time is
going to pass. Places are going to change. Let it all go
and just be there without telling the careless world
that you were. And the THIRD thing is, suppose you DO
"capture a moment". Suppose that finely-edited Instagram
photo or Facebook video or Snapchat story or whatever it
is you think you are so capable of capturing is finally
caught. Why do we feel the need to share it with people?
Why is it so important that the whole world is pelleted
with our meaningless details? Our trips to this place or
that and our non-GMO grilled chicken kale feta garnished
salad at that nice little hip restaurant in hippy
hipville where all of the unique hipsters look exactly
the same and our children's burps and farts and our Friday nights at the big game and our photo next to a dying
celebrity with a big molesting grin on our faces and our

thumbs held up high as boners. It is such a bizarre and
strange practice we have evolved into: posting the proud
moments of our lives for all to see. Plastering them
onto everyone else's little screens. And though this all
sounds pretty over-the-top, and most certainly it probably is, I ask these questions so that we as a collective
human entity can reflect upon who we are and why we are
here.

So anyways. We started walking toward the waterfall,
and one of the reasons was that it was quiet and isolat-
ed and we needed that for a moment. We were among the
very few on this path early that morning, so it was a
quiet walk. We walked slowly, entering green upon green.
The green lit up and then darkened. Silence slowly
swelled upon us. The vibrant verdance soaked us. And
speaking of soaking, the humidity deep inside the rainforest is unfathomable and stifling. We walked and
walked, first through trails of green, across bridges of
green, talking, discussing, thinking. We talked about
tourists. About capturing the moment. About water. About
nature. We discussed the heat. At some point into the
trail, it became difficult to breathe. We felt ourselves
slowing down. The globing green and solid air tensed
within our lungs. Our gait slowed and our breaths con-
gealed. We came to a set of wooden stairs to cross a
bridge and paused to observe this incredible lush prism
of unadulterated earth.

We stopped. Stopping and standing or sitting in silence, we looked out into the purest truth of nature.
Into places never touched by man. And as is common when
in the loins of nature, I experienced the truest sense
of reality, the one so often spoken to us by the great
minds that venture out into nature and into truth. I
watched the rising undergrowth, the soft caresses of the
tender wind, the leaves large and small, the birds and
bugs and butterflies, the trickles of bashful water, the
fortitude of humble stone, the mothering cradles of rich
soil. And then I felt it. Felt it starting deep within
me. Felt it in my center as slowly but surely it rippled
through my blood into my heart and then echoed into the
bustling universe:

Pulse. Pulse. Pulse. Pulse.

The world is pulsing. The sun and moon are pulsing.
Green and white, blue and red are pulsing. Leaves and
bark, sand and stone, soil and water, worms and snails

birds and fish green and green. Pulsing. Did you know
that? Did you know that earth has a beat of its own? Did
you know that that is precisely where truth lies? That
between the veins of the earth, amidst its bustling or-
gans, there is a voice? A ring? A pulse?

I watched this world go by. Slowly but surely. A
world careless of our iPhones and concrete walls and
traffic jams and Wi-Fi connections and bright lights and
CNNs and gas prices. A world pulsing slowly but surely
as we try to race past it. And in truth, what we search
for and fight for and struggle for and work for is right
here. But we will never see it because we fear accepting
ourselves for what we are. We are this. We are this
earth. And no amount of metal or concrete or frequency
or electricity or power can change that or replace it.

And when the tides of enlightenment settled and consciousness returned to us, only some moments had passed
and we continued slowly but surely toward the waterfall,
discussing beautiful and truthful things.

chapter one

We saw great green plants. Butterflies of the most
ingenious design: wings of black and red, yellow and
orange, and colors I never before did see. Adam bent
down to adjust his shoe and was startled to look up to
see a strange lizard just two feet from his face, resting lazily on a leaf. We carried on slowly, immersed in
color. We finally reached the waterfall, a small cascade
of fresh water, and we sat to observe this wonder. Other
visitors gathered as well, coming and going in pairs and
groups. We sat in silence and admired the holy wonder
that is this Planet Earth. A pelican or some other avian
variation wandered gently below. We finished and slowly
proceeded back up the path we had come, discussing many
things like tourists and travelers and this one single
shot we have at life and the City of Dearborn from which
we hail and why on earth I have an American Express card
and pay an annual fee of fucking $150.00 (to which the
answer is, I don't really know. So many times we make
such decisions without giving them much thought. And
half the world doesn't even accept that damn card! I
should cancel it). We talked about asses and beautiful
women. We witnessed the force of ants. Have you ever
just sat down and really looked at ants? These monsters
mean BUSINESS! I've always been fascinated, actually, by
ants, but the ones in the RAINFOREST?? Strong fierce and
fast forms of robust militancy marching without doubt or
chance of failure. Moving fluidly and hindered only by
certain death. Calculated federated regulated venerated
creatures of the hearty earth. Marching to the pulse
pulse pulse of the universe.

At one point Adam who is damn near half a foot taller than me looked out into the distance above me and
said with the wonder of discovery, "There's a sloth!" He
pointed it out and I looked in that direction and he
kept pointing and I kept looking and it took me what
felt like ten fucking minutes to finally catch sight of
what he was pointing at and sure enough, hanging off a

branch some several hundred feet away high above us was
an amazing sloth! We stood in silent wonder, minute by
minute, watching this thing we (Adam) had succeeded to
see and thinking, this beats a tour guide's constructed
directions any day! Then after a length of time without
motion the sloth slowly began to use one arm to lower
itself and we stood watching in the quiet holy density
of the forest as this strange little thing lowered itself with such a slow painfully dawdling sluggish pace
that a full minute later it was still goddamned lowering
itself and we stood there laughing in hysterics at this
awkward sight. Some time later we felt a motion in the
brush behind us and found to our right a woman of some
Latin origin or another craning her neck over our shoulders to see what we were gazing at. So Adam pointed out
to her the sight of the descending sloth in the distance, and then from behind her arrived a girl whom I
assumed was her daughter. So I whispered to this beautiful little child that we were looking at a sloth and
suddenly with a boisterous bark— nay, roar!— this obese
little Latin-American kid flailed out "Sloth?! Sloth!
Sloth! Where Where Where!" "Where where," she cried,
pushing through us, parting us with her girth as her
mother pointed out the little fucker for her and she
yelped like a blundering booming gorilla "Sloth Sloth—

(If I may intercede, allow me to emphasize that I do
not express this little girl's weight lightly, [Lightly.
Heh. Pun. Irony. Hah.] for I am no proponent of childhood obesity nor do I find it appropriate to mock those
who ail from this condition. I merely mention her weight
here because A) it is a fact of the situation and B) her
obesity serves not so much as an affront to her personally but rather as a grander metaphor for our greedy
grotesque conquestuous rank American Western consumerism
which this obese little girl was clearly a product of,
to no fault of her own. I hope I've been clear)
—Sloth Sloth!" and Adam and I just picked up and walked
the fuck away from the desecration of the beauty and
silence and sanctity of Mother Earth and for a second,
JUST for a second, I wondered if sloths attack people.
You know, like how baboons tear off people's faces?
Something like that.

As we headed back, and quite suddenly, Adam and I
noticed something: an experiment in the making that we
had been performing quite unconsciously but with star-

tling results. Without knowing it, we were saying "Hola" to everyone who crossed our paths. Couples, families, singles, men, women, children...we said "Hola". But it was hundreds of "Hola"s later that I noticed something: EVERY ONE I said "Hola" to said "Hola" back. It was reciprocated almost every time. In most cases, people were GENUINELY SURPRISED that a stranger had said "Hola" to them for no reason. Most "Hola"s were reciprocated with a smile. And in almost all cases in which someone DIDN'T say "Hola" back, it was for a reason. Like in one particular instance someone was putting on a jacket and was distracted with the zipper. Another was putting a water bottle to her mouth. Another was talking to someone and most likely didn't hear us. So we kept on saying "Hola" and people kept on saying it back! And the sum of our experiment was this: Say hi! People want to hear it, want to say it back, and want to connect with each other! So just start the happy chain, man!

Coming back from this short side-path to the waterfall, we found ourselves back on the big dirt road, so we continued down that path to the next trail up to the famous cliff viewpoint. By now the traffic had noticeably increased, but so had the things to see! Deer emerged from the brush to sniff around and returned back in. Sloths surrounded us in the distance. Strange beautiful birds soared above our heads. We witnessed a wild fascinating plant which grew on the branches of these wondrous arching trees and, prior to blooming, looked like enormous four-foot-long bright red centipedes! And then came the monkeys! They travel in troops of fifteen or twenty and you hear them rustling in the trees above. They come up close, hoping to eat your food or to steal from open bags, and by now those primates had MASTERED the intricacies of the zipper, so don't even try! Walking through long wooded bridges we saw the green brush around us sprinkled with shiny round ruby-red objects and we discovered later that these were LAND CRABS! Did you know that? Land crabs! Huge active crabs by the hundreds and hundreds, living on the lush soily land! Large and plump snails crossed our paths. Huge swelling mushrooms sprinkled the land and tree stumps. From the distance Adam witnessed an ENORMOUS SOARING black bird and though I didn't see it myself, his sheer shock and startle ignited my imagination. We carried on, reaching a fork in the path. Looking at the map, we decided to head

left up to a high and wonderful viewpoint and then to
come around to witness the rest of the park from another
angle.

The climb was hilly and laden with lush green
stairs. Upward upward upward we carried forth. At some
point Adam took on a fit of silliness and announced
"ConfyOOshus sey..." and then declared some silly word
of wisdom. And when I asked what he was saying he said
it again and it was "Confucius say..." in a stereotypical goofy Chinese accent. And so we carried on bantering
back and forth with things like "ConfyOOshus sey...dwink
wato when uou thustee" and other shamelessly stupid
phrases like that and we just kept at it for a while
until Adam pushed his imagination further and thought,
imagine if "ConfyOOshus sey..." was in the 21st century!
And fucking Confucius is standing in your living room
and proselytizing on and on "ConfyOOshus
sey...tewevishin shwink de mynd—" and you cry out "The
FUCK, Confucius, get out of the WAY you're blockin' the
TV!" and after a short pause he says "ConfyOOshus
sey...neveh fight fiwe—" and you shout "BRO shut the
FUCK! UP Confucius!" And I just couldn't stop laughing
imagining three dudes in filthy white tees in a cramped
and dirty dorm watching Netflix while this old Asian guy
in a twinkly dress and a stringy mustache and white muffin skin and hands crossed up his long sleeves stands in
the corner and tries to get a word in edgewise and just
repeatedly gets fucking shamed shot down like a nagging
wife and he's wondering how five thousand years of wisdom strangely isn't working in this particular situation! We laughed our asses off right up the fucking
green slopes of Manuel Antonio!

Walking past lizards, ants, birds, bugs, butterflies, strange little mammals, and other exotic wonders,
we reached a dense point in the woods and I started to
feel hungry. And since food wasn't allowed in the park,
we hadn't brought any. Adam said he had seen a sign for
coffee or snacks further back and offered that we return
that way, but I declined. "Toughen up and deal with it,"
I thought. We returned to the subject of hunger because
that inspired a question along the way which was this:
"Suppose we lose our way and have to stay out here in-
definitely and eat to survive. What would you eat?" Of
course, I posed this question to Adam because personally
I have NO CLUE what I would eat. I mean those leaves

looked pretty alright, all green and shit. But Adam immediately refuted that answer, saying chances are that
quite a number of these plants are poisonous. He spoke
thoroughly about numerous botanists of expert-level
knowledge, such as Chris McCandless from Into the Wild,
who had died of accidental poisoning THEMSELVES. Even
experts often erred when choosing leaves. So considering
the lack of nutrition in plants and the sheer risk of
poisoning, Ice said he would all but entirely avoid
plants.

"So...?" I asked.

With a twinge of disgust he said "I wouldn't want
to, but I'd settle for grub. Bugs and worms under logs.
A lizard. High in protein." And that was the end of that
conversation.

We had been climbing for well over an hour by now
and we were tired (Well, at least I was). So at one
point high into the hills we took a seat near these man-
made platforms and sat on the benches. We rested for a
moment, looking out into the virgin-green rainforest and
other tourists came and went. I was tired, hungry,
thirsty, and dizzy. Hours more of hiking and effort remained ahead of us.

Deal with it.

I got up and continued. I had no choice. But more
importantly, I was starting to understand this phrase
that Adam so often repeated to me (and to himself).
"Deal with it" isn't a scold or command to press on;
it's a life philosophy. It's an understanding and strategy of how to live in an unpredictable ever-changing
world. Because we humans either fail to realize or simply ignore the fact that very very VERY rarely do things
go "according to plan". There are too many variables out
there that conflict with our "plan". It's like trying to
dress a morphing baby, you know? You grab the squirming
squealing kid and put on his pants then reach for his
shirt and suddenly he's a giraffe. So as he kicks and
screams some more you lengthen the pants and stretch the
collar of the shirt and suddenly he's spaghetti sauce.
You scoop the fucker into the shirt and now he's ink so
he soaks the whole shirt. Know what I mean? That's life.
You can't plan for it. And if you actually think your
day-to-day is going "according to plan" then cousin, I
have some suggested reading for you: look up "cognitive

biases" and "hindsight bias" in particular. And call me
cuz we need to have a little talk.

"Deal with it" means that if you plan loosely and
just prepare to adapt to whatever situation you're in,
then you're never caught off-guard. How CAN you be if
the only "plan" is to deal with it when you get to it?
Like water! Water doesn't plan. It follows its natural
law and deals with whatever comes its way. Water flows
smoothly and without resistance. If objects are big, it
goes over and under them. If small, it pushes them aside
JUST ENOUGH to get by and then keeps going. If it is
caught in a crevice or chalice, it waits patiently until
it amasses the force to flow out. If it doesn't achieve
the force, then it hangs out there carelessly. Because
it knows that at some point, it is going to flow again.
Whether sucked up atom by atom into the clouds and
spilled out of the sky or sucked through the esophagus
and kidneys and out the urethra, soon enough it's going
to be back in action. It'll get there one day and it
always does. So it doesn't worry, man. Water is cool.

I got up and continued. Soon enough I'd have what I
needed, from food to drink to rest and beyond. For now,
carry on and deal with it. And that I did.

On and on we continued step by step on these stairs
into deep dense rainforest. We saw more monkeys, butterflies, lizards, and strange little rodentey mammals.
Adam and I talked more, chatting philosophically in
playful banter. At one point, suddenly, we found that we
had reached a huge platform full of people. We stopped.
And looked to our right. And there, we beheld a sight
too miraculous for description. Too beautiful for photos
or dialogue. Dense lush forest. Aged angel cliffs and
little islands. Water of blues and purples and greens
unnamed by linguistic man. Endless horizons of sky
spilled in blues of mesmerizing wonder. A cool breeze
from the pulsing ocean topped it all off. And there we
stood among tourists who snapped fervently against their
gadgets, watching them snap snap click clack chick ad
nauseam and then scramble for signal here upon Mother
Earth's shoulder only to fling and smear their grin-
tended faces back to a mulking careless world. We sat

and waited until this was all finished for a second.
Then we approached the edge of the viewpoint and just
watched silently. We watched and watched. And when it
was done and we had captured the moment there, we
went back down those stairs and into the rainforest.

On our way down I realized to my dismay that I NEED-
ED to get something to eat. Adam recalled the café or
booth from earlier and it was on our way to the next
viewpoint, so we would head that way to pick something
up. At least we could get a bit of coffee and some refreshment. So on we went back the way we had come, admiring the beauty of this vast verdant world, observing
snakes and monkeys in trees, ants and lizards in the
soil, and heavenly butterflies and insects in the air.
It is, my Most Auspicious Reader, a heavenly world out
there.

We finally reached the junction of trails where other visitors stood observing signs and directions. We
checked the signs ourselves and observed that there was
still a whole section of the park to be seen, so we
would head on that way to another viewpoint and a beach.
But also there was a sign that indicated that some type
of food stand was nearby so we decided to head that way
for a moment and get some. We carried on, walking and
saying "Hola" to passersby and joking and thinking until
we reached a narrow path in the woods. Ahead of us was
this entirely BATTERED little wooden shack that looked
like it had befallen a hurricane and a Detroit gang-
rape. To our left we beheld with astonishment an absolutely gorgeous beach, FULL of beautiful visitors swimming and playing and bathing in the sun. We pressed on
to find this coffee booth but noticed soon after crossing numerous raccoons and a tree-house/skyscraper and
endless dense thickets that there was probably nothing
left ahead, so we doubled back and found ourselves once
again between a gang-ravaged wooden shack and a heavenly
ocean beach. Behind the shack was a water pump for fresh
clean water (where we filled up) and beside it were some
benches where groups and families had gathered to eat
and relax (mostly Indians. I'll explain in a moment why
I mentioned that they were Indians). We gathered that
this booth USED TO BE where coffee and refreshment could
be found, but since the Apocalypse it had closed for the
time being. So we took a seat and witnessed among other
things on the beach a woman in a black swimsuit loading

things into her bag. The bag was on her left, and as she turned around to pick up some things on her right a swift and vicious raccoon emerged from the brush on the left headed STRAIGHT for her bag! We watched intently as this skirting little fucker went straight for her bag, literally crawling into it and digging for stuff! When she turned back she jumped in fright at the sight of this raccoon halfway into her bag. It took her a moment to process, and then she screamed. The raccoon didn't budge. She screamed, shooed, then stood there dumb and with a look of terrified panic as ANOTHER raccoon began to approach. And when a nearby tica saw this utter dismay she came and with a vicious yelp kicked some sand at the raccoon and the bag. Immediately the raccoon retreated, observed from a distance, and then returned into the brush.

(I gather from tica women that the way to deal with any sort of wild animal is to kick sand at it. I will not challenge the wisdom of the ages.)

We sat facing this beach and admiring the coastal sun and glimmering blue ocean and soaring radiant skies and canopied thicketed trees and sugar-silk white sand and the occasional but thankfully frequent abundance of ASS ASS ASS which plumped and pummeled our pulses. And since previously (as guys always do) Adam and I had explored the depths of our loins discussing women and our insatiable lusts for them, we had raised a question that had yet to be definitively answered and it was this: Is Adam an ASS man or a BOOBS man?

(Folks, I am most indeed a BOOBS man. Most indeedly so indeed. Ask me again and I'll tell you the same. Love ass. Love tummy. Love lips. Love love. But BOOBS man. I like them in a box I like them with a fox I like and love them here and there I like and love them anywhere I like and love them yes and damn I am indeed a BOOBY man). And Adam had asserted that he didn't have an answer to that question, for if he described what he liked about women, the answer would invariably be that he liked "Women". Just "Women". Nothing specific, nothing in particular, but all in one. He just loved the complete soft variable wonder that is God's hand-crafted Woman.

That's sweet, Ice. Heartwarming. I can't deny. But what makes your ticker totter, my friend? What gets the juices joltin', eh? What grinds the gears down there,

friendo?? There are three possible responses to this
question: Tits. Ass. Legs (arguably included with
"Ass"). We all love a pretty face. Glimmering eyes.
Cream skin and silk silence. The melting white darling
of a genuine smile. The glow of intense adoration as she
hurries by through quiet rain. We've all felt our knees
clap with helpless despair when beholding the elusive
face of heaven carefully meaded upon her tender head,
adorned with flowing hair and the bliss of being alive,
leveled with the yeah yeah yeah yeah WHAT PERKS YOUR
PANTS, ADAM??? And Adam loved it all and I knew that.
But sitting on the beach for a few minutes too many,
watching girl after girl after girl girl girl rise from
the water and into the water and run through the sand
and lift her arms to stretch and bend over to adjust her
towel, Adam finally found his answer. Yes, the inspira-
tion of the Muses finally beaked from the recesses of
his soul and burst forth into consciousness and he
blurted out with exorcism what would have been totally
random had I not been thinking the exact same thing: "I
like ass".

    Yes you do. Yes you do.

    Now on to the Indians. These are Indians from INDIA,
mind you, the REAL India. Not the one we accidentally
found and robbed and ravaged and raped and riddened with
our putrid diseases and carved up and decimated tree by
tree by rock by bison by mineral by deer by bone. Nope,
not that one, though we still call its rightful owners
INDIANS. No, not those. I'm talking about red-dot-holy-
cow-masala-spice-gupta-Brahman-Karma-No-tip-Thank-you-
come-again-Seven-Eleven Indians. THOSE guys. So if you
haven't gathered the fathoms of your intellect yet to
infer that I'm not a fan of Indians (well, at the TIME I
wasn't. That has changed. It changed fast. Long story.)
then by now you totally should. And you should know that
by all accounts I am WELL AWARE that I have a racist
view of Indians, that it is based on false, erroneous,
bigoted, and ignorant assumptions, and that it is shameful, evil, unforgiveable, and downright horrific. That
you should know going into this, my Most Beneficent Most
Merciful Reader, and in addition you should know that
though I am TOTALLY aware of ALL of this, I'm going to
tell you now what I told Adam then, which is this: I
don't care. I still am not a fan of Indians.

chapter one

    So if you're anything like Adam or any other sane
individual human being, you're a tiny bit offended right
now. WHY! HOW! How can you be this and that! What right
have you for that or this! Yes yes yes calm your crevices and listen up for a minute. So Adam and I sat on the
gorgeous ass-speckled beach talking about so many
things, but one of them was racism. And he asked the
Great Question, of course: "Then how do you feel when
people say that about YOUR people"... and so on. He is
right. Of course, racism is absurd. It is the act of
basing a conclusion about a whole group's behaviors,
beliefs, or characteristics on the actions of a few. It
is factually, logically, morally, ethically, and
everythingelse-ly WRONG. So how is it that I can know
ALL of that, know without EQUIVOCATION that I can't
judge Indians— all one BILLION of them, mind you— because just SOME of them are goofy-looking stinking cheap
rude inconsiderate demanding weird-accented froths of
masala shit? Because maybe after living for a time in
Kuwait where they are treated as a sub-species or waiting tables for them without tips or parking their cars
during valet with accusations of stealing purses and
without tips or trying to sell them First Wireless X
FIFO cell phone accessory racks without sales or tips or
watching them infest fucking Wayne State University
(which by the way SUCKS DEAD DONKEY BALLS for FARRRRRRR
more reasons than just Indians) for six years...maybe
after allllllllllllll that, I MIGHT have developed a
biased irrational unfair clearly ignorant grudge against
them. Because, my Dear Magnanimous Reader, I am a bad
human being. Let's move on.
    We got our rest and sipped some water and Adam told
me a couple of stories about good Indians and some racist friends he knew from work in Utah. Then he gave up
wisely, as one should in the face of a stubborn ignorant
shameless fuck like me, and we wrapped up and headed
back down our path away from the beach, back through the
thickets, and toward the next (ass-less) paradise of
Manuel Antonio National Park.

    We resumed our pleasant hike further discussing the
wonders of earth and thought and at some point arrived

near a VERY long flight of stairs leading deep down into
the thickets of the rainforest. And down there was sup-
posedly yet another beautiful viewpoint. But without
food or rest for hours I really felt myself panic thinking about descending (but much less about going DOWN as
coming UP) those stairs. I felt that whatever was down
there wasn't worth the venture. But Adam luringly coaxed
me with the wisdoms of Confucius, reminding me how
"ConfyOOshus sey" I should keep going and how
"ConfyOOshus sey" to take it step by step rather than as
an enormous whole and how "ConfyOOshus sey" I should
hurry up and quit being a frothy cunt, or something to
that effect. But anyways we went down those stairs and
my heart went down too with each endless step but eventually after a long haul we found ourselves at the bottom and down there amid dense verdant thickets of paradise we walked a bit and found great numbers of people
in bathing suits without shoes and they were on the
silky sands of a beautiful little beach surrounded by
mammoth rocks and jagged cliffs and glowing greens and
gemming colors of flowers. And the ocean, my friends.
That great blue crisp expanse of Mother Earth's darling
back extending as far as the eyes can see, peaked by
tall black islands of rock. We stood and admired for
quite some time the indescribable wonders of our swirling pale blue dot remembering what it means to be on
this earth and to be human. For many lengthy minutes we
silently observed it all as people and families roamed
about swimming and taking photos and climbing some large
boulders. Eventually Adam also proceeded to climb some
boulders, a giant pile that extended out into the ocean.
From afar I admired the view and took a few photos and
watched Adam watch life, which is a beauty in and of
itself. He returned to inform me that there were MANY
little crabs out there and we walked on as he explained
other geological earthly wonders about this great place.
At one point we found an enormous hollowed tree trunk on
the beach so Adam sat at one end of it and I tried to
climb up so he could take a picture. But folks, for the
fucking life of me I couldn't get my ass up onto that
log. I literally must've tried about twenty or twenty-
five times. Adam first laughed, but after a while he
seemed downright embarrassed and repulsed. But finally I
did get up there and he snapped the goddamned photo and
we moved on with our bane and putrid lives.

Coming back up the beach we saw a great troop of monkeys blasting through the trees to take a gander at these gullible little humans whom with such delusional authority had ventured into their domestic territory. The monkeys would scramble up close to us on the sulking branches, inspecting our sights and scents, as we flopped about ecstatically with our fuckface phones like sneering clown-cows snapping and recording their every gesture with alarming gullibility. Little did we know that these monkeys had evolved to exploit our stupid scramblings by playing a little trick in which two or three of them would come up really close to the humans, but only to distract them. Meanwhile, as we piled onto each other to capture them with our goofy gadgets, the rest of the troop would circumvent this mass of idiots to reach our bags which had been haphazardly strewn behind us, thereby proceeding to unzip our bags and steal our belongings and foods. It seems that even the raccoons had caught on to this trend (makes you wonder, though: how fucking predicable are we, exactly?) and by the time we had even noticed, they too had half of their bodies dug into our junk. Once they had taken or tried to take what they could, the troop was off through the trees to rob the next group of ape-mutated imbeciles. But I'll tell you, though: it was all worth it, for Adam managed to catch some mad footage, my friends.

And now the time had come to ascend those fateful stairs whose ferocious descent had remained on my bothered little mind ever since. On we went ascending step by step, encouraging one another with the great chants and maxims of all that "ConfyOOshus sey". And with every step I faced and thought I could no more, Adam reminded me to go step by step. Stop thinking ahead and deal with what's in front of you. Deal with it, I chanted. On and on I focused on the step before me and the gorgeous fantasy of the nature around me and the wondrous humor that is Adam's and my frivolous banter until at one point after one too many cries about what "ConfyOOshus sey" Adam finally asked, "Hey, what IS Confucianism?" In other words, what exactly the fuck DID ConfyOOshus sey? I thought this was hilarious and laughed heartily and before I knew it I found my feet back on damp soil and a mountainous trail of wooden stairs behind me and I couldn't believe how quickly and painlessly and downright pleasantly this whole dreaded process had passed.

God, do our worries so often disappoint, my Dear Most
Pensive Readers. My, what a letdown our worries are indeed.

We carried on back walking and talking about all
forms of religions, and I tried to explain to Adam the
little I knew about Confucianism and Taoism and Chinese
thought as a whole and then we branched out into Bud-
dhism and Islam and religions and morals and ethics and
all the beautiful things that make us such great friends
and make the tread through the years all worth it in the
end. We carried on walking and observing animals and
noticing more ants and bugs and butterflies, more snakes
and lizards monkeys raccoons and here and there a
quaintly strange little thing that looked like a cross
between a raccoon and a monkey and it moved in such a
strange way and Adam thought it to be an anteater but
though I felt he could be right I wasn't quite sure that
it was an anteater so I kept observing it ever-so curiously (it turned out to be a coati, a mammal indigenous
to South America). And finally after lengthy discussion
and exploration and the sights and sounds and talks and
thoughts of a lifetime, we found ourselves back on the
main trail of the park heading back the way we had come.
The sun had clearly shifted across the sky and it was
now positioned quite differently and the sunlight
spilled upon us at an acute angle as we carried on into
its heavy crystal beams.

And as we sallied forth beneath the green canopied
limey-light of the crisp rainforest, at some point somehow the topic of prostitution came up— namely, the act
of exchanging money or other barter for sexual remunera-
tion. We discussed hookers and strippers and other means
of prostitutory practice and Adam took a pretty firm
stance as to its immorality yet I took a stance to the
contrary, and I argued that besides religious reasons,
there were no moral or ethical grounds for a group or
government to deny people the choice to trade for sex. I
mean, what business does anybody have telling me I can't
trade for sex? What indeed is wrong with an agreement
between two consenting adults to carry on for a prede-
termined amount of exchange? It seems bizarre to me that

this would require the blessing of the federal government, wouldn't you say? In addition, if indeed the matter is settled on mutual terms between both parties (as
opposed to rape or slavery) then what's the problem? (I
might note, my Chanceably Perplexed Reader, that most
but not all of my opinions about the permissibility or
legality or morality of prostitution stem from my reading of the graphic novel Paying For It by Chester Brown.
I thought the guy made an exquisite case for it and
frankly, he had me reasonably convinced). But despite
arguments that I felt to be fairly sound and reasonable,
Adam was not the slightest bit deterred from his stance
and argued pretty solidly that rationalizing an immoral
act such as prostitution doesn't make it acceptable,
soundly as one may construct the case. No matter how you
choose to semanticize the matter, it's wrong. Well,
those were all the cards I had for THAT particular conversation so we agreed to disagree and carried on.
    Finally, our ventures through Manuel Antonio Nation-
al Park had come to a close and we found ourselves back
among the priestly park guides and souvenir salesmen and
fresh juice and coconut water vendors and scampering
children and tourists and booming restaurants with
charming bombastic little men serenading us in. After
passing quite a number of them whose charms didn't quite
catch, I must admit that one guy finally TOTALLY swept
me off my feet! He was this absolutely explosive little
tico in a hat and polo shirt and sunglasses who swayed
and swung with the energy of an acid trip and in seconds
he had us laughing and joking and following his smooth
enervating ass into the shades of a canopied little patio and before our butts had hit the chairs and our feet
had placed under the tables the fuckers were already
blending our mango smoothies and asking us if we needed
a couple more minutes. And I won't lie, the hatted
sunglassed tico dude had it right because we hadn't
quite known how absolutely STARVED we were. So when the
smoothies came out we looked over the menus and I wanted
some fish (which Adam at some point informed me that my
keenness for fish and vegetables could mean that I have
a "pescatarian" inclination. Which I so fucking do!) So
out came our food and I went at that tasty meaty filet
of fish and sides of vegetables like no other and I
sipped with raging gusto my mango smoothie and before I
had slurped out its last darling droplets I already had

another papaya smoothie coming up and I washed it all
delectably down with cool fresh water and gorged further
on conversation and memories with my buddy Adam and we
lounged the FUCK out, my friends, in pleasures I recount
euphorically of sun and green and laughter and music and
food and the joy of being alive.

Then, suddenly and without any warning, my deep and
genial gratification was solidly blindsided by the realization that it had been HOURS AND HOURS since I'd
looked at my phone. My face warped and I dug into my
pockets for my phone and held it up to get signal but
the little thing didn't catch. So I set it down on the
table and waited eagerly with tapping phalanges for signal but it still wouldn't catch. Meanwhile, Adam was
sitting there with all the signal in the world checking
HIS internet and HIS Whatsapp and HIS social media and I
dunno what else but what I DID know was that I was growing absolutely LIVID with my damned T-Mobile iPhone cunt
crap piece of shit which wouldn't goddamned fucking
work! I just wanted to send home a message letting the
family know we hadn't died or been half-devoured by a
Costa-Rican lion but I couldn't do that until this tight
fucker caught some damn jungle signal! So I sat there
fuming and steaming until finally I just asked Adam if I
could use HIS perfect little gem and with great aggrava-
tion I found the means to text someone back home that I
was fine. Then I gave it back to him and shoved my crack
piece of piss phone back away and thought, fuck satel-
lite and signal and the whole of the shitty human race
that can't do ANYTHING RIGHT!

The food was great and so were the smoothies and the
setting and the conversations so after paying our tab we
were ready to carry on with our day. So as we were heading back to our hostel we found ourselves crossing back
through town in Manuel Antonio and slowly the gorgeous
ocean and its sandy paradise of a beach emerged on our
left and the shops bustled on our right and looking out
into the glistening afternoon we saw in the heavenly
distance a multicolored parachute being dragged about by
a speedboat and thought PARASAILINGGG!!! We raced down
to the beach and found the white booth where we could
inquire about parasailing services and there we found a
tico and a VERY American woman who was like a divorced
lawyer from New York or something and they were jolly
and merry and answered all of our questions. So our op-

tions were a fifteen-minute ride (is a parasailing session called a "ride"? A "session"? A "slot"? I'm not
sure. Well we could parasail for fifteen minutes) or a
thirty-minute one. Prices varied significantly, but we
thought WELL WHAT THE HELL how many times in a man's
life does he get to PARASAIL OVER THE COAST OF A CEN-
TRAL-AMERICAN RAINFOREST?? It turned out that they had
an available time slot right then and there so we selected the maximum time and it was time to head out! But
before we could do that I needed to head back to the
hostel to change into waterwear (and Adam didn't because
this guy has on clothes that are designed for every ele-
ment in the universe. If we had to ski through fire this
fucker's fabrics would suffice. His pants and characteristic tattered orange hat were dipped into the River
Styx or something). But instead of having to walk back
the lady at the booth offered to drive us there and back
so we could make our session on time. Before we knew it
we were driving back uphill to our hostel and I was running into our room and changing and grabbing a towel and
slippers and cash and I was back in the truck and we
were driving back downhill and leaving our stuff under
the booth and suddenly we were strapped to a fucking
parachute! People. It all happened as fast as I describe
it. One second I was fishing for my cash and Chase Freedom card because for the one-hundredth time they'd declined my American Express and the next second I was
strapped to a fucking PARACHUTE. A bunch of charming
ticos scurried about us hollering commands and signals
and disseminating careful instructions about how to sit
and where to hang on and what to grasp and who to what
and as they talked I felt my blood all drain to my knees
and it became hard to breathe and I felt a shiver and I
thought "What in God's name am I doing here? If something goes wrong I'm going to die out here dragged down
to the depths of a hungry ocean am I fucking crazy? Get
me out of this thing how did this all happen so fast"
but before I could finish my inner monologue ramble of
terror I was under the sun strapped to an intricate net
of harnesses and clamps (Are these going to HOLD??) and
behind me was a goliath outspread parachute and before
me a speedboat VROOMED and suddenly I was dragged to a
jog and one of the ticos yelled "JUMP!" and holy shit I
jumped and holy   holy   HOLY!   ah   AH!
AHHHH!!! And the beach was under us.

chapter one

We were soaring through the sky, my friends. Gliding through the blues of heavenly God, sailing into the winds of stratospheric space. Higher and higher. The mammoth waves of the Pacific were but microscopic flakes in the infinite ocean blue. We glided into the horizon, which by now was streaked and streamed with the infinity of blessing blue and then padded with monolithic clouds. The brushed blues of above crashed glassly against the horizon into the channeled coast of the ocean below. We were flying across the sky.

We soared. The parachute fluttered noisily behind as the almond-sized speedboat cruised below. To our left we saw for the first time an aerial view of the national park. Towering solid greens against sharp black-brown boulders. Fluttering patches of azures and aquas below us, crashing as a frothing white line against the forest. Here and there peaked mountainous islands, jagged and sharp and brown and black, jutting from the crystalline sapphire waves with warm and welcoming smiles. The amazement of it all didn't fade for one second. Still it doesn't.

And then in all of this midst of indescribable skysailing aerial beauty, Adam took out his waterproof-encased phone to capture in photo and video all of this magnificent wonder (And at the time, I was incredibly glad that he did. See, back before they strapped us into this potential but beautiful death-trap, I had considered my sunglasses and outright nulled my phone from coming out on this soar with me. Bison-balled Adam brought both. He pocketed his sunglasses and held out his phone which was safely enclosed in a waterproof case, and he gleefully snapped pictures of indescribably majesty and beauty, catching us as well in its midst. And I appreciated all of this tremendously at the TIME, mind you. Meaning AT THAT MOMENT. What happened NEXT is an entirely different story).

We soared and soared. I looked down, wondering how
high up we were, squinting to observe the miniscule
waves and wondering, of course, if we would survive a
fall into the ocean from such a height. Adam said it
would be impossible. A fall from all the way up there
onto a watery surface would equal the impact of falling
onto concrete. He said your only chance of survival
would be to fall in a way that your body would be perfectly straight. If a single limb, a single toe, were
out of place, it would shatter on impact. So I enjoyed
the wonderful sky-cruise and hoped that the speedboat
wouldn't malfunction or a small accidental tear in the
parachute wouldn't rip the thing into tatters and I
wouldn't have as my last lesson in life a physical
demonstration of what it might feel like to jump off a
twenty-story building. Educational, I'm sure, and quite
riveting. Real hands-on experience right there, of
course. But I'll gratefully pass, thank you.

And after the great soar of heaven had quelled us to
humility and wonder, we were once again facing the shore
and yawping aloud with vitality and euphoria and a couple of jet-skis raced out toward us from the shore as we
felt ourselves slowly descending. The speedboat slowed
and we coasted downward closer and closer to the breaking waves as the jet-skis positioned themselves for our
arrival. We took one last lustful look out into the distance into the blues and pearling horizons then braced
ourselves for watery impact! And when we finally crashed
into the waves, the ticos reached out for us just in
time to clip us out of those huge metal bars which
rigged us to that expansive parachute. We bobbed around
in the cool water for a moment, and then each of us swam
toward a jet-ski for our ride back to shore.

The next three things that happened were bizarre beyond the scope of reason. The first was this: the tico
on Adam's jet-ski tossed a phone to a tico on the speedboat. I watched this happen: jet-ski tico threw the
phone to speedboat tico, and the phone bounced right off
of the side of the boat and into the water! Holy shit!
For a moment none of us seemed to have processed what
had just happened, but once it finally clicked a couple
of them dove into the water searching for it. It was
nowhere to be found. And I know I'm an idiot myself (as
this tale is all but PUMMELED with examples and cases-
in-point), but as dumb a fuck as I am I think I would've

known that that was a bad idea. I found myself baffled that someone would attempt such a stupid thing.

In the meantime, Adam was patting about across himself realizing that during his descent into the water he had lost his sunglasses. Somehow during the whole shuffle they had fallen off and now they too were swallowed into the roaring belly of the sea. Holy shit!

The jet-skis raced off, with me clinging to one and Adam to the other, and the ride was nice and brisk. A great way to end a parasailing experience! I got off in a thrill, shaking off the water and hooting joyously as Adam headed off toward his pile of things under the white booth. And as I stopped to catch my breath and bask in my glee, I stood bent forward gazing at Adam's back from a distance and I sensed that something wasn't right. Something was off about him. I headed over and when I neared him I saw that his attention was on the waterproof phone case and it turned out that the waterproof case hadn't been so fucking waterproof at all!

"It's soaked", he muttered, dangling his dripping-wet Samsung. I was blown away. Two phones and a pair of sunglasses all in less than five minutes. He held out his phone, trying to turn it on but in vain.

"It's alright," Ice said.

"The fuck it is," I thought.

What now? That phone was now water-damaged and it had been our everything. It had tracked and downloaded our maps, booked our hostels, stocked our videos and photos, settled our purchases, and if needed JIGGLED OUR BALLS, for Christ's sake! Adam had fucking EVERYTHING on that phone. What now...

Nothing, I suppose. Somehow, I found myself following Adam back into the water to play in the waves. We'd hoot and holler as waves crashed over us and dragged us back, immersing us beneath frothy foam as we laughed and careened about. But after a laugh or two, I'd catch Adam from the corner of my eye looking back toward to beach. And he was thinking what I was thinking. Adam listed off the fallen pairs of sunglasses he'd lost at sea— maybe five of them— but then we'd be back spiraling in the waves in no-time and laughing and hollering away. But then, our minds trickled back to the fallen soldier on the beach.

This wasn't ok.

chapter one

"We can try to get it fixed," I tried to reassure
him. "You've got everything backed up on there, right?"
I don't remember what he said, but I remember the look
on his face. No, it wasn't ON his face at all. It was
beneath it.
But beneath that, beneath all of it all, I saw something truly amazing. I saw the thing that makes my dear
friend and hero Adam the great man that he truly is.
Like the crashing waves before us, his mind would careen
toward the beach, but not with regret. Not with anger or
spite or despair or bitterness or malice toward an un-
just fickle world, nay! Not with the slings and arrows
of outrageous fortune and the thousand natural shocks
that flesh is heir to, nither nay! None, but only with a
calculating assessment of how to proceed. A clarified
acceptance of the present reality and a brief computa-
tion of the forthcoming effects. And when the test of
life had come, Adam had lived up to his holy mantra:
"Deal with it". And deal with it he did. This setback
wasn't going to ruin his trip or his day or even his
moment. Life happens, as it always does. And when it
happens, you deal with it. And that he did. I thought
back to my breakdown at the rickety chipping hostel the
night before and felt quite humbled. I could now see
what it really meant to "deal with it".
"We can put it in a bag of rice," I suggested. After
all, we could at least try to salvage the fucker, right?
"Yeah," he said, noting though that salt water was
NOTORIOUS for annihilating electronics. But we finally
decided to give that a try. So we exited the crashing
waves toward the beach and retrieved my shirt and towel
and slippers and what remained undestroyed or ocean-
fucked of Adam's belongings and as I dried off and
started up toward the street (Adam doesn't "dry off" by
the way; he air-dries. Meaning he just waits for the
water to go away on its own. Fucking guy) the ticos from
the parasailing ride approached us asking about our
rides and chatting and serenading us and after a minute
I thought they had overstayed their welcome and I started to wonder what exactly the fuck they wanted. But Adam
isn't as fucking STUPID as I am and through his decade-
plus of service-industry experience he knew EXACTLY what
they wanted. And DESERVED! So he asked me how much cash
I had on me and I didn't have much and once he tried to
explain to them that we were low on cash and would go

back to the hostel to grab their tips THEN my peanut-
sized lightbulb turned on and I thought, Jesus man
you're such a damned blundering idiot I swear to GOD!
And how ashamed and Down-Syndrome-Asperger's-Doy-Rave
stupid I felt that had Adam not slammed it into my face
I would NEVER have figured out that I was supposed to
tip these amazing young gentlemen, let alone that that's
precisely what they were hinting at! My GOD, I would've
walked away not noticing a thing I'm so STUPID!!!
   Anyways, we embarked from the beach with the inten-
tion to buy a bag of rice, head back to the hostel for
some cash, and come back down to tip the guys all before
sunset. So we headed over to the little grocery shop
across the street— the only one in town— and went up and
down the aisles looking for a bag of rice. We came to
realize, however, that everything in the store was king-
size, ESPECIALLY fucking bags of rice. We were talking
twenty pounds or more here! I mean, we're trying to dry
a Samsung phone, not fucking COTTON, you know what I
mean? Finally we managed to find a bag of rice small
enough for the purpose, so Adam got in line to buy it
and I stepped outside to wait. There I noticed that my
wet feet were covered with scratchy itchy sand, as were
my slippers, so I went about smacking myself across the
legs to get it off. But then I noticed a nice little
tica who was hosing down the walkway, so I waved to get
her attention and when she looked at me I smiled and
pointed at my shins, saying "Puede usted?" which I supposed meant "Could you?" She nodded and I walked over to
her and she hosed me down from the knees down like a
delighted elephant. Once she was finished I nodded and
smiled thankfully and when Adam emerged from the market
holding a bag of rice with his phone inside, we carried
on our way.
   We headed back uphill toward our hostel as the sun
set sweetly to our left and the clouds dutifully amassed
overhead for the evening's showers and the warm winds
waltzed about in content and we walked and talked with
this bag of rice cradled in Adam's hands. And as we continued uphill I heard faintly the gently-purring roars
of the ocean in the distance and suddenly it hit me with
profound shock and anguish and desolation that tomorrow
we would be heading out very early in the morning to La
Fortuna, a city inland in the mountains, and that that

would mean that this was going to be the last time I
would get to behold the ocean and the Costa-Rican coast!
    Whoa.
    We reached our hostel and Adam set down his bag of
rice and other things and it was time to unwind. But
first, Adam had to run back to the beach to tip the dear
tico parasailing dudes. Now, I wanted to stop by the
grocery store again and pick up some food so I told Adam, why don't I go ahead and kill two birds with one
stone by tipping the guys and picking up my groceries?
Adam asked if I was sure and I said YEAH! And he said
ok. I asked him if he wanted anything and he said no, so
I took the 10,000 colones of tip money and started back
downhill and as I neared the beach I looked out toward
the setting sun and the easing darkness and realized
that I probably would arrive back on the beach quite
near nighttime. And sure enough, when I finally got
there after a ten- to fifteen-minute walk from the hostel, the sun was just about gone and so were all the
previous inhabitants of the beach. The ticos in question, by the way— the parasailing crew and their white
tent— were nowhere to be found. With great remorse I
realized that they wouldn't be tipped after all and even
sadder, gone would be the Pacific coast of Costa Rica
which had been for the last five nights my home and base
and soul and alma. I stood there alone and silent unable
to imagine life out of reach from this motherly ocean
spirit and I watched the sun and its beach and ocean
slowly fading into the jacket of night, quietly slipping
away from my vision into oblivion only to slowly but
surely emerge again tomorrow. But tomorrow, I wouldn't
be there.
    There is a sadness beyond howls and sobs and tears,
my friends, and it is known best to those on a setting
beach.

    Here we are. Another night at the rickety white
paint-chipping wretchedly-lit mosquito-ridden veranda
with rolie-polie giggly Spaniard chicks and EuroBitch
roommates and Adam's genial conversation and laughter
and my sweat-stanked seething quirky awkward assness. On
my way back from the beach after my solemn goodbye to

the Pacific Wonder I had stopped by the grocery store
again and picked up some snacks for the night: a large
bar of dark chocolate, a block of white gouda cheese,
and some hand-sized soft tortillas. What was to come of
this odd assemblage of edibles would be among the most
delightful and memorable dishes that Adam and I would
eat on this joyous trip. So there we were! Amid the
grand Manuel-Antonian night upon a rickety veranda
laughing and joking talking and playing as folks ambled
in and out of their rooms and the night coolly built up
to an upcoming midnight crescendo.

Earlier when I had returned to the hostel with the
bad news that I hadn't found and tipped the parasailers
Adam wondered if he could run down there early the next
morning to get them their tips. But since the last bus
to La Fortuna would depart FAR sooner than the
parasailers would be out to set up their tents, this
wasn't going to be feasible and we really WEREN'T going
to be able to tip them. We were just going to have to
stomach this blunderous entanglement of misfortune and
we hoped those excellent professional kind gentlemen
could know that we really didn't mean to stiff them at
all and that we were intent upon tipping them but in
vain and we'd tried our best to get them their well-
earned tips. But they'll never ever know...

That's laying it on pretty thick, of course. But for
a split second that's how dispiriting it felt. And after
that split second had passed it didn't quite feel like
anything anymore. So there you go.

So here we are again! The Spanish chicks are playing
around laughing loudly and some people are gathering
around the common table and here and there other folks
are doing stuff and it's all going on. And there he is!
Adam talking and mingling and socializing and
awesomizing with other human creatures while I avert eye
contact and shuffle around the common kitchen looking
for a knife to cut the cheese with. No sign of Ezekiel
or Samantha tonight, whom I believed must've left, so
there wouldn't be any debauched card tricks or chess
lessons or Sermons on the Mount tonight. No, tonight was
going to be a totally different thing altogether.

I was in the kitchen shuffling around for a knife to
slice up the cheese block with when I noticed behind me—
yes, wouldn't you know it! Yes, ladies and gentlemen,
coming to you live from across the Atlantic, yes hereee

theyyy areee the ONES! The ONLIES! EUROOOOOOO
BITCHEZZZZZZZ!!!— yes, our unresponsive rude hostel
roommates, Miss TimberBlonde and Miss GreyGas. There
they were in the holy flesh! In the corner of the communal kitchen before the stove fiddling with a pan trying
to cook some eggs. I looked their way and then turned
back around to resume my search for a knife and then
something quite bizarre happened. I mean something TRU-
LY. TRULY. Unexpected.

GreyGas spoke to me.

Yup. That she did, my Most Astounded Reader. I
turned around and said, "Sorry?" And she repeated her
request: "Could you help me light this stove?" So I
walked over and there she was with a pan filled with oil
and raw egg batter and she was fiddling with a lighter
and the gas knob on the stove and because of the way she
angled her lighter she kept burning her thumb. So I came
over and inspected the stove and figured out that her
method really wasn't going to work out too well. So I
asked, "Do you have a stick or some paper?" She looked
about and didn't have anything. So she tried it again by
putting her hand to the gassing stove and lighting it
up, but it only burned her thumb even worse and she
looked very much in pain. "Thanks anyway," she told me,
and she and TimberBlonde were back at it trying to light
this damn stove with great agony. Now, in my head I KNEW
what to do, but they wouldn't understand; I was just
going to have to show them. I fiddled through my pockets
until I found a piece of paper that would be perfect so
I tore off a long piece of it and rolled it up and went
back over to them and said "May I see your lighter?" and
when they handed it to me I lit up the tip of the rolled
paper and hurriedly said to the rude little bitch "okay
now turn on the stove!" and when she turned the knob the
gas let loose and I simply and painlessly placed the end
of the burning paper onto it and voila! I MADE FIRE!

They seemed a bit amazed actually and were quite
grateful and thanked me. I said "no problem" and shuffled back on to find that knife. But somehow that act of
kindness and genius (I suppose) broke the ice (thick the
fuck as it was for these EuroSpats) that opened up some
conversation between us. I asked them what they were
making and they said "eggs" which is always a great dinner. On we talked and they asked my name and I said
"Joe" of course and without remorse as Adam wasn't in

the room and they said their names but somehow I forgot those names the second I heard them (and so going forward I'll just continue to call them the EuroBitches TimberBlonde and GreyGas, if you so may oblige me, my Most Cerebral Reader). And then we struck upon the subject of our origins and TimberBlonde said she was from Scotland, and when it was GreyGas's turn to answer she said something that made all the sense in the world: "England."

England! England! She's English! And then it all made sense.

You see, my Most Venerated Most Auspicious Reader, the riddle all makes sense. GreyGas isn't a bitch. She's just English. Which explains why she's a flat square unresponsive stained urch of gas and pale air. Nothing personal or bitchy about it. It's just genetics. And I don't say this with prejudice or stereotype, either, for I've been to the United Kingdom many times and folks? Those people are ALL TOTALLY greygas. No exaggeration. The same goes for the Scot, too, though not entirely. TimberBlonde's just KINDA English, that's all. She's both SO English and SO NOT English at the same time. It all makes sense!

I felt much better at that point because these fine young ladies weren't so much Euro-BITCHES as they were Euro-BRITS. Kind of different. We chatted back and forth for a minute more, then they went on to their egg dinner and I returned to find a knife for my cheese and when I finally did I joyfully walked over to the counter and went at it! First I pulled out a few tiny soft tortillas and set them out. Then I opened the cheese with the knife and sliced off a generous portion. Placing the cheese onto the tortilla I broke off a large chunk of the large chocolate bar and when those three things came together I observed and admired this wondrous discovery— this chocolate cheese tortilla wrap— and with two hands I took a bite and with great thought beheld this marvel of rainforest cuisine!

Now you may think me insane for thinking up such a late-night snack, let alone ENJOYING such a thing, but let me assure you that I wasn't crazy. For in my excitement I wrapped one up for Adam as well and though Adam THINKS he's done eating for the day I must admit that the guy for the most part doesn't say no to food. So I gave him one and he actually really praised me all over

about it with things like, "My man!" and wow was I so
proud! So I wrapped up another cheese chocolate soft
taco and stood in the kitchen listening to people talking and EuroBrits cooking and just basking in the jolli-
est mood there can be. And Adam and I enjoyed our meals
and the delight of everything started to really build up
in me so I started to hum to myself. I hummed music of
all kinds, then Latin music struck me and I hummed to
the salsa and bachata and merengue and cumbia that was
all orchestrating in my head. And the music was just
awesome and my mood was on holy fire!

So I started to move. A girl walked in to grab something from the kitchen and when she turned back to
leave, our eyes met and she smiled. And this girl's
eyes, her smile, her spirit, immediately impressed me
with a jolt of life. Some people have the power to do
that. And goodness it wasn't so much that she was necessarily pretty or kind or anything at all; she just had a
spirit that snapped you to attention and wonder. I would
never see or speak to this girl again, but I'd later
discover that her name was Cathy and that what little
wonder she had impressed upon me she would soon detonate
onto Adam. But that's a different story that is soon to
come.

For NOW, here I am. Slowly I found myself moving to
the music in my own head. I sauntered out of the kitchen
onto the veranda and to my right some guests— Adam among
them— were seated laughing and chatting at the communal
table. To my left sat the Spaniard chicks, dressed up it
seemed as if about to go out. They looked pretty lovely,
considering they were outside of their oversized T-
shirts and not rolling around on the ground like deranged snails hooting and honking like drunken hogs. No,
I admit I liked them better this way.

I moved and hummed. I found myself facing a stack of
books, reading the spines of them and dancing to the
music blasting in my head. Oscar De Leon and Willie Colon and Celia Cruz and Marc Anthony and Buena
Vista...track after track song after song just Latin
Bamba blastering through my brain! In no time I was tapping my feet and moving my hips with my eyes closed! So
I pulled out my phone and I had some salsa songs stored
on there so I just played them and danced! Yes, there
all alone with my eyes closed I just stood on that veranda and started to dance. I danced and danced without

regard for anyone or anything around me. Moving shaking
tapping flowing with the moment that I was in. At one
point I walked over and took Adam's hand to join me. But
I found that he quickly and firmly refused. At the moment it didn't quite strike me as odd but slowly and
then abruptly after about fifteen minutes, something hit
me: Is this weird?

And suddenly self-consciousness and doubt, with the
craft and silent creep of the most unsuspecting leech,
started to curdle my spine: "Do I look weird? Is this
normal? Why hasn't anyone talked to me or joined me? Why
am I facing away from everybody (my back was completely
turned to them)? Why did Adam refuse? He refused pretty
firmly. Maybe it's because this is stupid. Am I bother-
ing anyone? I'm being a nuisance."

I thought, "Maybe I could go over there and ask the
Spaniard chicks to join. But then, would they think this
was all a coy to seduce them? It's too late to engage
people NOW, you've been dervishing by yourself for the
last twenty minutes! Maybe I can reach for Adam again.
HE knows how to be social and defuse awkwardness and
shit. But GOD, what if he declines? If he doesn't jump
in for a SECOND time then this must be REALLY bad. I
mean, does anybody think this is bad? God, do I STOP??
Yes, how FUCKing awkward would THAT be?! Just STOP dude
yes and walk away. Yes into the dark woods just keep on
walking yes until your worthless ass falls off the edge
of a jagged cliff into a black roaring ocean and sharks
rip you to shreds you stupid idiot!" And that was when
the long-burning fire of joy and passion and life of the
moment suddenly extinguished within me and in an instant
I found myself standing there, facing the woods, my back
to EVERYone, my inner flame vanished and gently smoking,
and my phone blaring away like a fucking siren. Carefully I picked it up, gently hit the "stop" button, and
walked off toward my room across the driveway. And I was
possessed with the certain and fortified realization
that I wanted to be, for the time being, completely and
utterly and silently alone.

I got up to my room and the two EuroBrits were there
on their beds being their usual cunty selves or whatever. I didn't say a word to either of them. Why say anything? They're genetically predisposed to being antiso-
cial snobs, so fuck them. I grabbed some underwear and
headed back downstairs to the bathrooms. It was time for

a shower. With tranquil and liquid silence I took a nice
comfortable private shower right there with fulming med-
itation. It was perhaps the most peaceful private moment
of the whole trip and I found myself insatiably relieved
to be away from people. And it dawned on me that
throughout this entire trip I have had yet to really
have a moment all to myself. With the washes of that
gentle shower spray, my self-consciousness and bitterness and anger and awkwardness and strain all melted
away and trickled off my back and down the drain. I
breathed deeply and with great restful relaxation. I
dried off with Adam's kind and darling gift— the neon-
green quick-dry microfiber towel— and dressed for bed. I
slowly and calculatedly ascended the stairs to my room,
crossed the Bitch Ass EuroBrits without so much as a
glance (and whom by the way I would never actually speak
to ever again), dropped my dirty clothes in the corner,
and genially glided across the cool white sheets into my
bed. Sitting up grazed by the light breeze from my room
fan, I reviewed and edited some of my photos from the
day and posted them onto Instagram and then I took out
my dear book and travel companion, The Dharma Bums by
Jack Kerouac, and I sat in stolid and soothing silence
reading chapter after chapter of this delightful little
book, listening tranquilly to the sounds of birds and
monkeys in the forest night, enjoying every sweet dulce
second of solitude in the night. And when I felt ready
to turn in I set my book down lightly, rolled over, and
drifted off to sleep.

    Periodically I would roll over in bed and awaken to
the maniacal rage of the thunderstorms outside. I'd peek
a glance out the window as the tempestuous hells of
night pattered the trees and leaves, pelleted the gush-
ing ground, and rattled with violent lightning roars the
black silence. I'd smile and drift off back to a sweet
and oh-so-restful sleep.
    Oh yeah. And the night was freezing. My sheets were
hardly enough to keep me warm. So much again and forever
for air conditioning.
    I arose early the next morning to the same silent
introspective solitudal feeling: I wanted nothing to

fuck to do with ANYONE. Nothing pleased me more than
being left the fuck and entirely alone. It was time to
ditch this rickety-white shamble shit-hole so I started
packing my bag and discovered that all I had to pack was
a sopping heap of sweat-wetted dirty laundry. And with
no time or place to wash them I would have to carry these moist sagging heaps all the way to La Fortuna before
I could get them cleaned. So I sacked up and marched
past the slumbering EuroSkanks out of the room and headed down for another tasty breakfast serving of pancakes
and melon. I waited in line, grabbed my plate, and sat
down to eat quietly. Adam showed up very soon after and
he got his grub and took his place next to me. We sat
for a moment in the tranquil shade of the veranda in
peaceful stillness and then the exchanges started to
roll. First Adam said something in regards to our
EuroBritCunt roommates: "Our roommates weren't very
friendly" or something like that and I said "DUDE I KNOW
RIGHT??? FUCK THEM!" Then he asked "How was your night?
What did you do?" and I answered and asked him similarly
and it turned out that he'd had a great night as well.
Apparently that communal table was bustling with fantastic laughs and enlightening conversations. He mentioned
meeting some very cool new friends and one of them was a
girl named Cathy. And when I saw his eyes sparkle and
his spirit skip a beat at her mention I recalled very
well whom this was all in reference to:

*"And this girl's eyes, her smile, her spirit, imme-
diately impressed me with a jolt of life. Some people
have the power to do that. And goodness it wasn't so
much that she was necessarily pretty or kind or anything
at all; she just had a spirit and snapped you to attention and wonder."*

"The whole time," Adam recalled, "I kept thinking
that I wished you were there." And that, my Dear Senti-
mental Reader, hit me right in the feels, I tell ya.

A chubby friendly American couple was eating at the
table across from us and they started asking us how long
we'd been here and if we had been to the park (which we
had, as you read about pretty extensively, my Most As-
siduous Reader) and we gave them all kinds of tips and
suggestions about how to make the most out of their visit that afternoon. Funny, I thought. If people are
asked, they're so happy to answer and help. Sometimes
you should just ask! Then Adam sort of asked me about

the whole dancing episode from the previous night and
kind of apologized for not jumping in with me which was
totally alright of course. Then he asked, "Didn't it
seem a bit contrived?" And I just thought "You know man?
How do I know? I don't know what it 'seemed' and don't
quite care who thought it was or wasn't fucking 'contrived'. What I DO know is that it was all perfectly
natural and good-spirited as far as I was concerned and
I went with it and it felt right and when at one point
it didn't then I just stopped and walked away". It's
just exhausting to me to do things while wondering what
others might think of it. I lived that way for YEARS,
folks, and it quite literally drove me insane. Whether
people that night thought I was cool, stupid, annoying,
arrogant, pretentious, hilarious, charming, douchey,
profound, or insignificant really didn't and doesn't
matter. It was what it was, and that was it.

And now came the great and riveting news! Once again
Adam's charm and conversational charisma brought about
great fortune. During the night's excellent roundtable
chats Adam had met and befriended a dude named Clarence.
To describe him as straightly as possible, he was a
short smiley black guy (which in my possessed dervish I
do recall grazing my sight over a black guy). Clarence
was also heading to La Fortuna that morning but here was
the difference: while we were taking the bus route which
would cost less than ten bucks but total a travel time
of seven to eight hours, Clarence had booked a shuttle
which though costing fifty bucks would get him there in
one piece in less than four hours. And guess the fuck
what! THE SHUTTLE WAS AIR-CONDITIONED! So Adam asked me
if I wanted to switch plans from the bus route to the
shuttle and of course without the slightest hesitation I
hooted for the shuttle. Adam agreed, for at this point
in the trip as we neared the rising finale, time became
more precious than money so if we could trade money for
time we should most certainly do it. So since I had the
working phone (Adam's was still bleeding out moisture at
the bottom of a bag of rice) we looked up some local
shuttle companies and I tried calling them to find something. I called a few of them but none would be able to
service us under such short notice. It seemed that this
brilliant idea had come too late.

But wait! Adam had an idea. Since Clarence's shuttle
was coming soon anyway, why didn't we just ask the driv-

er if he had room for two more? Maybe we could ride out with Clarence! So Adam waited eagerly by the hostel entrance to make sure he could catch the shuttle and I went back in to wait for the news.

I took a seat at the communal table and grabbed a book off the shelf which turned out to be an anthology of great Australian short stories. Really cool! I sat there skimming the book and I did something I greatly enjoy about stories, which is that I would read the first lines of a story and just imagine what would happen next. So without reading the complete stories I just jumped from page to page reading the first couple of sentences to myself and then moving on to the next story. Somewhere in the midst of this nerdy-but-damn-so-satisfying pleasure a young thin white girl showed up and sat next to me. She was from New York and somehow we started talking all about great first-liners from various books. I shared a couple of my very favorites like this one from The Stranger by Albert Camus:

"Mama died today. Or yesterday maybe, I don't know."

Or this one from Vladimir Nabokov's Lolita:

"Lolita, light of my life, fire of my loins. My sin, my soul. Lo-lee-ta: the tip of the tongue taking a trip of three steps down the palate to tap, at three, on the teeth. Lo. Lee. Ta."

(Just so you know? Those lines were spoken by a middle-aged man about a twelve- or thirteen-year-old girl. Who happens to be his stepdaughter. Funny story, that one.)

Or THIS one from Fahrenheit 451 by Ray Bradbury:

"It was a pleasure to burn. It was a special pleasure to see things eaten, to see things blackened and changed."

(He's talking about firemen, my friends. And no, these aren't the firemen who put OUT the fires! No, these are the firemen who START THEM! Yup because they live in a futuristic dystopian world where books are illegal. And if you are caught reading any book of any kind [as you at this moment are my Most Screwed Reader] then you and the book and the house and everything in it are set

on fire! Yup with fire hoses that don't spray water but
KEROSENE! Yes I love telling my student eighth-graders
that story. They perk up with wonder and thrill and exchange looks of mouth-watering awe and cry out "Wow,
that's 'lit'! or 'savage'! or 'ratchet'! or
whateverthefuck...a world where we don't have to READ!"
Ignorant fucks.)

And she and I laughed with great delight and passion
for great literature. Then she shared a new one with me!
One that REALLY knocked me sideways. She had trouble
recalling the title or the author but finally with a bit
of internet help we found that she was talking about
Carson McCullers' The Heart is a Lonely Hunter which
begins like this:

"In the town, there were two mutes and they were always together."

Wow.
Adam came up behind me and cried "Let's go" and it
turned out that Clarence's shuttle had room for two
more! So just like that we grabbed our stuff and hustled
over to the shuttle and met the driver whose name we'd
later discover was Eddie and I loaded my Hoodoo Red Osprey Porter 46 Pack into the back and Adam loaded his
bag as well and carried the bag of rice with him into
the shuttle and we paid by credit card and folks, it was
time to head off inland to La Fortuna! And as we finally
climbed into the shuttle I witnessed from afar from
across the driveway our former EuroBritBitch roommates
and it seems they too were leaving the hostel that morning. And for a moment I was so grateful and thought,
what a relief that I would never have to see these two
quite offensively rude and standoffish little cunts
again.
Until I saw them again.

chapter one

I greeted Clarence the smiley black guy and he and I
got into the very back of the shuttle and Adam got into
the front back (as in, not in the passenger's seat but
in the first row of the back seat, as I'm sure you reasonably inferred, my Dear Imaginative Reader). And as he
climbed in with the bag of rice in his hands and his
dead phone at the bottom of it wouldn't you know, the
stupid rice bag tipped over and a bunch of the rice
poured out onto the shuttle floor! So we spent a minute
or two scooping that shit up and putting it back into
the bag and I thought, what a funny couple of idiots we
must seem like to be traveling across Costa Rica balancing an open bag of rice. But overall this unnerving
tragedy was quite amusing, on the whole.

So it was me and Adam and Clarence for the time being driven away from the coast by a strong and charming
middle-aged tico named Eddie and it turned out that the
four of us really hit it off! Clarence was quite a hilarious fellow from D.C. who had an absolutely fascinating background and just about the most charming geniality of anyone I'd ever met. And with Adam's sheer buffa-
lo-balls awesomeness and what I assume to be my fairly
astute and pleasant disposition and Eddie's wonderful
kind generous charming ticoness and an almost miraculous
abundance of SWEET SEXY SLUTTY LUSTY DRIPPING-WET AIR
CONDITIONING this was turning out to be one sweet treat
of a road trip!

So let's talk about Clarence for a moment for he is
a FASCINATING guy from D.C. as I mentioned and who happens to have worked with and campaigned for Obama and
was an active part of getting President Obama elected!
We laid back and chatted and he relayed with a great
white smile and genial laughter and emblemic energy such
merry tales of D.C. politicians and the political world
and all the things one wouldn't know without being in
D.C. As Clarence talked Adam slowly began to exude feelings of discomfort, uneasiness, and sheer pain and when

I asked why, he notified me that he was prone to motion sickness which I did not know! So as this van rocked and rattled through the streets of Costa Rica and Clarence carried on about the wonders of our nation's capital, Adam's demeanor shifted from leaning forward to laying down to downright curling up into a fetal position. And here again was my hero living up to his code of honor: bearing the whips and scorns of time, shuffling through this mortal coil "dealing with it" with no complaints, no resistance, and no worry, aware of the fleetness of each present moment and living immersed within it, allowing it— however pleasant or unpleasant— to take its course. What a stud.

Adam was off to a brief and agonized nap as Clarence and I carried on talking more about our nation and its state of affairs. Clarence talked about joking with Obama back when he was a candidate and about the current election, regarding which he said with all gravity (still smiling): "I think for a long time everybody thought Republicans were batshit crazy...and now everybody knows they're batshit crazy." We laughed heartily and then Clarence very interestingly talked about how "human" our politicians are. "They're just people", he repeated, just folks out trying to do their jobs. Normal folks with worries and wives and children and fears and deadlines and irks and termination dates. Just Barack steppin' out for a smoke cool as the fucking day and Hillary hustlin' about haulin' her purse over her shoulder and so-and-so forgetting his keys and so-and-so laughing his ass off and so-and-so rushing because he's late. Just people. And it all got me thinking about this flaring orange pubic-hair-headed racist dumb demagogue and his bitch-faced corrupt phony opponent and that fat left-testicle of an ulcer Chris Christie and that Holy Sellout of a shame sold-to-the-devil brain-surgeon-turned-tampon Ben Carson who could use a lobotomy himself and all of these other horseshit phonies with ovaries for balls and how after all of this, when it really comes down to it they're just desperate scared-shitless folks nervously applying for a job. Nothing more.

"What's the one thing everyone in the States should know about our politicians?" I asked Clarence. With a shake of the head and a smile he said "They're just people, man. Just people".

"You alright?" I'd occasionally ask Adam and with a
clutch in his voice he'd reply "I'm good" and you KNOW
he was. But he remained curled up and laid down to sta-
bilize his sickness and he held it all down very well.
Now you may be thinking "isn't there a medication for
that?" (which indeed there is and it is called Drama-
mine) but Adam again is complete Buffalo-Bison down
there and he ain't a lil bitch takin' no pussy-ass "Dra-
ma", know what I mean? He stuck it out.

But fret thee not, my Apprehensive Reader! Our noble
hero is far from fallen! For soon after, just about an
hour into the ride, my good pal Adam's cure finally arrived! Yes, in seconds our dear hero was back upright as
a tree-stump erect as a flagpole, his prayers for respite fully and firmly and tight-assedly answered! Yes,
there it was! His cure! Ascending the shuttle and taking
the available seat next to him, causing him to sit up
stiff as the mast of a raging sail, my friends. The
cure! A slim trim robust athletic pony-tailed young German blond named Ana. And as we all greeted our new passenger Clarence and I found ourselves taken quite aback
by the sudden and stern vitality of Adam's return. And
certainly as boys would and should do we teased our comrade pretty harshly about his miraculous recovery. But
he didn't seem to hear a word of our taunting for he was
for now and onward quite thoroughly occupied.

The shuttle continued for some time past farms of
palm trees in neat stolid canopied rows and large fields
of cows and cattle and surging hills of verdant green.
We carried on laughing and joking and telling funny stories and Clarence continued his tales of D.C. politician
hilarity and Adam, fully recovered, sallied forth in his
discussions with our new friend Ana. A short time later
we quite suddenly found ourselves startled to be in familiar territory and when we felt the road narrow into a
small yellow bridge we practically jumped out of our
seats with exhilaration! It turns out that on our way
back northwest from Manuel Antonio we were crossing
through Jacó once again! Yes! The surfing city of beautiful beaches and strange whores at bars! The town of
the lion-fierce Laura and chillin' Gary and Riva Jacó
and Elías Rachel Santiago Diego Julián Juan and Hola
Maria! Yes, the town of all the fun of our first nights
and days in Costa Rica! Adam and I laughed vivaciously
and with fond nostalgia as we passed through this idyl-

lic place, and Clarence and Ana joined in as well, commenting that of all things to remember about this town the most outrageous was how verminly it crawled with prostitutes. Exchanging glances of confirmed realization, Adam and I finally understood what was up with that weird first night at the coastal nightclub in Jacó: those chicks had indeed been prostitutes after all.

On we drove, at which point Clarence mentioned quite observantly "You know? I haven't seen a street sign or name since we left Manuel Antonio." And truly this was so and it inspired great awe among us, for it seemed bizarre and downright impossible that whole towns with all their streets and busy intersections could be so devoid of indicators. How did these folks get about anywhere? But our thoughts were quite brusquely disrupted right then as riding uphill through this small town Clarence sighted something out the window and literally jumped with surprise. And when I managed to catch his gaze I saw crossing the street an astoundingly flamboyant homosexual boy craned like a flamingo twisted like the letter S itself stamped with a short pink shirt and sutured with ripped-jean booty shorts along the seams of his flesh dangling a plastic bag off the tip of one fingernail and crowing in Spanish and then with the suavity of the very wind he literally twirled around! Like with a kick-back of the head he did a spin right on the street there as he crossed! My friends, we threw our heads back and wailed out from our loins and stomachs the most outrageous astounded guffaws we could charge, for in all the fuck of Costa Rica that was one sight we wouldn't soon forget.

And with great jollity we exited from the good the darling the charming town of Jacó and as we barreled into its outskirts our driver Eddie decided to pull over at a rest stop. Getting off the phone with some folks from dispatch, I assume, he announced to us that this was the next pick-up stop; however, the next passengers were running late on their other shuttle and they would need approximately twenty minutes to arrive. Therefore he suggested that rather than sitting on the shuttle waiting for them it would be far more pleasant if we all

got out and stretched our legs and grabbed a bite to
eat. Well that sounded good to us! We walked across the
parking lot over to the rest stop which included a gas
station, a convenience store, some bathrooms, and a buf-
fet-style carry-out diner serving all kinds of Latin
dishes. With a sudden surge of appetite everyone lined
up to pick up some food and I excused myself to wash my
hands. Returning, I saw many things on the menu including open empanadas, pintos con arroz, numerous styles of
chicken and pork, and a couple of stews of which the
contents were absolutely impossible to identify. Knowing
full well that my stomach is a tender little thing I
surveyed the selections and decided to stick to what I
knew and also to keep it vegetarian, for the last thing
I fucking needed right then was a bad stomachache due to
rank pork or diseased chicken. So after some careful
consideration I ordered an open empanada and some rice
and beans and played it safe this time (Adam ordered the
fried chicken among other things. He has buffalo balls,
magic clothes AND an iron stomach. Fuckin' fuckin' guy).
Once we each had our trays of food we went back outside
to sit at a table under the shade and we talked about
many things but among them and the most engaging of them
was trying to guess what the FUCK was in Clarence's
stew! So it goes without saying then that Clarence did
select the mystery stew and we honestly sat there dis-
secting that shit speculating with every muster of our
intellect and couldn't for the life of us figure out
what the fuck was in it. After lengthy debate and minus-
cule inspection we collectively decided that it was lamb
and just moved on with our lives. And can you believe
it? This dude Clarence fucking sat there eating it chewing carefully with an inquisitive smirk on his face trying to discern from its texture and taste what it could
be. Insane!

Once we had finished eating we all got up to go to
the bathroom to wash up and dispose of our refuse and I
got a sudden craving for something sweet (to call it
"sudden" is a bit misleading, for I ALWAYS have a craving for something sweet. I merely mean to say that this
time my craving got the best of me) so I took my big
heavy full CamelBak Chute 1.5L Sky Blue water bottle and
crossed over to the small convenience store next door to
pick out some candy. I walked in and said "Hola" to the
young hefty female attendant in a yellow shirt at the

cash register and then proceeded up and down the aisles
trying to decide which candy to choose. Moving along I
noticed that bachata music was playing on the speakers
so I shuffled about to that for a moment and then I cut
it out pretty darn quick from fear of having another
fucking episode like the one at the rickety white veranda hostel of the night before. I carried on looking for
a spot-on choice for candy and just before I had settled
my mind on some Kit Kat— my very favorite of all candy
bars— I noticed a small shelf with a section of packaged
local treats such as those you may find in grocery
stores containing things like chocolate-covered almonds
and white-chocolate pretzels and salted cashews and the
like. But skimming the fresh delicacies I noted with
dejection that the containers were too large for a small
post-lunch snack so I continued searching until I found
from among the large packages what looked like locally-
made M&M's in petite decently-sized containers upon
which the labels read "botonetas". And I figured, well I
can't say for sure what "botonetas" means but looking at
this package all I see are some locally-made M&M's! And
these would be shareable and decently portioned and also
quite delicious and soothing to the sweet-tooth palate!

I grabbed a package and walked over to the counter
to pay for it and with my usual jollity I greeted the
portly young attendant-lady in the yellow shirt with a
smile and the little Spanish that I knew. And when she
responded back to me in Spanish she made me question
everything I had ever known about the entire Spanish
language, for I understood virtually nothing she said. I
later figured that she was speaking in a local country
dialect and that was why I couldn't quite understand
her. But I did catch one thing she said which was "Que
bonita tu botela" which means "how nice your bottle is!"
And though I highly doubted that I had understood her
correctly she indeed was complimenting my big blue
CamelBak Chute 1.5L Sky Blue water bottle as she repeated the phrase and pointed to the bottle with a coquet-
tish smile. I smiled back and thought it charming but a
little part of me inside wondered, what the holy fuck
kind of a compliment is that? Are water bottles rare in
these parts of Central America? Or is there something
particularly special about this water bottle? Is "water
bottle" a metaphor for something else? This young honky
seems thoroughly turned on by my water bottle, no pun or

figurative language intended. What a strange young girl this is in this quaint little town. Are these water bottles valuable in this neck of the woods? How much could I pawn off said water bottle? And so on.

So we tried to communicate a little bit more but beyond the water bottle compliment I couldn't understand a thing she was saying and finally she just gave up and waved me off so I shrugged and walked out with my conspicuously awesome water bottle and a small package of "botonetas" and returned to the table with my fellow travelers.

Adam and Clarence were not around when I returned to the table, for they had gone off to the bathroom or something. So I sat and chatted a bit with Ana and I offered her a bit of the candy which she pleasantly accepted. Soon after, Adam came back and joined us and I asked him "Would you like some M&M's?" and he said "Sure" so he reached his hand into the package of "botonetas" and took one out and put it into his mouth and seconds later I noticed with somewhat of a start that his face had totally twisted and convulsed into sheer disgust and agonized contortion and with all the strength of hate he could muster he squealed "What IS this??" and I was thoroughly baffled! "Those aren't M&M's!" he protested and I couldn't understand what he meant. I looked back at the package and saw that they were round chocolate bits coated in various colors! M&M's, right?? I put another one into my mouth and tasted it and thought, tastes to me like chocolate-covered goodness that melts in your mouth and not in your hand! I pressed Adam to explain but he insisted "Those are NOT M&M's!" and I figured, well sure they're not REALLY M&M's, just the way Hannaford Fruit Rings Cereal isn't REALLY Kellogg's Froot Loops or the way Market Pantry Tomato Ketchup isn't REALLY Heinz Tomato Ketchup, sure! But shit, they're more M&M's than they are anything else, wouldn't you say? But Adam firmly demanded that they were NOTHING like M&M's and going forward he wanted nothing at all to do with them!

We asked Ana what she thought and though she agreed with Adam that it is misleading to call them M&M's she also understood where I was coming from. So in the heat of this debate we saw Clarence returning and we figured we'd have HIM settle the matter once and for all so we shuffled ourselves back to normal and resumed our talks

and after Clarence had been seated for a time and had
joined unsuspectingly into our conversation I took the
package of "botonetas" and reaching out to my right
where he sat I said with an evil grin "Clarence, would
you like some M&M's?" and reaching innocently into the
package he took hold of one blue piece of candy and responded graciously "Sure, thanks man" and as the tiny
blue morsel neared his lips we all leaned forward in
great anticipation excited and bubbling with certainty
awaiting this metacosmic verdict of incontrovertible
truth and then with grand crescendo there it was! Clarence the Supreme Justice of discernable candy treats!
Jurors have you reached a verdict! We have your honor!
We find the defendant... and Clarence's face twisted
swirled spiraled squeejed crunched cringed cranjed
cranked curled mutated muddled misshaped malformed and
with a gag of dejected hate he cocked back his head and
literally spat out the deformed blue-brown saliva-gunked
morsel right onto the curb!

Somehow this whole ordeal gave Adam a hankering for
some real M&M's (go fucking figure) so he excused himself from the table to go do some convenience-store pe-
rusing of his own. As he was leaving I thought with
cheerful gaiety, you know what would be funny?? What if
Ice took my apparently all-desirable CamelBak Chute 1.5L
Sky Blue water bottle with him into the store and the
plump little chica in the yellow shirt saw HIM with one
of those? What would she think?? So I gave Ice the bottle and he decided to walk in casually and see what
would happen. How delightful!

Meanwhile I returned my bewildered attention to
Clarence who seated beside his gucky blue-brown
"botonetas"-filled wad of spit was still writhing in
disgust and outrage and utter confusion and looking on
at this insane muddle of irony I thought to myself the
following: "Let me get this straight, Clarence my Afro-
American pal. You sat there chewing endlessly over a
mystery stew, the contents of which will remain the subject of debate well into our old age, chewing and peck-
ing at this horrific abomination of gas-station muck,
and now after having consumed the inscrutable clot in
its enigmatic entirety you are seriously going to gag
and choke and spit out a perfectly decent piece of chocolate candy? Dare I ask, what the fuck is wrong with
you, kind sir? Such a strange fellow you are!" I mean

seriously! He had just before my naked eyes fully consumed what looked like would be scraped off the hide of
a muddy dead donkey's wet ass! It was horse- or dog- or
cat- or mule- or lemur- or ferret-meat for sure! Hell
knows that stew was as country-local as "sautéed raccoon's assholes on a stick", as the Great George Carlin
once so profoundly put it. But after all, the look on
Clarence's face was downright hilarious and we all
laughed heartily about it for quite some time.

Adam returned from the convenience store quite
amused, for his short visit had indeed proved eventful!
He had gone in, picked out some candy, and approaching
the cash register had found our lovely clerk in the yellow shirt quite startled by this befuddling coincidence!
Adam said that she had been quite excited and surprised
to see this same notable CamelBak Chute 1.5L Sky Blue
water bottle in another person's hands. So she told him
that someone had just walked in with the very same kind
of bottle! Then she had gone on to explain something
that he couldn't quite pinpoint but from the little that
he did understand he gathered that she was telling him
that there were many young girls in the village. He concluded with great awe that she was trying to hook him up
or marry him off to somebody in town. Now I found this
quite arousing, for nothing would thrill me more than a
darling union with a señorita loca, but if such fucking
dazzlement could be aroused by these ladies simply over
a plastic water bottle then what would they do for a
dollar??

Well, we weren't going to stick around to find out
because it was time to hit the road again and Eddie
gathered us around to get back on the shuttle where we
met and greeted the new arrivals to our journey— a blond
German family consisting of a man, his wife, and their
rather adorable child— and we all hopped back onto the
shuttle ready for departure.

It goes without saying that this next portion of our
shuttle's journey was far less eventful and sociable
than the former. On the way there it was mostly me, Adam, and Clarence (followed by the polite pleasant Ana)
chatting comfortably and casually. But now with a stolid

silent stoic igneous-stone German family stiffly erect
and forward-gazing in the back seat it seemed to follow
quite naturally that this was a time for quiet and mannered introspection. So we all turned our attentions and
gazes out of the window to behold the glory of the passing towns of the Costa-Rican inland. We beheld with awe
the swerving roads, the wavy hills, the diving cliffs,
and the dim and fading greenery, for as we rose farther
and farther upward we fondly glimpsed the darling nos-
talgic coast fading into the distance and into the recesses of our minds and we instead cuddled into the descending fog and the terrain which gradually shifted
before us. We gazed out across the verdant hills spotted
with little blue and yellow and pink and red and orange
boxes. Farther and farther up, the fog descended upon us
and before long our visions were filmed with nothing but
dim beautiful hazy waves of pale green and distant mystery.

Around this time we started to approach narrowing
streets and numerous buildings and we found ourselves
swerving through the mountainous and hilly cliffs of
small rural towns. And it was at this precise moment as
we slowly ventured through these narrow weaving bustling
simple streets that a series of words assembled themselves in my mind and without warning my Muses began to
sing and the words which came to me were these:

"The next week of my life was packed into one (red)
osprey backpack Plane Det-ATL. Stress balls shirt and
jeans. Aisle seat Cute girl tired not very interested in
chatting Atlanta recommended midtown"...

The stream began and it would not stop. Notes upon
notes upon notes. Memories of the most minute details
and stringed swirling sentences streaming sizzling gliding oozing through my cerebrum as I typed frantically
into my phone before I lost it all. Memory after memory
flowed swiftly and like molasses honey-like cool running
water each idea fizzed through my mind across my shoulders down my arms and wrists and moltenly out through
the faucets of my thumbs onto the tiny fiddling screen.
Forty-five short minutes later I was still staring at my
phone frantically typing every possible memory of this
trip that I could muster. And before I had it all down
it dawned on me that I hadn't looked up or out the win-

dow in a significantly long time. It seems that Adam had
been thinking the same thing because the moment I realized it myself he said to me "You might want to put your
phone down and look at this. You are missing some pretty
amazing small towns".

So I pushed the Muses aside for a moment and sat observing these passing towns. But just as I brought my
attention back to my surroundings it seemed that we had
passed the last of them. And looking back over my shoulder as we drove out of the streets and back into the
open fields I was suddenly overcome with grief and remorse and doom and the terrible feeling that the world
had passed me by. And though what I had been doing in
the meantime bore tremendous significance (since after
all, those very notes are what form the skeleton of this
very tale through which you vent, my Sojourning Reader)
I could only imagine with much heartbreak how much more
enriching that ride would have been had I witnessed
those once-in-a-lifetime towns and beheld those locals
about their daily businesses and all of the architecture
and simplicity of rural Central-American life and I truly felt with great despair that it had all passed me by
and the chance to see it would never come back again.
But from that incident I was reminded of the valuable
lesson in all of our lives: that every moment is passing
and never coming back and if you are spending it lost in
thought or detached or distracted then it will pass you
by too. And it won't be until the end of the road that
you finally realize how much of its richness and beauty
and mystery is now gone from you forever.

So I sucked it up and learned my lesson and knew
that going forward I would not allow myself to be distracted, for my time in this glorious paradise was short
and fleeting and therefore every moment was to be absorbed in its present entirety.

Then the time came for our next and final rest stop
so Eddie pulled over at this lengthy diner / convenience
store and we all got out to use the bathroom and purchase water and get our blood flowing a bit. After pee-
ing and washing my hands and face I came back out and
perused the store's products and beheld with amusement
all the Latin-American produce and packaging and candy.
People sat about eating and others shopping and others
yet loitering as employees joked around and laughed behind the counters. We purchased some water and Adam and

chapter one

I sat near the door on a lacquered wooden bench chatting
about familiar things and in the midst of this conversation I felt quite suddenly a sharp itch emerging tena-
ciously on the back of my right leg and with a start of
panic and rage I screamed out to myself: Mosquitoes!
ZIKA! With fervent manic rage I scribbled and scratched
against my leg flaring to rid the demon from my flesh. I
turned to Adam seeking consolation and asked "Hey so do
you think mosquitoes around here are something to worry
about?" to which he replied with an all-comforting cud-
dly-motherly "Oh, absolutely" and I gritted my teeth
with the rage of a hemorrhoidal wolverine.
    I might as well inform you that I have a vindictive
vendetta against mosquitoes. I've been told that apparently the scent of my blood type attracts them to me
more than to others and they bother me more than anyone
I know. Besides, there's nothing worse in the world than
a fucking flaring flaming itch along your netherlimbs.
In the past my solution had often been to scratch the
motherfucker until it bled and no longer itched, but in
this case I felt it wiser to use my Cortizone 10 Maximum
Strength Easy Relief Applicator with Healing Aloe which
I had packed nicely for just this sort of purpose. But
when we went back to the shuttle to get it we discovered
that the shuttle had been locked (wisely so, of course)
by Eddie so we waited (now with a far more urgent more
nuisanced anticipation) for Eddie to finish his Costa-
Rican dump or whatever and unlock the fucking shuttle
for us. He emerged some time later from the bathroom
ready to go but darling Adam took it upon himself then
and there to exercise his curiosity once again and ask
the middle-aged tico about his fucking life. Meanwhile I
was teeth-clenchingly grating the vamp of my left shoe
against my right calf in a tumbling boil dreaming of
shotgunning my fucking legs away, itch and all. But Eddie spent the next ten minutes or so telling us all
about his wife and kids and the many woes of a Costa-
Rican shuttle driver and all about his wonderful precious employer— a company called "Interbus" and pronounced "een-tar-boos"— and about how Interbus was a
fabulous provider of shuttle services throughout the
glorious nation of Costa Rica and that we should definitely contact Interbus for our future commutes. And as
the darling guy just kept talking about Interbus my
flaring little mosquito bite malformed into a fire-

breathing face that cackled up at me from a throbbing
red calf and all the goddamned fuck I wanted was to get
that stupid shuttle unlocked and to rip the fuck into
tatters that whore bitch Hoodoo Red Osprey Porter 46
Pack and to gnash open with my wolf teeth the plastic
pink sack that bore my Cortizone 10 Maximum Strength
Easy Relief Applicator with Healing Aloe and to cum its
icy-cool creamy contents down my limbs. Finally Eddie
shut the fuck up and got back to the shuttle so we sallied forth again prepared for a final departure to our
next destination.

Once we had all collected ourselves back onto the
shuttle I called back to the German wife behind me (who
happened to be closest to the luggage) if she would be
so kind as to reach over into the trunk and hand me the
big reddish-orange backpack. Indeed she turned out to be
very kind and very good at fetching backpacks. I ripped
apart zippers and tore aside balls of cotton and vora-
ciously slashed out the pink first-aid sack like a Mayan
king tearing out from the sacrificial chest a beating
heart and with the rattling bulgy-eyed fervor of a frantic diabetic reaching for his insulin I shoveled up the
Cortizone 10 Maximum Strength Easy Relief Applicator
with Healing Aloe and whiddled off the red end-cap and
with a breathless yelp I doused the medicine over the
flaring red mosquito bite and in seconds I felt the misery subdued and the fire quenched and I fell back into
my seat cackling gently, hysterical with relief. After a
few deep breaths and a moment of repose I gathered myself to return the items back into my bag. But as I
reached down to put it all back in order I paused and
found myself staring with great reverence at this Hoodoo
Red Osprey Porter 46 Pack which lay before my feet. Rattling through the vining streets of Costa Rica I became
suddenly hypnotized by the realization that for the last
five days I had lived securely and comfortably out of
this single 46-liter 9 x 22 x 14-inch 3.1-pound backpack. That I had befriended and beloved this item as an
added organ to my sacred body. That despite its size and
despite your skepticism, my Most Incredulous Reader,
this single backpack had been all that I'd needed and
all I would ever need for the duration of this trip.

Then what of drawers? What of cupboards and shelves
and closets and boxes and racks? What of crates and bar-
rels and cellars and sheds garages basements attics and

vaults? What in the wasteful wizard hell are we storing
out there? What is this possessive neurotic abundance of
shit that heaps our corners and nooks and crannies? What
is with this delusion that we are of so many material
things in "need"? Many years ago Adam had told me that
everything he ever needed could fit into his car and
that that was the most liberating feeling in the whole
world. Sitting there rocking to the rhythm of the road
upon this silent shuttle I felt that I could finally
understand what he had meant. For let me impart unto
you, my friends, what is perhaps the greatest realization of all: we are greatly delusional about what we
"need".

Upon this transformative travel I was forced to face
this predicament of "need" and it turns out— not theo-
retically, but tangibly and demonstrably so— that what I
"need" fits right into this single portable 9 x 22 x 14-
inch 3.1-pound Hoodoo Red Osprey Porter 46 Pack. Nothing
more. That is indeed about all a single human being really "needs". And realizing this I was overcome with one
very strong stern scolding certainty: I was ashamed.
Ashamed of my closets and racks and shelves and drawers.
Ashamed of my tens of pants, my scores of shirts, my
rows of shoes, my drawers of socks and underwear, my own
personal fuel-efficient fully-insured tinted-window low-
mileage private motor vehicle. Ashamed of my twelve-inch
subs and double-patty burgers and extra fries and gargantuan shelves and aisles of family-pack jumbo-sized
buy-two-get-one-free mounds of produce and sixty-inch
screens and needle-perfect Wi-Fi and indestructible
electricity and air conditioning. Ashamed, my friends.
Ashamed.

I gazed on at my Hoodoo Red Osprey Porter 46 Pack
with tender gratitude and just as I thought to hoist it
back up to the German wife, I decided instead to just
let it rest beside me keeping me company as I turned
back to the ambling green valleys and languid grey fog
of these holy hills.

chapter one

I sat drifting through my thoughts and the green
waves of the land and the misty slumber of the fog and
the rocking melody of the quiet coasting shuttle and
would have carried on infinitely so were I not startled
back to consciousness by a nudge from Adam who passed me
a black hardcover notebook and a pen. The notebook was
filled with many handwritten comments of thanks and ap-
preciation to Interbus and to our dear driver Eddie. I
skimmed through a few of them and then thanked Adam for
sharing it and as I leaned forward to pass it on to the
next passenger Ice said "Aren't you going to write anything?" And in retrospect I can't for the life of me
understand why the hell I was so confused by all of this
but in that moment I had no idea what he was talking
about or what on earth was going on. But finally I managed to calculate this cluster of seemingly unrelated
occurrences and put together the following conclusion:
this black hardcover notebook was a company notebook for
customers to write their comments and thanks regarding
their experiences with the driver (herein being Eddie)
and at this moment it was my turn to write my comments
expressing my gratitude and satisfaction with Interbus
services. So I rolled my eyes with humiliation and sheer
black self-loathing and proceeded to think very carefully about how I wanted to express my infinite regard for
this pleasant sojourn. Yet all I managed to concoct from
my exceptional education and my bounteous vocabulary was
this: "Eddie is the MAN!" And staring blankly at this
linguistic abomination of a tribute I mentally spat at
myself and rolled over again in my self-hatred and
passed the damn book on and spent a moment wondering why
the fuck such a stupid rancorous nematoded maggot like
me deserved to fucking exist.

And as this final hour tumbled by and after we had
exchanged some pleasant conversation we found ourselves
rolling steadily uphill and the terrain narrowing into
one single long bustling street and we sensed the shops

and buildings tightening and the traffic congesting and
our sally shortening and soon we stopped before a bustle
of boisterous ticos and ticas hustling about carrying on
with their evenings. Adam pinpointed our location on my
phone and discovered that we had indeed arrived at the
town of our next destination! Eddie pulled over to the
left and to my deep sadness Clarence and Ana exited the
shuttle, for they had reached their journey's end. With
sincere and darling farewells we saw them off as they
left and once they had departed our shuttle carried on
and in passing Adam waved sillily back at Clarence who
returned the silliness with a smiley jumpy flamboyant
wave of his own. But very soon just a few blocks away
Adam confirmed our new lodgings over the phone and we
pulled over once again and dismounted into the cloudy
dimness of La Fortuna's cool bustling sunset. We saluted
this dear good man Eddie and wished him the best of
luck, then carried on. At first we had some trouble
finding our place but we knew it was around there somewhere and that it was a hostel with the word "Arenal" in
the title so very soon after, just a few steps farther,
we spotted the Arenal Hostel Resort and marching forth
we entered the gates of our new and exciting home.

Within the very split second that our bodies crossed
into this hostel we knew with assured fact that this was
not our destination. There was indeed no possible way.
Palm trees. Hammocks. Overhanging balconies. Running
streams of water. Birds. Marble. Cascades of warm sparkling sunlight. Angels. White fluffy clouds. The lascivious pleasings of a fucking lute, if I recall correctly!
We shuffled toward the metal and glass door on the right
to the registration desk. And since Adam's phone was
still dead as a doornail and buried ritually beneath a
foot of white rice we had used my phone to register this
next accommodation. I stepped up to the front desk and
the kind folks greeted us with honored smiles and asked
"Name?" and since I was in no mood to employ my efforts
in the spelling and exegesis of my name I just handed
them my credit card. The bespectacled gentleman in the
suit behind the desk typed my name into his computer
with elegant fortissimo and a cordial smile but then his
smile flipped and his brow curled and he held the credit
card near to his eyes to verify the spelling and when
his mind had run out of possibilities he inquired "Sir,
it appears your name is not turning up". I shuffled

through my pockets and Adam searched my phone and pulled
up the Hostelworld.com app and verified the name and
asked "Is this the Arenal Backpackers Hostel?" And suddenly it looked like an entire house of cards had collapsed around us, for they all suddenly dropped the act
and shuffled about and half-turned away from us and a
stern blond-haired ponytailed woman who had been standing to our right sort of moved toward us pressuring us
away from the reception and toward the hostel's exit and
with the smile of a hotel bellhop but the force of a
nightclub bouncer she announced as she scurried us out
"No, this is the Arenal Hostel Resort. You are looking
for the Arenal Backpackers Hostel" and I swear to God
she almost rolled her eyes with disgust as if this exact
episode happens to her a hundred times a day and after
she firmly pointed uphill to our left the goddamn fuck
away from her precious hoity-toity resort the door
closed behind us and we stood before the Arenal Hostel
Resort facing uphill and toward the Arenal Backpackers
Hostel.

Welcome to La Fortuna you scrappy motherfuckers.

So once again I found myself hiking uphill behind
Adam in his invincible red shorts and jagged green shirt
and gang-raped-to-tatters orange hat and battle-scarred
grey and orange backpack through the bustling street of
cars and honks congestion and bikers pedestrians and
cabs and cloudy misty grey skies and suddenly from over
Adam's head I was slammed with surprise when I beheld in
the hazy distance the sight of an enormous silhouetted
single-peaked mountain. I practically jumped with delight and awe, and once it had all finally registered in
my head I understood what it was that I was looking at.
I was facing the next physical challenge of my trip
through Costa Rica: the climb up Volcan Arenal, the active volcano.

The rest of our walk toward the hostel remains but a
smoky memory sprinkled around the vast godly giant of a
presence that from this titanic volcanic peak loomed.
But as our venture continued the congestion began to
scatter and the buildings became sparser and distances
grew wider until finally we neared a long metal- and
aluminum-barred fence on the right with a large electric
gate at the entrance. And when Adam started to slow down
near this place I thought, now THIS is more like it.
Yes, THIS is how REAL travelers lodge! Flutter thee not

among the soft and pampered, nay! THIS is the lodging of
TRUE travelers! Yes THIS is the great terminus of all
who hath by stern and gravelly feet fed forth!

We waited before the large electric gate to be
buzzed in but once that buzzer went off and we opened
the gate, what we saw inside immediately furled our
brows. We entered modestly into an expansive grassy
field ranging long and wide in open tame and spacious
green. A red-tinged chipping tile path lead the way to a
vast open-air patio. On our left stood some vibrant palm
trees from which hung numerous brightly-colored hammocks. We gingerly heeded the path to the patio until we
reached the open-air space which served as a reception
area, lounge, and restaurant. Big-screen televisions
whirred above us. American music pulsed in the background. Boisterous youth reclined on extended wooden and
straw sofas or sat at tall tree-trunk tables. A barista
took orders for pizza and beer. Adam nudged me to look
left where I beheld in gasping awe a beautifully-lit
crystalline swimming pool buzzing with bodies and vitality.

Palm trees. TVs. Music. Couches. Hammocks. Tables.
Food and drink. A pool.

Where the hell am I?

We stood amid the crowd of vivacious youth gazing
raptly about waiting our turn for reception. Once we
were called we approached the young female receptionist
who received us kindly and looked up our reservation to
check us in. And as she took my credit card and her eyes
fluttered lightly between the computer screen and the
spelling of my name I gazed on at this girl and realized
with quite an innocent start that she had just about the
most sweet and beautiful little face I had ever laid my
eyes on. Adam verbally (and nonverbally) confirmed this
and we stood engaging with this indescribably pretty
little receptionist who presented a professionalism,
beauty, and charm that no reasonable man could possibly
defer. She checked us in and with a rosy melting smile
reviewed the rules of the hostel and the guidelines regarding our stay, but I just hoped Adam was getting all
of it from her because I wasn't processing a single word
out of this glorious angel's sweet Latin mouth. I just
stood there fluttering like a feather in the wind allowing her lyrical voice to lute through my loins and rip-
ple me like a silken flag in the ocean mist. And when

with a slight giggle she excused us my legs indolently dragged me away and I slinked off half-smiling half-drunk with love.

When I regained consciousness I found myself standing at the door of our first-floor room which directly faced the shimmering pool and with a smooth revolution of the key we beheld with grandiose spectacle our new room! The door opened to giant sliding-glass windows and in onto four bunk-beds. Jutting from the top-right corner of the room overseeing this glorious quad was a large and regal divine and holy hallowed grail of deific glory: a single bedroom air conditioner. Just below this sacred monument, this holy Manna of majestic beneficence, was another door.

We couldn't believe it. There was more.

We opened this next door and were smitten with disbelief. We stood before our own personal bathroom. A bathroom! Do you understand what I'm saying to you? There was a personal bathroom in our bedroom! On the right was a series of large lockers. Mounted on the wall was a large clean mirror. A mirror? A mirror! Then a sink. A large sink with knobs to regulate the temperature of the water. And then...God how do I even say it all? Would you even believe me!!... a... a shower. Holy fucking Buddha Jesus Allah Zeus and Brahman! A personal shower! In our room! A shower! And it had knobs! That's plural, motherfuckers! KNOBS! That means multiple temperatures. That means I can CHOOSE the temperature in which I wash myself! DO YOU UNDERSTAND WHAT I'M SAYING!

It was all just too much. I was downright hyperventilating absolutely revolted by the extravagance and sheer excess of this luxury-teeming palace of kings. We left our bags on our bunk-beds and headed out to explore what other indescribable indulgences this glorious estate had to offer. We found multiple toilets. Extra shared sinks and at least four more showers. Granted these were public spaces, but for just $15.00 per night I could actually choose from one of many porcelain toilets, mirrored sinks, and temperature-regulating showers. And for the most part I wouldn't have to because all of those things were already available in my own fucking sleeping quarters! Do you goddamned holy hell understand that??

Once the shock of our good fortune finally settled we sensed our hunger and beheld the sun gently easing

into the horizon. Few guests were about then so we figured it would be a good time to head out and explore our
options. We returned to the open-air patio where some
mostly college-aged youth reclined on the couches eating
pizza and sipping beer. We scanned the menu and found it
decent, but also thought it worthwhile to explore the
town of La Fortuna a bit to see what it had to offer. So
as we were crossing the patio to leave my eyes grazed
over the darling receptionist who had in the span of
typing my long countless-letter surname stolen my heart.
Quite involuntarily I walked back over to her to engage
her in conversation. We talked about the hostel and
nearby places to eat and after I got a few giggles and
smiles out of her I asked for her name and she said
"Berenici". It took me many attempts and countless embarrassing mistakes to impress that name into my memory,
for I kept forgetting it and asking her to remind me and
she kept laughing at me. But finally I had the holy name
inculcated and then the name and the roses and clouds
and winds and open grassy pastures of romantic daydreams
surged my mind's eye and I stood there a bit longer than
one should carrying on and thinking, Ay Berenici ay
Berenici! Que linda mi amor! Mi alma mi señorita hermosa
que dulce mi corazón! And once I had exhausted the whole
of my romantic Spanish vocabulary I just switched to the
next stage of falling in love: rationalization. Which
went like this:

"If I manage to spend enough time with her these
next two days then I can propose on our way out of town.
Why would she say no? Look at me, I'm a keeper! The
girls down here would love me. Sure she may be coy at
first but that'll change! Right? I could write her poetry and leave it on her desk in the morning. Or I could
show her my CamelBak Chute 1.5L Sky Blue water bottle
and certainly there could be no respite from that! We
could stay in touch through email or text message and
that would give her some time to break the news to her
ailing father and her weeping mother and siblings. Yes I
know she has been the breadwinner of the household for
so long but ever since she met "José Mi Amor" she can no
longer resist the migration to her sweet American beloved! This wouldn't be easy, of course, but she will
promise to send money back whenever she can. And I will
vow to sustain them despite the odds! Sure, my family
won't be too thrilled about all of this but I'm sure

they would eventually understand. They've been through worse. It will take some serious coaxing but I will not take no for an answer! Once I secure an apartment for us then she can move in by Christmas and we can begin arrangements for the summer wedding. She can enroll in college classes by next fall and I'll provide for us until her English is satisfactory for employment. We can name our first boy after HER father but our daughter will be named after MY mother, dammit!"

And so on.

I texted my friends the "3 Blind Mice" a photo of this astounding grand court of a hostel and commented: "My home for the next two nights. And a receptionist named Berenici who inspires poetry and daydreams. She melts the heart. Ay, mi amor Berenici. Que sonrisa mi alma!" And it seems this flight of passion for Berenici got ALL my juices flowing all at once and suddenly I was swirling twirling ramping romping with desire and it turned out my undying love for the peligrosa Berenici spilled out over everybody and I suppose my devout and faithful adoration wasn't so devout and faithful after all, for the next text I sent said "The fucking women women women girls girls damas damas AAAAHHHHHHHHHHHH!!!!!! Nudity? Hah! In my underwear 70% of the time. So's everyone else. We did only hostels this trip. Best experience of my life. Never traveling outside of hostels again."

And finally I just ran out of shit to think about and moved on to the next darling love of my life: food! We decided to head back down to La Fortuna to find a decent meal.

Arenal Backpackers Hostel is located on the farther western side of town, closer to Volcan Arenal. We headed back east away from the volcano to get to town and though it seemed like our hostel was placed on the fringes of the action this certainly had its advantages, for the view of the mountainous behemoth was gorgeous from the poolside and defied description, my friends. Once we had crossed the chipped red-tinged tile path and exited the buzzing gate we turned left heading back into town and just minutes later we found on our left a small

green information booth about the tours and trails of
Arenal and then just a bit farther we spotted a luxurious tiled Venetian-themed open-air restaurant advertis-
ing pizza. The place was completely empty, yet so seemed
the whole of this tiny town. So we decided to give it a
shot.

We took a seat closer to the wall where we were
hosted by a gracious pudgy-but-not-quite-fat youthful
waiter with a face straight out of a Raphael painting
and whom I could only describe as "cousinly". Yes,
that's the word. In an instant you felt as if you'd
grown up with the guy. Like he was your dear chum and
that you had to make sure he was home before sunset and
that his mother thought very highly of you and that if
any of the boys on the street ever hurt him then you'd
beat their fucking asses. Yes, you wanted to take the
guy out and show him around. To invite him over for dinner. To laugh with him about all the great childhood
memories. Yes instantly he made you feel warm and at
home and as welcome as family and as we settled in and
ordered our pizzas and smoothies we felt such comfort
and warmth indeed.

And as we sat in quiet solitude awaiting our dinner
my mind reeled back with daunted humility to that godly
pyramid, the all-seeing monolith of the ancient fire-
breathing volcano. Ever since I had laid eyes on it, it
had enraptured me with wonder and terror. I thought back
through the thousands of years to all the indigenous
peoples who must've looked upon this towering memorial
and called it their god. We tend to look back on such
people today and call them stupid or ignorant or uncivi-
lized because they worshipped the sun and the winds and
moons and trees and mountains. But maybe we say that
because we haven't seen mountains, because we haven't
experienced what the greatness of these things can to
the human spirit do. I sat there knowing that had I been
brought forth from this earth knowing nothing, being
told nothing, having no instruction of who or what or
why, and then later had my eyes fallen upon this spectacular structure which now hovered gloriously behind
me, then I too would call it my god. And I too would
have fallen to my knees in fear and surrender. And I too
would have named it and sung of it with great passion
and poetry through the fires of night and I too would
have burned incense and gathered feasts and danced in

its holy honor. And had that tremendous inescapable cauldron suddenly heaved forth unstoppable seas of flaming red fire and spurted them into the dark and trembling heavens and shoveled them down toward me creaming the visible world into black ash and cindered bone (as it certainly has done many times before, including this very decade) then I too would have sacrificed every sheep and goat and captive and virgin and son to make it stop. No, these primitive servants of the volcano were not stupid; in some ways they were smarter than we are today.

So I turned to Adam and asked "so tomorrow we're going to climb that thing?" and he replied "Yezzur!" After a slight pause I said "Look man I am going to be honest with you: I'm scared." And without judgment or surprise he began the conversation with his characteristic "okay...okay..." which he states a couple of times in a very soothing and considerate tone whenever he mentally prepares for deep conversation. Adam is a profound listener so his next question was "why?" I thought very carefully about why. We are seldom aware of why we are afraid and to find the answer we really must dig deeper. So after some thought I realized this: when beginning any new task, I don't feel comfortable in circumstances of the unknown. I don't like taking action while uninformed. However, once I am informed of the reality, great or terrible as it might be, then I am able to deal with it— even if that reality is utterly hopeless. So I started asking some factual questions and Adam responded clearly and practically:

"Am I going to die?"

"No."

"What are the odds that I will fall to my death?"

"None. It's not as steep as it looks."

"What if I slip?"

"Be careful not to."

"Is it difficult to breathe up there?"

"No, it's not nearly high enough."

"How high up is that thing?"

He searched the pamphlet from the information booth. "5,400 feet. But that peak [Arenal] is active so we won't be allowed to climb it. We're climbing nearby Volcan Cerro Chato. 3,700 feet."

"How long's the whole hike?"

"We can choose. One trail is estimated to take four
to five hours. The other runs ten to twelve hours."
"What should I bring with me?"
"We'll shop after dinner."
And thus we carried on chatting about hiking and
travel and friends and asshole-friends and high school
as our pizzas arrived— our delicious hot cheesy baked-
to-perfection pizzas, brought forth still steaming mo-
lecularly sizzling with sauce, tomato, cheese, and mush-
room. We carried on with delectable gusto biting into
our morsels of joy with the same melting delight of a
baby tummy-rubbed to speel. We enjoyed the interjections
of loving camaraderie from our new cousinly waiter-
friend chum Joseph who brought out our pizzas and with
great propriety announced "Buen Provecho!" And I said
back "Buen Provencho SIIIIIIIIII..." But Adam corrected
me saying it is not pronounced "proVENcho" but is actually pronounced "proVEcho" without the "n". I respect-
fully disagreed but when we asked Joseph for the correct
pronunciation he verified what Adam had said and what do
you know! I learned something new there!
So there we sat in the cloudy murkiness of La Fortuna when suddenly my eyes grazed a sight of vertical linear movement behind me against the white plastered stone
wall. I turned around and even pizza couldn't hinder my
marvel. I saw ants marching up the wall in a sporadic
hurry. Their vigilant and frantic activity struck me. I
looked more carefully. Somewhere near the bottom of the
wall along the black line of ants there was a very big
ant, at least double the size of the others. It was im-
mobile, but was being moved. I looked even more carefully and then I understood: along this vertical plastered
white wall in this Venetian-scened Italian restaurant at
the base of a towering deific volcano, an ant had fall-
en— a large significant ant, the queen of them all— and
they were marching her up the wall. Marching in frantic
funereal shifts. Marching solemnly for their martyred
monarch. By now they were halfway up the wall and my
face was two inches away. They moved in rotary shifts in
which five or six of them carried the sacred lifeless
burden and after a few seconds once they had tired out
they rotated from beneath their venerated matriarch and
another five or six carried on. They continued thusly
inch by mourning inch up the wall while Adam and I sat

gawking at the wonder of this everyday miracle of Planet Earth.

We finished our delicious dinner and paid our tab happily, but when Joseph witnessed the gracious tip we had left him he was awestruck and tried to refuse. We wouldn't have it; he had earned it and we were honored to be his guests. We bid him a gracious and heartfelt farewell then proceeded across the street to a small market. There we would purchase all of the food and water needed for the upcoming adventure.

Adam instructed: "We are looking for nonperishable power foods. High-energy foods. Fruits, cheese, protein."

I reached out and grabbed a large tin. "Nuts?"

Adam cringed. "Man, I'm sick of nuts."

"Okay then," I thought. "What about cheese?" We scanned the coolers for cheese but found only sizes too large or textures too soft. We finally settled for peanut butter as our source of protein. We coupled it with some soft tortillas on which to spread it then crossed to the opposite end of the shop and scanned for fruits. Apples? Grapes? Bananas? We settled finally for little clementines. Soft, small, and refreshing. I picked out a water bottle from the fridge and Adam laughed. "That's not gonna do it." He pointed to a multi-gallon barrel of water: Four? Six gallons? "We need THAT."

"Fuck," I thought. I heaved it over and got in line to pay, but Adam had saved the best for last.

"Now," he said with a bubbling excitement reserved for a child's surprise. He explained the idea: we should each pick out something we want to enjoy once we reach the top.

I didn't understand: "Enjoy how?"

He gave an example of a friend who held a tradition that whenever he'd reach a summit of a climb he'd celebrate with a treat. So basically, I was now to choose my "victory treat". We considered other examples: cigars, colas, pints of rum. But no, these weren't quite what hit the spot. Then Adam gave me the clue that hit the nail on the head: "It should be something that keeps you going. Something that motivates you, rewards you when you reach the top."

"Yeah?" I thought. "You know what fuckin' motivates ME? CHOCOLATE!" And with tongue a-dangle and eyes agape I strutted in a pin-straight line right up to the candy

aisle and grabbed my favorite chocolate bar of all time:
Nestle's Kit Kat. (Mind you, my Most Perceptive Reader,
we are talking about NESTLE's Kit Kat. Not HERSHEY's Kit
Kat, no fuck THAT shit motherfucker! This is NESTLE's
Kit Kat. NESTLE's Kit Kat.) I grabbed the smooth glistening red square block of orgasmic deliciousness and
rejoined the line, my smile beaming.

Carrying our bags we ventured back west toward our
hostel beneath the looming shrine of the hallowed honor.
By now the sun had almost set and the heavenly mist of
gold and blue now silhouetted Volcan Arenal which hailed
before us. I paused for a moment to observe this breath-
taking view, realizing that on the morrow I would mount
this towering wonder, that I would face it and ascend
its back to stroke its stone and be among its lizards
and shrubs. I took a picture of this black mammoth
against the golds and blues of heaven and then posted
the image onto Instagram and announced valiantly: "Tonight we sleep. Tomorrow we climb. Hasta mañana". And
with that we buzzed ourselves back into the Arenal Backpackers Hostel (which is not the fuck to EVER be confused with the Arenal Hostel Resort not EVER) and entering, we found it pulsing with energy and bustle.

A lot had changed since we had left it! The hammocks
were all taken, fully occupied by lounging youth and
chattering laughter. Music pumped and pulsed through the
open-air lounge. The pool's refreshing splashes startled
us to delight and skipped the beats of our spirits.
Glasses and dishes clinked, chairs shuffled. The air
permeated with cheers and laughter, howling and hooting,
and everything in sight pulsated in a rip-roaring blast
of energetic excitement. And it is precisely these kinds
of rousing thrilling spontaneous wholly happy gatherings
of people that make me want nothing more on earth than
to be left severely and entirely the fuck alone.

chapter one

We entered our room and found it buzzing with excitement. The bunks were all taken now. The precious
personal bathroom was occupied. We greeted our fellow
roommates genially as we shuffled toward our beds to get
to our bags. Adam borrowed my phone to research and update while I dug through my bag to get myself in order.
The first thing I noticed was that I had almost no fresh
clothing left, for I had left the shit town of Manuel
Antonio carrying back all of my dirty laundry. I shoveled out the hardened caked balls of cotton sphere by
sphere and piled them up before me. I asked Adam "you
got any laundry you want to get done?" and as if the
thought had never crossed his mind, the prospect of it
seemed to perk him up. He found a shirt or two and a
pair of shorts and threw them into the pile. One of them
was the navy-blue cutoff T-shirt that he had worn for
the past couple of days and once that thing came within
an arm's length of his face he recoiled grotesquely and
flung the dangling sulk away from his body, writhing in
disgust.

"Hoof! That thing stinks!" he exclaimed.

Now personally I didn't mind, for you see I was born
without the ability to smell (Yes, that's right. I can't
smell. It's a rare condition called anosmia that affects
one in every few million people in which we are born
without the sense of smell. It's sort of like nose-
deafness. I will answer your follow-up questions in the
order in which you will ask them: 1. Yes I can taste. 2.
Yes I know taste and smell are connected, but still I
can taste. 3. No I have never smelled ANYTHING before.
That includes roses and farts. 4. To my knowledge there
is no known cure or treatment for this condition. 5. Yes
I am lucky). And indeed at this particular moment I was
incredibly lucky, for if my dear friend who hardly
sweats at all was that disgusted by HIS single shirt,
then what the fuck did my heap of the sweat-caked fabric
smell like? I thanked God for my infirmity and quickly

scooped our items into a plastic bag, sealing it with every muscular fiber of my upper-body strength, and then carried it outside to the front desk.

Berenici was no longer there, to my lamentable and desolate dismay, and instead I was greeted by a towering bowling violently large man with a titanic belly and scruffy old hair and a dirty white T-shirt and a huge grin of gaping teeth (by the way, I would later meet this fantastic man whose name is Raphael, and he is among the coolest and most entertaining fellows in all of my experience in Costa Rica! But at first glance I am ashamed to say that that was what I saw). I greeted him and asked if he knew of any nearby laundromats that were open this late in the evening. His response was one of the most astonishing things anyone has ever said to me: "We can do laundry here".

What.

What?? Here??? You mean you will do my laundry? You mean that you are a hostel that does laundry? Are you fucking kidding me? Is this the Taj Mahal? Is this Buckingham Palace? Is this the White House? What did I do to deserve this? And with coursing tears of gratitude and trembling humility I handed our laundry over to this grinning man who never seems to let down his smile and I almost fell to my knees and bowed. He told me it would be ready by the next day so I thanked him profusely and giggled hysterically all the way back to my room.

I returned to find Adam standing there undressed and adjusting his Greek mythology red shorts. Everything else lay casually on his bed. "Gonna hit the pool, you wanna come?" he asked.

I politely declined. "Nah," I said. "I think I'm just gonna shower and chill." Then, as my palm gently scuffed across my rough and hard face, I added: "And I need to shave", to which my dear Adam promptly howled in indignation and protest.

"WHAAAAT," he cried. "NO, man." He explained scoldingly the euphoric benefit of letting the scuff grow right past the itchy stage to where it looked great and finally smoothed out. But frankly I wasn't itching for any more discomforts (pun intended) and I took his bullying for a bit but just decided to shave anyway. With an interjection of disappointment he went off to enjoy the pool and I delighted to have this time to enjoy my solitude. I just wasn't in the mood for happy people.

I gathered my shaving kit and a dry change of
clothes and with nothing on but my grey Hanes I marched
out around the corner toward the stalls and showers,
greeting people along the way. You may find it strange
that I ventured out in my underwear, but I and the rest
of this nation have been half-naked ever since I got
here. Frankly, there was no other way to be about. I
reached the lovely tiled hallway where five or six individual bathroom stalls awaited my choosing. I entered
one and stood staring at this marble marvel, this personal private space, clean and sweat-free, that I had
all to myself. And suddenly for no reason and without
any warning, S.J. came to mind.

I finished up and strutted over to the showers from
which again I could choose from any number of empty
spots. I picked one and after hanging my clothes on the
outer side of the door, I entered and turned on the
shower. A myriad of water temperatures tickled my nerves
and once I had chosen the ideal degree of cosmic warmth
I stepped in and stood in its glorious comfort in a
great span of heavenly timelessness. I just stood there
naked as the day, my eyes closed, my child-like smile of
joy whitening my stupid happy face, with water cascading
across my limbs cooling and soothing my flesh and bone,
my blood and soul. Finally I gathered the strength to
break this trance and I began to wash. And once I had
savored the delight to my satisfaction I reemerged,
dried off with my legendary gift (the neon-green quick-
dry microfiber towel) and headed down in my underwear to
the communal sinks to shave.

For the first time in recent memory I found myself
standing full-bodied before a mirror. I was barbarically
unshaven. I had noticeably lost weight. My face, particularly my brow, appeared unfurled and stunningly at
ease. This was surprising given the strains of the past
week. I looked at the scuff that jagged my face. Did I
want to shave it all off? Did I want to keep something?
I finally settled on shaving but leaving a light mustache and goatee. After all, it was more so the neckline
and the cheeks that bothered me than anything else. So I
dampened my face and with a quick spray of the travel-
size Barbasol Beard Buster 2.25 Oz Shaving Cream I lath-
ered my cheeks and neck and gently enjoyed a nice calm
quiet shave, and what remained once I had finished was a
light grazing circle around my lips and chin: a goatee.

I returned to my room to pack my things and take
some time to chill. By now the pool was swarming with
happy guests, and I observed that most of them were thin
fit bikini girls. So I went back to my room and checked
again the bathroom and air conditioner just to make sure
they were real and I greeted some of my roommates. Finally I felt there was nothing left to do but to join
Adam so I grabbed my Brazilian-colored shorts and headed
out to see what all the damn ruckus was about. I approached the pool and saw instantly a great many people
hooting and hollering joyously as they jumped into the
pool. Getting closer, I realized that they weren't jumping; they were falling! Across the center of the pool
hung a slack line upon which swimmers competed to walk
across. I stood aside observing this boisterous game.
Adam of course had already made friends— five or six of
them, and all of them attractive girls. One by one they
would approach the deck of the pool and mount the slack
line, but three or four steps in they would fall into
the center, splashing everyone around them as spectators
hooted and hollered with laughter and joy.

A slack line is a long, wide, flat surface similar
in width and material to a seatbelt that fastens at opposite ends. The challenge of walking this beam is that
it is fastened loosely, rendering flat balance impossible. Instead, one must engage multiple muscle groups to
achieve the slinking balance required to walk across it.
So Adam approached the slack line! He mentally prepared,
then ascended the step and began to walk. Knees jangling, hips wiggling, arms extended outright, he endured
with careful mental concentration. But three steps in,
his weight overpowered him and he collapsed hysterically
into the cool beaming water. His joyous fans cheered him
on.

A girl followed, prepared to defeat his record and
riveted for the challenge. She was a tall slender girl
with long limbs, clean pure white skin, long blonde
hair, and sparkling blue eyes. Her smile radiated across
the pool, her laughter uplifting the most dispirited of
souls. Her genial smile and warm laughter would be her
trademark and my most vivid memory of her throughout the
whole trip. Her name was Kylie.

I was stunned by Kylie's skill as she mounted the
slack line. She balanced nimbly, her long limbs suave
and smooth. She stepped daintily and with the gentle

precision of a ballerina. Her unmatched physical
strength was smoothed over by her grace and step by step
she made her way along the slack line. But she too could
not defeat the swinging forces of gravity and eventually
she too plunged to her watery finale. The spectators
applauded her vivaciously.

She was followed by her extra-smiley friend, a girl
of shorter stature and darker skin, dark and small but
cavern-deep eyes, Polynesian features, and robust curly
black hair. But like Kylie, she too bore a smile of a
thousand miles. It was a smile that brought you back to
childhood, a sweet warmth of the face that made her ir-
resistible to hug and smile along with. Her name was
Tia.

Ascending the pool's edge and establishing her feet
against the base of the slack line, she approached the
challenge with a starkly different mindset than Kylie's.
Contrasting the swan-like grace and precision of her
partner, Tia began with a hard and determined affront.
Her strength came not from her strong frame or her solid
core, but from deep within her, from a staunch fortitude
and intrepid resilience that seared beneath her shimmering smile. Her steps were firm, determined, her arms
masted and grail. With a few steps she too fell, but she
emerged from the blue pool laughing soulfully. She loved
the challenge, but she loved even more the wrestle with
looming defeat and the slow but inevitable triumph of
perseverance. The spectators all cheered. I cheered. And
somehow unconsciously I found myself too close to the
pool. Too close to the slack line. A thin young guy and
his European girlfriend cheered me on from behind, urg-
ing me on. Somehow I had ended up in line. And now it
was my turn!

Standing there facing the base of the slack line I
was now at the center of the pool's attention. The
cheering happy faces appeared grim and grotesque, clown-
like actually. Sneering! if I may put it plainly. I wondered, how did my efforts to avoid attention lead me
right into the fucking center of it? I felt goofy in my
Brazilian-colored shorts, my stupid goatee which did
NOTHING to ease my brutal Hispanic vato look, and most
of all my deep self-consciousness about the fact that I
had never been on a slack line before and was about to
make a hideous fool of myself. Why am I always making a
fucking fool of myself?

chapter one

No time to turn back now! This wasn't middle school.
For I had been in this situation before and had learned
from it. Once back in the eighth grade I had attended an
after-school dance. Now how a bunch of 90's middle-
schoolers happened upon a private dance party without
adult supervision (let alone how the fuck I of all people ended up there) still evades me. Anyways, asshole
Billy Danigan was on DJ and we had formed ourselves into
some kind of grinding line in which girls on one side
would hop into the center and boys from the other side
would hop behind them and grind them across the dance
floor, hip-humping their asses from one end of the hall
to the other. After Paul had hip-humped Ashley into the
dim distance of the hall, I suddenly found myself right
there at the front of the line with a pubescent female
ass plunked up high before me and the cheers of the
whole eighth-grade student body quaking the walls of the
hall! I politely declined, smiled sheepishly and raised
my hand with a toothy grin and an Elizabethan "no, thank
you" gesture, crossed my legs, scooted past the preteen
ass mounted before me, and cordially exited the center
of the circle out into the fringes.
    Yeah. You learn a lot in fucking middle school.
    So fuck it! I stood mentally analyzing what I could
from the mechanics and techniques of the slack line,
stood up on it, barely balanced, and fell sprawling and
laughing hysterically into the pool. The entire congregation laughed with me, and excitedly I swam back to the
pool's edge and hopped back in line.
    Adam tried again. Kylie and Tia tried again. I tried
many times again. After over an hour and virtually hundreds of attempts, I only recall one or two times in
which someone succeeded. But it didn't matter. It didn't
matter because it doesn't matter. After a good hour of
this nonsense we got hungry so I went back into my room
to grab some money. I entered the room and was greeted
with emphatic excitement by two guests on the bunks to
my left. On the top bunk lay a lovely young woman in a
tank top with striking hazel-brown eyes, a sweet smile,
and a small light birthmark above her left eyebrow. Below her sat a dude in a T-shirt who for all the world
looked like a white dude from Iowa (and wouldn't you
know? He turned out to be a white dude from Iowa!) Immediately and with great excitement the girl on top fired
off questions:

"How are you?"

"What's your name?"

"Where are you from?"

I answered accordingly, and she explained that her name was Lena and that she was originally from Portugal but lived in Switzerland. Wow, I exclaimed. I am originally from the Middle East but I live in America! In Michigan, to be exact. And from that simple exchange I ended up standing in the center of that room for almost forty-five minutes talking to Lena and this dude from Iowa whose name fails me and later a couple of other dudes from France whose names also fail me and we talked about America and the Middle East and Muslims and the Arabic language and Europe and the world. To my surprise, Lena found Arab and Islamic culture fascinating and told me that she would love to learn Arabic. Come to think of it, she looked a bit Middle-Eastern herself and she had the darling warmth and genial charisma and spiritual eloquence of the Levantine people. She would have fit in quite well. Yet though this conversation was fascinating and engaging I was eventually forced to cut it short, for I had been gone far too long from the folks at the pool and needed to get a bite to eat. So I politely excused myself and eagerly hoped to continue our conversation another time.

I returned to the pool which had by now almost entirely emptied out and saw that all that remained was Adam still going at that fucking slack line with some other dude. Kylie and Tia were not to be found so I assumed I would catch up with them later. Meanwhile, two sexy girls were lounging in the far corner of the pool sipping drinks and from where I was standing they looked pretty astonishing. One in particular had long dark chestnut-colored hair and wore a cherry-red bikini which fit nice and taut against her skin, ornamenting her sweet stomach and slim limbs. On her face she wore the nonchalant resting-bitch pose that really gets me going. But quite instantly once I noticed that she and her darker-skinned black-bikinied friend were taking selfies in the pool (which if you think that's an acceptable practice for anyone over the age of fifteen then frankly, fuck you too), my fires receded and my juices sulked and that was all the excitement I had up for that evening.

139

So I joined Adam and his new buddy who was a short, fit young man wearing glasses (yes, glasses in the pool) and as he mounted the slack line and struggled for balance the two bikini selfie-chicks in the corner cheered him on, drinks raised, and this was when I made the connection that these three were all traveling together. Eagerly I thought, what a lucky young man this bespectacled gallant fucker must be! Traveling across the world with two fine-ass chicks by his side! God, what a dream that would be! If only I had two fine-ass bikini-brazen pool babes along MY side to cheer me on as I rodeoed the slack line then I would perpetually keep one under each arm and strut about like a bold barrel-chested rooster! Boy, how enhancing THAT would be! And instantly I was endeared to this gallant young son of a bitch who before my eyes manifested my youthful dreams— that is, at least for a while.

I jumped in with Adam and this bespectacled young lad and once we had tired out of the slack line we sat in the pool and introduced ourselves. His name was Christian and he was traveling from New York with his two young selfie-taking friends, whom he finally introduced us to. The darker-skinned smilier one was named Samirah and she was from Pakistan; the other (the fine-bodied one in the red bikini) was originally from Turkey and she must have pronounced her name three or four times for me, but whether it was because her name was utterly foreign to me or because she talked like a horse with broken glass in her mouth, for the life of me I couldn't make out what she was saying. So I asked her to spell it and it is spelled "Dojuh". So I introduced myself to Samirah and Dojuh and we chatted pleasantly until they decided to leave the pool and change. After they excused themselves Adam was off again doing something more active (I don't know what he was doing but I recall him in the background physically shuffling around and laughing a lot. Would this fucking guy sit down please?) while Christian and I chatted amiably in the bright crystalline lights of the pool amid the music and the dancing and the buzzing of the hostel and the stillness of the Costa-Rican night.

While talking to Christian, I found myself struck by this young man's intelligence and profound introspection. He expressed himself with dignity and poise. He spoke openly and thoughtfully and I found him to be an

exquisite pleasure to talk to! That is not to say that
he isn't a complete and total nerd; no, Christian is
very much a dork. But then again, so am I as you have
invariably witnessed, my Most Judicious Reader. So
Christian and I consolidated our joint nerdiness to discuss with poignant analytics the crises of the modern
age, the perils of this worldly life, the complexities
and hypocrisies of social constructs and expectations,
the inevitable fall of civilized man, and the existential realities of what it means to be a young man in
21st-century America. Amid all of this sizzling discussion, something came up that quite rightly stumbled me
with surprise:

"...it's like, sometimes you just need a buddy to
talk to," Christian said.

"What do you mean," I asked.

"So for instance," he explained, "They [Samirah and
Dojuh] are cool to travel with. I mean they're nice and
everything, but I can't really talk to them. They're not
really the "conversation" type...

[Yeah no shit, Sherlock. Unless by "conversation"
you mean pillaging their budding genitalia, I more-than-
emphatically agree with you]

"...All they want to do is go out and party and meet
guys. But I look at you two [referring to me and Adam]
and you guys can have conversations and just hang
out..." Now I don't recall the rest of the exchange ver-
batim but the general gist of it was that Christian felt
a bit cursed to be stuck with two girl acquaintances
while I was so lucky to be traveling with a male friend.

Yes oh yes, indeed I sense your surprise, my Most
Astounded Reader. This guy?? This guy!! Traveling across
the coasts with those two bomb-ass beauties fluttering
beside him? Sharing luggage and beds and days and nights
with them? And HE would rather be ME?

I digested what he said and concluded that it seemed
the man was right. I reflected upon all those times when
I saw a man in the company of sexy women; how many of
those times was that man actually happy? How many of
those times had I assumed that I'd wanted to be him? But
what use could beautiful girls be if one cannot connect
with them? What good are bikini babes and parties and
drinks and vacations if they leave you feeling all
alone? And in that instant I turned to gaze upon my dear
friend and brother Adam who sprung about splashing or

flipping or whatever the fuck he was doing, his face
elastic with a great wiry smile, his hearty chuckles
echoing in the distance. Would I trade him for four
moist tits and two bouncing asses? I wouldn't. I
wouldn't trade him or us or all of this for absolutely
anything.

I looked quite pitiably back to Christian who now
sulked beside me drowned in thought. Just over his
shoulder there had sat two glistening girls, drinks held
high, scrunched together to take a selfie, smiling only
with their bellowing teeth. And I'm not sure if you know
what I mean by that, but a real smile isn't just a physical construct. It has nothing to do, in fact, with the
shape of the mouth or the crinkle of the eyes or the
visibility of the teeth. A real smile is a warm light
that glows from deep within you. And that, my friends,
wasn't there. It wasn't there at all.

Christian and I parted ways to change and shower and
carry on with our evenings and we hoped to connect again
very soon, for our evening's conversation had been quite
enlightening and pleasant. I returned to my room to
change, exchanged further discourse with Lena and Iowa
and French dude, then returned to the open-air lounge to
find Adam seated at a table with a young lady amid riotous music and bombastic television and cheerful socia-
bility. By now it seemed like the whole hostel had become one big perpetual party and the enthusiasm was contagious. I joined the pair at the table where Adam introduced me to his new friend, a girl named Lori. When I
heard Lori's accent and as soon as she mentioned that
she was from England, I shut down like a nuclear war
bunker. "Ohhh no!" I thought. "Not again! No sir, I'm
not getting back into THAT again. I've had enough of you
Euro-Brit bitches for one lifetime, thank you very
much!" I was just going to excuse myself and scoot away
to the other end of the lounge when I noticed that she
was smiling. She made eye contact, spoke in complete
sentences, and asked questions! Dare I say, she behaved
like a normal civilized fucking human being! Dare I admit, here was a person from England who didn't behave
like a person from England! Well I'll be god-damn
damned! Lori turned out to be an awesome person whose
company I dearly enjoyed. Her friend joined soon after
and we all sat around the table chatting and laughing
heartily. Kylie and Tia came by too, now dressed in

shorts and a T-shirt, and Tia now donned a baseball cap
that would come to characterize her fashion, for it fit
her very cutely and emblemized her smile even further!
Then Christian came by as well and before we knew it, we
had a huge gang of folks sitting around mingling and
chatting together.

I went over to the lounge's bar to get something to
drink and found Samirah and Dojuh ordering dinner themselves. However, now that they were not clad in flaming
bikinis dripping wet in a sparkling pool, I must say
that they didn't look quite as good. In fact, they
looked pretty darn average to me. In FACT fact, they
looked slightly and recoilingly disappointing. Briefly
we exchanged some pleasant small talk and while I commu-
nicated pretty fluidly with Samirah, I really couldn't
figure out at all quite what Dojuh was saying. I mean,
she talks like her tongue has been chewed on by a mule.
I honestly mean no disrespect, but that's about as accu-
rately as I can describe what I was hearing. Anyway,
once the ladies had ordered their food I brought them
back over to our table where we all sat together immersed in laughter and conversation.

So the first thing we all talked about was plans for
the next day's hikes up the volcanoes. Kylie and Tia
were going to attempt the full ten- to twelve-hour hike.
Samirah and Dojuh affirmed the same decision and Adam
and I said that we were still thinking about it. But
secretly I was hoping that Adam was thinking what I was
thinking, which is FUCK. THAT. and instead would agree
to hike up Volcan Cerro Chato, a challenging feat that
would last between four and five hours. So since we all
were going to need our energy for the next day, we decided to turn in early that night and spend the rest of
our time lounging at the hostel. And that turned out to
be one of the greatest decisions of our entire trip.

After that, we hopped around across many different
topics and at one point we came upon a highly engaging
and entertaining discussion about the modes of communication. Someone mentioned a recent survey which found
that millennials strongly preferred texting— even face-
to-face interaction— over talking on the phone. They
would prefer almost ANY mode of communication over
phone-calling, and for the most part we all agreed. We
had one digressor, however, and that was Christian, who
insisted that he actually preferred pleasant telephone

conversation over all else. Sadly for him, none of us
were buying it.

Now let's all be clear about something here: Christian is technically and logically correct. Texting is a
far less effective mode of communication than calling.
Texting is horrible, actually, in that it greatly limits
such aspects of basic communication as tone of voice,
nonverbal expression, and the means of constructing sentences and ideas effectively. Texting causes more fights
than public intoxication, even! (an entirely made-up
fact, by the way. Complete bullshit but you get my
point.) But here's where poor intelligent innocent
Christian went wrong: he assumed that we were technical
and logical people. That we were open to reason. That we
construct our beliefs and opinions with any shred of
intellectual calculation. Not so, my poor puddling pal;
we are stubborn impulsive indecisive creatures pre-
programmed by mutated genes and vile traditions. Don't
even bother.

So in response to dear Christian's bold, rational,
lucid, erudite, and articulate conclusion, Adam and I
politely but firmly disagreed, and Samirah and Dojuh,
his close friends and travel buddies, violently castrat-
ed and demeaned him before the whole music-blasted fes-
tively-spirited congregation.

"WOW, you're so WEIRD", Samirah urched, practically
vomiting up the phrase with vile disgust. "You're like
an old MAN..." Her mouth contorted into such vindictive
contempt that it hurdled my stomach for a second.

"Why are you LIKE this," Dojuh I think said, and
they both glared daggers at him and seeped bile and
carved him to slivers with smoldering hatred.

Then they laughed at him. Connecting glances of
spurning disdain they cackled at his mutated oddity and
guzzled up rickety black guffaws of sizzling sardony.

That's fucking bitchy, I thought. With great astonishment, head tilted in confusion, I wondered, were these REALLY the two girls from the pool who seemed so dip-
shitting sexy to me earlier? I recalled how grotesquely
correct poor Chris had been about the miseries of traveling with these young broads. I thought that in his
shoes I'd trade a kidney to be alone and away from these
little gems than to have the whole world think I was
lucky. There's plenty more to life than people thinking
that you're lucky.

chapter one

    I henceforth dubbed this dear young man
"ChrisKafka". We excused ourselves for bedtime.

chapter one

I woke up with a start just to be sure. In the dead
of night amidst seven other sleepers I jumped up, eyes
gaping, JUST to be SURE. But no, it wasn't a dream.
There it was before my eyes: a fucking air conditioner.
Do you understand? A fucking. Air. Conditioner. I rolled
over and went back to sleep with a gaping smile
stretched from ear to ear. And shivered.

I woke up bright and early the next morning, among
the earliest risers in the whole hostel. Adam was asleep
and I didn't want to disturb him so I rose and walked
out into the cool morning. Birds chirped and the sun was
hardly visible and everything was still and silent. I
walked over to the reception desk where a fresh face was
preparing the day's proceedings. The open-air lounge
sans the music, televisions, people, and lights casted
an air of delicate tranquility and I felt tremendous
peace. Behind the desk I saw a couple of shelves of
books so I asked if I could read one of them, but after
flipping through a couple that didn't strike my interest
I decided to just head over to the hammocks and mellow
out in the silent Costa-Rican morning.

As I approached the abandoned hammocks I saw from
across the grassy dewy field two palm trees and between
them hung, low to the ground, a slack line! Next to the
palm trees was a simple series of blue metal bars, most
likely serving as gymnastics beams. So I thought, what
better way to start my day than with some exercises and
a bit of slack line practice! I approached the blue metal bars and did some chin-ups, exercising in the crisp
silent morning mist of the volcano's base, my feet wet
with the morning dew, my breaths echoing in the stillness of the blue fog. Soon after, my wrists began to
hurt so I decided to lay off the chin-ups for a moment.
Then I approached the palm tree and mounted the slack
line and began by trying to stand upright for as long as
possible. With flailing arms outbound and knees jangling
I finally managed a grip on that, so then I started to

take short and gentle steps. It was a definite struggle
and I made very little progress, but the mental and
physical dauntings of the task refreshed me and aroused
me for the morning's greater challenge. Once I had tired
out I dismounted the slack line, but setting my feet on
the wet grass I slipped backwards and fell solidly on my
ass. The impact ricocheted throughout my body, even
slightly dizzying me, and I rose a bit rattled by this
sudden fall laughing heartily at myself.

I stumbled back to the open-air lounge where I found
a few of the guests stirring languidly. In our room Adam
was up and ready for departure. We exchanged greetings,
freshened up, and after emptying out his bag we started
to pack it with our basic essentials: a few liters of
water (and my CamelBak Chute 1.5L Sky Blue water bottle), peanut butter, clementines, tortillas, some napkins, and my precious NESTLE Kit Kat bar. He zipped up
and we left the room and headed out to grab a good solid
breakfast. We were certainly going to need it.

We headed down into La Fortuna to the nearest open
restaurant, which was still technically closed that early in the morning but the host agreed to accommodate us.
We seated ourselves at the far end and ordered some eggs
and beans and fruit and coffee. We ate heartily and
talked pleasantly. A dog ambled in from the street and
approaching our table crawled right under our feet,
curled up, and went to sleep. Once finished we headed
back out into the street and found a cab, loaded up,
hopped in, and began our journey west.

Our driver that warm crisp morning was a chatty one
and extremely friendly. We talked pleasantly en route to
the volcano. After passing just a few scattered hotels
we found ourselves amid endless green pastures with the
summit of the holy volcano well within view. Beyond its
imposing fortitude dazzled the clear blue sky, brushed
with puffy white clouds that harnessed the warm splashing sunshine. Driving around the volcano which jutted
before us to the south we beheld it with wondrous mesmer
and the cab driver pulled over for us to get a better
look. We emerged from the cab and stood beholding this
grand and marvelous sight: a great and monumental volcano with oceanous blue from above and radiant green from
below. We took some photos and got back into the cab and
some thirty minutes later we found ourselves headed uphill past grandiose resorts and hotels, then diving into

the thickets of towering trees and emerging before the
gates of the Volcan Arenal entrance. We thanked our
driver and tipped him graciously, then emerged with Adam
hoisting our backpack of provisions and we marched forth
with the strains of steep elevation beneath our calves
and thighs toward the reception office where we would
begin our day's journey.

At the reception desk two kind charming ticos politely gathered our information and presented our terms
and options. Adam handled the booking and the technicals
while I eyed down the baskets at the front of the counter which were filled with candies like Kit Kat and 3
Musketeers and Twix and Snickers and tiny bags of Doritos and I drooled hangrily and thought, oh baby fuck
yeah. Then I went into the lobby which contained couches
and chairs and a large checkers table and bathrooms and
televisions. Two young Latin maids hovered about in
brown uniforms sweeping, cleaning, and dusting and
drooling hornily I thought, baby just come fucking back
with me to America for Christ's sake— and the serenade
ended right there as Adam came from behind and handed me
our entrance information and a map and went to the bathroom to empty his canisters before we headed off into
the forest. I followed after to empty a couple canisters
of my own and once we had both finished our business it
was time to head off!

Adam asked "are you ready?" and I announced
"SIIIIIIII" and he proclaimed "SIIIIIIIIIIIIIIII" and I
affirmed "SIIIII SIIIII MUCHO SIIIIIIIIIIIIIIIIIIII" and
we marched laughing out past the parking area and down a
flight of stairs into a large beautiful garden which led
to the path where we would commence our adventure.

So this whole "SIIIIIIII" thing had sort of evolved
over the course of our trip and was by now in full swing
and it had come to Adam during his trip through Spain
along the Camino de Santiago some years ago. Apparently
he and some buddies had picked up this emphatic
"SIIIIIIII" thing from the Basque folks of northern
Spain (whom I came to learn much more about from Adam
and boy what a fascinating mystery THAT whole thing is!)
and I had really latched onto that whole "SIIIIIIII"
thing so I was romping around all over Costa Rica declaring and proclaiming "SIIIIIIIIIIIIII" and "MUCHO
SIIIIIIIII" and strutting and blastering my chest and

perking my lips and squinting my brow and cooing
"SIIIIIIIIII" to anything and everything in sight.

So as we came down the stone steps which funneled
like a sweet weaving stream through the thickets of this
magnificent garden I looked out into the distance and
beheld the Holy Tower and vast greens and solid browns
and fortified rocks of the distant forests and volcanoes. Looking up I also beheld a strange sight: very
long and tall spears of posts which had large pieces of
watermelon hanging from the top. Bees and flies swarmed
these dripping dewing watermelon slices and passing by I
wondered what could be the purpose of this strange operation. But I shrugged my shoulders and carried on and
soon Adam and I were hiking uphill on a large paved path
into enormous tall dense green woods. Adam opened up a
large map to guide the way and as I glanced crudely over
his shoulder I was struck by my confusion. Here I realized that all things considered I really didn't know how
to read a map. So I asked him to show me and he first
turned the map sideways saying "Well first you want to
orient yourself" which was something I didn't know. Then
he pointed to all the weaving pink and orange and blue
lines and said "So next, find which trail we are on" and
we saw a colored arrow that matched the ones on the map.
"Now that we know where we are we need to find where we
are going" so he pointed on the map to the distant large
black triangle that read CERRO CHATO and with that we
carried on and what do you know, I learned how to read a
map!

The path gently shifted from paved asphalt into
wood-chip graveling into warm brown dirt and above us
the trees grew taller, the sky bluer, the shade deeper
and denser. We observed the landscape shifting, the tall
trees taking on characteristically different forms and
structures. One type in particular we found remarkable
and a few times I had to just stop and stare: it was a
strange tall type of tree, barkless and smooth, with odd
greenish and brownish stains resembling the patterns of
military camouflage that streaked vertically down their
long stemmed trunks. We stood gazing on, stroking these
miraculous patterns of God, gawking insatiably at the
peculiarity of these arborous magnificents (Let's get
real, though. There's most likely a very simple scien-
tific explanation for all this but I don't know it and
didn't know it then. So it amazed me the way the rising

and setting of the sun once so amazed the primitives,
though most likely there's nothing to it that hasn't
already been explained on a Wikipedia page. But at the
moment it was a miracle of nature).

Twenty minutes into the walk I started to feel the
soreness in my legs and the aching in my back and insatiable dying thirst and horrible fatigue and I wondered
how much farther before we could go home and lie back
down in the hammocks and for a split second I suffered a
slight panic attack and wondered if I might die up there
halfway to the summit of this fucking volcano and I fu-
riously pondered why people do this kind of shit to
themselves and I admonished myself for being in this
insane situation and I started to list the hundreds of
ways in which I would invariably die in the next few
hours. Then of course all of that bullshit passed as it
always does and I found myself once again along a gorgeous and lengthy path with waving green pastures all
around me and a long steady endless row of military camouflage trees assembling a natural fence to my right.
The ambling hills, the weaving contrasts of sun and
shade, the beaming moist greenery, the crisp cool morning air, and the warm soothing white sun propelled me
into elated and fluttering wonder. To our left the mammoth behemoth of Volcan Arenal soared above us and now
with the eloquent splashes of sunlight we could discern
the rocky sandy crevices and weaving grooves of the
mountain's skin. And the sight of it all reminded me of
great places I never before had been, places that form
in our dreams, places we assemble from the pages of sto-
rybooks and fiction novels. In the midst of this glorious natural setting I envisioned myself a daring knight
crossing the pastures of the Basque countryside (which
I've never been to nor have ever seen nor could confidently place on a map). I imagined myself venturing
through a Steinbeck novel through the hills and valleys
of California, wandering through great Spanish pastures.
I quoted passages from Don Quixote and pictured us upon
a valiant quest to tilt at windmills and rescue fair
maidens from their oppressive fathers. I declared and
proclaimed left and right "SIIIIIII" and "SI SEÑOR
SIIIIIIIII" and "CLARO QUE SIIIIIIIII" and marched about
with chest brazen and spirit lifted, marching boister-
ously in my white CSG T-shirt and brown Old Navy Cargo
Stretch chino pants and black K-Swiss shoes and black

bandanna and stupid light eerily Hispanic goatee. And I
declared "Sí Don Quixote SIIIIIIIII!" and I called myself Sancho Panza and poor Adam wasn't quite sure what I
was talking about or what the fuck was wrong with me so
I briefly summarized Miguel de Cervantes' Don Quixote
for him and strongly recommended that he read it and we
carried on cheerfully into the dense thickets of the
volcano's edge.

We passed by a horses' stable and a bridge and a
barn, then found ourselves marching along a crude wooden
fence which looked out toward the volcano. We paused and
took some pictures and proclaimed many things in broken
Spanish and then after a few steps we halted quite suddenly before an enormous dark gaping green wall of towering trees. Trees upon trees hundreds of feet into the
air like green giants staring down at us pathetically,
skeptically, declaring "Who do these pitiful youths
think they are? What bringeth these impish nurslings
hither, these sort of vagabonds, rascals, and runaways,
a scum of Americans and base lackey peasants, whom their
o'ercloyéd country vomits forth to desperate ventures
and assured destruction? Go to, ye cankered ill-fated
scut! Dissemble thee henceforth!" I approached this in-
fantry shuddering because I don't know about you but I
ain't fuckin' with an army of angry forest trees, ya
heard? Slightly to our right was a small and dark hole
within the walls of this forest, like an accidental cavern, a careless cavity in the cracks of a valley's fur-
rows, and next to it stood a crude wooden sign, crooked
and limp, on which some letters were slapdashedly
carved. It read: "CERRO CHATO. LAGUNA LAKE CHATO".

We had reached the base of the volcano.

"Cerro Chato SIIIIIIIIII" I proclaimed, and with a
deep breath and a strong forward step we entered the
uphill forest that is the sloping backside of El Cerro
Chato volcano.

So there are some things you need to know about this
incredible natural wonder that is El Volcan Cerro Chato.
Located in Alajuela right beside the grander and active
Volcan Arenal, Cerro Chato is a dormant volcano that has
remained inactive for over 3,500 years. Over time and

without the volcanic lava to smolder its surface, the
rising sides of this great monument gradually started to
collect shrubs and bushes until after some millennia it
had all formed into a large and lavish uphill forest.
Now overgrown with lush wildlife, it is home to countless species of birds, mammals, reptiles, and amphibi-
ans, as well as thousands of varieties of bugs and insects. This is fascinating in and of itself, but it
isn't nearly as fascinating as what occurred INSIDE of
the volcano: thousands of years of dormancy allowed millions of gallons of water to accumulate within, so that
now the center of the volcano's mouth has formed into a
misty and silent lagoon. It is fresh and swimmable, especially so for the numerous forms of water life that
have evolved to live in its shallows. Annually, thousands of climbers transcend the sloping forest walls of
this monument to celebrate at the summit by swimming in
its cool depths. On this day we would be among those
conquerors.

   We pierced the dark dense thickets and began our ascent, the whole of which proceeded at about a thirty-
five-degree upward angle into endless weaving caverns of
green wood. The path was practically unmanned by human
hands and had pretty much been formed by enormous hori-
zontal roots of aging trees whose unders had been exposed by centuries of erosion. This natural circumstance
left behind a long continuous stable path of tree roots
which served as steps upwards into the forest.   Within
the first few steps I felt myself panicking.

   "Shit man," I said. "How the hell am I going to do
this for 3,700 feet into the air?"

   Adam said, "You're not. If you think of it that way
then you'll never make it. When I was on the Appalachian
Trail, had I headed out from Georgia aiming for Maine, I
would never have made it. You focus on the step in front
of you. You proceed in small goals. Baby steps."

   So I did just that: I forgot about the summit and
focused on the steps in front of me. And as we ventured
forth diligently, Adam would periodically share with me
some hiking wisdom:

   "Keep sipping water. If you start feeling thirsty
it's already too late."

   "Keep your heart rate down by taking small steps."

   "Exert as little energy as possible. Choose the path
that requires the least effort."

So I did what anyone else would do in my position: I ignored his advice completely. I carried on hopping about and lunging in large strenuous steps and climbing with my hands until just minutes into this idiotic approach I was already entirely out of breath. I paused, regained my composure, and proceeded then exactly as he had instructed. And what do you know! It seems that after a decade of rigorous experience and knowledge, Adam knew what the fuck he was talking about after all! Hell, whaddya know about that! So I carried forth in baby steps. Sipping water. Keeping the heart rate down. Conserving energy. Enjoying the view.

At some point in our upward sally Adam bestowed his gracious wisdom upon me once more when we came upon a sharp ascending slope that was streaked with giant roots and jutting rocks. Here he commanded me to pause and think: observe the situation before us and try to determine which course would be the best for upholding the basic tenets of hiking (which for purposes of this discussion we can narrow down to two things: keeping the heart rate down and conserving energy). So we stood there calculating intently and deliberating about which of the numerous courses to take and once I had calculated my own conclusion, Adam said "go for it". So I lunged over this rock and tripped over that root and found myself six feet higher, but when I turned around I saw that Adam had chosen a different angle and had transcended the obstacles I'd faced with far less exertion. Here he explained to me his thought process and I could see where I had erred in my decision. So some feet farther up we did it again: we stopped before the next few feet of climb and deliberated, and once I had chosen my path I went forth with it and to my utter elation Adam also followed suit!

"Good," he said, for my calculations had proven successful.

We continued on doing this every few minutes and it became quite an exciting mental game, almost a physical manifestation of chess. After some more practice I had developed some very intricate theories and wild evaluations about the pros and cons of rock formations and the multi-angular growth of tree roots and pretty soon I had overcomplicated the matter entirely and had fallen into grave over-analysis, and once Adam recognized this he brought the whole house down on me at one point when he

asked "Ok, so which path should we take here?" Once I
had mapped out an insanely detailed intricate lucid
strategy he quickly pointed in another direction and
debunked me. So I recalculated and reorganized and reas-
sembled my meta-theories and once I was certain enough
to bet my life on it he flung the whole matter around in
yet another direction and stumped me again. Finally I
was mentally drained and thoroughly puzzled and it was
then that Adam imparted the greatest wisdom of this entire climb: "The lesson here is that there isn't a
'right' or 'wrong' path when climbing. Sometimes there's
more than one way to walk the trail".

My friend Adam is a wise motherfucker, my friends.

We had been marching solidly for quite some time before I started to feel the incline tugging my shins and
calves. It was time to look around for a walking stick,
a tool to help alleviate the tensions of the climb and
to support my footing and balance. So since in the dense
forests of Costa Rica one is never lacking of the boun-
ties of large heavy sticks in no time we came upon a
great many fallen branches and one of them was of the
perfect length and strength to do the job. I picked it
up and held it forth and carried on with Adam following
behind me. I wondered frequently if my urban sedentary
pace might be slowing him down or holding him back but
he insisted that the pace was comfortable and that I
wasn't holding him up. So I carried on with my trusty
walking stick and my steady tread and the dazzling de-
lights of isolation and silence and nature and the wondrous sounds and colors of verdant oblivion until eventually I came upon a slight slippery slope in the mud.
But here my dear dependable walking stick served me very
well in resisting the fall. Thereupon I resolved to
christen this valiant courageous hiking hero of mine, to
title him, to strew his holy honor, and I named my walking stick "Herman". I proclaimed magnanimously "Ándale,
Herman!" and I cried out to Adam from above "Eso es Herman SIIIIIIIIIII". And for the official record let me
be clear, alright? The walking stick's name is "Herman"
which is NOT pronounced "hur-men" but instead is pronounced "ehr-MANN"! Herman! Herman! Say it correctly you
uncultured swine! So we sallied forth— I and the celebrated knightly Adam and our new and steadfast companion
Herman ("ehr-MANN"!)— onward and upward through the glorious thickets of the volcano's sloping graze.

It was at some point after much time had passed that
we realized that we needed to pause. We seated ourselves
against some trees and reclined peacefully and silently
catching our breaths, sipping water, and sharing a clementine. Between the rustling cracks of the leaves above
I beheld nothing but blue; this assured me that we were
very high up indeed and for some unusual reason brought
about the incontestable revelation that here and now I
needed to pee. So I told Adam that I needed to pee and
he directed me away from the trail and into the foliage
of the trees where I emptied my canister and proceeded
forth thence, I and my loyal companion Herman, sallying
onward and upward tiny step by tiny step behind Adam who
led the way for the duration of the venture.

Soon after, we came upon a dangerous precipice and I
found myself quite frightened to realize that the only
way forward from this point was a three- or four-foot
vertical lunge which if missed or failed could result in
a six- or eight-foot life-threatening vertical dive.
Here gripping the earthly wall before me my primal im-
pulses took over and I was suddenly doused with trembling terror. My breaths came short and quick, my legs
quivered, and from above Adam looked down on me waiting
for me to go.

"I can't make this jump," I said.

"You can," he replied.

"What if I fall?" I whimpered.

"You won't," he replied, and after a lengthy pause I
sensed the ultra-confident soothing tone of his voice
syruping through my veins and steadying my nerves. So
with a deep breath and eyes clenched I made the jump and
I landed with a success and grace that genuinely surprised me. In a word, I had no idea my body could do
that. And these, my Good Gracious Reader, are the moments that life and travel are made for.

By now the merry hours of the morrow had come to
pass and my throat was sore and sweat soaked my clothes
which were now stained with dirt and mud and my feet
throbbed and my arms quaked with strain and my calves
squealed for mercy. With a great howl of despair I cried
"How much farther," but how could one know? As we passed
a rounding curve in the trail we saw a couple of climbers heading back down. Quite excitedly I asked, "Hola,
how far away are we?" And with contagious excitement
they cried "Not far! Fifteen or twenty minutes!" I

yelped with joy and jumped into the air. Some minutes
later a woman and her children also descended before us
and when I saw this blond-haired American of no older
than four or five years I held my hand out to him and
cried "Awesome job, Superman!" and he smiled and gave me
a high-five and we laughed and boy did it feel good to
be alive!

Adam called to me "Hey can I see your phone?" and
with it he started taking some incredible pictures of
our marvelous ascent. But before long I found myself
struggling to keep up with him and then quite suddenly
he was nowhere to be found. I squinted and glared intently into the mounting distances yet saw nothing. I
kept on with sweat streaking and soaking my cotton and
my breath heaving with every forward lunge and my heart
thumping to the strains of my leg muscles. Then as I
started to believe that all was lost I looked up and I
came to a startled halt. Some forty feet ahead, high
above me, I could make out the silhouette of my dear
tall friend and mentor with our bag on his back and his
hands held up as if he was holding up my phone and recording a video. Behind him I could distinguish less
brush and more light. The top? The top!

"No hay manera." The words of frenzied shock and
disbelief oozed from my lips as my gaping eyes processed
the reality. "No hay manera." I hoisted Herman up into
the air and lunged forward with the vigor of a Roman
conqueror. "No hay manera!" I had forgotten that this
journey would ever end! "No hay manera!" Sprinting
striding lunging sliding like a maniac! Fuckin' FUCK
"sipping water" and "keeping the heart rate down" and
"conserving energy" and "enjoying the view"! "No Hay
Manera! NO HAY MANERA!!!" I hollered it with a joy known
only to children and war heroes. His silhouette expanded
before me, his great grin now visible, the light of the
sun and open sky blazed forth! And then!

Blasting past Adam I ran into an open expanse of sky
and soft grass and blazing sun. Before my eyes lay a
deep and wide blue-green lagoon. "WOOOO!! Oh my god!" I
approached the edge unfastening the soaked bandanna from
atop my head and plopped to the ground and beheld in
silence the victory and satisfaction of a 3,700-foot
volcanic climb.

chapter one

After a brief and blissful rest it came time for another short ten- or fifteen-minute descent into the
mouth of the volcano where we could swim in the lagoon.
We eased ourselves down the watery slopes of the volcano's lips yet despite the short length of this descent
it was a strikingly grueling terrain full of slippery
wet clay and mud, sharp curves, and perilous narrow
paths that required slender crawls and highly calculated
maneuvers. After descending one final long and steep
ravine through which I almost broke an ankle we finally
reached a misty bottom where before us extended a circu-
lar blue lagoon enshrined with thick dense forest. A few
climbers had already plunged the icy cyan waters of the
volcano (and one of them was a smiling pudgy young woman
in a blue bikini with absolutely bodacious breasts, but
I digress) and before I knew it Adam was fully undressed, his shirt and shoes strewn against the limb of
a tree, and clad only in his Greek-god red shorts he
gingerly eased himself into the freezing waters of the
lagoon.

Here, despite the insatiable temptation to celebrate
our triumph with this ceremonial rite, I let my senses
get the best of me and decided not to take this swim. If
I had to hike back down those jagged slopes in wet cotton and develop a chafing rash then that would be the
end of the pleasures of this trip, my friends. I was
simply unequipped for a swim. So I defeatedly washed my
hands and doused my face in the cool waters of the lagoon, then removed my shoes and immersed my feet in its
icy pleasures. But this had to be the end of my festivity and with beaming contentment I retreated to a large
boulder and sat to observe the elated swimmers. I
watched my dear friend paddle himself into the distant
center of this expansive misty pool as his little head
jutted out from the water among all the other little
heads and I thought with disbelieving astonishment, my
God, we have climbed to the top of a VOLCANO! And now we

are SWIMMING in it! I leaned back gleefully and watched
a company of Italian guys wrapping up their swim and
horsing around and taking pictures while a perfect family unrolled their perfect picnic and washed down their
perfect triangular sandwiches in perfect napkins with
perfect cans of Coca-Cola. From the other side of the
lagoon other victors howled out to us in celebratory
triumph and we cheered back ecstatic with our common
conquest. To my left a fresh arrival, a slim fit black
girl, dropped her large black backpack and slowly undressed herself down to her tiny neon-green bikini, and
with that blazing lime hue taut against her tight moist
coal body she was a mesmerizing sight. With tender care
she removed her socks and now stood bare before the
misty cyan lagoon and began her timid approach like a
fawn in the brush.

Adam emerged from the lagoon dripping wet and invig-
orated and kneeling to unzip his bag brought out our
much-anticipated lunch. One by one he handed me the jar
of peanut butter, the packet of soft tortillas, some
clementines, some water, and most importantly the prized
Nestle Kit Kat bar which would be the trophy of our summit's celebration. We sat upon a damp log and unloaded
our humble spread and as I ripped through a clementine
and Adam tore off the red lid of the peanut butter jar
we realized that we had not brought anything to spread
the peanut butter with. Quite casually Adam searched
around for a stick. I found a small twig which he inspected and decreed "it's wet" so we searched a bit more
until we found a small dry twig and we took turns dipping it into the jar and smearing its contents onto our
soft tortillas. With both hands fully occupied with delicious morsels of food we dug in! Nearby a hungry raccoon scampered about sniffing clothes and bags but he
found little and ventured off soon after. We ate peacefully in the grace of this magical murky wonderland and
any residue of our feast that remained— be it the orange
peels or crumbs of tortilla— we collected meticulously
and placed back into Adam's bag.

"Ideally," he instructed, "things should be left exactly as they were before we arrived. Nothing taken
away. Nothing left behind."

I felt quite ashamed thereafter recalling the hundreds of times in which I had haphazardly (or even right
deliberately) disregarded this sacred adage and I pon-

dered what this planet would have looked like today if only we as a species had honored this simple sacrament.

This of course spotlights the peculiarity of what happened next: as we were splitting the Nestle Kit Kat bar Adam openly and ofcoursely struck up a chat with a pretty girl in shorts and a blond ponytail and I sat there politely listening to their exchange licking up every sexual morsel of this fucking Nestle Kit Kat bar right off of my hands and lips and fingers and the spaces between my fingernails. And this girl was snacking on something too when suddenly she dropped a napkin and a slight gust of wind blew it away. Adam's dynamic eyes flashed at the tumbling rubbish which skidded to a halt some ten feet away.

"You shouldn't leave that there," he said to the blond-haired girl who with a slight German accent giggled and returned to the conversation. But when her eyes fell back upon his and she realized with the start that my buddy Ice wasn't fucking around he repeated, "You should go pick that up."

Her face creased with puzzlement and not sure what to do she reluctantly got up and teetered over to pick up the trash and in my mind I cheered my buddy on and thought "That's right! You get your gingerbread-house Franziskaner-Hefe-Weissen ass up and walk over there and pick that shit up! Pick it up, this is the ENVIRONMENT! YEAH!"

She came back trash-in-hand and slightly bummed at being bossed around, but the incident also happened to build up a repertoire between them and before long they were laughing it up like childhood friends.

Meanwhile I kept my eyes fixed on the slender damsel whose sweet tender black figure had so recently graced the silky shore of the lagoon, but I was stumped to see that her visage had changed starkly. She stood trembling ringing ricketing with cold and fright, her long leg extended outward to peck at the dense blue water which with every dab of contact would jolt her away yelping with anguish and terror. Her eyes flitted horridly, her mouth contorted downward with miserable remorse, her arms and legs veined crossly against the stump of her frame. She almost cried.

"It's OK," I called out to her. Meaning, unless you're being forced to do this at gunpoint then it's safe to get dressed and leave.

chapter one

"NoOoOoOoOo..." she protested with a whine and a
shudder and pranced daintily and poutingly back toward
the water. But well before reaching it she once again
hurled back with a terrorized start, scurrying to her
belongings muttering "no no no no no no..."

(This dumb bitch's name is Sonia. I'll introduce you
all in a moment and forewarn you that her dumb ass will
soon become a big part of this story.)

So she dressed herself in a floundering frenzy then
scampered over to our direction where the blond-haired
German girl sat talking with us and she stood there
still shivering, waiting patiently and flitting her eyes
about psychotically and cowering sporadically as if at
any moment she was going to be mauled by a bear. From a
tiny Ziploc bag in her hand she brought out some morsels
of a pinkish-grey prickly plant and holding it out offered us to eat. We gagged and politely declined and she
bellowed "They're gooooooood" as she took one out and
cracked its prickly sharp shell with her teeth then
picked out its contents (which to me looked like chest-
nut-sized puss-filled goo balls of the color and texture
of a gangrene cyst) and proceeded to put the gacking
morsel into her mouth, chewing the plastic fruit and
delighting in its putrid phlegm.

"Well, I'm Adam," he finally said to the blond German and she replied "yohana" which is how it is pronounced but definitely not how it is spelled (it is
spelled "Johanna"). Johanna then acknowledged the hovering trembling black girl beside her and she stood up
ready to head off. We stood up as well prepared to depart and within seconds Adam had convinced these girls
to spend the rest of the day with us.

"Are you guys getting a cab to get back to town?" he
said. "If we head back together we can split the fare."

Before I knew it we had ourselves a pair of fine female travel companions who were going to pay half of our
cab fare! So Adam and Johanna quite naturally paired up
and lead the way and I followed loosely behind the misery march of this mopey scaredy young woman who trudged
along limply and with great dejected woe.

Ten minutes into our descent Adam and Johanna were
submerged in enrapturing conversation and I was airily
sauntering along with my trusted sidekick Herman admiring the lax wonders of this joyous journey, frequently
interrupted by the seething mutters of this wretched

woman beside me who carried out her death march with
doling indignity.

"It's so hot", she spat. "This bag is so heavy." "My
feet hurt." "I'm so thirsty." "I hate bugs." "Look at my
shoes." "I hate rocks." "I'm so tired." "How much farther?"

In an attempt to shut her the fuck up I asked "So
what's your name?"

"Sonia," she replied and with such a rank phony
cheeriness that I had to resist the godly impulse to
kick her down the side of the mountain. "I'm a writer
and a world traveler," she added, proudly firing off a
series of pointedly shallow accomplishments ranging from
a master chef to a rescuer of children in Ghana. She
sounded so pathetically insultingly outrageous that I
laughed out loud. Has that ever happened to you? Have
you ever encountered people so recklessly idiotic, so
foully pretentious, so banely banal that it was impossible to take them seriously? Well that was this little
precious right here and frankly that's just too bad.
What a waste of a sultry solid midsection, tight firm
ass, and sweet little titties.

The descent down the slopes of Volcan Cerro Chato
was much harder than I had imagined. Apparently a bit of
rain had fallen during our ascent and now the trail and
its paths were slabbed with mud and clay and the whole
terrain had achieved the consistency of peanut butter.
Rocks loosened, branches wired, mud laxed, and every
step was a worrisome progression of timid dread.

"Trust nothing," Adam advised. "Trust no step."

He was right. Every assumptive step I took resulted
in a startling slip, so I had to calculate my every
move. To my great remorse, Herman my trusted and faithful walking-stick confidant had been much more of an
asset going up than he was coming down and now he served
as a great nuisance and an obstruction to my progress.
With a heavy heart and cries of shameful betrayal and
guilt I tossed my fallen friend into the brush, crying
out tearfully "Adiós Herman mi hermano de alma! Lo
siento mucho mi amigo. No quiero esto mi compadre!" And
sobbing I treaded down and left Herman crooked and forgotten in the woods.

(Una plegaria por Herman y un momento de silencio)

Covered in mud, clay, and sweat, the treacherous descent became grueling and strenuous. Adam and Johanna

had advanced well ahead of us as I crept down the slopes
with Sonia some ten feet ahead of me spattering complaints and dissents and protestations like a baying
terrier. And would it have delighted me so to take just
two of the millions of logs that surrounded us and clog
one down her esophagus and chuck another up her rectum
and toss her spiraling into a ravine and off the wet end
of a precipitous waterfall. But instead I asked about
her life back in Boston and to tune out my murderous
plots and to steady my nerves I concentrated on her ass
but soon even THAT provided no reprieve, for sweet as it
was there was a vomitous ejection of choleric shit spew-
ing perpetually out the other end. Once I was able to
accept that this was just going to be a fact of our trip
back I managed to come to terms with this inevitable
reality, this puzzling troubling ironic wonder that is
in one word "Sonia", and I began thence to tune out all
of the whining and moping and drawling and droning and
focused instead on the wondrous nature surrounding me.

Like a cowardly cat I pawed my way down each mud-
sliding slope, and indeed I had a ghastly feeling that I
was going to fall and every micro-slip rattled me with
terror. That is, until at one point despite the best-
laid schemes of mice and men my foot slipped and I fell
solidly onto my hip. At this moment I realized three
profound and transformative things: 1) a fall is just a
fall and not the end of the world; 2) my body had so
nimbly and agilely foiled the fall, as if I had been
pre-programmed for such things (which I had; it's called
DNA); 3) I had overcome my fear of falling. And when
these three realizations had seeped into my consciousness I rose to my feet and the hike down became a skipping amble of merry melody. I jumped and skipped and
sang carefree until even Adam asked me to tone it down a
bit and to try to be more careful. I fell at least two
more times after that and one of them quite hurt my elbow but I no longer cared because I discovered to my
relief that if you do fall, all you have to do is fall
with grace, land with style, and get back up and do it
over again.

In no time the four of us had reached the bottom of
the volcano.

Back beside the "CERRO CHATO. LAGUNA LAKE CHATO"
sign where this whole volcanic voyage had begun we sat
down together to rest. Adam scanned his map while Johanna sat to rub her feet. Sonia stood prattling on about
something involving herself and some foreign success she
achieved somewhere. Out came that plastic bag of cactus
gack-spheres again and thrusting them into each of our
faces she asked if we wanted to partake in this nutritious wholesome all-natural snack.

"They're healthyyyyyyy" she cooed.

It should've bothered the three of us enough to bash
her prickly head in with a rock and eat the puss out of
her skull but to be honest by this time we had really
gotten over her and found her nuisances ridiculous and
dismissible. I discovered that I could totally pretend
to be listening without hearing a word she was saying;
more importantly, I discovered that she wasn't quite
interested in anyone listening because she was intently
listening to herself, completely unaware of anyone or
anything else. Meanwhile I noticed from the corner of my
eye that Adam was looking at me curiously and when I
asked what was up he said "Man, you look scary." I
wasn't sure what he meant but he asked me to consider
myself in someone else's shoes who coming up the slope
would have seen a figure such as myself emerging from
the green brush: a hardened grimy man with a carved
face, a haphazard goatee, a guerrilla bandanna and muddy
military pants, covered in mud and sweat, lunging down
the mountain toward them.

"I mean, there are families here. There are children," he said.

We laughed hysterically and to prove his point I
went and sat on a rock near the brush so he could take a
picture. I grabbed a large stone from the ground and sat
with muddy pants and shoes exposed, face carved into
malicious hate, and after he snapped a few photos they
all laughed heartily and I beheld myself for the first
time and was indeed terrified of myself. Clearly José no
viene hogar, my friends.

We gathered ourselves and marched on back toward the
exit but on the way Adam noticed on the map that if we
took a longer route we could encounter a beautiful waterfall.

"You guys want to go see the waterfall?" he said.

"Sure," Johanna cried excitedly.

I agreed as well, and from somewhere behind us came a mutter of disapproval which did absolutely nothing to sway our decision so off we marched to see the waterfall!

Itching and swatting and kicking and lumbering her way before me, Sonia followed the conversational carefree Adam and Johanna across a long and large field past a few hills and trees into a dense trail and up a set of stairs along a precipitous cliff.

"STAIRS???" howled Sonia lamentably. "I got to go down the STAIRS!? And come back UP?" and she wailed like the woe of the Holy Virgin Mary was upon her.

"Not necessarily," I thought. "I'll gladly kick your ho ass down there and it won't be much use coming back up. If you so graciously desire, madam." But that all turned out to be quite unnecessary for before we knew it we had reached a small viewpoint with rocks and grass and a slight fenced drop-off from which after an eighty-foot descent you could dive into the winding torrent of the raging waters and swim under the seventy-foot waterfall. Before I had taken in the spectacular view Adam and Johanna were already undressed and descending the rocks. A hysterically happy couple was already swimming below and they howled up at us and we howled back.

"Come on man," Adam called out without waiting to see if I would join, and due to my slight cotton-water problem I skipped the chafing yet again and politely declined. So I stood from above watching them dive into the rafting surge and swim under the whole of a marvelous waterfall! Eagerly I wished to join them but decided to keep sensible. Sonia meanwhile had seated herself, legs crossed, facing with her BACK to the waterfall and moping piteously and with great gloom about her fate's misfortunes. She proceeded to take out her phone and tell me all about her photography skills as I watched Adam and Johanna hoot and holler down there. From within the clutches of the flowing water I saw Adam's hand go up waving me down to join them and when I gestured a polite decline he became vigorously insistent. I waved him down again and suddenly realized that Sonia was still talking to me; in fact, she was showing me pictures on her phone.

She offered to take a picture of me so I posed near the viewpoint and she snapped a couple photos. But when she showed them to me my stomach jumped, for in some strange uncanny downright creepy way her pictures were absolutely revolting. Almost every basic rule of photography had been shattered to produce a crooked blurred disfigured choppy Picassocsque atrocity which marveled Quasimodo in its hideousness. I offered to switch places and photograph the dumb trudge herself so she went over and sat looking away, and aggravating every skill of modern photography I adjusted the focus and shadows and colors and rule-of-thirds and calculated symmetry and after a few snaps I proudly brandished my artistic masterpieces to her and as she stared at the pictures I asked "How do you like them?" and she slightly cringed and looked up apologetically at me and said "I don't like them. Sorry". I handed her back the phone and smiled.

Adam was marching back up the rocks from the waterfall dripping wet and with the anger of a disappointed father. Meanwhile a group of ten or twelve hikers was descending the stairs to our viewpoint and reached us just as Adam stomped up to me declaring "You're going down there, man."

"Ice I can't," I said amid the racket of the new arrivals.

"Why not," he cried in frustration.

"My clothes man," I pleaded. "They'll never dry."

"Here!" he exclaimed, taking out an extra pair of shorts and jabbing them into my hands. "Put them on and let's go." And with that he returned to plunge the raging currents.

So off came my pants and my shirt and then amid all the commotion on that viewpoint I hobbled into a corner and exchanged my sweaty cotton grey Hanes boxers for these shorts and dug my sweaty socks into my muddy shoes and said to Sonia "Hey, can you watch my stuff?" and nimbly I pawed my way down across the jagged stones toward the rafting waves and when Adam and Johanna spotted me coming down they cheered wildly for me and a few strangers also cheered. I finally reached the bottom and eased myself into the raging stream which was both freezing and refreshing. And by this point in the trip I had gotten over the notion that we should choose our water temperatures. Fuck off you spoiled reeks, if it's water then praise God and use it, goddammit!

So here I was wading stiffly through the foamy rafts
of the waterfall dodging sharp rocks beneath my feet as
Adam guided me toward the cascade where we treaded directly beneath the falls. We swam up real close amid
furious surges and the hoots and cheers of the other
swimmers and finally after numerous tries I managed to
mount the rocks beneath the cascade and sit directly
under the falls. It was difficult to breathe and wildly
chaotic down there but what a spiriting feeling to be
seated under the falls of a dashing volcanic rainforest!
After a few minutes we plunged back into the gasping
waves and treaded gingerly to the sloping rocks and as
we climbed up to dry off and change I thanked God that
Adam had insisted on taking me down with him. Never say
no, my friends.

Changing back into cotton underwear was difficult,
especially in a small corner surrounded by tourists, but
finally after multiple calculations and considerations I
just gave up and down dropped the wet shorts and up went
the grey boxers and if by some chance anyone happened to
spot my tight firm hairy ass in the process then, well,
you're welcome.

We headed back up the stairs through a dense thicket
and a trail and a bridge and past the sights of watery
streams and strange creatures and vast green countryside
until after a long and gorgeous walk we found ourselves
back at the reception office. We called for a shuttle
and took a seat outside to wait and rest. Adam went back
to use the bathroom and I developed a sudden hankering
for those Doritos on the front counter so I bought a
small bag and munched on it with great disappointment,
for sure the bag said that they were "Queso"-flavored
but they didn't taste like no "Nacho Cheese" to me! Nevertheless I scarfed down the whole bag and Sonia once
again recovered her plastic bag of prickly puss pebbles
and offered us for like the fifth or sixth time and when
we declined (this time quite brusquely) she went on
about the myriad benefits of nutritious whole-food
snacking and the glorious biological virtues of a vegetarian diet which Johanna celebrated with rolling eyes
and Adam with that look of puzzlement he usually gives
when something sounds too stupid to be true.

We loaded up into the shuttle and Adam and Johanna
climbed into the back and Sonia sat in the middle and I
sat closest to the door and the shuttle might've been

air-conditioned but I honestly didn't notice or quite
care. Sonia lounged back and dropped her bag and threw
herself against the seat and heaved a sigh apt only for
Odysseus' return to Ithaca. Then she hummed reminiscent-
ly with a peaceful smile "That was such a pretty blue
horse..." and I really thought it was time to collectively strangle her to death.

Let's back up. On our hike back we had passed by
some of the stables that I mentioned to you earlier on
our way to Cerro Chato. There we saw a few horses grazing near the barn and Sonia had called out "Wow that's a
blue horse! I always love seeing blue horses!" So we
stared and squinted and gaped our eyes but we saw no
blue horses so we said "a BLUE horse?" and Sonia said
"Yes that blue horse right there" and we squinted and
gaped and leaned about to adjust our angles but still we
saw no blue horses. So we finally made her walk up to
the stable and point at the blue horse so she did and
her finger fell upon a horse that was quintessentially,
definitively, and indisputably grey. Johanna declared in
a monotone that only a strong German could rightly convey: "It's grey." And with a hearty delighted chuckle
Sonia declared "No it's blue. What a beautiful blue
horse." The three of us exchanged glances and looked
back at this grey horse and it was still fucking grey,
my friends. But the more we tried to show this senseless
cunt that she was looking at a grey horse the more she
delighted in the blueness of the blue horse before her
darling eyes. It is to this blue horse that Sonia is
referring.

So finally Adam and Johanna were done playing around
and prepared to press the matter and with tones of
staunch assertion and unflinching reason they insisted
that the horse had been grey and that there are no blue
horses and that the horse from earlier was totally grey
and jointly they managed to talk this dumb puss-sucking
yap down to at least needing to explain herself so she
said this: "Well it was KIND OF blue" to which Johanna
stalinly stamped "It wasn't blue at all. It was grey."
So Sonia took a different angle and said "Well a LITTLE.
It's kind of like bluehounds. You know? Like how you
call it a BLUE hound?" And Adam's puzzlement look
creased over his brow and he said after a pause of dumb-
founded disbelief "They're not BLUEhounds. They're GREY-
hounds." And then he added with an almost choke of

astonishment "and dogs are not horses." So finally with no other hope she turned to the only refuge of a defeated arguer: changing the argument from an objective one to a subjective one, and to that effect she ended the conversation with a coy smile and this: "Well I don't know...The horse is blue to ME." And with a pause of silent introspective calm I had a mind to just wrap my unyielding claws around her neck, saddle the circulation from her head, and holding a mirror to her face exclaim "BITCH DAT HORSE WA'NT NO BLUE! SEE YO FACE BITCH? DAT DERE WAT BLUE IZ! YO BITCH-AZZ CHOKIN GAGGIN OXYGEN-DEPRIVED FACE IZ WAT BLUE IZ! GIT A GOOD LOOK TOO CUZ IT GON' BE DA LAST MO'FUCKIN COLOR YO HO AZZ E'ER DONE SEEN!"

After a few more laughs and Sonian wisdom we arrived at our hostel and we decided to exchange numbers and meet up with the girls later so Johanna punched her number into my phone and we agreed to connect later that night. Bidding them a pleasant farewell we exited the shuttle and entered the Arenal Backpackers Hostel dirty, damp, dizzy, and drained but triumphant and victorious.

chapter one

The evening was coming in fast and heavy angry clouds tumbled over us assembling for a night of down-pour. We reached our room just in time to dodge the sudden cascade that plunged about us. The room was empty, as was most of the hostel, for since we had taken the shorter trail that day we had been among the first guests to return. It was a relief and a blessing to have the whole place to ourselves to relax and unwind before a night of partying and celebration. Adam hit the bunk and borrowed my phone to use, for after excavating his dead phone from the bottom of the rice bag he plugged it in and found little sign of life and we knew then and there that if it wouldn't turn on by now then it probably never would. I kicked off my shoes for a bit and changed into some dry clothes and sat quietly watching the rain pellet the pool and deck before us, immersing the whole visible world with a slant blue haze. After a relaxing spell I took out my harmonica and went out to play for a bit, but after a couple of tunes I just felt awkward and self-conscious so I returned to my room and put it away. Then I decided to leave the room to do something else and as I stepped out I looked into the room next door and there stood a little man in a white shirt emptying out his bag onto his bunk. The second we made eye contact his face lit up and he marched straight toward me with a geniality and warmth that instantly captured my heart. Climbing right through the open window to me he announced with enchanting sincerity and hands extended out to shake, "Hi! I'm Marco."

His forwardness was unusual but refreshing and honest and he instantly had the most positive effect upon me. "I arrived just now," he said with a slight European accent, with a forthright stance and a dignified bearing and warm green eyes and a gracious smile and just an overall conviction that he loved you and loved life and it took me virtually no time at all to decide definitively, "Jesus, I really fucking love this guy!"

Marco and I jumped right into it and he told me that
he was vacationing from northern Italy and lived and
worked in Rome for a large accounting firm. We chatted
pleasantly and when Adam emerged from our room I proudly
introduced him to Marco and they both also hit it off
right away! I was so excited to hear about Marco, for I
too had an Italian friend: my best friend E who has been
my dear comrade since the sixth grade and is nothing
short of my sister. And I too had a brother who worked
for a large accounting firm and his name was Kal and if
you piss him off, well, he might kick you in the balls!
So we had much to talk about standing there at that window fully immersed in conversation and as the rain
around us gently subsided Adam asked "Hey are you guys
hungry?" and Marco said "Yes I arrived just now and haven't eaten." So Adam said "I was thinking we actually
try some Latin food for a change," and I thought "Yes!
Fucking yes!" I was indeed by this point entirely fed up
with the fact that across the whole of this Latin-
American country there wasn't one bit of Latin food or
music or dancing or even language! For God's sake, what
the hell did we come down here for! To listen to fucking
David Bowie and Britney Spears on the radio and gorge on
super-sized pizza and burgers and converse with English-
speaking servants and cab-drivers? Fucking hell! Let's
at least dab into even a bit of the Latin culture while
we're out here! Might as well, man!

The unfortunate reality is that there are two things
that the Costa-Ricans do just as well— if not better—
than any American city: American music and American
food. The whole entire country has ingeniously morphed
itself into one big all-too-familiar theme park for stupid uncultured Americans. Everywhere— from the airport
to the shuttles to the streets and shops to the waiting
areas— everywhere, you hear the blaring boom of 80's and
90's American hits. In fact, I heard some of the best
American music playlists ever in Costa Rica— better even
than anything I've heard in the States. And the Costa-
Ricans top off the music with an endless barrage of unhealthy uncultured fatty oily deep-fried American grub:
hot dogs and hamburgers and pizza and steak and chicken
and nachos and fries— so much so that if you want to
hear or eat anything that is un-American then you really
have to go out of your way and search for it. And though
one is bound to appreciate this surreal familiarity I

170

must admit that for me and my buddy Adam this was totally not what we came here for. But it turns out that the
Costa-Ricans are quite ingenious, my friends, for they
have been enormously successful at building their econo-
my and their country at our expense.

Adam patiently allowed me to finish my rant and then
suggested we grab dinner at a "soda", which is the Spanish name for a small hole-in-the-wall Costa-Rican diner
that serves authentic Latin dishes and drinks. Marco was
down as well so we agreed to change and freshen up and
meet up to get going. As we were getting ready I texted
Johanna: "We are heading out now. We will let u know the
name of the soda." She replied "Ok. It's next to your
hostel right? How far is it from the center?" but I
didn't know yet so I waited to text her once we had
found the place.

We left the hostel together heading east into town
through a dark rainy night which had set in far sooner
than we had expected. The rain drizzled lightly and
would do so for the rest of night as we carried on chatting with this astonishingly charming and mannered young
man named Marco. Eventually we were able to locate Soda
Mima which had been hard to find because it really was
quite off-the-grid and you had to really look for it to
find it. It turned out to be a very small battered shack
with a green awning far off from the road across an
abandoned lot. We walked up and took a seat at a table
outside and since we were the only people there we were
greeted and served in no time. The waiter only spoke
Spanish (thank God) and menus were of little use to us
so we just ordered a bunch of dishes and offered to
share them together. I texted Johanna "We came to Soda
Mima. Next to al paseo ricas. If you head toward our
hostel it is a little place on your left next to big
blue 'Farmacia' sign. We will find you outside." I went
out across the dark abandoned lot to the main street to
retrieve her and on the way I began to wonder about the
cleanliness and healthiness of a diner like Soda Mima
and worried if my dinner was going to make me sick. This
was a terror I couldn't quite afford at this point and I
didn't want to deal with it.

I came back with Johanna who had come out alone
without Sonia for reasons I couldn't possibly care about
and Johanna greeted Adam and met Marco and the four of
us rejoiced and sat laughing and chatting as the humble

waiter brought out our dishes, first serving Marco and
Johanna. Adam's and my dishes were taking a bit longer
to arrive so we just sat chatting and sipping coconut
juice but after a few minutes I sensed that Marco was
growing slightly anxious. Before I could ask him what
was wrong he blurted out: "Everyone, I apologize. But
may I ask that I go ahead and begin?"

For a second he stumped me and I wondered what he
was talking about, but when I realized what he meant I
was humbled and venerated: Marco was asking our permis-
sion to begin eating his food, for it was customary for
him to wait until everyone had been served in order to
begin together. But since our food was taking longer and
his was getting cold, he was politely requesting that he
breach this customary courtesy and begin his meal. And I
thought that this was just about the most polite and
courteous gesture I'd seen throughout this whole trip. I
recalled fondly my childhood days when these manners had
been instilled by my parents in our household. Where had
all these great things gone: the courtesies for the meal
and manners for the guests and respect for the food and
meal and one another? It had been so long since I'd giv-
en any regard to the manner in which I eat, for I eat
too fast and too much and I hardly chew and I shovel my
food into my big open face and I talk and reach over
others and throw away what I haven't finished. Compared
to this delightful young man I'm an ogre. Marco humbled
me that night and reminded me of an idyllic past in
which manners and great conversation superseded selfish
materialistic whoredom.

All of our food did eventually arrive and we delved
into these delectable ethnic dishes, enjoying them with
gusto and grateful delight. In the midst of our meal we
were interrupted by little meows from near the table and
a sweet little kitten approached us, courteously pleading to be invited for dinner. Johanna downright lost her
shit and jumped up to play with the kitten. I gave it a
little of my fish and Adam threw it something as well
and Johanna was on the verge of tears but eventually the
kitten got her fill and headed off.

We wrapped up our meal and paid thankfully and decided to head back to the hostel where many of the other
guests would by now be arriving. Johanna said she was
tired but asked that we update her if we decided to do
anything later. So we bid her farewell and returned

through the puddled dark streets of the town to our hostel which by the time we arrived had already started to
look like the crazed party from the previous night. In
the open-air lounge we found Kylie and Tia and Samirah
and Dojuh and ChrisKafka and Raphael the large smiling
friendly tico receptionist and we introduced them all to
Marco and they were happy to meet him. Once we had all
gotten together and asked what we were going to do, I
said "I'll tell you! We're going dancing! It's time for
some salsa and bachata and merengue and reggaeton and
some serious Latin partying! I haven't partied once this
whole trip and we are going to put an end to that shit
right now!" And apparently everyone loved the idea because suddenly we were all quite frazzled with excitement so I approached Raphael at the front desk and
asked, "So is there any Latin dancing in town tonight?"

He replied "Yes there is a place right here down the
street. La Terraza. Tonight they have Spanish dance.
9:00."

"Wow!" I exclaimed. "Really?! And it's just around
here?"

He nodded emphatically and pointed as if it was
within arm's reach: "Here. Here, it is right here it is
on second floor here."

I thanked him and by then it was right around 7:00
PM so I announced to the whole crew that we could meet
there tonight and finally get the Latin experience we
had all come here for!

La Terraza is an open-air two-story restaurant and
bar on the farther western side of La Fortuna and no
more than a five-minute walk from the Arenal Backpackers
Hostel. From down the street it blazed with multicolored
globing lights and grandiose music. After quickly fresh-
ening up Adam and Marco and I were ready to head over
there, but since the rest of the crew had so recently
returned from their full-day hikes they all still needed
some time to clean up and get ready so we decided to
head over there ourselves and allow the others to catch
up later. Running into my room to grab some extra cash I
greeted Lena who was kneeled beside her bunk packing up
some stuff and I said "Hey Lena! We're heading out to

grab some food and dance! Wanna come?" And though she
seemed interested she politely declined, complaining of
a stomachache, and said she would be turning in early.

"I'm sorry to hear that," I said and I really meant
it, for though I had spent very little time with Lena
the previous night talking about the Arabic language and
Islamic culture I had taken a tremendous liking to this
sweet and charming girl. "I hope you feel better and if
you change your mind come by and see us!" I said.

I wished her a good night and rushed off to find Adam and Marco waiting at the gate. But on my way I saw
ChrisKafka crossing the open-air lounge as he raced
right up to me and stopped me and asked where I was going and looked very eager to be going there with me re-
gardless of wherever the hell it was. Poor ChrisKafka
practically tugged at my sleeves with pleading eyes like
he'd had about all he could take of his two female
friends and was dying for a half-intelligent conversation with some pragmatic testosterone. The poor existential fuck! Climbing dismally up the hill of monotonous
shallow banality all day like a curséd Sisyphus! I
couldn't wait to satisfy this need for intellectual discourse, and he had certainly found just the guys for it
because Adam and I could hardly stop our philosophical
discussions. Everything to us was an existential question to be dissected. So I soothed his tremors and eased
his angst and practically petted his brow with maternal
warmth and I told him to get ready and just meet us at
La Terraza, for there he would find all the mind-blowing
scholarly interchange to gratify his famished mind! Once
he had been suitably reassured we were off!

On the way through the faint drizzles of rain I
texted Johanna that we were heading out to eat and dance
and she said she didn't really feel like it. So I texted
her "If u change your mind we are at la terraza in town"
and she said "Yeah ok I'm already in my bed. LOL Have
fun". La Terraza stood amid the silence of a slumbering
town exploding with music, psychedelic colored lights,
and blaring televisions and we arrived to find ourselves
entirely alone. I mean NOBODY was there except a single
bartender on each of its two stories. The rainfall
smothered the open-air restaurant with stifling humidity
and the first thing I did as we walked in was race to
the bathroom to mop the streaming sweat off of my face
and douse myself in cold water. After a quick piss I

went back and found the guys heading up the stairs to
the second floor where there was a bar, some couches and
chairs, a women's bathroom (men's was downstairs), and
more televisions and hallucinogenic lights, but nothing
else beyond that. Especially people. So we placed our
orders and sat down on the vacant couches chatting and
laughing and watching the televisions that on one screen
aired the 2016 Olympics and on the other screen blared
episodes of Tom and Jerry. And I thought that was absolutely brilliant! Cartoons at a lounge? I was thrilled!
So we sat back watching cartoons and the Olympics and
chatting and every few minutes or so I excused myself to
run back downstairs to mop my face. It was well into the
night before people started showing up and before long
the first floor grew completely packed with diners and
large parties. Soon we could see some stragglers coming
up the stairs to take a peek at the second floor but
spotting three dudes on the couch watching Tom and Jerry
in an empty lounge like some kind of scene from The
Shining or something they all shuffled right the fuck
back down.

I was growing pretty irate and damn frustrated by
this point, for although I was having a spectacular time
with Adam and Marco I still really couldn't understand
what the hell was going on. How could this be the only
club in town on a Friday night and yet be so deserted?
Why the hell of all things were they playing AMERICAN
music in here? Didn't Raphael say this was LATIN night?
Was I EVER going to escape this hyper-American plague of
hamburgers and Backstreet Boys and find for one second
some Hispanic authenticity around here? I came all the
way to the Latin world to practice my Spanish and dance
a bit of salsa and so far I had done WAY more of that
back in Detroit! For God's sake, get it together people!

Finally I came to terms with the possibility that I
wasn't going to dance the salsa in Latin America so I
redirected my attention to my good friends Adam and
Marco who were talking about their travels and Marco's
life in Italy and all the great things that guys sit
around and talk about on a Friday night. Meanwhile La
Terraza was quite gradually starting to fill up with
folks just returning from their hikes and travels, and
by now the first floor was absolutely crammed with diners who slowly trickled up to the second floor where we
were. In no time the place was packed and suddenly to my

revitalized enthusiasm the music finally switched to
merengue.

Let's talk a bit about Latin music for a moment, before we go any further. I was introduced to Latin dance
one time entirely by accident when I was out with my
friends W and Doc in Ann Arbor some years ago. Stumbling
accidentally into the basement of a small restaurant (to
use the bathroom, I believe) I beheld with delighted
disbelief couples dancing to foreign and vibrant music.
I was hooked on sight and stood beholding the cyclical
vivacious movements of these glorious dancers who
twirled and whirled and slid and laughed and I watched
intently until I thought I had the hang of it. Finally I
mustered up the courage to jump right in and try it out,
but after stomping the crap out of a few girls' pretty
little feet I retreated in forsaken injured shame determined thenceforth to master this beautiful lively human
art called "salsa". Two years and hundreds of hours of
practice later, I could walk onto any Latin dance floor
I chose and be the life of the party.

Latin dance comes in three main forms: merengue,
bachata, and salsa (here listed in descending order of
complexity). Merengue is a fast-paced Caribbean two-step
march and the easiest of the three to learn. Bachata—
once considered a peasant dance of the Dominican Republic— is a four-step horizontally linear dance, markedly
more passionate and romantic than merengue. The most
complex of the three— salsa— came into its modern form
from the Puerto-Rican nightclubs of New York City (and
the influences of Afro-Cuban dance) and is a twirling
whirling eight-step dance and most likely the one you've
seen on Dancing With The Stars and America's Got Talent.
Now what really distinguishes Latin dance from most other dance forms is the center of motion, which for both
men and women is the hips. Basically, the hips rock in
the direction you want to go and the body follows. This
was of course the most difficult aspect of the dance for
me by far, for no self-respecting male of my cultural
background has ever attempted such a physical feat without being arrested and possibly stoned to death. But
after great and laborious practice I nailed it and now I
dance as precisely and as skillfully as any Latin man.

By now the second floor was fizzing with motion as
couples and large parties poured in to check out the
dance scene. Most sat along the bar and balcony while

others stood in place and rocked lazily to the music. I
for one was now consumed by the energy of Los Toros Band
and Oro Solido and La Banda Gorda and quite involuntarily found myself standing beside my friends tasered,
electrified by the merengue. Adam and Marco playfully
cheered me on and Marco was quite impressed by my moves.
"We must find you a partner now," he said and I started
to think the same thing, but looking around at the couples and seated parties I really didn't see anyone
available to dance. So I did then what I did back at the
hostel in Manuel Antonio and what I often do when I'm by
myself which is to just dance alone, so I danced and
danced and stomped and clapped as "Las Mujeres Lo Bailan
Bien" and "Tu Muere Aqui" and "Tu Sonrisa" and
"Abusadora" razed through my limbs electrocuting my
loins jolting my heart and others around me soon caught
the waves as well and in the midst of my stomping rever-
ie I saw Samirah and Dojuh ascending the stairs to the
terrace, followed by ChrisKafka who instantly spotted us
and shuffled across the dance floor to greet us. The
girls jiggled over to the bar smiling and glancing about
and certainly they attracted some looks which didn't
surprise me but I'll admit, it did make me laugh a bit
because I for one understood the bigger picture.

And now came the moment of shifting dynamics, my
friends, the do-or-die make-it-or-break-it now-or-never
split-second moment in a man's life when the chance ar-
rives to dominate the scene and declare oneself king of
the jungle. The time had come and the moment was right
to step forward and claim the night's dominion for myself. So without the slightest warning or hesitation I
marched right over to the bar and grabbing a genuinely
startled delighted Samirah by her wrist I took her and
dragged her right to the center of the dance floor and
there my Most Incited Reader the game began.

Now ladies and gentlemen, let's go over a few basics
of nightlife social interaction. The most important aspect of any man's domination of the center stage is to
act like he knows what he's doing— no matter WHAT he's
doing. The slightest second-guessing or hesitation will
instantly result in a mental collapse of mind and body
and everything will unravel into string. Thus the domi-
nator must approach the situation with unyielding confidence to strike with a wave of incontestable energy. In
this way like a sweeping tsunami I stole Samirah to the

dance floor without the slightest regard for her approv-
al or consent and there before them all she was dancing
in the spotlight.

Now be advised that girls rarely go along with this
approach willingly. Over time women have evolved— intel-
ligently so— to challenge the approaching man's confidence by resorting cleverly to a series of "girl tests"
which are designed to weed out the wimps from the roost-
ers. When the man approaches the first thing that most
girls will tend to say is "No thank you. I have a boyfriend" or "Not right now. Maybe later" or "I don't know
how to dance". Most men at this point shy away, but
those who don't can advance to the next stage. So some
perfectly appropriate witty responses to these "girl
tests" include "Good! Your boyfriend can join us!" or
"Now is better than later. Let's go" or "No problem! I
will teach you" and the man must respond swiftly and
without the slightest retreat or hesitation— and I really mean the SLIGHTEST— for if for a microsecond she
senses any second-guessing on his part then the game is
instantly and permanently over.

So with one fell swoop of an eagle's wing Samirah
found herself on dead-center stage in the arms of a guy
who didn't ask and didn't care. She went for the third
of the "girl tests", laughing aloud, resisting, and crying out "No, no, please I don't know how!" and hardly
looking at her and certainly not slowing down I replied
"No problem, it's easy" so I stopped and made eye contact and standing square to her as she giggled and shook
with excitement I said "Follow me" and I began to march
in place counting "One. Two. One. Two. One. Two. Right.
Left." And once she managed to march along with me I
pointed to the speakers and said "Now to the music! One.
Two. One. Two. Right. Left. Right. Left." and she went
right along laughing her head off and before she knew it
she was dancing merengue! I then said with a smile "You
just do that. I'll do the rest" and I went about swinging, twirling, dipping, and sliding this hysterically
overjoyed girl who couldn't believe she was dancing and
before she knew it she had become the center of attention and the life of the party and everyone on that se-
cond-floor terrace was taking notice. As the song came
to its final crescendo I cried "I'm going to dip you!"
and before she could shriek in terror she was strung out
horizontally with head and hair flung down to the floor

and she was pulled back up absolutely ecstatic. Then I
politely excused myself and walked away.

Samirah returned to the bar still laughing and I
strutted back to the couches in the corner where Marco,
Adam, and now ChrisKafka, Kylie, Tia, and a new guy were
all standing around laughing and high-fiving and con-
gratulating me on my dance skills. But to keep the momentum going I didn't stop and reaching out to grab both
Kylie and Tia who were reclined comfortably on the couch
I cried out "Who's next!" They both laughed and giggled
and writhed and politely refused, and to every "No I
can't" and "I don't know how" and "I just got here" I
replied "Yes you can" and "I will teach you" and "Come
on before the dance floor crowds up". But no matter how
hard I tugged at their arms I would have had to dislo-
cate their shoulders to get any action out of them so I
finally got the hint and laid off, for they genuinely
weren't interested in dancing and I could respect that.

Thus the momentum eventually faded and that was alright. Sure I'd have to wait for the next wave of opportunity to arrive but frankly I could've used the break
because I was dripping with sweat. So I sat down with
this amiable crew and we conversed pleasantly and Marco
in particular was quite visibly impressed by my dance
skills and had a whole bunch of questions about how and
where I learned to do that. So I stood around chatting
with them all and quite relieved that I had finally
scored some salsa dancing in Latin America! However, the
greater part of the night lay soon ahead, for my efforts
for domination and roostering and feather-flaunting had
actually worked. Now everyone on that terrace— including
and especially all of the other potential dance partners— had beheld my successful approach and dance with
this mesmerized and clearly charmed young lady. Thus I
was no longer a singularity creep floating around piteously and meekly requesting the pleasure of one dance—
Nay, I had established my credibility! My authority! I
am KING! Come thee hence, dubious wenches, and line thee
up in silence! Now I shall have my pick of the lot.

So I lounged about with my dear friends laughing and
drinking for a while but I also kept my eye out for any
potential dance partners. You may wonder then, my Most
Admiring Reader, how I determine if someone is a suitable dance partner? Well, the answer lies in universal
physics: "an object in motion tends to stay in motion".

Girls who are moving will most likely keep moving, while
girls who are seated or standing motionless are less
likely to engage. So I scanned the terrace for those who
were dancing in place or floating around near the dance
floor or tapping their feet or just finishing up their
dance with someone else and if those girls had come with
a group of other girls or a mixed party of guys and
girls then as far as I was concerned they were fair
game. And if they had come exclusively with male partners and stayed in close proximity to them then the approach would have to be a bit different. So I spotted
one girl dancing with her girlfriends and snatched her
up and we danced a bit. Then I saw another seated on a
barstool but moving about in her chair so she too became
my most willing next victim. Finally after I had had
enough myself and was thoroughly drenched in sweat it
came time to sit down and rest so grabbing the seats
between Marco and Adam I joined the large enthralling
group of dear hostelmates who laughed and joked and had
a wonderful time. I scanned their joyous faces and felt
safe and happy, completely blessed to have met and befriended such wonderful people.

It was then at that precise moment that I spotted
her from across the floor. She arrived with what seemed
to be a double date: she and one guy entered with another couple. Her long silky dark hair blew in the wind,
rustling against her crisp white blouse and taut blue
jeans, her slim figure ornamented by her perfectly selected heels.

She would be the one tonight.

I danced in place for a little while longer and
tried to coax Kylie and Tia into joining me again but my
God those two were really good at saying no without
hurting your feelings! In truth, they seemed to be having a wonderful time just hanging out on the couch
laughing and talking. And as their darling smiles illu-
minated the whole of that pumping lounge I figured
thence to quit harassing them and let them enjoy their
night as they pleased. No sooner did I turn around to
approach the dance floor again than I beheld suddenly a
barreling large man, hair curled and grin jokerly
stretched across his face!

"AHHHHH RAPHAELLLLL!" I cried and gave him a huge
enthusiastic hug, for it had greatly surprised me that
our hostel receptionist had come to join the party!

"Pura Vida! Que tal, amigo!" I cried. He was equally
excited to see me and sipping on his bottle of Imperial
he joined the group to laugh and chat of familiar
things. He wore a shirt that said "Harvard: School of
Music" so I said "Cool shirt man!"

"Yes. They send it for me." he replied. "I apply
and was accepted!"

I couldn't believe my ears. "Really??" I exclaimed.

"Yes I apply and was accepted. I am a musician" he
announced proudly and posing his arms like a guitarist
he went on to tell me about the many instruments he
could play (one hundred instruments, he said) and about
his short career with a band and his interests in music.

"Well then, if you were accepted to Harvard then why
didn't you go?" I asked. But all he did was shake his
head solemnly and bemoaningly with that huge grin still
on his face (it literally never faded from his face, by
the way. He grinned from the second I met him until the
second I bade him farewell) and didn't answer. It seemed
he couldn't answer because the reality was too painful
and tragic to be spoken. So we left it at that.

It was then that I noticed from the corner of my eye
that the girl in the white blouse and the beautiful dark
hair was dancing alone with her friend right on the side
of the dance floor. Their male partners were turned away
slightly, watching the girls and eating. Call me crazy
if you'd like, but I knew this was my perfect chance. I
started to move alone, dancing to my own rhythm and
watching them from afar trying to establish eye contact.
I saw that they were stumbling to dance merengue but
their step was slightly off. Marching forward with a
fake air of disappointment I walked clear across the
dance floor right up to them, jokingly scolding them,
and declared "No, no! No es así!" and I pointed to their
feet and shook my head vigorously. They sure looked surprised but their cool smiles permitted me to continue.
"Hacerlo así!" I said: "Do it like this!" I started the
merengue march and they followed suit and though they
actually got the hang of it I pretended that they were
still slightly offbeat. "Ay Dios," I declared in mock
despair and throwing my hands up in hopeless discontent
I took the dark-haired girl in the white blouse by the
wrists and announced "Así!" and suddenly without any
warning we were standing square, face-to-face, marching
to the beat of the music. Her friend, quite heartily

excited, started to clap for us and so we marched! "Uno!
Dos! Uno! Dos! Muy bien! Otra vez!" She marched and
laughed and her friend cheered and clapped and there we
danced for a few short moments right on the edge of the
dance floor. Finally her self-consciousness took over
and she mustered up the courage to shyly wave me off, to
which I surrendered with a hearty laugh and placing my
hand on her shoulder I said "Cómo te llamas, señorita?"
    She smiled and replied "Florencia".
    I said "Hola Florencia. Soy José" (yes that's right.
To family I am me. To strangers I am Joe. To cute smiling timid candy-sweet Latinas? SOY JOSÉ!) I nodded and
excused myself politely, waving over to the two gentlemen behind her in pleasant camaraderie, and as I walked
away I asked "Bailes salsa, Florencia? You dance salsa?"
    "No," she responded. "Sólo bachata".
    I nodded chivalrously and returned to the group.
    After a bit more conversation and discussion and
hearty laughter and Tom and Jerry the merengue finally
shifted to a bachata song and then the moment of deci-
sive action descended upon me once again as Florencia
and her party of four grabbed their things and headed
for the exit. With one suave fell swoop I rose once more
and cried out from behind them "bachata!" and before
Florencia had turned around or had time to propose any
objection I had her by the wrist and pulling her to the
center I cried "uno más!" and she smiled without protest. There alone on the dance floor she and I rolled
and rocked sweetly to bachata.
    I held Florencia firmly against my body and our two
embracing frames rocked swingingly in the manner of a
baby's cradle. With my left hand palming her upraised
fingers and my right arm steering her thin stalwart form
from behind we gently rocked to the swing of the tender
melody. We swayed like feathers in the wind, like a car-
dinal's beating wing, like the soaring waft of a conduc-
tor's baton. Two stoll significant separate souls united, ignited, recited, delighted into one swooping gale
of marveling motion. Her hair grazed my neck and shoulders, her sweet cool cheek kissed against mine own, our
hips linked and locked, our breaths pulminated as one
solid silent pulsing blue mist. We were the wind, the
whirl, the winding of space and time. We were the blue
centrifuge of rotary infinity, drowned in the fluid flow
of syruping sound. And once the kaleidoscopic whirr of

the universe folded and felded and melted into the next
song we gently opened our eyes and I whispered softly
into her ear "Grácias, Florencia" and she whispered back
"Grácias, amor" and with a gentle gust we parted like
parting lips like parting water drops like parting whis-
pers in the wind's icy drift and her sweet dark hair and
crisp white blouse and taut blue jeans floated away and
drafted daintily down the stairs and I never saw her
again.

And now that I had fully satisfied my dream of salsa
dancing in Costa Rica with a beautiful Latin woman I
could finally relax and actually enjoy the company of my
good friends without the relentless interruptions of
unfulfilled wants. I fell back into the chair fully at
ease and thoroughly exhausted by the heat and a full
night of dancing. I joined the chat listening laxly to
the wonderful conversations and laughter and it seemed
everyone was enjoying their time. I looked around from
face to beautiful face: Tia's smile and Kylie's smile
and Marco's smile and Adam's hearty laughter and
ChrisKafka's fully stimulated acknowledgments of camaraderie. And towering over us stood Raphael the looming
grinning mammoth with his charming tico accent and as we
sat chatting the dynamic of La Terraza slowly began to
shift and little by little folks like Florencia and
Samirah filed out and after a slight patch of emptiness
some quite barbarous-looking dark-clothed smileless wom-
en filtered in and they staggered about in their leather
and fishnets and spandex and towering heels glaring
about and saw that they totally reminded me of that
overtly conspicuous patch of prostitutes back in Jacó.
Then once the music shifted to ragged reggaeton (Spanish
club music, more or less) I knew full well that that was
what was going on and I felt quite uneasy and exposed.
Meanwhile much of the attention had turned to Kylie and
Tia who by now had become the only girls remaining in La
Terraza without an ostensible venereal disease so we sat
surrounding them asking if they would like to dance and
when they politely and playfully declined, well, we
asked a bit more firmly. And one pulled along one arm
and another tugged with serenading words and after they
had really plainly declined us all they unknowingly ac-
tivated the male egos among us and it now became a matter of challenge. Raphael had particularly taken keen to
Tia and after much coaxing and serenading and swindling

he was just about demanding she get up and dance with
him. And frankly I thought the girls stood their ground
exceptionally well because once she finally made it
clear that she didn't want to dance he threw his hands
into the air and with his characteristic grin howled
"okay, okay. You are sure? Okay," suggesting that she
had just missed the opportunity of a lifetime. Finally
he finished his second Imperial and the perpetual fun-
neling of leathered fishnetted cleavaged black souls
finally urged us to leave before the humping and brawl-
ing and cocaine and gunshots could get started so we
gathered our things and stepped back out into a deserted
street, wading through the puddles and drizzles of rain
back to our hostel.

Along the way ChrisKafka asked me something about my
name, something along the lines of "So do you prefer
José or just Joe" and I said "Well actually my name
isn't Joe. But just for convenience I introduce myself
as Joe..." and suddenly from before me there came the
heaves of the dragon and as the last straw finally
snapped Adam took a deep breath, paused to collect his
words, and then finally surging out the flames from
within he said "I don't think you should be telling people that your name is Joe". And I thought, well we finally got to THAT conversation, and anticipating this
moment for quite a few days now I assembled myself and
straightened my belt and mentally prepared my many
streams of logic and lines of defensive reasoning and
calculated the various conceivable counterarguments and
dissuaded them overtly in my head, I raised my index
finger and prepared my sermon of protest, when suddenly
Tia cried "Well you know, my name actually isn't Tia.
It's Tamaliah. I just tell people it's Tia because it's
easier to remember." I paused and after allowing her
perfectly simple response to seep in I said, "Right.
Exactly." ChrisKafka said "Yes exactly I totally understand." And my extended index finger slowly came back
down and I exhaled lightly and that was that.

The next thing I knew my head hit the crisp soft
pillow in cool heavy air-conditioned darkness.

chapter one

Travel is just as much a journey inward as it is a journey out. As we soar the skies and sail the waters and crack the virgin soils of the earth, we too delve into our own caverns, peek around the corners of our dreams, tremble before our fire-breathing terrors, axe to splinters our biases and judgments and beliefs, and discover the uncharted wonders of our psyches and our hearts. My stay in Costa Rica was soon coming to a close, but of the myriad of emotions that pelleted me upon realizing this fact, sadness was not one of them. Longing was not one of them. For although I was leaving Costa Rica, Costa Rica was not leaving me. It and everything in it was coming home with me. For in the course of true travel, my friends, you might be afraid to lose the place or leave it behind. But trust me: the place comes right back with you. And stays.

In all of my stay in La Fortuna, what I will remember most of all are the smiles. The mountains, forests, volcanoes, lagoons, the pools, the nightclubs, the hammocks, and the fun— that all will pass. But I'll grow old and rotten and shrivel and dry and I'll never forget the genuine happiness of those smiles. Of Tamaliah's sweet smile— that wide Polynesian shine that encompasses half her face with sheen and heartwarming bliss. Of Kylie's— that beautiful blond-haired blue-eyed sweet-home-apple-pie American smile that reminds you of all that's beautiful back home. Of Lena's— whom I so wished to have spent enough time with, for I had really connected with this grand human spirit and felt that there was so much more to have done with Lena. I wouldn't forget her smile. And mi amor mi alma mi sangre mi corazón Berenici who hasn't the faintest idea that I exist and never will and will forever be the emblem of all that is lovely and sweet and indescribably stupid in a man's heart. And el tico Raphael! His wild grin so pasted and plastered and spaded against the chars of his face that one could not forget the chumminess he brought forth. And Marco! Such

a man of manners, of kindness, of endearing friendship
and joy. And Joseph, the dear cousinly waiter! Even
ChrisKafka, in all his existential angst and grief, was
a smile from the world. And even dear Samirah and Dojuh,
despite what little was behind their smiles, indeed had
unforgettable smiles nonetheless. What I'll remember
most of all are the people, my friends, and so shameful
it is that we have forgotten that. It's all about people. And if you don't know that little secret of life
then I truly and sincerely pity you. Because if you had
met people in your life like Kylie and Tia and Lena and
Marco and Joseph and Christian and Raphael then maybe
you wouldn't give a hog-washing whore-fucking shit about
material things. Maybe you would be a hair-thin bit happier, my friend.

These are just some of the many thoughts that sailed
the coasts of my mind that next morning as I sat resting
in the near-empty open-air lounge of the Arenal Backpackers Hostel beside my fully-packed and zipped Hoodoo
Red Osprey Porter 46 Pack sipping cool fresh water out
of my CamelBak Chute 1.5L Sky Blue water bottle and
waiting for Adam to wrap up the checkout process. We had
woken up quite early that morning and I got up to find
that the bunk behind me which yesterday had bedded one
single young Hispanic man now contained that same single
man and two half-naked girls strewn about him. But before the egotistical dreamlike macho awe of this young
man's admirable conquest could hit me I recalled
ChrisKafka and thought it best to withhold my judgments
in the absence of further information. Slowly I rolled
out of bed and found Adam seated upright on the bunk-bed
above me, his face stolid with panic and dread. He shook
his head in disbelief.

"I woke up and saw that girl unpacking her bag. Lena? It freaked me out man," he uttered as the horrors
flashed before his eyes. "She had so much shit that it
really freaked me out."

At first I thought it hilarious but then I realized
his point and recalled the tremulous terrors that hoard-
ing could cause, for I'd witnessed it piled along the
walls of my parents' garage and heaped in the cluttered
corners of our home. That shit is no joke.

We got up and changed and now I was sitting in the
open-air lounge and Tia sat nearby wearing an oversized
T-shirt and her characteristic baseball cap and chowing

down watching TV. I had been ready to go for quite some
time now and was waiting for Adam when after a while he
came out looking exhausted and aggrieved and limp with
excruciation and he announced with great suffering,
"Sorry for the holdup man but I just took a chapter one
shit." We both cocked back and erupted in laughter as
this description hurled me over in hysterical glee, for
this was a most apt and most honorable reference!

So let me back up and explain in case any of you are
not familiar with what a "chapter one shit" is. The reference, of course, is to this very narrative through
which you now strum, my Most Bibliophilic Reader, and of
course it is my most great and tremendous honor that my
work has now become the source of allusion. I am quite
honored to be quoted thus! But what is a "chapter one
shit"? Well, the very idea of Chapter One was born— as I
have previously professed in my Preface to Chapter One
at the advent of this ranging tumble— sometime back in
April of this year after a series of incredibly bizarre,
irrational, and literally insane events changed the
course of my mind and my life forever. On the day in
question I was taking a walk through Corktown in Detroit
after my usual weekend cup of coffee and delicious egg-
herb-aioli sandwich at Astro when right on the corner of
Michigan Avenue and Levrette near Brooklyn Street the
Muses screamed out the following words into my head and
I was so overcome with their truth and brilliance that I
literally spoke them aloud to myself:

"4/17/16 The problem is this: I am too much of a
free spirit. All beliefs and values have vanished or
collapsed. All goals have been accomplished or abandoned. And this has placed me in a position of infinite
choice: the choice to do everything and to do nothing.
The choice to go anywhere and to go nowhere. The choice
to spend my time or to waste it. The choice to race past
the clouds or to watch them go by. And here begins the
next chapter of my life, one of a potentially infinite
and utterly absent future."

It is true that great art can arise from great suffering, for a prime example of this comes from none other than my very own literary hero Jack Kerouac who begins his masterpiece On the Road with the following:

chapter one

"I first met met Neal not long after my father
died...I had just gotten over a serious illness that I
won't bother to talk about except that it really had
something to do with my father's death and my awful
feeling that everything was dead. With the coming of
Neal there really began for me that part of my life that
you could call my life on the road."
    (By the way, that double-"met" at the beginning is
not a typo but literally quoted from what Kerouac tran-
scribed onto his legendary 120-foot scroll during those
fateful spring weeks in April 1951.)

    And so indeed is true great writing born. But back
to the subject at hand. I continued these sporadic rants
pretty much as they came to me. And some time later after a significant binge on coffee and fiber I composed
the following Chapter One entry:

"4/12/16 Want to see my feces? I just let out a
flashlight. I mean how this fucker was in me in the
first place is incredible. How does this much go in, let
alone come out? There's no way my plunger can take this
down. It's all like a porcelain white bitch
deepthroating this black turd. And cousin? Diz bitch is
GAGGIN! I'm gonna need an axe to break this bad boy up.
Or a chainsaw. But not an electric one. I wouldn't want
to risk it against the toilet water. I should call an
ambulance or something. What the fuck did I eat? Oak
bark? I have some genuine concerns about my home plumb-
ing at the moment. Fuck lead— I think this turd is what
caused the Flint Water Crisis— this fucking thing right
here. I think it's time to sell the house. There is no
way this thing is biodegradable.
    Wow. It actually went down. If this were a white
whore throating black dick, then it's a fucking fucking
champ."

    And it is to this entry that Adam was referring upon
his sore and tender exodus from the piteous lavatory.
The pain would afflict him for the remainder of that
day, as he so aptly cared to inform me throughout its
progression.
    Adam said that we weren't allowed to check out just
yet and even if we were we would be stuck with our bags
all morning. So we might as well leave them in the room

and grab some breakfast until it was time to go. With
just over an hour to spare we decided to head back down
into town and grab ourselves a light and scrumptious
meal. We found a small open-air diner (is it just me or
is everything "open-air" in Costa Rica?) serving breakfast, pastries, and smoothies so we took a seat and
grabbed a light meal and some smoothies. Once we had
settled ourselves and relaxed it dawned on me that I had
no idea what we were doing next. All I knew was that our
flight would be departing from San José the next morning
(Sunday morning) and I had to be there in order to be on
the plane. I asked Adam "What's the plan today?" But he
was already on the case and was looking up many things
on my phone. After gathering some information and veri-
fying his sources he said "Before we go we should check
out the hot springs. They're just down the street."

"Cool," I said, not knowing exactly what "hot
springs" were. Referring to the phone Adam continued:
"We can catch the 2:00 PM bus to San José which should
get us to town right around nightfall." Adam opened up
the Hostelworld.com app and looked up available lodgings
and as soon as he said "So as far as air conditioning—"
I announced "No worries. It's cool." And to my astonishment I actually meant it. So he looked up something
cheap and clean, booked us two beds, and we were all set
to enjoy the remainder of our day.

As we carried on a little dog roamed in from the
street and settled right beside our table. After throwing him a small piece to eat he decided to sit right
beside us and guard us. We finished our meals and as we
headed back toward the hostel we found the amiable dog
strutting behind us, charmed and pleased to be in the
company of his new friends. Now I practically sobbed
with delight because when it comes to dogs I pretty much
turn into that little warm-hearted boy from "Lassie" so
I was thrilled to have him follow us and I kept looking
back with delight at him trotting along but eventually
he got distracted and left and I sulked back into adult-
hood.

We returned to the hostel and reception was finally
ready to check us out. We went back to our rooms and bid
our roommates farewell and we found Marco and gave him a
big hug and we saw Kylie and Tia and wished them well
and I looked around to find Lena to wish her well and to
ask about her stomachache but I couldn't find her. Even-

tually I did spot her from a great distance so I called
out to her and she came back and she said her stomach
was still uneasy but hopefully it would get better before she left inland for Monteverde so I gave Lena a big
hug and wished her well and hoped that we could stay in
touch, for I felt I didn't get enough of this kind and
gracious young woman. With that, I returned to the hostel reception desk, bag-in-hand, and as Adam was wrapping up his conversations and goodbyes his eyes scanned
some new arrivals at the front desk and a flutter of
recognition splattered behind his eyes and when I looked
up and realized which pair of arrivals he was looking at
my heart skipped and I gasped and I fumed with the rage!
My Most Indignant Reader, I shit you not! Checking into
the hostel before us stood the rude aloof insufferably
bale bland and blighted British EuroBitches:
TimberBlonde and GreyGas! Our former roommates from Manuel Antonio! My stomach twirled intestines corkscrewed
lips writhed bones sickled and I frothed at the mouth
with contempt, for I have never in my being met a pair
of foul dungs who stunk of venomous stale so badly as
these two pungent cunts. Then to my utter astonishment I
saw TimberBlonde's eyes meet Adam's and she did something that absolutely blew me away: she smiled! I mean
her face lit up and her eyes sparkled and she actually
smiled with genuine joy and waved to Adam and cried out
"HEYYYYYYY"! They smiled and laughed and chatted and the
commotion of it all caused GreyGas to turn around from
her engagements at the reception and when she saw us
both she smiled too and turned to another one of their
travel companions and said "Hey, those guys were our
roommates back in Manuel Antonio."

My jaw hit the floor, my friends. My legs slabbed to
stone. Are you kidding me! Fuckers, we spent two days—
two. whole. days— stifled and gagged by the bitchy silent treatment from you two and now you're all suddenly
happy to see us?? Dammit, I just don't understand people
sometimes. So I just nodded my head in recognition and
walked away in bafflement and once Adam had finished we
looked back and scanned the beauty of the wonderful
Arenal Backpackers Hostel of La Fortuna and with a sigh
of joy we set out to carry on with the next steps of our
journey.

A cab picked us up at the front gate and drove us
west for about ten minutes to a place on the side of the
road where I followed Adam out to a sign and a metal
fence that read "SAN CARLOS". These were the free hot
springs that coursed from the Tabacon Hot Springs near
La Fortuna. Now when I had heard "hot springs" back at
breakfast I had thought that we were checking into a
resort for half the morning. You know, with baths and a
pool and possibly some tuxedo butlers and umbrella
smoothies and Latin bikini girls oil-massaging our
butts. But instead we had come to a pass under a road
bridge which we would have to wade through in order to
get to a steaming creek in the woods.

We paid the cab fare and descended a series of stone
steps to a flowing ravine under a concrete road bridge.
Somehow within that instant of time Adam had already
undressed with his bag and slippers in-hand and was wading upstream into the ravine toward a wide and raging
river. Ten minutes later he was long gone and I was
still balancing on my toes trying to remove my clothes
and socks and shoes, terrified to set down my non-
waterproofed bag which if dropped would soak and ruin my
life. I finally managed to get down to nothing but my
Hanes and once I was finally able to step into the
streaming water I jumped up and yelped with smiting
pain, for the stream was absolutely scalding! I eventually managed to adjust my toes to the flaming temperature and started my trudging begrudging march upstream
toward the other side of the road bridge, all the while
dodging sharp rocks and gaping cracks and slimy moss. I
reached the streaming river which now surged at me with
a far stronger current than I had earlier weathered and
now I was climbing step by creaking step upon slick
rocks against the coursing current of a fire river. The
only way forward now was through a large gap in a solid
concrete wall which I only managed to surmount with the
toiling help and guidance of some French tourists. But
once I had passed that last horrendous obstacle and had
forgotten why the hell I had attempted this grueling
misery in the first place, I looked up and before my
eyes streamed a wide and shallow coursing river. Banked
along its shores were clothes and shoes and piles of
luggage and tons of tourists laid out against its rocks

and boulders, their heads pillowed against large smooth
slates of stone, their muscles soothed and kneaded by
this natural spa. Crispy lime sunlight twinkled the
rushing waters and canopies of lush green and yellow
trees domed above us. I managed to slip and tap and balance my way to the riverbank where I set down my shoes
and my Hoodoo Red Osprey Porter 46 Pack against the soil
between two strong tree branches and hoped to God that
they would still be there by the time we left. I spotted
Adam laid out in the damn center of the stream so I waded over to him and eased myself into the boiling tor-
rents and laid down to relax.

   We sat in soothing silence, enjoying the sun and the
green and the streaming misty massage of the racing waters. Nearby a mother played with her two kids on the
bank while some teenagers hooted excitedly behind us. A
Latin couple— seemingly honeymooners— reclined beside us
relaxed and rested and though the white-bikinied female
of the pair was of the size and stature of Penelope Cruz
she had the round heavy firm melonous bust of fucking
Dolly Parton and I couldn't help but marvel if such a
disproportionate protruding miracle of God was naturally
possible or if those things were just well-engineered
mastodons of a surgeon's hand. But soon my inquisitive
angst receded and I was once again absorbed into the
beauty and wonder of the nature around us. I asked Adam
exactly what a "hot spring" was and how such a thing was
possible and he explained it all to me and I was quite
amazed and pleasantly informed and finally after we had
thoroughly enjoyed the wondrous merriment of an all-
natural flowing outdoor jacuzzi we got up and marched
toward the riverbank to get our stuff and then marched
clear across the stream again to the other side where we
climbed up the slant of the bank and found ourselves
back on the side of the road dripping wet in our underwear.

   Adam tacked on his slippers and his shirt and his
hat and there he was done, and I thought "Fuck you man
you perfect fucking traveler" as I trudged barefoot and
smited across the road past fleeting traffic to a small
brick building where I hoped I could find a bathroom or
something in which to change. When I found the door
locked and the whole building closed I chuckled in despair and as Adam called for a cab I took a minute to
change and assemble myself for our return to town. So

without a better alternative I started dressing right
there on the side of the road before passing cars and a
giggling tourist lady and I tossed on a shirt and fresh
Hanes and some shorts and just threw my old wet underwear into a rubbish bin because I wasn't going to deal
with that anymore and just before I could fiddle on a
pair of black socks the taxi had arrived and I hustled
across the street to catch it.

On our way back into town Johanna texted me and
asked "Heeeey What are u doing?" and I replied
"JOHANNAAAA! We r heading to the bus terminal but we r
free until two! What's up :)". She said "I'm free until
two as well. We're just in town are you at your hostel?
Maybe I come over ;)" and I couldn't help but wonder
what she was suggesting there exactly but I replied "We
are no longer guests. Are u at yours?" but she said
"Where are you? We're at your hostel hahahahaha." I
asked Adam what the plan was and he said we were going
to buy our bus tickets and once we got those we would be
free to meet. So I texted back "We're coming back from
hot springs. Just got to la fortuna" so Johanna said "Ah
okay. Let's meet somewhere. At the same place like yesterday? At the pharmacy?" I didn't mind that idea, but
since at this point I was still in a moving cab and well
into town and not quite sure yet, I said "Give me five
minutes! We will let y know." We arrived and looked into
purchasing our tickets and there Adam spotted a cell
phone shop and had a great idea! If he could find someone who could work on his dead phone for a couple of
hours then maybe he could get it fixed before we left
town! He asked around a bit but couldn't seem to find
someone to meet our time frame so finally we decided to
head over to meet Johanna and save the phone repair for
later.

Johanna texted us her location and we finally met
her on the side of the road and to our illustrious delight the sweet little darling had brought along a
friend! Oh yes she had— had brought right along a wonderful little gem to keep us company. There she was
again: Sonia! Oh joy! Oh merriment! Oh welting delight!
We greeted each other and stood about debating where to
eat until finally right in front of us I saw a sign that
read "Pupusas" and I cried out "Oh wow! Pupusas!" And
they all said "What?" and I said "Look, pupusas! Let's
eat pupusas!" and without waiting I marched right up to

the booth and started scanning the menu. There was little objection and quite a lot of confusion and curiosity
so we took a seat outside in front of this rickety booth
and looked over the menu and I said "Guys, you gotta get
the pupusas!" and they finally demanded "What the hell
are pupusas?" so I said "It's an El Salvadorian dish!
Basically it's a baked pastry filled with cheese, beans,
and any meats or vegetables you like! Think of it as a
Central-American calzone!" Now I had no idea what a
pupusa was myself until about a year ago when my dear
friend Benny invited me to get some Spanish food and
told me I might enjoy going with him because all of the
waitresses and chefs there only spoke Spanish. So to
help him order and to practice my Spanish and to try
something new, we finally went together to the place on
Livernois called simply "Pupuseria" which means "pupusa
place" in Spanish and I conversed in Spanish and ate a
whole crap-ton of pupusas and sipped coconut juice and
later our other dear friend Tucker joined us and we ate
more pupusas and talked about classic films. But anyways. That was when I learned about pupusas.

We ordered a scrumptious variety of different
pupusas of cheese and beans and chicken and vegetables.
Johanna was a vegetarian so she stuck with the veggie
options, but despite her enormous and piercing appetite
(as she so insistently cared to inform us), Sonia on the
other hand wasn't very impressed with pupusas and was in
fact quite disappointed with our boorish tastes. "I'm
craving eggs" she drawled in a whining fume. "Ever since
last night all I wanted was some eggs. I'm really craving eggs!" So she carried on and on for the remainder of
our mealtime writhing and reaming about her insatiable
craving for eggs. And whenever we told her "Well then go
get some eggs" she spattered in recoiling disgust "Oh,
not from any of THESE places. I don't trust their eggs"
and whenever we said, "Well why not go to the grocery
store, buy some, and cook your own eggs?" she said "Well
I don't eat eggs. I'm a vegetarian." So once the colossal fogging shock of her outrageous stupidity subsided
we went on with our pupusas and well after we had embarked onto another topic Sonia slammed down her palm
and erupted in a yearning rage "God I'm so craving
eggs!" and she went on and on about her insatiable hankering for eggs and her gratitude for her wonderful successful career as a writer and her pursuits in world

photography and did I mention how badly she was craving fucking eggs???

Johanna and Adam and I chatted gayly and avoided as best as we could the inevitable confrontation for as long as possible until finally after one plea too many for eggs Adam said to Sonia "So where are you from again?" and Sonia replied "I live out in Boston".

Now let me be quite honest: from the MOMENT Sonia had introduced herself the previous afternoon atop the peaked lagoon of Cerro Chato as an American from Boston, I KNEW that didn't sound right. Actually, her accent was distinctly un-American and quite ostensibly African. We pressed her a bit further to explain where exactly she was from in Boston and hard as she tried to keep the conversation general, eventually she was forced to confess (dismissively and casually) that in fact ever since she was nine years old she had lived most of her life in Kenya and had only resided in the U.S. for a few short years.

Well then.

But thankfully now she was living in Boston as a successful writer— and here I had had about all I could take of THAT bullshit so I said "So you're a literary! Who are your favorite authors? What are some of your favorite books?" And this little bundle of joy fired off a list of titles so trivial and juvenile that to a Master of Education in ESL and a Major in English Literature and Shakespearean tragedy such as me, it sounded like this week's list of tabloids at a Meijer checkout counter.

I went on: "So tell me a bit about your writing. Where have you published?" She said she was still finishing up her works in her creative writing class and would soon start submitting them for publication. I smiled and said "so have you been published yet?" and she said no, she was still working with her creative writing professor on revising and editing her work. I asked, simply for purposes of discussion, "Well THAT'S weird! How can someone 'revise' or 'edit' creative writing?" And she said, "Well, you refer to the rubrics and your development of plot and character and setting" and by this point to settle my sizzling ulcers and to spare shattering my plate of pupusas against the side of her fucking jaw and to afford her rot and worthless life, I just took a deep breath and let her finish her sentence and went back to conversing with Adam and Johanna who was asking all about the pool at our hostel and whether or not we could get back to the pool (which now explained Johanna's earlier message about "coming over ;)" to our hostel. I'm such a fucking dumbass).

Soon our food was brought out by an adorable boy in a red T-shirt with a blue jersey over it and a smile that could light up the world. He was a striking little gentleman who served us with exquisite professionalism and charm. If I may say so, he was the cutest damn boy I ever saw. He spoke English fabulously and seemed to run the entire restaurant all by himself, though he couldn't've been older than ten or eleven. Adam and Johanna took notice of this as well, and at one point when we asked him "What's your name?" and he said "Alan", Adam's face lit up with recognition and he hollered "Alan! Oh my God, that's him!" He explained to us that back in Manuel Antonio, the girl with the radiant smile named Cathy had told Adam about the cutest little tico boy who ever lived who had waited on her back when she was in La Fortuna. Cathy had loved the boy and had taken pictures with him and had been blown away by his charisma and demeanor. And we sat there thinking, who could blame her! This kid is the man! So Adam called Alan over and asked him if he remembered perhaps a week ago a girl he had served and before Adam had even finished his sentence Alan's face beamed with recognition and delight and he was so excited to hear about Cathy and to meet her mutual friend. Adam snatched a selfie with Alan and he shared it with Cathy and we all found ourselves that much happier to meet little Alan from La Fortuna.

We paid our tabs and thanked Alan dearly and headed back into town to relax for a little while. We arrived at a small open park in the center of town which was packed with locals about their daily business: women walking home with their groceries, men heading to and from work, solicitors haranguing pedestrians in the streets, and children running and riding their bicycles. We laid out in the park together joking and laughing and I took out my harmonica to play a few tunes and Adam then said "Can I see that" and I said "Sure" and he took a crack at it. Then I put it away and realized that Sonia was talking and probably had been for the last forty-five minutes at least. Adam had laid down and Johanna had laid down next to him and for a split second their eyes met and I thought to myself, this would be the absolutely perfect moment for Adam to move over and put his arm around her. He did nothing of the sort, but I thought in the universal scheme of social interaction that that would have played out quite nicely. Then I thought, perhaps if he kissed her then I could kiss— but looking over at Sonia who was TOTALLY still talking I thought, you know? I'd rather kiss a rhinoceros.

Then came the time to head back toward the station and to look into getting Adam's phone fixed, so we got up and gave each other warm hugs and I told Johanna that now that I had her number I would share it with Adam as soon as he got his phone fixed and we would all definitely stay in touch! Then to Sonia whom I never wanted to see ever again I said "We should stay in touch! Do you have an Instagram or something?" She said "Sure" and took my phone and plugged her name in. I beheld her Instagram page, plastered with photos of all her travels and a whole bunch of her relatives from Kenya and so on and looking at it I knew right then and there that the moment I walked away from this girl, I was going to unfollow her account. So we smiled and hugged and laughed and wished each other well and before I had turned a complete 180° from her I smashed my thumb upon that "unfollow" button so hard I damn near cracked my fucking screen.

chapter one

Now with a little over an hour to kill before our
bus departed for San José, our first orders of business
were to get some cash from the ATM, find a cell-phone
shop that could repair Adam's phone, and enjoy a bit
more of this town of La Fortuna before heading back and
wrapping up this trip for good. We found a bank just
across the park next to a church where we saw the blue
awning and got in line to get Adam some cash. Then we
headed back to the bus station to verify our departure
times and to check out a couple of cell-phone shops.
After two or three unsuccessful attempts and negotia-
tions, we eventually found someone who was up for the
task: he promised to repair Adam's phone in less than an
hour and for a reasonable fee. We agreed, and leaving
the phone in his trust we went off to kill some time
before our departure.

Adam laid down against the concrete wall of the bus
station and resting his head on his bag, he crossed his
long legs at the ankles and crossed his palms over his
waist and lowered the brim of his orange cap over his
eyes and fell asleep. I, however, was much too energized
and hot and subconsciously horny to take that route so
to kill an hour I went off to saunter through town
checking out the shops and mingling with the locals.

After mooching through shops observing beautiful
items and Latinas and creeping out a few of them by
walking straight up to their bronzen skins and crisp
smiles and uddered bazzooms bulming beneath their scant
spaghetti-straps and stating head-on and with direct eye
contact "eres hermosa" (to which they replied with jutting frowns and reorienting recoils), I returned to find
Adam blooming from his nap. We grabbed our bags and went
back to pick up his phone from the shop only to find
that not only was it still not working but it now had
developed a long and mysterious crack along its crisp
screen. The shop attendant raised his hands in helpless

pity and genuine remorse at our misfortune and wished us a good day. Clearly we were not in the U.S. anymore.

Our departure time was soon arriving so we headed back to the bus station discussing all of the new textiles that I should purchase upon my return to the States (such as, for instance, the synthetic-fibered "No Boxer Boxer" from Lululemon Athletica in Birmingham with silver-lacing technology to repel bacterial growth and odor, as well as various socks, shirts, and undergarments of merino wool), and there we discovered to our illustrious joy that Kylie and Tia were waiting for a bus as well! We greeted them and their big beaming smiles that brightened up our spirits and the day, and when the bus arrived we all poured in with the other streams of countless locals and travelers toward our final destination of Costa Rica: the shit city of San José.

Boarding the bus and finding that there were no more seats available, we cramped ourselves into the small luggage section (which on most local busses is a tiny platform near the bus entrance) where Adam dropped his bag and sat on it while I stood over him grasping the handlebars and flirting with the bus' wavering imbalance as it rocked out of the station and onto the ambling roads of the country. With no more indications of distress— not from the airless cramped city bus nor from the oppressive humidity nor from the incessant standing nor the questionable sanitation nor the relentless rigor of a traveler's day— I beamed with every progression of the ride and smiled gayly back to Kylie and Tia who had managed to snatch some seats and now sat cutely beaming back at us.

So we swung and rumbled to the rocking rhythm of the city bus as it careened away from the volcanoes and back toward the ambling misty green hills of the countryside and we chatted up a pleasant young blonde lady who sat before us clutching her bag and delighted by our company. She appeared to be a traveler (and a fit one at that) named Meghan who ventured from South Africa and she was joyful and friendly and of easy conversation and though she was more Adam's type of gal I did find her quite charming and cute myself. We chatted and laughed about our travels and about the merits and horrors of American culture until after a few more stops we spotted Tia from afar pointing ecstatically to a few open seats

so Adam and I shuffled over there and found a couple of
seats, but they were aisles apart so we bid each other
farewell and from our distant huddled hampers we exchanged friendly glances over the heaps of heads and
luggage between us, then turned back to beaming Tia and
blooming Kylie and did the same. Soon after, the brim of
Adam's orange hat came down and I would be on my own for
a little while, so I read some more of The Dharma Bums
and closed my eyes for a moment and kept my sights
peeled to the roads, for I was not missing any small
towns THIS time! As we rode the godly coasters of the
country we tumbled along past swelling hills and sulking
valleys and narrow streets sprinkled with colorful home-
boxes and grocery stores with DJs blasting their
reggaeton from the parking lots. After another brief nap
I opened my eyes to find us towering over the valleys of
the countryside, sunk beneath a deep blue fog which had
so softly descended upon the crops and cattle and capped
straw homes and had sprayed the earth with a murky cool-
ness. I gazed on, mesmerized by this earthly wonder,
unable to digest enough of this dazzling visage of God.
Finally I could no longer resist this entrancing sight
so I rose from my seat and trolled back to the luggage
platform where I could stand and get a full view of this
murky melancholy. I stood beholding and admiring the
rolling momentum of the bus as it ebbed and flowed like
a raft among the ambling hills of this dazzling landscape when from behind me I heard someone say "It's a
beautiful sight, isn't it?" and I turned around and responded to Meghan with a smile, "It totally is. I can't
believe it." I turned back around and gazed on further
until Meghan asked me another question, so I turned back
around to answer her and before I knew it I was standing
over her seat balancing against the handlebars chatting
with her all about Costa Rica and the Olympics and various interesting facts about her homeland of South Africa
and about the unspeakable amazement of the Trump phenom-
enon.

"Fucking Americans," Meghan said. "I tell you, you
are idiots if you vote for that guy."

With unchallenged and unflinching confidence, I replied "If we vote for that guy, then we deserve him". We
both laughed.

Eventually I bid Meghan a pleasant farewell, then
returned to my seat and spent the rest of the drive in

quiet easy introspection, reflecting upon this epochal century of a lifetime in Costa Rica that had been altogether but seven fleeting days. I rode the tides of my mind just as the bus rode the surfs and sprays and whitecaps of those ambling hills and the dark blue mist faded gently and drooped into the dimming blackness of night. From within, the bus's interior lights beamed our buoyant bounces; and from without, the black sheet of night was now sprinkled with the tiny golden sheens of the streetlights and porch lamps. After a few stops through bustling towns Adam arose from beneath his hermitic shell of an orange brim and examined my phone to verify our location and it turned out that after many languid sailing hours of bus travel we were very soon arriving in San José. I looked around and saw that the bus had quite completely emptied out by this point and that Kylie and Tia were also grabbing their things to leave. With sunset smiles they waved us goodbye and departed the bus on to their next adventures.

With only a few minutes remaining until our own stop would come, Adam moved over to the empty seat next to me and asked "How was the ride?"

"Good," I said. "Relaxing."

So we chatted on and on until we settled back into quiet and we heard behind us two sweet voices chattering jovially in Spanish. Eventually we were able to pick up a bit of their conversation and turning around we were startled by the dazzling beauty of these two young ladies. So with Adam's lead we hopped right into their conversation and they welcomed us right in! They were both from Spain— one from Barcelona and the other from Madrid— and they too were traveling across Costa Rica. Adam had much to say about that, for he had traveled to Spain before on his venture across the Camino de Santiago. So they chatted all about the wonders of Spain, and most engaged in the conversation of the two was the brunette named Laura (who was an absolutely stunning beauty, my friends). Her blonde counterpart went along and was strikingly beautiful as well, and we all carried on chatting and laughing until we finally reached our stop. We wished the damsels farewell and Laura smiled— holy Laura from Dante's Inferno who was the inferno de mi alma y corazón mi amor— and then we exited the bus and crossed the station to find a cab.

It was a cool and humid night, or at least it seemed to be. We emerged from the bus station onto a side street to find a troop of small red taxicabs lined militarily along the curb of a vexed and chaotic road. Fervent and fiery young tico cab drivers scurried up and down the curb in a frenzied hyper crying out "TAXI! TAXI!" with bulging hot eyes and simmering stomach ulcers. We approached the one closest to us— a short-haired fat tico in a tight polo— and asked "taxi?" and without even looking at us he yawped and hooted and twitched and flung open the trunk of his tiny red cab, chucked our luggage in, pried open the back- and passenger-side doors, hurled us in, ran around to the driver's seat, and was suddenly swerving around the corner to our jostled startle and clinching terror. He jetted down the dark swerving streets of oblivion, hammering defiantly against speed-bumps and potholes and whiplashing around corners and over curbs to the shrill maniacal screams of reggaeton on the radio, rattling us about like beans in a maraca. He sizzled and steamed as the hollers and yawps of pent-up verve chugged out of his simmering red face and bursting temple-veins. Finally he stomped to a skidding halt when we reached a congested main street that chiseled like a canyon fault line through the crumbling concrete stub that is San José, Alajuela, Costa Rica.

If the city of San José had one week ago been a trashy nightmare by day, then by night it was a decrepit Fuselian horrorshow of ghoulish bleak soot-black dubious terror. Could this really be the same country?— the same hemisphere?— as that of all of those passionate ocean coasts and ambling green hills and fit lush forests and shimmering white smiles of recent days? The cab driver punched the steering wheel and howled at the moon as Adam and I laughed hysterically and beheld the wonders of Red Bull and cocaine. But the horrors from within the cab could not contest the repulsions from without: decrepit crumbling old buildings mortared with chipping paint and crudding stone. Grimy streets strewn with heaping hateful trash, their corners patched with piles of rubbish. Congested cars and streets fuming their hot ashen gases against the reeking locals.

And speaking of the locals: hysterical half-dressed maniacs strapped in leather, fishnet, and plastic— stamped with tattoos, bandannas, chains, and coiled rings all roaming half-wittedly on a dark warm wet Saturday night like Halloween ghouls. Masses of rambling Spanish-speakers and guffawing mock-hookers in cheap imitation-leather and stabbing heels that protruded from beneath their popping hines like the lances of Satan. Long lines of dark shady hunched men with flipped collars and flitting eyes and clinched frowns waiting along the streets and around the black corners for fragmented misshapen doors to open. Oozing chlamydia and syphilis, they all hooted and howled and screamed like baying dogs and snorting pigs back and forth across the choking streets among the heaping trash surrounding them. We passed by closed shops with cheap fluorescent lamps of blue and yellow tinge that brazened half-naked mannequins laced in leather and rope, strapped in tight black fishnet, and sprinkled with glitter and metallic chime. When I beheld those female mannequins with their GG-sized busts— their offensively ostensible nipple-jutting titties— I felt only revulsion and hatred. What craft would possess a local business to stage a mannequin of such swelling distended proportions before the sights of the general public? It was a sight suitable but for the sex shops of Bangkok and Calcutta.

It was busy. It was ugly. It was shady. It was unsafe. It was Shanghai-ey. I wanted nothing more than to be gone from there.

Above our heads, the angels of heaven rolled out large heavy clouds like mountainous boulders and with a sprint bowled them toward us in a hurry to wash away the sin and vice and stink of this pungent Saturday night in San José.

Our cab driver could stand the wait no longer; villainously he veered off down another side street around a deserted corner and halted before a dark metal gate. Here we got back to our feet, retrieved our belongings from the trunk, and watched him zoom off into the darkness from which he came. The night glimmered near and far with patches of whirling red and blue lights, signaling a heavy police presence that seemed helpless and comical against this cyclone of diseased insanity. We were relieved to have been abandoned on the curb of an empty street in the darkness— away from it all— so we proceeded past the large rusty metal gate into what would be our night's lodging.

But immediately upon entering this place, I knew
that we would fare no better here than on those streets.

The hostel was cold and impressed upon me a xylo-
phonic jangle along the spine. Like the reeking streets
beyond it, its lobby was piled with old broken rubbish:
dusty cracked red-tinged tiles, chipping ceilings, an
old broken television, dust-mited cushion chairs, blan-
kets and old crudded travel books, high looming statues
and aboriginal masks. Yet despite the heaps of junk it
still exuded a chilling sense of vast and muted emptiness. The corners were too dark, the rooms too boxed and
huddled behind heavy wooden doors. The place echoed with
the howls of dead spirits and ancient sin and emitted
the numb dreaded pulse of an altar of sacrifice. Besides
the ponytailed American dude in the blue shirt who stood
stoically at the front desk, there wasn't a soul in
sight.

He greeted us politely and warmly, I must admit
(though it wasn't his fault that the merriment of Santa
Claus and the love of Jesus Christ couldn't dispel the
black vacuum of this place's spirit), and took to pen-
ciling us in and charging our night's stay. After an-
swering a few questions and setting a few ground rules,
he lead us down the open echoing half-lit red-tiled
junk-infested lobby-hall past black rooms beneath heavy
unrelenting doors.

"To the left," he said, "is the bathroom and the
shower." Then coming to an enormous wooden slide door,
he forced it aside and opened us up to a dusty stone
stairway that overlooked a large open basement space
which seemed to serve as the communal kitchen and
lounge. The whole space— a jumbled mess of rickety
blood-painted wood and rusting metal— was piled with
dishes, pots and pans, busted televisions, ancient 80's
electronics, rickety dirt-caked gardening tools, heaping
wooden and plastic furniture, and the overarching stench
of stale primordial death. A large old television blared
a Chinese news network as three little Chinese men hovered around it fiddling with wires and remotes. Next to
them sat a black woman chatting with another brown man,
possibly an Indian. Beyond them was another door with a
window.

"Right this way," said the attendant, marching us
down the steps past the chatting dark couple. He opened
the door and there we found two bunk-beds, two queen-

sized beds, and no windows or access to the outdoors
(except for the window that overlooked this junky basement). The walls were painted with childlike images of
the jungle: lions, giraffes, tigers, elephants, and lush
green forest for the children. Sure enough, there
against the wall was another broken television.

We wondered why in such an empty decrepit hostel we
had been placed in a windowless escapeless basement
closet. The only advantage I could see was that since
the entire room was empty and devoid of any luggage, we
could pick our own beds comfortably. Adam plopped his
bag onto the farthest top bunk while I went for the
queen-sized bed closest to the door. You know. Where I
could get the fuck out of there when the ghosts of the
Mayan dynasties arrived with their chant charms and ma-
chetes. Besides our own bags, there was nothing else in
the room indicative of other guests. Except this:
against the farthest wall near Adam's selected bunk,
piled into the corner, were two bags. And gazing on at
these items in a sudden and Shining-like trance, I was
overcome...possessed...by a realization and a certainty
that to this day defies understanding or explanation.
The very instant that the whites of my eyes fell upon
those bags, I came to the following conclusion: "whoever
owns these bags right here is going to kill us tonight."

The night was young and it was time to grab some
dinner and scope out our surroundings. We left our bags
and took with us our personal documents, cash, and keys
to the basement room, then went back up the stone steps
overlooking the Shanghai Triads and the chatting brown
couple to discuss with the hostel attendant our upgrade
to the upper demon floor. He said he would be happy to
reassign our accommodations, but that there would be an
extra charge. After brief deliberation, Adam and I figured sensibly that there was no point in upgrading since
we would only be staying for one short transient night,
so we thanked the ponytailed blue-shirted American attendant and exited the door and the metal gates out into
the street.

We ambled through cold sharp raindrops and the ambi-
ence of whirling police lights and the distant honking

of maniacal traffic as we ventured to the nearest open restaurant that didn't look like a pawnshop, nightclub, rave, or butcher house. We found at the end of our hostel's street a well-lit colorful two-story restaurant which appeared to be of a more prominent standard, so we entered and were greeted by a sweet and charming young waiter. We were the only customers there and I couldn't help but notice the exotic drapes, multicolored carpets, and terraced ethnic design of this charming light place. Was this a Moroccan restaurant? Spanish? Andalusian? We scanned the menu and discovered that it was Peruvian. We asked about the menu and they had numerous options, among them the most famous and authentic of Peruvian dishes: chaufa, which was essentially a fried rice scramble of vegetables and choices of meat. We thought it looked fantastic so we ordered two dishes of chicken and shrimp. In no time the waiter brought out our steaming dinners and they looked more delicious than we could've imagined. We ate heartily, devouring each succulent morsel with tender delight.

And with incredible fantastic meals comes incredible fantastic conversation. We reminisced about our youth: high-school days and basketball on the Lowrey school blacktop. Hilarious memories of adolescent stupidity. We descended into much earlier memories of grade school, which Adam recalled far more precisely than I could. We exhumed the memories of our teachers: Ms. Garrison's second-grade class (where Adam and I had actually first met, and which I had shamefully forgotten). Ms. Cozka. Ms. McLaren. Ms. Darany and Ms. Barrett. Dr. Harden. And then the names and looks and hilarious anecdotes rolled right on out: Kadim Ramadi with the big glasses. Stanley Asmat, whose poor Vietnamese ass I kicked one too many times in the third grade and whose suffering actually landed me a suspension. Theresa Ware, who even in her gentle and tender childhood emitted an unmistakable destiny of cluttered trailers and bountiful babies. Sharon DeMarco. Christie Masterson. Nancy Dunham. Ali Bazzi. Charlie Corwin. Lina Rouhani. Jeffrey Bulger. Sarah Mackie. Matthew Martinson. And Hank Karam HK, who had been a dear friend of Adam's back in elementary and who remains a dear friend of mine today. Through the rolling coasters and whooping rainbow tunnels of our past we laughed and groaned and winced and reminisced with unquenchable delight. We talked about relationships and

the nature and form of infidelity: namely, what exactly
does it mean to be "unfaithful" to another? Boy, did
that question raise some astonishing intellectual discourse, my friends. Our conversation carried on well
into the remainder of the evening— an intense philosophical moral dialogue. On and on it rolled as we paid our
tab, finished our drinks, thanked the waiter and the
hostess, and walked out into a boisterous reckless
night.

Having now the rest of our night— our last night on
this trip in the holy country of Costa Rica— to enjoy
exactly as we pleased, we hit the streets in search of a
venue for entertainment. We first approached a lime-
green balcony which overlooked the black empty street.
Up a dark steel flight of stairs was loud bombastic music and rowdy chatter.

"That looks interesting," I said.

"Yeah," said Adam. We turned around and walked the
other way.

We passed by the doors of our sanctuaried Peruvian
restaurant once again, and then turned another corner
and started uphill along another dark empty street. And
in the middle of my sentence about the psychosocial ram-
ifications of undisclosed or undiscovered adultery, Adam
stamped his foot and cried out in a frustrated rage exactly what the fuck I was thinking: "Let's just go back
to the hostel and continue this conversation." Without
objection or hardly a response, I reoriented my body
completely toward the hostel and marched on. Last night
in Costa Rica or not, we weren't going to spend it in
this trash heap of shit among low-class hoodlums and
cheap whores waiting to get knifed or mugged or hassled
by these Spanish-speaking riffraff.

As the clouds finally assembled their ranks to soak
upon this damnéd Gomorran pit of sin the sanctified tor-
rents of heaven and as the wrath of God thundered and
quaked the call of the imminent tempest, we hustled back
down the street smited by icy pellets of acidic
raindrops. The wrathful fire and brimstone spanked my
neck and skin, and just fleetly dodging the cascade that
pummeled the roofs and heads and hoods, we came to a
stop before our hostel's metal gate. We entered to find
the hostel even emptier than when we had left it. Neither the attendant nor any of the guests were to be
found. We crossed the sacrificial death-hall of wailing

indigenous ancestors and hoisted aside the heavy wooden
door, then descended the dusty stone steps into the
high-ceiling sangre Shanghai basement-garage. We saw and
heard no one. And so in the seemingly empty hostel we
entered our basement-room and it, too, was bone-
chillingly vacant. There was no new luggage save our own
bags left right where we had placed them and the third
guest's luggage still heaped in the dark corner.

We settled down to the raging rat-tat-tat of the
downpour outside which had commenced with the shrieks of
Poseidon and the fire-bolts of Zeus. Our conversation
continued, branching out from the philosophical to the
practical to the theoretical to the personal. We sat
near the doorway beside my charging phone which nursed
merrily the electric flow from the child-painted walls
and napped sweetly atop the old busted 80's television
set that slumped over a crippled wooden table. Then in
the split midst of our sentence, as if to snap us to
silence, the whole room cracked to darkness and my phone
buzzed as its nourishment was torn from its charging
snout.

"Power out?" I said to the cringes of the surging
waters that pounded and pierced the aluminum roof outside, snare-drumming my nerves and my sanity.

"Yeah," said Adam in the pitch-blackness.

"How long?" I asked.

"Don't know," he replied.

We carried on in blind darkness until some moments
later my phone buzzed back to life and the room's tart
florescence thrashed back against our corneas.

It was then that he walked in: a large burly man who
trudged in with a heavy gait and a calm face chiseled
with Polynesian features. He wore a T-shirt, shorts, and
a long dangling ponytail behind his head. He held a
black camera— perhaps a Nikon. With manner and charm he
greeted us both. And here came the point: Yes, you may
think me vain or senseless, my Most Venerated Reader—
you may think me foolish and paranoid, and who could
blame you since you weren't there? But I tell you this:
the split-second my glances fell upon the frame of that
man, I knew it. I knew it with divine conviction. I saw
it flittering behind his eyes, pruning back and forth
along his frame, looming like a grey wolf, like
waldeinsamkeit between the leafless black thickets of a

winter wood. This I knew: "This man is going to kill us tonight."

He extended his hand. "I'm Pat," said the ponytailed Polynesian.

"Adam," replied my friendly pal.

He turned to me. "Hey. Pat."

"Hi Pat," I replied, smiling as his large cold hand gripped my palm for a shake.

This man is going to kill us tonight.

Pat approached his luggage in the corner as Adam climbed up to his bunk. I sat up in my queen bed smiling, clutching the mattress beneath me, spading my nails into its fabric, flitting my eyes about in search of a potential weapon to use at the imminent moment of reckoning, and wondering if my pillow would suffice to fend off the descending battle ax of this murderous brute. Pat placed his camera gently upon his luggage pile and then sat down on the bunk beneath Adam's. "Where are you guys from?" he asked.

"I'm from Michigan," I said.

"Well," Adam said, "Utah." I agreed that he was from Utah, for we both weren't going to bother to explain that we were both in fact from Dearborn which is a small-town suburb of Detroit, Michigan, but that Adam had moved to work in Utah and now lived there— meaning that technically he's from Utah, but in actuality he's FROM from Michigan. Get that? Why bother explaining that to a stranger? And you know? That's the same fucking reason I don't tell people I'm from Dearborn because that conversation always goes like this:

"Where are you from?"

"Dearborn."

"Where is that?"

"It's a suburb of Detroit."

"Michigan?"

"Yes."

[Thinks to self]: "It wouldn't happen to be the terroristville Sharia-law Dearbornistan from Fox News, would it?"

And that is precisely why I tell strangers that my name is "Joe" rather than telling them my real name! Because it takes the ignorant bastards forever to comprehend my name and they seldom remember it and often they need it repeated and Good God does that fucking get annoying! Case-in-point, my pizza delivery exchange for the last fifteen years:

"*Paisano's. Pick up or delivery?*"

"*Delivery please.*"

"*Name?*"

I say my name.

"*Sorry?*"

I say it again.

"*Can you spell that?*"

I spell it.

"*What can I get for you?*"

[Thinking to myself]: "*The same goddamned fucking thing you have gotten me every month for the last cocksucking decade and a half, motherfucker!*"

So some time ago when I changed up the game on them, things ended up going more like this:

"*Paisano's. Pick up or delivery?*"

"*Delivery please.*"

"*Name?*"

"*Joe.*"

"*What can I get for you?*"

There! See? Shorter common names equals faster fucking pizza! Understand?? Now back to the show.

There I sat facing Pat on the bottom bunk and Adam on the top one as Pat talked on and on for the rest of the night. Adam rolled over and Pat lay down on the bed looking up at the bottom of Adam's mattress reciting the memories and visions that flashed before his eyes. He put up his feet, which I swear to you and shit you not looked like this: the toenails on his left foot were painted blue and the toenails on his right foot were painted yellow. Pat said "My dad was from the Singapore but my mom is actually in Michigan. What a coincidence. She lives up there somewhere. Haven't been up there myself but she seems to like it. Come to think of it, haven't been to Singapore either..."

And I thought: "Jesus, I think he's going to kill us."

"...But I'm living in Hawaii and I take a bunch of pictures. There's my camera over there. I came down here to check out some of the surfing. You guys surf? Yeah I surf back in Hawaii and they said there were some pretty

cool coasts around here. Just got in myself so I'll be
heading to the coast tomorrow..."

"Jesus Christ, this fucking maniac is going to fucking kill us."

"...And it was cool and all but then I joined the
Marines and since then I've been in Hawaii..."

"Holy fucking shit, this blood-drooling psychopath
is gonna kill us PROFESSIONALLY."

From the top bunk I faintly heard Adam snoring. I
was now on my own.

"...But I'm still in college, you know, and that's
cool. I should've graduated a while back but I'm actually still there because there's a bunch of Estonian babes
at the University. Shit man, I love Estonian babes. You
guys got many Estonians in Michigan?"

"Diz. Motha. Fucka. is gonna block me up with an ax,
man. He's gonna strip me to shreds with a machete and
then shave the fat off my bones and wear my skin."

"...And then I think I'll head back to Panama because I wanna get some of that surf in. So far I heard
it's pretty cool down here..."

Ten minutes later, Pat was still talking. I slowly
wedged my fingers out of the mattress and as casually as
possible I announced "Well, I'm going to go take a shower and get ready for bed. Good talking to you man."

"Oh, cool man," said Pat the Butcher. "Yup you have
a good night."

I snatched a pair of underwear, jerked up my pink
bag of toiletries, and hurdled out of there. I knew Adam
was dead as a roast hog and I lamented my dear brother's
untimely and gruesome end, but maybe if I could escape
before Pat the Slayer got to ME then I could at least
identify the son of a bitch. I slinked rattlingly up
those stone steps in stoic terror, my stomach wrenched
with dread and panic, and standing nude and wide-eyed in
the stream of the hot shower I wondered why in the hell
a complete stranger would impress such a terrifying
foreboding upon my spirit. I had met hundreds of complete strangers this week, slept peacefully among them
in their beds, shared with them their meals and laughed
with them with hearty joy. Why, then, would he of all
people entrench in me the unflinching assurance of
blood-thirst? I showered among the red-tinged tiles of
this demonic hostel-hell beneath copious hot water and a
flittering light-bulb. I brushed and flossed digitly,

then descended back down the stairs to find that the
lights were off and the room was silent. Timidly I
opened the creaking door and entered the black vulcan of
the void. Pat the Shredder was lying in a fetal position
on his mattress, uncovered, his back toward me. I listened intently for Adam's snoring, and though it seemed
eerily faint I could be sure that he was still breathing. Stiffly I crawled under my sheets. In the silent
darkness, to the pulsing huffs of both of their snores
and to the incessant dings of downpour, I found it impossible to fall asleep. Eventually I drifted off into a
hazy tar slumber, but no sooner was I plunging into terrible dreams of black cats and dark wet puddles in
screeching alleys than I was startled awake with a gasp,
expecting Pat to be towering over me with an ax or a
chainsaw cackling hysterically to the sweet smell of my
coursing veins. Finally after repeating this horrific
cycle three or four times I witnessed the distant thin
red haze of sunlight and I figured it was as good a time
as ever to get up and get the fuck out of there.
  I exited the dark room into the orange haze of dawn
and the chirps— nay, shrieks— of hysterical birds croak-
ing cawing baying irately. To the maniacal barks of a
livid rabid dog. To the strange distressing wails of an
animal dying nearby, which after intent deliberation I
concluded to be a cat, though I've never heard before
from man or beast such excruciating bloodcurdling
screams of looming death. I slowly trudged away from the
horrors of the silent morning up the stone steps into
the dead dark hall of the hostel lobby. Again there
wasn't a soul in sight, so I took to exploring and observing this strange setting: the stiff dusty cushioned
chairs, oversized and ugly. The poorly-painted and plastered ceiling. The cracked and tempered red tile, chipping and crumbling along its edges and corners. The
stacks of travel books crinkled and water-damaged and
strewn haphazardly on a poorly finished wooden table. An
enormous grey 80's television, its electric wire hung
over its top like a fanged black snake. The looming indigenous statues, large and etched with rage, staring
from the towering walls into my soul and riling my sins
with hollow shadow-eyes. Finally once the terror of the
place subsided and as the sunlight came to splash
through the windows near the ceiling I managed to sit
down upon a dusty chair and enjoy the eerie silence and

the downright comical creepiness of this place. For
nearly a half hour I sat meditatively in peaceful silence observing my surroundings. Then once the sun had
risen enough, I rose and returned past the large sliding
wooden door and down the stone steps again into the
basement lounge. There I sat staring at the floor wide-
eyed as the crows of hateful birds and the rage of a
revolting dog and the last cries of a dying cat oceaned
through my ears and through the washes of my veins. The
birds flew off, the dog ceased its barking, but the cat
carried on wailing and meowing and pleading and sobbing
in excruciating death as inch by inch its morbid soul
was wrenched from the latches of its bones and stripped
from the tanglings of its pin-needled fur. Wide-eyed and
stiff-boned I sat there enduring her pleas and weeps and
whimpers as they grew fainter and fainter and breathless
and hopeless and finally waned to silence. I listened
until her final breathless cough of death pinged my ear-
drums and wrung my heart and awakening from my trance I
noticed that for all this time, mosquitoes or gnats or
something of the sort had been nipping away at my toes
and ankles. I smacked at them for a bit but then soon
gave up, for if I had finally caught the Zika or malaria
or whatever it was that could finally end this day of
suffering, then I could just go lie down out there next
to that cat and join the choir.

    I had been up alone and in silence for over an hour
when from above descended a kind-looking Hispanic woman.
She was enormous and draped in a lovely simple red
dress. "Hola," she announced and went to the kitchen
behind me to begin the daily preparations. I watched her
shamble past upturned pots and stained dishes and half-
full cups and piles of scraped toast and crudded silver-
ware and hovering swarms of fruit flies. But she carried
on as if she'd done this all her life. She set out some
fruit and toast and scrambled some eggs and switched on
the coffee pot. Then three Chinese men also came down.
One immediately began adjusting wires and antennas and
technological boxes until moments later he had retrieved
from the air a bona-fide Chinese channel hailing from
Shanghai or Hong Kong. The other two stood outside in

the yard barefoot chattering in Mandarin and I wondered
if these fuckers ever got to scenting that dead cat out
there if they would proceed to boil it for lunch. Again
the gnats or mosquitoes had at my legs so after scratch-
ing slightly I stood up to go rinse off my feet. Some
other guests also arrived and soon Adam woke up and came
right out of our room and into this basement kitchen
Chinese theater.

"Been up long?" he asked me.

"Not long," I said. "How did you sleep?"

"Good," he replied. "What's for breakfast?"

Looking over my shoulder at this filthy fruit-flied
dish-caked crud-plastered kitchen with the amiable boulder hostess preparing our grub, I said with a smile
"Let's go out to eat."

Adam didn't mind so we went upstairs where an elder-
ly lady now tended the reception. It wasn't yet time to
check out so we emerged out onto the now sunny deserted
street to get some breakfast, but after passing two or
three closed restaurants and numerous patrolling police
cars, we presumed that Costa-Ricans still honored the
Sunday Sabbath and still took seriously the holy day of
rest, so we returned to the hostel. Now a score or so of
guests had gathered in the basement-kitchen-lounge to
eat and Pat the Chopper was nowhere to be found. I decided to stick with coffee and to set aside my appetite
for the concessions at the airport, so once breakfast
was over we grabbed our bags, marched upstairs to the
front desk where the attendant checked us out and hailed
us a cab, and before we knew it we were on our way to
the airport! And here, my Most Beloved Most Genial Reader, comes the beginning of the end of this glorious trip
to Costa Rica!

chapter one

As the cab volleyed gently through the town's silent
Sunday streets, my mind glazed over the passing homes,
the unkempt waving verdant fields, the winding cramped
roads, the silent man biking freely through empty slumbering neighborhoods. But unlike the riotous filth and
dubious chaos of the antenight, I saw in this quiet des-
titute morning the charm of simplicity, the freedom
which had permeated the whole of our stay and our trip
across this great and glorious country. Here, one felt
alive. Here, one was living. And thinking back to the
grid-lined streets, the teeny-trimmed square patches of
even lawn, the venerated street signs and unflinching
street lights, and the gunpoint automobile lanes of our
home, I started to wonder if our suffocating sense of
perfection and order was really "living" at all. Were we
really "living" over there inside our square buildings
with square doors and square windows and square rooms
staring at big and small square screens, eating out of
square fridges and square ovens and off of square
stoves, retiring to square dressers with square drawers
full of folded cotton squares plotted on trim green
square lawns in square neighborhoods at the intersections of square grid roads? Let a weed grow, motherfuckers. Skip a haircut. Laugh at the crud underneath your
fingernails for once. Get off of the sidewalk and wet
your bare feet in morning dew. Leave footprints in the
snow. Scream where nobody can hear you. Say "fuck" and
"shit" and "piss" and "asshole" every once in a while.
Kick a ball. Do something stupid and senseless, you
know, to limp a bit that corked lead metal pipe that so
erectly spines your rectum. But no, we wouldn't dare,
would we?

With these thoughts simmering in my liver I cried
out with livid disgust: "We are so repressed in America." Adam smiled at me and said, "I was thinking the
same thing." And here I remembered something my dear
friend E once told me about her friend from Guatemala:

after he had studied in America for half a decade, she
had asked him: "So do you think you will stay in the
U.S.?" He had shaken his head with anger and sadness and
said "No. I don't feel free and I don't feel safe." Now
I knew what he meant.

Coming to a halt before the Main Terminal of Juan
Santamaria Airport (SJO), I emerged back into the hot
Sunday air of Alajuela and knew for the first time since
this trip had begun that I was now changed forever. That
whoever I was before this week, I would never be that
person again. And entering the terminal behind Adam, I
gazed intently at that tall rugged man with the orange
hat and the green shirt and the blue pants and the brown
slippers and the grey-orange-blue backpack who now
walked before me and who I wouldn't see again for many,
many months. And in the hustle of entering the sliding
doors of the terminal I yelled out to him: "Adam."

"Yeah," he said.

"Adam I fucking love you man," I said. And I meant
it with such passionate conviction and such outpouring
honesty that I could have cried.

We entered the airport to check in and worm through
security and here we bade one another a temporary farewell as I approached the Delta line and Adam went off to
Copa. Ten minutes into the line I was asked to fill out
some international travel documentation so as I was
leaned over scribbling down the last of my name and
passport number and criminal history, a blonde American
girl smiled at me and asked to borrow my pen. "Sure," I
said as she and her two other travel companions— a pretty, dark-haired girl in a hat and shorts and a white
dude— scrambled to fill out their forms and I returned
my attention to the Delta line, assuming I wasn't getting that pen back. But quite suddenly the blonde girl
was back again with a smile and she gratefully returned
my pen and thanked me and we chatted and it turned out
that she and her friends were heading back home to Salt
Lake City.

Finally I checked in and met Adam at the security
line where we shoveled along past smiling tico officers
and genial travelers and soon found ourselves inside the
terminal. Passing by a remarkably wholesome bakery-café
that brandished delicious-looking French pastries and
wildly appetizing sandwiches, I was caught dead by surprise and howled with hunger! I declared "That looks

GREAT! Let's eat here!" So we got in line at this well-
lit booth that announced "Brioche Dorée" in red and
white pride and I ordered a breakfast egg-and-cheese
croissant, a black coffee, and a large and scrumptious
chocolate-chip muffin. We sat in the corner as I took to
devouring with avid glee this enchanting and satisfying
meal. I offered Adam some and he took some of the chocolate-chip muffin and we ate and laughed and discussed
comedians and laughed heartily and braced for our return
to civilization until suddenly Adam was smitten by the
sight of a beautiful woman passing by. And when I looked
up I jumped from my seat with delight, for Adam had
spotted none other than the blond American and her pair
of friends from the Delta line!

"Hey, I know them!" I said to Adam. "They were in
line with me at Delta! And they're from Utah!"

Adam's eyes settled upon the dark-haired one in the
hat and shorts (who was indeed a remarkable beauty, my
friends) and we sat swooning about her and them and all
cute, beautiful, pretty girls. Then once we had finally
wrapped up this incredibly delicious meal we left Brioche Dorée and went off to explore the terminal. To our
grave disappointment we found that the whole of the Main
Terminal at Juan Santamaria Airport (SJO) was but ten
gates long! JUST TEN! We walked its entire length in
four minutes, then went back and did it again! We went
to the bathroom and standing outside of it was a man in
a colorful shirt playing a marimba and next to him were
some massage chairs and two ticas in grey uniforms and
welcoming smiles greeted us. And emptying my canister
into the urinal I thought through my splattering tinkle,
"My, what could be better now than a nice relaxing massage to wrap up this amazing trip?"

I washed my hands and found Adam and said "Hey,
let's get a massage." He seemed reluctant at first and
uninterested, but I felt that he was resisting the temptation so I made him stop and tell me about it.

"Why not, man? It's good for you!"

"Yeah," he rationalized and carried on explaining
the pros and cons of succumbing to comfort, but I insisted and said "Let's do it."

He finally agreed, so we approached the booth and
the ladies welcomed us and seated us gently and soon
they proceeded to knead our shoulders and mold our lats
and tenderize our traps and though these women weren't

at all arousing, they were MASTERS of the human touch
and their massages were truly liberating and rewarding!
Fifteen minutes later, we got back to our feet slack-
ened, mashed, and slinked into euphoric mist. Sauntering
airily away from the darling masseuses whom we thanked
abundantly, Adam came to inform me in a half-trance that
this massage had been the first massage of his entire
life!

"WHAT!" I exclaimed. "WHY?"

"Well, I don't like to spoil myself," he said. "I
worry about getting too comfortable because then there's
no way of going back."

It was true. Adam still slept on an air mattress and
willfully ignored food education for that very reason:
so that he wouldn't get too comfortable or allow his
body and mind to soften. And I don't blame him for this
fear because indeed the coffins of comfort are things of
terrible dread. But he learned that day that every once
in a while it's alright to treat yourself, and I was
honored and thrilled to have been the instructor of that
lesson.

And now we came to the final destination of Costa
Rica, the end of the line, the moment of farewell:
Flight DL 903 to Hartsfield-Jackson Atlanta Intl Airport
(ATL), departing on Sunday, August 14 at 12:55 PM. We
approached the gate and Adam said "I can wait with you
here", for his connecting flight to Panama was not departing for another five hours. So I took a seat beside
a charging station and Adam laid out on the floor in the
corner before the large glass terminal window in his
characteristic napping position by resting his head on
his bag and crossing his legs and palms and lowering his
hat's brim and drifting off to peaceful slumber. I
plugged my phone in to charge, then went back to the
bathroom to pee again and to wash my hands. I returned
and retrieved my metal baoding balls and sitting there
in meek silence I watched the other passengers chatting
and eating and wrangling up their wild kids and blaring
over my head was yet again the "news" and none other
than the orange face of a farting anus.

USA, here we come.

I looked back at Adam who lay sleeping beneath his
orange hat's brim, crossed in peace and tranquility upon
a green-and-beige striped carpet. Looming over him to
the left was a massive Starbucks mural, and behind him

the orange roof of the terminal and the ambling green and silver hills of the countryside and the blue and white sovereign vastness of the heavens served as his holy backdrop. Here I took the last and final photo of this sacred pilgrimage to Costa Rica and I looked on at my dearest friend and soul-brother and declared with a warmed heart and a tearful eye: "Adiós, mi amigo mi hermano de alma. Hasta luego."

It was time to go.

Then to our amazement, there they were: the blonde American girl, her cute dark-haired friend in the hat and shorts, and their white-dudey friend. They were boarding my flight.

"Talk to 'em, man," Adam said. "Give 'em my number and I'll meet 'em in Utah."

"Fuck yeah!" I declared, and with a big warm hug I bade Adam farewell and said "See ya later, man. Safe travels."

"You too," he said. And that was the last time I ever saw Adam again.

Just kidding. We see each other all the time.

I approached seat 24D and plopped my Hoodoo Red Osprey Porter 46 Pack into the overhead compartment and when I looked down to take my seat, I beheld the most amazing most incredible miraculous coincidence of this entire god-blessed holy trip: the blonde American girl was seated next to me.

"Hi!" she cried.

"Hey!" I yelped with surprise and delight. "What's up! You guys are on this flight?"

"Yeah!" she exclaimed. I looked over my shoulder and the other two waved at me. "I'm Millie," she said. "And that's Katie and Bjark. His name's Raymond but we call him Bjark. Where are you off to?"

Before I could answer, I had to take a moment to muster up my hatred for a fucking rock-thumping fucktard named Raymond who walked around calling himself BJARK. But then I said, "I'm heading back to Detroit. What about you guys?"

"Utah," said Millie. "We're from Salt Lake City. Wow, so you're from Michigan? My grandparents are from

Michigan! Well, they're originally from Germany but they
lived in Michigan."

"Wow that's cool, what a coincidence! You know, I
have a buddy living out in Utah! I'm not sure if you
noticed the guy who was with me—"

"Yeah! Oh, he's from Utah?"

"Yeah, he lives and works in Zion National Park."

Millie's eyes lit up like sapphires. "We've been
wanting to go to Zion! I've heard it's beautiful!"

"It is! It's amazing! You guys should definitely
check it out," and I hinted at Katie as well who smiled
at us from the opposite side of the aisle. "Let's exchange numbers and I'll connect you with my buddy. His
name's Adam. He'll hook you up with everything you
need." And as Millie and I exchanged numbers to my
astonishment, I thought, "Adam is not gonna believe
this."

The flight soon filled up with boisterous youth all
chatting and laughing and the whole cabin permeated with
an intoxicating air of festivity. I spoke a bit to Katie
and fucking BJARK and Millie turned around to beckon a
giddy young girl in glasses who seemed to want to move
up to our row. So Millie turned to the third person in
our row— a French man in a black shirt and who I assumed
for some reason must've had a big dick— and asked "Excuse me, would you mind trading seats with my friend
over there? We were hoping to sit together." The Frenchman smiled pleasantly and did not mind so he chivalrously rose from his place and moved to the other seat as
the bespectacled girl scampered over excitedly and plop-
ping herself ecstatically between us she turned to me
and cried "Hi! I'm Doris!" Doris was from Phoenix and
she was such a cheerful delight and as the rest of the
cabin filled to capacity we all charmed at meeting one
another and settled ourselves in for the flight.

As the flight attendants prepared us for takeoff I
sat observing the cabin and all of the cheerful passengers and I suddenly noticed that the little screen on
the back of the seat before me was blaring in my face. I
turned it off, but looking around I saw so many other
screens still blaring on. In fact, it seemed as if every
damn screen on the flight was on and every passenger's
head was plugged into a set of headphones and most of
them were already well into full-length movies even before the plane had started taxiing. I, however, pre-

ferred to spend that time with a clear mind, and as our
seats kicked back during takeoff my eyes glazed from a
tiny round window the green hills and the blue horizons
and I said goodbye to Costa Rica. But though it was a
goodbye, I didn't miss it and I certainly wasn't sad
because I knew that Costa Rica was coming back with me.

So this fucking Delta Flight DL 903 had full Wi-Fi
and state-of-the-art air conditioning and a complete
line of Coca-Cola products and a waterproof tear- and
stain-proof high-gloss heavy-stock fusion polyester full
Starbucks menu so I snapped a glance at my blank screen
which seemed to be the only dead seat-square on the
whole flight and I looked over at Millie and Doris who
were no longer talking and giddy but instead now hunched
over their personal fucking screens and phones entranced
entrenched in the color and sound. I missed them. I
missed humanity.

I took out my trip's itinerary and a black pen and
turning it over onto its blank side I began to scribe by
hand the very first words of this whole weird and winding yarn, and I wrote this:
   "   8/14/16
And so I suppose now, my fellow reader, comes the
moment
   I assume you've all been waiting for— the Magnum
Opus of
   this merry tale of absurd and (offensive) nonsense
in which our
   holy Protagonist sets out for adventure..."

Then after I had written a paragraph I put that away
and played a game of chess (Yes on one of those evil
screens) and I lost that game but I no longer cared.
Then I ate and I was surprised by the small quantity
that did so fully satisfy me, but I suppose I didn't
need very much food. I then typed into my phone the
notes that formed the skeleton of this holy tale and I
wondered during the process that if someone were to see
me on my phone, would they think that I was a mindless
screen junkie like everyone else? I hoped not. Then
again, I thought it funny that we all think of ourselves
so apart and distinct from the rest of the world. I put
the phone away and retrieved my book The Dharma Bums and
continued to read from where I had left off, which was
the part in which Kerouac was tearfully and fearfully

climbing the mountain with Japhy and about all of the
terrible fears and worries that he had to surmount and I
found that I could totally relate to all that he was
describing. Kerouac is a very honest and truthful writer, my friends. I noticed that a gentleman to my left
was also reading a book: his was called "el extraño caso
de Dr. Jekyll y Mr. Hyde". So I leaned over and asked
him about his book, and he turned out to be an awfully
charming and kind young tico. His name was Roberto and
he had "negocios en Atlanta hasta viernes". Then he
asked for my pen and wrote down his email address and
told me with a straight face and overflowing sincerity
that if I ever had any questions about Spanish or travel
that at any time I was welcome to reach out and ask him.

I thanked this saint named Roberto and then returned
to my book and continued reading. Then I set down The
Dharma Bums and played some Sudoku. Finally I closed my
eyes and napped for a bit and before I knew it the
flight was over and we landed safely and soundly in
Hartsfield-Jackson Atlanta Intl Airport (ATL). With warm
farewells I wished Millie and Doris and Katie and Bjark
and Roberto safe travels and the best of luck and without further ado we were on our ways to our next destinations.

Compared to my last eight days in Central America,
U.S. Customs seemed to be UNBELIEVABLY fast and effi-
cient. It took these hootin' Yankees ten minutes what
took well over an hour in Costa Rica. They herded and
hustled us from one obstacle to another, from one
snaking mazing stream of stanchions (you know. Those
ropey velvet line dividers at banks and airports) to the
next, from one blaring kiosk screen to another. Herding
herding calling herding and at some points I found myself literally scrambling to a jog. Finally I felt the
pressure ease and I had a moment to look around and before me stood a petite young lady with pretty black hair
and a large black-white-grey shawl over her tiny shoulders. But this particular shawl caught my eye, for it
looked pristinely exotic. Arabian? Spanish? Finally I
asked her:

"Excuse me," I said. "But where did you get that
shawl?"

She smiled and replied "It's from Spain."

"I see," I said. "Are you Spanish?"

She giggled sweetly. "No, I'm from Nice. In France. But I traveled to Spain."

"Cool!" I said, and through the winding stanchioned line I chatted with the pretty girl from Nice in the Spanish shawl and I just loved how nice and sweet the whole world was. In moments the whole ordeal was pin-needle-efficiently done and the entire herd of us was silently ascending a cold steel escalator back to American civilization.

We do it hard and we do it fast in the USA. But at what cost? And for what gain?

The first thing that struck me about it was the sheer size and speed of it all. Why is everything so big? And why's it all moving so fast? Huge overstuffed suitcases on wheels. Jogging hustling travelers with stoic faces and iron frowns. Booths tables televisions chairs meals— all so big! What's going on??

In slow molasses motion (or so it seemed compared to my surroundings) I seeped through the bustling terminal to spot my gate. Then with a couple of hours to spare I decided to grab a quick bite for dinner. First I scoped my options: Grindhouse Killer Burgers. The Original El Taco. Popeye's. McDonald's. P.F. Chang's. Chick-Fil-A. For fucking eight dollars you could feed a starving family for a day. It all revolved my winding stomach. I turned instead to a deli and decided to settle for a single sandwich (you know. Sans the bucket of fries, the keg of soda, and the trunk of side dips). But approaching the Boar's Head Deli, I couldn't help but wonder if these guys were serving fucking sandwiches or halved triangulated textbooks. I mean, am I supposed to eat that thing or sleep on it? Fucking insane. So I turned instead to the Boar's Head Kiosk which was half a fridge and after great deliberation I finally settled for a tiny hummus-olive-dressing wrap. Then I went to another shop and ordered a small iced coffee. Standing in line I spotted an Udi's muffin and I jumped with delight and thought "Udi's for my mom!" (Udi's makes gluten-free baked goods and since my mother has celiac disease, these tasty treats are always a delight). So I bought my iced coffee and my mom's Udi's muffin and I walked over to the farther end of the gate's waiting area and I set down my wrap and drink and took out my Delta Lotus Biscoff cookie and my tiny chocolate piece for dessert and bon appetit! Dinner was served.

chapter one

I took off my shoes and sat on the floor, for those
airport chairs were much too luxurious and spoiled for
me and I felt ashamed to sit in them. Little by little I
munched on my hummus wrap and sipped my iced coffee and
delighted in the sweet delicacy of my Biscoff cookie and
chocolate piece and the whole meal took me over forty
minutes to finish and left me feeling distended and ach-
ingly full! And as I ate I just sat there in silence
observing it all passing before my eyes. And truly, it
all made me feel painfully sad: they all move way too
fast, some at a steady jog and others in a panicked drag
and others hustling on the verge of tears racing against
the clock and the sun and the pivots of the earth. And
they hustle and bustle and frazzle and trudge and skid
and roll about never stopping to wonder why or how or
what they just keep going going going after fabricated
purposes and secure goals and measured outcomes and da-
ta-driven analysis and empty veins.

But they don't know. They've never stopped. They've
never defied the fears of hunger, thirst, sleep, sweat,
heat, pests, heights, filth, cold, seas, strangers, exhaustion— and conquered it ALL! And sitting there cross-
legged and barefoot before a passing surge of lighting-
speed, it was this I dreaded: that I had to go back.
Back to a life of ease and drawers and shelves and
trunks and infinite shameful abundance. Back to a world
of likes and comments and apps and boxes and squares.
Back to a "no" world full of "can't" people. Back to a
void that sucks you in and sucks the life out of you.
And seated on the floor before the fleeting flitting
world of techno-seismic sprints, I heaved a sob and
swallowed it.

Flight DL 1290 from Hartsfield-Jackson Atlanta Intl
Airport (ATL) to Detroit Metro Airport (DTW) served as a
reinforcing reminder of what was yet to come. Everyone
was fat. Nobody smiled. All of their clothes were misfit
and malapportioned and mismatched and clownish. They
evaded eye contact and sulked with heavy dejected
frowns. To revive my spirit I tried to chat with a group
of older women in Jamaican dresses who were boarding in
line before me. But their standoffish snobby snubbing

responses were unflinching testaments to the world that they were just a cinco of fat huffing bitches, and as one of their gargantuan asses turned around (or rolled over, but who can tell?) I thought, "Now don't turn TOO far now cuz every time yo fat ass turns around it's yo birthday again". God, some people are so venomously toxic that they only bring out the worst in those around them.

The flight was dark and too fucking crammed and a fucking bunch of them were loud and screaming and obnoxious as they slogged their oversized clammering crammed-with-bullshit trunks up and down the aisles and chattered and sneered and yawped and hopped and you could hear their horrific and ghastly excuses for music blaring from their dumb fucking onion-sized headphones and you know what? Fuck it, they were black—

(Now don't give me that "racist" political-correctness bullshit right now, you understand? Just listen and be honest with your repressed self for a moment. Now, it is wrong, UNDOUBTEDLY and CERTAINLY wrong, to take a stereotype about a group of people— Afro-Americans, in this case— such as dirtiness or lasciviousness or poverty or laziness or ignorance or delinquency or anything else, and to proclaim that this stereotype applies to ALL of the individuals in that group. That is wrong. BUT! When a small and particular number of people who happen to be black are actually behaving in unmistakably and unabashedly stereotypical ways, then it is NOT wrong to acknowledge what is happening with the recoiling raging disgust it so aptly deserves. THAT isn't racist. What is RACIST is to ASSUME that this is a predisposed trait of an entire group of people— which it certainly is not— and to apply those ignorant conclusions upon the population as a whole. Am I being clear? Okay good. Now back to these hood-ass jumbo fucks on the plane).

So I sat there silently in seat 28B between two white women and the one to my right was certainly going to vote for Hillary in November and the one to my left was certainly going to vote for Trump. And if you're an American who lived to witness the 2016 campaigns and election then without any further explanation you know EXACTLY what the fuck I'm talking about. So frankly, with all of these horrors jangling about me I really didn't want to exist for two more hours in this den of

shit and I felt myself suffocating and growing claustro-
phobic so I did what I do best when I feel like shit: I
slept. I closed my eyes and focused on my breathing and
I managed to reduce this horrific nightmare down from
two hours to twenty minutes and when I woke up and the
plane had finally touched down on Michigan soil I knew
that I was finally home. Home and never. Ever. The same
person again.

chapter one

What shall I say more than I have inferred? Remember
who I am to cope withal! I will not bore you with the
details of my return to my former life: of my silent
stroll through an empty airport amid echoing white tile
and steel frigidness and flaring fluorescent lights onto
a squeaking steel escalator and out into a black night.
Of my ten-minute wait for W who insisted kindly upon
picking me up that night as I sat mutely upon an icy
steel bench beneath the blaring beams of glimmering
white light grinding my baoding balls in a mucking
sticking steaming Michigan heat that after this trip
would forever be but a spine-chilling tickle in compari-
son. Of my dear reunion with my heartwarming friend W
and of our drive back to town in which he asked me "How
was the trip?" and in which in an effort to explain what
had happened to me I convinced him within seconds that I
had gone ravingly insane (He coaxed me back to silence
and ease, but he would think me insane for months after). Of my tapping amble back to my house, bracing to
my chest my dear Hoodoo Red Osprey Porter 46 Pack, and
of my entrance through the back door into the arms of a
mother who bubbled with delight and relief and fizzled
her woes and worries upon me with laughs and chugging
sobs. Of my reunion with other family members whom I
vaguely remembered and my numb farewells to them as they
returned to their beds and I descended into a wide and
silent freezing-cold basement clutching my Hoodoo Red
Osprey Porter 46 Pack and knowing what was now inevita-
bly to come. Of my silent stand in a dark basement in
which I didn't bother to turn on the lights, but instead
set my bag down on the red-and-gold Persian rug and
without the heart to go on any further retreated into
the bathroom to shower. Of my most shameful temperature-
regulated water-pressure-precisioned indoor private
shower with the revoltingly extravagant bathroom fan and
wistfully wasteful waterfall and flowing streams of soap
and shampoo. Of the moment of truth, the funereal cere-

mony of the exhumation of the holy Hoodoo Red Osprey
Porter 46 Pack, in which I emptied piece by piece and
pocket by pocket the content of my most beloved and most
devoted friend, and staring at his autopsied sulking
corpse I took him in my trembling arms and bore him back
up the stairs into a plastic shroud and with the drag of
a choking grey breath I buried my beloved friend under
the dusty cavern of my bed. Of my shameful return to my
own personal private quarters where I found a blaring
fifty-pound personal air conditioner which I dared not
turn on and a spongy-soft crisp white memory-foam mattress which I fell upon and shuddered with morbid dis-
grace until I drifted off to unacceptably comfortable
slumber. Of my rise the next morning to chirping birds,
and the rest of that week in which I showered in ice-
cold water "just because" and ate for days straight
plentiful servings of huevos con pintos y arroz y café
negro. Of my frequent cruises around Michigan Central
Station past 16th Street and Newark Street into the Mexican bend of Vernor Highway around Los Galanes Restaurant
and Gloria's Bakery and my pleading yearning hopes for a
split deceiving second of honorary revival— but finding
nothing of the sort of my dismal march into La Carreta
Market where a darling clerk squalled to me "Hola primo!
Bienvenidos a Mexicantown!" and where I picked up the
week's copy of Latino Detroit and went back home to sit
on my porch and read with slunked nostalgia. Of my attempt to buy my merino wool socks and Lululemon
Athletica silver-laced "No Boxer Boxers" and of my question to my brother Kal: "Hey, have you ever heard of
Lululemon?" and of his response: "Yoga pants! So, you
wanna buy yoga pants?? Huh???" (I guess he figured, why
KICK me in the balls if he can just do away with them
altogether, you know?). Of my numerous failed attempts
to explain even one simple anecdote of my prophetic experience and of the endless recoiling smiles and embarrassed smirks and quizzical interruptions of "Chill out,
man. You were only gone a week".

No, I'll not bore you with any of that. Instead,
I'll leave you with the message I sent to Adam via Facebook on the night of my return since his phone was yet
to be repaired:

"Adam you are not gonna FUCKING believe this. Remember that Salt Lake trio with the cute girl in hat and
shorts and the one in the white shirt? Well the white

blouse girl sat NEXT to me on MY PLANE! We talked the
whole time shes so cool! her name's millie and her
friend's name is Katie. They have your number and will
reach out yayyyyyyyy. lemme know when you're home lol
and if u message back here i wont see it until october
so text or whatsapp lol. Safe travels bro!"

afterword

By Assam Saidi

In the summer of 2015, Yousef came out to visit me at Zion National Park where I live and work. He seemed pretty down at the time after having just come out of one of the worst years of his life. Although he wasn't his usual self, we had a great week anyway and got out and explored the park. When the trip was over, we discussed some possible destinations that we were interested in traveling to. After having talked about traveling together for years, we finally decided to make it happen, and since I had been learning Spanish and he had been dancing Salsa, we looked into visiting a Spanish-speaking country. Cuba, the Dominican Republic, and Costa Rica were all options, so we finally settled upon Costa Rica because it was convenient for tourists, cheap to fly to, and suitable for improving our Spanish.

Or so we thought. We came to find that you could get by in Costa Rica without speaking a lick of Spanish.

Also around that time, Yousef had started to express to me his frustrations with writing. He had been an author for years, self-publishing two books and writing other poems and stories, but he was frustrated with the conventional writing process and fed up with the bureaucracy of the publishing industry. He just wanted to write freely without having to worry about those things. Through our conversations, some thoughts began to surface about how, in this day and age—the age of the internet, blogs, YouTube stardom, and social media—he *could* just write, and the platforms for getting his work out there existed in abundance. This realization, combined with the absolute lack of fucks that Yousef gives about what people think, is what led to *Chapter One*.

It started as a blog where he wrote his thoughts on a day-to-day basis in a stream of consciousness. Some weeks, he would write every day; some weeks, not at all. Some entries were lengthy and introspective, while others were silly and a waste of time. But that was the beauty of it: it didn't matter! Whether you read it or not, liked it or not, they were *his* thoughts and *his* words in *his* own form of artistic expression without planning, direction, or revision.

At the time, I didn't know that these rants would become a book one day. Neither did he, I think.

Chapter One is full of surprises, but what has surprised me most of all about it is just how vulgar my friend can be. The eloquence, word choice, and degree to which he can insult people and things is, quite frankly, impressive. I didn't actually know this side of him because this isn't the way he speaks or carries himself in everyday life. And although we often have conversations that lean toward the comedic, I've never actually heard him speak the way he writes. As I read, I find myself blown away by how he can articulate his frustration and disdain.

It has also been interesting to read his side of conversations that we had in real time, and it has given me the opportunity to witness what goes on in another person's mind. Back at the time, I knew what *I* was feeling and *thought* I knew what he was feeling, but reading the book revealed to me that I could often be way off the mark, and it has been very cool to compare my own perspectives of the trip to the ways in which he describes them in the book.

Several instances of this kind stand out to me, like that moment when we arrived in Manuel Antonio and Yousef broke down and confessed how he was feeling. As he describes in the book, we arrived in a downpour and hiked up and down this winding road looking for our hostel and once we found it, it didn't turn out to be this beautiful place in the mountains where you could take reprieve and relax, but seemed instead like a shoddy dump fit for Queens, New York in the 1970's. But in that run-down room, Yousef sort of dropped his bag and let it rip.

I suppose I can understand why it all happened. I think he was simply unaware of where exactly we were headed and how things were going to be in that part of the world through this form of travel. I can understand that there's only so much a man can take after a rough day before it all bottles up and he just has to let it all out. But nevertheless, it caught me off-guard to find out just how frustrated he had been feeling and I wondered how long he'd been feeling this way. So I dropped my bag and we sat on our beds and talked. I listened to everything he had to say and he very eloquently talked it all out. And when it was over, he felt better and realized that everything was okay again.

Moments such as these have helped me reflect upon myself. I try to be more intuitive of others' feelings and how they experience uncomfortable situations. Since a big part of my job is to take people out into nature and help them work through their discomforts and fears, I try to pay more attention to their thoughts and feelings throughout the process.

And it's very exciting when they succeed! I watched my friend approach many of the trip's challenges doubting himself, saying things like "I can't" or "This is crazy". But time and again, I would watch him say these things and yet still manage to go out and do them, only to realize over and over again that he is perfectly capable of achieving whatever he sets his mind to and that he is only breaking the limitations that he had set for himself for no good reason. I watched him grow in this way through every stage of the trip, and it was an amazing thing to witness firsthand.

The trip has also solidified a notion that I have been developing for a long time: that life experiences are more enriching and rewarding when shared with others. After having traveled around the world to many places both alone and with company, I've learned that it's far better to share our life experiences than to experience them alone. Since Costa Rica, Yousef and I have already traveled again together. In 2017, we went to Alaska and after ten full days of travel, we came to a profound realization: despite being together through every waking and sleeping moment, we never once got at each other's throats, fought about anything, or grew irritated by one another. We always had plenty to talk about, and if we didn't, then we sat in comfortable silence. We also pushed some boundaries that Yousef had never explored before, like sleeping out of our rental car night after night (I'm not talking about an SUV here; this was a tiny Kia Optima where every night we'd pull over, put the back seats down, and lay down with our heads in the trunk). Our friendship has been strengthened by these trips and as a result, traveling together has now become an annual tradition that we plan to uphold every year during Yousef's summer vacations. I am grateful for this opportunity and I wouldn't want to share it with anyone else.

At this point, you might expect me to wrap up by going on some crazy-long tangent about "the nature of being" and what-not. Maybe if I was in a more philosophical state of mind, I would. But I'm not gonna lie to you: I don't think anybody really fucking knows. What I try to do for myself, however, is to always remember to not separate myself from the environment around me. I think this mindset should set the pace and track on which we move through life. It should frame how we view people and plants and animals and everything else, so that we can maintain that connection to the Earth and everything in it. It brings us back to the idea that we are a part of it all and not separate from it, so that it's no longer "Earth" and "me" on it, but rather that it's simply "Earth".

So, we're here to figure it out together and monkey-fuck our way through it and ask the questions that need to be asked and search for the answers that sometimes simply aren't there. Then, we'll have to make it up as we go along and pretend that we're doing well. But through it all, we make it a point to maintain kindness and empathy for one another and to do good in all situations. We are going to fuck up time and time again, but those moments should not define our lives. After all, who we are is the *sum* of our doings, both "good" and "bad" together.

And as for "the nature of being"? It's something that we're all trying to figure out.

acknowledgements

Thank you, Assam Saidi.
Thank you, Fatema Alqamoussi.
Thank you, W Design and Development.
Thank you, Agnes C. Fischer.
Thank you, Dearborn, Michigan. Thank you, America.
Thank you, Shakespeare, Kerouac, Lao Tzu, Whitman, Melville, Muhammad, Burroughs, Bukowski, Picasso, Ginsberg, Joyce, Watts, Salinger, Shakur, Hemingway, Ellison, Coltrane, Carlin, Kafka, and Twain.

YOUSEF ALQAMOUSSI is the author of several collections of fiction, poetry, short stories, and essays, including *The Massacre of Heartbreak Morrow*, *Renegade Rebel*, and the "GenEd" series on education. He earned his Master of Education from Wayne State University and teaches Secondary English and History. He lives in Detroit, Michigan.

Visit www.alqamoussi.com for more information.

71172496R00149

Made in the USA
Middletown, DE
22 April 2018